XENOPHON

The Education of Cyrus

Translated by H.G. Dakyns
Introduction and Notes by Richard Stoneman

J. M. Dent & Sons Ltd
London
Charles E. Tuttle Co., Inc.
Rutland, Vermont
EVERYMAN'S LIBRARY

First published in Everyman's Library, 1914
This edition published in 1992

Introduction and Notes © J.M. Dent & Sons
1992

This book is set by Cambridge Composing (UK)
Ltd, Cambridge
Printed in Great Britain by
The Guernsey Press Co. Ltd, Guernsey, C.I.
for J.M. Dent & Sons Ltd
Orion House, 5 Upper St Martin's Lane,
London, WC2H 9EA
and
Charles E. Tuttle Co. Inc.
28 South Main Street, Rutland
Vermont 05701
USA

Everyman's Library
Reg. US Patent Office

ISBN 0 460 87154 4

CONTENTS

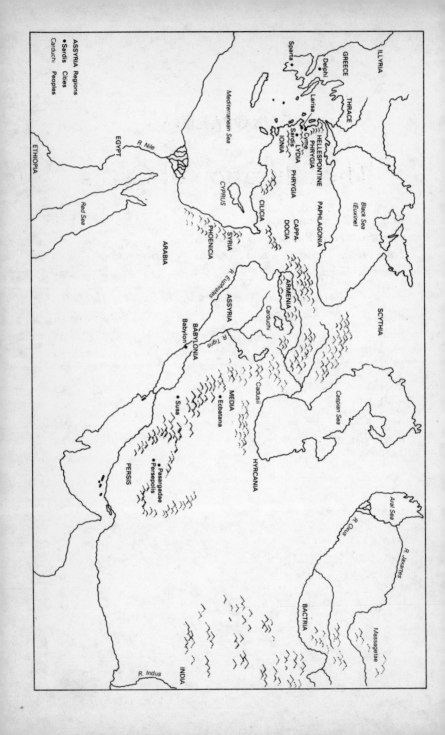

CYROPAEDIA

The Education of Cyrus

INTRODUCTION

XENOPHON the Athenian was born into a well-to-do family in the early 430s BC, soon after the outbreak of the conflict between Athens and Sparta which became known as the Peloponnesian War. Too young to participate in the first fifteen years of the fighting, one of the formative experiences of his boyhood was his encounter with the teacher Socrates (born c. 469). According to the brief biography by Diogenes Laertius:

The story goes that Socrates met him in a narrow passage, and that he stretched out his stick to bar his way, while he enquired where every kind of food was sold. Upon receiving a reply, he put another question, 'And where do men become good and honourable?' Xenophon was fairly puzzled; 'Then follow me,' said Socrates, 'and learn.' From that time onward he was a pupil of Socrates.[1]

Xenophon thus became one of the younger members of a coterie which included a number of men later to make careers out of their opposition to the democracy of Athens – men such as Critias (born c. 460), Alcibiades (born before 450), Charmides, and others. Socrates' most famous pupil was the philosopher Plato (c. 427–348), a man of about the same age as Xenophon, whose portrait of Socrates the seeker after wisdom and virtue is one of Greek literature's greatest achievements. It is clear that Socrates, like many excellent teachers since, liked best to share his wisdom with young men of good family who were likely to make successful careers in the wider world. The influence of Socrates' attempt to define the nature of the good man (and perhaps the good ruler, a topic which exercised his pupils Plato and Xenophon), combined with Xenophon's experience of the misfortunes of democratically ruled Athens under the onslaught of the monarchic Sparta, turned Xenophon into a committed anti-democrat.

When Athens was defeated by Sparta in 404 and a vicious cabal known as the Thirty was installed, in which Critias was one of the leading figures, Xenophon threw in his lot with the tyrants. Shortly afterwards, democracy was restored. Xenophon's career was blighted, and in 401 he accepted an invitation from his friend Proxenus (who had been a pupil of another great teacher, Gorgias of Leontini (485–375)) to join a mercenary force being assembled by Cyrus, the younger brother of the newly acceded king of Persia, Artaxerxes II, ostensibly to subdue a revolt in Pisidia. Xenophon consulted Socrates, who advised him to accept, and in spring 401 Cyrus' expedition departed from Sardis.

It quickly became apparent that the expedition against Pisidia was merely a pretext, and that Cyrus was in fact engaged in a revolt against his brother. By autumn 401 the army had penetrated deep into Mesopotamia. Here Cyrus' army was defeated by Artaxerxes at the Battle of Cunaxa, and Cyrus was killed.

Despite the failure of the expedition, Xenophon conceived a warm admiration for Cyrus and his qualities of leadership, and there are many parallels between his descriptions of Cyrus in his account of the expedition, the *Anabasis*, and those of the other Cyrus, the founder of the Persian Empire, whom he made the hero of *The Education of Cyrus*.[2]

Xenophon was now a member of an army without a cause, stranded half a year's march from home in hostile territory. Slowly the Ten Thousand Greeks began their march back to Greek lands. Before long they chose Xenophon as their commander and by late 400 the troops had reached the safety of Thrace. Soon after this the democracy at Athens condemned Socrates to death (early 399). It was probably at this time, also, that a decree of exile from Athens was pronounced against Xenophon, on the grounds that he had taken arms with Cyrus who was friendly with Athens' enemy Sparta.[3]

Clearly Athens was a state which could offer little to a man of Xenophon's type. In spring 399 he led the remnant of the 'Cyrean' troops to join the Spartan general Thibron in Asia Minor. He probably remained in Spartan service until the new Spartan king Agesilaus (who had acceded in 399) took command of the troops in Asia in 396, and continued under the new commander. His relationship with Agesilaus became a close and important one, and – if he had not been exiled already – it may have been as a result of his association with Sparta in campaigns against Athens from 394 that Athens pronounced Xenophon's exile.[4] For his service to Sparta the Spartans granted Xenophon an estate at Scillus in Elea. He seems to have married around this time, and he had two sons (who were of military age in 362). In 386 he retired to his estate at Scillus, and we must suppose that it was in his retirement that he wrote the numerous and diverse works which have come down to us.

After Sparta was defeated by a Greek coalition at the Battle of Leuctra in 371, Xenophon's estate was seized and he had to leave. The Athenian decree of exile had very probably been revoked in 386 on the conclusion of the King's Peace, but Xenophon had no thought of returning to the city. Instead he moved to Corinth where he spent the remainder of his life. One of the works of his later life, the *Hellenica* or *Affairs of Greece*, concludes with his despairing assessment of the outcome of the Battle of Mantinea in 362.

Both sides claimed the victory, but it cannot be said that with regard to the accession of new territory, or cities, or power, either side was any better off after the battle than before it. In fact, there was even more uncertainty and confusion in Greece after the battle than there had been before it.

To the despair of Xenophon's orderly military mind at the incessant warring of the Greek states was added the tragedy of the death of one of his sons, Gryllus, in the battle. Xenophon lived only a few more years and died some time after 355, the year of his last datable work.

There are few clues to the date or order of composition of any of his works. The *Constitution of the Lacedaemonians* (*Spartans*) was written after 381; his encomium of Agesilaus after 374 (it was influenced by Isocrates' *Evagoras* which can be dated to that year), and probably after Agesilaus' death in the 360s; the *Revenues* can be dated by contemporary references to the year 355. A number of references in the *Hellenica* suggest it was written in the 350s. The works on horsemanship and hunting, as well as that on household management, probably belong to the idyllic period of his life at Scillus. On the major works there is really no evidence. The works on Socrates, the *Memorabilia* and the *Symposium*, may have been written at any time after Socrates' death. The *Anabasis* is commonly thought to belong to the late 370s or even 360s, an old man's memoirs of the great exploit of his youth.[5] This, like the *Hellenica*, is memoirs not history, written, or at least revised, in the last years of his life.

As far as *The Education of Cyrus* is concerned, the interesting question is whether it precedes or follows the *Anabasis*. It has been argued that the *Education* is the earlier work, because it presents a rosier view of the state of Persia than the *Anabasis*;[6] the judgement seems supported by the obviously greater literary care and elaboration given to the *Education*. The work is that of a man who still thought the Ideal Ruler worth describing, though he cannot have harboured much hope of finding one in the 360s; it should be remembered nevertheless that his contemporary Plato was still actively searching for the Ideal Ruler in real life in his visits to Sicily in the same decade. Some references in the *Hellenica* also point to a continuing interest in leadership and virtue in action (mainly exemplified in *Agesilaus* V.1.3–4, IV.3.19, 5.4, and in Jason of Pherae). However, the last chapter of the *Education*, VIII.8, is datable by internal references to after 362/1. The inconsistency of the view of Persia in this chapter with the rest of the work has often been remarked, for in the earlier part of the work Xenophon regularly refers to Persian customs which persist 'even to this day'; in the epilogue he is concerned rather to paint a picture of shocking decline from a heroic past, in which the men of Persia are less religious than they were of old, less dutiful to their kindred, less just and righteous towards other men, and less valiant in war. The epilogue reads like the postscript of a disillusioned man. It may possibly have been influenced, too, by a clear criticism levelled at *The Education of Cyrus* by Plato in his last work, the *Laws*.[7] This work was published only after Plato's death in 348, but may have been circulating unofficially before that (though it must be admitted there is no evidence of any contact between Plato and Xenophon). Plato denies the adequacy of Cyrus' education and administration, and further paints a picture of decline from enlightened monarchy into despotism, just like that outlined by Socrates in the *Republic*. If Xenophon was aware of this criticism, it may have influenced the epilogue he wrote in his declining years.

The Persian Empire

The Education of Cyrus is not a work of history, but it contains a considerable amount of historical or apparently historical material, and has been eagerly quarried by historians of ancient Persia. In order to evaluate what Xenophon did with his material, it will be useful to give a brief outline of the career of Cyrus the Great and his position in Persian history.

The Medes and Persians, two closely related Iranian peoples, first appear in history in 836 BC when they are listed among peoples paying tribute to Shalmaneser III of Assyria. The Medes dwelt in Media with a capital at Ecbatana (I use the familiar Greek forms of the Old Persian names; the ancient Persian name of the city is Hangmatana, modern Hamadan), while the Persians occupied the more southerly Persis with a capital at Pasargadae.

In the late seventh century Cyaxares (Uvakhshatra), who was king of Media, led the final overthrow of Assyria, with the destruction of Nineveh in 612. His son was Astyages (Arshtivaiga) who had a daughter named Mandane. She was married to Cambyses I (Kanbujiya), the son of Cyrus and king of Persis. The son of Mandane and Cambyses was Cyrus II, our subject, who became king of Persis in 559.[8] He became ruler of both Media and Persis.

In 562 Nebuchadnezzar of Babylon died, and after a series of brief reigns Nabonidus (Nabu-naid) came to the throne in 555. Nabonidus, leaving Belshazzar (Bel-shar-usur) as ruler in Babylon, entered into alliance with Cyrus for a campaign against Media, in which Cyrus was successful, capturing Ecbatana in 550 and transferring its wealth to Persis. Media became a satrapy of the new enlarged Persian kingdom. The Persians, however, continued to be known to Greeks as the Medes.

On the fall of Media, king Croesus of Lydia made an attack on Cyrus. Cyrus repelled him and continued on to the Lydian capital of Sardis, which he sacked in 547. At this time Cyrus also obtained control over the Greeks of Asia Minor, who in their disunity offered little resistance. In 546 the Babylonian general Gobryas (Gubaru) revolted and switched his allegiance to Cyrus and this was the opportunity Cyrus needed to begin his preparations against Babylon, which he captured on 13 October 539. Gobryas was appointed as ruler in Babylon.

Cyrus' main achievement as an administrator was the creation of the system of satrapies, provinces and regions ruled by a satrap (governor, usually hereditary) for the Great King. He met his death in a campaign against the Massagetae, a people located east of the Caspian Sea in modern Turkmenistan. The manner of his death is disputed by our sources, but Herodotus gives what he regards as the most likely.[9] Before the final battle, queen Tomyris sent the king a message threatening that, if he would not retreat on the basis of his present conquests, 'I swear by the sun our master to give you more blood than you can drink, for all your gluttony.' Cyrus refused to withdraw; a battle followed in which Cyrus was killed; queen Tomyris searched among the bodies until she found that of Cyrus; she then severed the head and flung it into a skin full of blood, crying as she did so, 'See now – I fulfil my threat; you have your fill of blood.' Nothing could be more at variance with the peaceful and noble death in old age which Xenophon attributes to the king.

The Education of Cyrus

The Education of Cyrus has been somewhat out of favour in recent years, particularly among historians[10] who are apt to be impatient with its divergences from historical truth and who compare it unfavourably with the *reportage* of works like the *Anabasis* and the *Hellenica*. This is a very modern judgement, and for much of history *The Education of Cyrus* was regarded as one of the most important, timeless and enduring of Xenophon's works, and the one that most entitled him to the appellation, given him by Diogenes Laertius, of a philosopher. A newer perspective still, perhaps, is to see Xenophon as the author of the first historical novel; James Tatum has most effectively traced its importance in the development of the romances of the seventeenth and eighteenth centuries.[11] Renewed interest in, and information about, the Greek novel has made this perspective particularly appealing; but it is important to see the romance-like elements in proportion to the work as a whole. Cicero[12] regarded the work as a most useful one for the aspiring administrator, and with that in mind recommended it at length to his brother Quintus. He saw Xenophon's hero as:

> a really great man, gentle by nature and cultivated by instruction and devotion to the highest pursuits . . . Such a one was Cyrus as described by Xenophon, not according to historical truth but as the pattern of a just ruler; in him the philosopher created a matchless blend of firmness and courtesy. With good reason our Roman [Scipio] Africanus used to keep that book always in his hands.

And it is as a Mirror for Princes that Xenophon perhaps saw this treatise on leadership, at least when he began it.

For that, albeit in narrative form, is what it is. The 'Education' of the title is the resonant Greek word *paideia* which connotes not just schooldays but a way of life devoted to the improvement of the self, physically, mentally and morally. The real topic of *The Education of Cyrus* is not simply Cyrus' upbringing, which is disposed of in Book I, but his practice of military command and of imperial administration. It has less in common with history, as practised by Herodotus, Thucydides and Xenophon himself elsewhere, than with a number of other genres. One important influence is the encomium, of which we have examples from Xenophon's pen, the *Hiero* and the *Agesilaus*. These take the form of a funeral oration, giving a brief account of the hero's career and an enumeration, often rather mechanical, of his various virtues. In comparison with these rather wooden productions, the *Education* is a highly skilled and structured exposition of the salient virtues of the ruler.

Another parallel is the more discursive mode of Xenophon's own work on Socrates, the *Memorabilia*. Though this differs again, being in the main a series of anecdotes, it shows the same interest in conveying ethical insights, ideas and dilemmas in a discursive form. The figure of Socrates also suggests a further comparison with Plato's dialogues. It is notoriously hard to determine what in Plato's portrait of Socrates is really Socrates and what is Plato's interpretation or extrapolation, or even what Plato has simply put into Socrates' mouth. The figure of Cyrus in the *Education* may be viewed similarly, as a peg on which Xenophon has hung the philosophical ideas he wishes to convey, while showing no objection to using actual historical characteristics of the hero and his milieu where they fitted his theme.

It was not the first time Cyrus had been the hero of an ethical treatise. He had also been the subject of a work by Xenophon's contemporary Antisthenes, but unfortunately we know nothing of its content.[13] Persia had more influence on fifth-century Greek culture than many Greeks liked to acknowledge, and its characters provided an additional resource, besides Greek history and legend, for tales with a point.

In the fourth century, as Plato makes clear, the Persian Empire could be viewed as an example of one kind of Ideal State:

Under Cyrus, the life of the Persians was a judicious blend of liberty and subjection, and after gaining their own freedom they became the masters of a great number of other people. As rulers, they granted a degree of liberty to their subjects and put them on the same footing as themselves, with the result that soldiers felt more affection for their commander and displayed greater zeal in the face of danger. The king felt no jealousy if any of his subjects was intelligent and had some advice to offer; on the contrary, he allowed free speech and valued those who could contribute to the formulation of policy; a sensible man could use his influence to help the common cause. Thanks to freedom, friendship, and the practice of pooling their ideas, during the period the Persians made progress all along the line.[14]

Xenophon certainly knew a good deal about the Persian Empire. He had marched through it with Cyrus the Younger and had learnt much about Persian life in the process. He is the first Greek author to make correct use of certain Persian terms, such as satrap and paradise. He gives some reliable information about the Zoroastrian religion, and even seems to give a reliable account of that controversial Persian official, the 'King's Eye'.[15] He also clearly admired the Younger Cyrus for certain characteristics he regarded as distinctively Persian, and projected them onto his historic namesake.[16] It was perhaps his experience of Persia and of Cyrus that led Xenophon to choose the Elder Cyrus as a model for his Ideal Ruler.[17]

At the same time Xenophon is not immune to anachronisms, inappropriate inventions and even outright falsehoods. Anachronisms include the use of siege-towers by the Persians, a military technique introduced by Philip II of Macedon late in Xenophon's lifetime, and the use by the Persians of coins called darics (which of course were introduced by the fifth-century Persian king Darius).[18] The covenant made with the Persians at

VIII.5.24–7 is anachronistically based on a similar passage in Xenophon's own *Constitution of the Lacedaemonians* XV. The battle scenes show signs of invention (for example, VII.32), but this is a trait not confined to this work; the Battle of Cunaxa in the *Anabasis*, in the words of G. L. Cawkwell, 'will not do';[19] and fiction can be detected even in the *Hellenica*.[20] Xenophon does not follow through even his accurate information: though he gives a correct account of the triple division of the Persian army, he does not employ this division in his account of actual battles.[21]

There are several notable places where Xenophon diverges from the other sources in his account of Cyrus' career. These concern the birth of Cyrus, the method of his seizure of the Median throne, and, as we have seen, his death. The account of Cyrus' birth given in the previous section follows that of Herodotus, who says (I.96) that it is the most plausible of four that were known to him. A different version from that of Herodotus was given by Ctesias, whose account lies behind the narrative of Nicolaus of Damascus.[22] According to this version Cyrus was the son of a bandit, Atradates, and his wife Argoste. Herodotus incorporated in his account a folktale about the exposure of Cyrus as a baby, and his upbringing by peasants. Steven Hirsch[23] argues that Xenophon's more commonplace account is closer to those Persian sources which make Cyrus the offspring of Cambyses, and that Xenophon was well acquainted with Persian oral traditions. This view is supported by Xenophon's frequent appeal to unnamed sources – 'Cyrus famed in song and story'. It may well be, however, that these references are simply ways of adding verisimilitude to the narrative; there is really no way of telling which version (if any) of the birth of Cyrus is correct. Xenophon's version does, however, carefully remove all dishonourable elements from his hero's origins.

Cyrus' acquisition of the throne of Media is in the *Education* a management problem involving the conciliation of Cyrus' uncle Cyaxares (a fictional character). A coup is, at most, hinted at (VIII.5.19). In all the other sources Cyrus seizes the throne from Astyages by force. In Herodotus Cyrus overthrows Astyages but thereafter treats him with consideration and keeps him at his court. In Ctesias, as reported by Photius,[24] Cyrus pursues Astyages to Ecbatana, but after his victory treats him as a father and marries his daughter Amytis. In Nicolaus of Damascus, Cyrus' victory is the result of a bitter battle in Persis. The incidence of battles in the story is confirmed by two passages in Polyaenus describing stratagems used by Cyrus against Astyages.[25] Xenophon's version is designed to enhance the virtuous character of his hero, and seems less likely to be true than the other versions.

The third striking divergence from other sources is the peaceful death of Cyrus. As in Ctesias, Xenophon's Cyrus dies in his bed surrounded by his chief courtiers and successors. In Herodotus and Diodorus, and other writers, he dies a violent death in battle against the Massagetae.[26] Hirsch argues[27] that even in this Xenophon is to be preferred to the other sources, because of the existence of a tomb (as distinct from a cenotaph) of Cyrus at Pasargadae; but the weight of the evidence is against him. In all these cases Xenophon may be deliberately setting out to give a version different from his predecessors. Another example is his account of the fall of Sardis, which again has ethical overtones. (See note on VII.2.)

Yet there are many aspects of Persian mores as described in the *Education* which we know to be authentic: the importance of hunting as a preparation for battle – hunting scenes are one of the most popular subjects in Persian art of all periods;[28] the kiss on the lips as a greeting between peers;[29] the importance of eunuchs. Xenophon also knew of the Persian devotion to gardens and gardening, though he mentions this not in the *Education* but in the *Oeconomicus* (*Estate Manager* IV.20 ff.). There are also wanton attributions to Persians of characteristically Greek customs, such as institutionalised pederasty. The latter was important at Athens but also notably at Sparta; this, combined with Xenophon's admiration for Sparta and for Agesilaus, has sometimes been taken to suggest that Xenophon's Persia is a disguised portrait of Sparta, and Cyrus of Agesilaus.[30] The praise of self-control and temperance, and its contrast with Median luxury, may also be no more than a projection onto the Persians of a contrast the Greeks, and especially Socratics, Cynics and later Stoics, felt existed between themselves and the Persians or Medes.[31] However, the authentic elements are too many to allow for such Spartan traits to be more than incidental to Xenophon's view of the well-ordered state.

Some of the characters in the *Education* are historical: Cyrus himself, his mother Mandane, Gobryas the ruler of Babylonia.[32] Others are fictional, most notably Cyrus' uncle Cyaxares, one of the most important figures in the plot. Many characters are introduced anonymously – 'a certain Persian' – only to be given a name later in the narrative: a piece of verisimilitude reflecting the way one does come to encounter people, and may be seen as a subtle device to distance us from the idea of the omniscient narrator, who becomes a participant in the plot. The most famous of these invented characters is the unfortunate Pantheia, the heroine of a little romance within the structure of the whole.

Xenophon's aim of portraying the Ideal Ruler is conveyed not only in Cyrus' adeptness in inventing stratagems (for example, III.2.22 – a characteristic he shares with another fictional-historical character, the Alexander of the *Alexander Romance*), but through frequent echoes of ideas we can recognise as Socratic (for example, VIII.2.5, VIII.7.22). The most conspicuous echo of Xenophon's teacher is the philosopher friend of Tigranes who had been put to death by the king of Armenia (III.1.38).

One influence on the narrative, of which one should never lose sight in reading any Greek work, is Homer. Homer's *Iliad* is, like this, an account of individuals involved in warfare and leadership, in a war whose details, then as now, could only be conjectural. Homer wrote of an 'ideal' Greek war as Xenophon writes of an ideal Persian Empire. Many narrative devices directly recall Homer: the frequent use of dreams to forewarn or move the action on;[33] Pantheia's farewell to Abradatas (VI.4.7) which irresistibly recalls Andromache's farewell to Hector in the *Iliad* (and has the same tragic consequence); the games of VIII.3.25; the consolation of love after suffering at III.1.41 seems like an echo of the experience of Odysseus in the *Odyssey*.

An important feature of this, as of all Greek historical works, is the use of speeches. Thucydides used speeches to draw out the underlying motives of his actors as well as to express the arguments they put forward at crucial junctures of his story. Xenophon has no such sophisticated approach to speeches. In the *Hellenica*, as far as we can tell, he confines himself to the duties of a reporter or uses speeches as a minimal means of scene-setting or advancing the narrative. (There are more, and more significant, speeches in the part of the *Hellenica* which is concerned with the fall of the democracy at Athens than in the later, military parts.) In the *Education*, however, speeches play an important role. They are used to emphasise important turning points in the narrative, such as a major battle (III.3.43 ff., IV.2.38), but equally importantly as a means by which Cyrus can express directly his ideals of rulership (I.5.7 ff.). VII.5.72 ff. is virtually a treatise delivered as a speech, VIII.7.6 a testament in spoken form. At the same time, Xenophon is enough of a pupil of Socrates to allow the dialogue to play an important role in narrative and character-drawing as well: a good example is his debate with Araspas in V.1 about beauty. Dialogue can also turn to conversation and raillery (VIII.3.26 ff.): Xenophon is skilled in using direct speech to lighten the texture of what is a very long work, and the variety of his uses of direct speech marks the *Education* as an important forerunner of the novel.

Enough has been said to show that Xenophon uses Persian material in the service of a thoroughly Greek concept of *paideia*, even if he found that better exemplified in the Persian than in any available Greek model. How far, then, is education really important to the development of the 'good and honourable man' whom Socrates invited Xenophon to study with him ?[34] It was a commonplace in Greek aristocratic thought (as evinced by Pindar, for example) that education or training was only as valuable as the quality of the material it had to work on: a man's inborn nature had to be good before it could be developed. Does Xenophon suggest that training could do more than this, as perhaps the democratic ambience of Athens suggested that it should ? Socrates' own choice of pupils seems to deny his principle. The experience of democracy must have suggested to Xenophon too that 'top people' really were better at running states. Yet his very emphasis on education suggests that Xenophon was more of an Athenian than he realised.

Perhaps, too, he realised that his ideal Cyrus could never be more than an ideal. Perhaps that despairing epilogue is not an admission of the failure of his programme for leadership, but an admission that all that had preceded was really only fiction. His ideal, like that of Plato, must be conceded as unreachable in the world of men. Perhaps, too, the epilogue indicates a recognition of the inadequacy, in Platonic terms, of fiction as a means of approaching reality. That has not stopped many succeeding centuries regarding Cyrus as a worthwhile ethical model. We owe it to Xenophon to believe that he was aware of both its demands and its shortcomings as a realistic programme for living.

NOTE ON THE TRANSLATION

The translation of H. G. Dakyns is here reprinted unchanged. In the notes I have not aimed to construct an interpretative commentary, but simply to draw attention to points of historical interest or importance, and to give some hints, where appropriate, of Xenophon's relation to other writers on the subjects he covers in *The Education of Cyrus*.

NOTES TO THE INTRODUCTION

1. Diogenes Laertius II.48.
2. E.g. *Education* I.2.2–12 with *Anabasis* I.9.2–6; see Steven W. Hirsch, *The Friendship of the Barbarians* (Hanover, N.H. 1985) 64.
3. See Cawkwell's edition of *Hellenica*, p. 12; Diogenes Laertius II.58; *Anabasis* III.1.5, VII.5.7. An alternative view holds that Xenophon was exiled after 394 BC when he threw in his lot with the Spartan enemy under Agesilaus.
4. Cf. n. 3.
5. E.g. *Hellenica* III.1.2. A parallel that occurs to mind is Patrick Leigh Fermor, living in retirement in rural Greece, following his major discursive works on Greece with an account of the adventures of his youth (though his own story of his part in the Battle for Crete remains to be written).
6. Cawkwell's edition of *Anabasis*, p. 16.
7. The relevant passages are *Laws* 3.694c; 694ab; 697ce. See Hirsch 97–100.

8. Herodotus I.91, 107–8, 111. Olmstead 38–40, Frye 85–94, Cook 25 ff.
9. Herodotus I.202 ff. See also note on VIII.7.27.
10. G. Cawkwell, 'A Diet of Xenophon' in *Didaskalos* 2 (1966), 50 ff.; cited by Bodil Due, *The Cyropaedia: Xenophon's Aims and Methods* (Aarhus 1989) 9 n. 4.
11. James A. Tatum, *Xenophon's Imperial Fiction* (Princeton 1989).
12. Cicero *Ad Quintum Fratrem* 1.1.23 ; Tatum 9.
13. Diogenes Laertius VI.16. Cf. R. Hoistad, *Cynic Hero and Cynic King* (Uppsala 1948).
14. *Laws* 694.
15. Hirsch 101 ff., 149 n. 3, 89 f. See notes on VIII.1.23, 2.10–12.
16. Hirsch 74 f.
17. Due 38 ff.
18. V.2.7. This is an anachronism Xenophon shares with the author of I Chronicles 29.7 : Cook 70.
19. Cawkwell's edition of *Anabasis* 38 ff.; J. K. Anderson, *Xenophon* (London 1974); Xen. *Agesilaus* 2.9 ff.
20. Anderson 155 ff., noting his differences from the *Hellenica Oxyrhynchia*.
21. Cook 101.
22. Nicolaus of Damascus, FGrH IIA 90 fr. 106.
23. Hirsch 76 f.
24. J. Gilmore, *The Persika of Ctesias* (London 1888), 122 ff.
25. Polyaenus VII.6.1, 45.2.
26. See note on VIII.7.27.
27. Hirsch 84.
28. VIII.1.34 ; though whether the attendant virtue of physical fitness is a Persian one is less certain, despite *Oeconomicus* IV.24 : it sounds like the Greek passion for athletics superimposed on a Persian custom, and is not independently attested as a Persian attitude. It is one of the Persian customs abandoned in Xenophon's time according to VIII.8.2. See Due 108 f.
29. Herodotus I.134.1.
30. E.g. Anderson 152 f.
31. Due 170–81.
32. On Gobryas, see Cook 168.
33. Though Xenophon does have important dreams in the *Anabasis* too : e.g. IV.3.8.
34. The question is raised by Due 147 ff.

SELECT BIBLIOGRAPHY

Anderson, J. K., *Xenophon* (London 1974)

Chahin, M., *The Kingdom of Armenia* (London 1987)

Cizek, A., 'From historical truth to literary convention; the life of Cyrus the Great viewed by Herodotus, Ctesias and Xenophon', *L'Antiquité Classique* 44 (1975), 531 ff.

Cook, J. M., *The Persian Empire* (London 1983)

Due, Bodil, *The Cyropaedia: Xenophon's Aims and Methods* (Aarhus 1989)

Frye, Richard N., *The Heritage of Persia* (London 1962, 1976)

Gilmore, John, *The Persika of Ctesias* (London 1888)

Gray, Vivienne, *The Character of Xenophon's Hellenica* (London 1989)

Higgins, W. E., *Xenophon the Athenian* (Albany 1977)

Nicolaus of Damascus in F. Jacoby, *Fragmente der griechischen Historiker* IIA 90 (frr. 66, 67)

Olmstead, A. T., *History of the Persian Empire* (Chicago 1948)

Tatum, James A., *Xenophon's Imperial Fiction. On The Education of Cyrus* (Princeton 1989)

Todd, Joan M., *Persian Paideia and Greek Historia. An interpretation of the Cyropaedia of Xenophon Book I* (Pittsburgh 1968)

Trenkner, Sophie, *The Greek Novella in the Classical Period* (Cambridge 1958)

Xenophon, *A History of my Times* (i.e. the *Hellenica*), with introduction and notes by G. L. Cawkwell (Penguin 1979)

Xenophon, *Conversations with Socrates* translated by Hugh Tredennick and Robin Waterfield with introduction and notes by Robin Waterfield (Penguin 1990)

Xenophon, *The Persian Expedition* (i.e. the *Anabasis*) with introduction and notes by G. L. Cawkwell (Penguin 1972)

Xenophon, *Scripta Minora* (Loeb Classical Library 1968)

CYROPAEDIA

The Education of Cyrus

BOOK ONE

The Education of Cyrus

BOOK I

C. 1 WE have had occasion before now to reflect how often democracies have been overthrown by the desire for some other type of government, how often monarchies and oligarchies have been swept away by movements of the people, how often would-be despots have fallen in their turn, some at the outset by one stroke, while those who have maintained their rule for ever so brief a season are looked upon with wonder as marvels of sagacity and success.

The same lesson, we had little doubt, was to be learnt from the family: the household might be great or small — even the master of few could hardly count on the obedience of his little flock. 2. And so, one idea leading to another, we came to shape our reflexions thus: Drovers may certainly be called the rulers of their cattle and horse-breeders the rulers of their studs — all herdsmen, in short, may reasonably be considered the governors of the animals they guard. If, then, we were to believe the evidence of our senses, was it not obvious that flocks and herds were more ready to obey their keepers than men their rulers? Watch the cattle wending their way wherever their herdsmen guide them, see them grazing in the pastures where they are sent and abstaining from forbidden grounds, the fruit of their own bodies they yield to their master to use as he thinks best; nor have we ever seen one flock among them all combining against their guardian, either to disobey him or to refuse him the absolute control of their produce. On the contrary, they are more apt to show hostility against other animals than against the owner who derives

C. 1 advantage from them. But with man the rule is converse; men unite against none so readily as against those whom they see attempting to rule over them. 3. As long, therefore, as we followed these reflexions, we could not but conclude that man is by nature fitted to govern all creatures, except his fellow-man. But when we came to realise the character of Cyrus the Persian, we were led to a change of mind: here is a man, we said, who won for himself obedience from thousands of his fellows, from cities and tribes innumerable: we must ask ourselves whether the government of men is after all an impossible or even a difficult task, provided one set about it in the right way. Cyrus, we know, found the readiest obedience in his subjects, though some of them dwelt at a distance which it would take days and months to traverse, and among them were men who had never set eyes on him, and for the matter of that could never hope to do so, and yet they were willing to obey him. 4. Cyrus did indeed eclipse all other monarchs, before or since, and I include not only those who have inherited their power, but those who have won empire by their own exertions. How far he surpassed them all may be felt if we remember that no Scythian, although the Scythians are reckoned by their myriads, has ever succeeded in dominating a foreign nation; indeed the Scythian would be well content could he but keep his government unbroken over his own tribe and people. The same is true of the Thracians and the Illyrians, and indeed of all other nations within our ken; in Europe, at any rate, their condition is even now one of independence, and of such separation as would seem to be permanent. Now this was the state in which Cyrus found the tribes and peoples of Asia when, at the head of a small Persian force, he started on his career. The Medes and the Hyrcanians accepted his leadership willingly, but it was through conquest that he won Syria, Assyria, Arabia, Cappadocia, the two Phrygias, Lydia, Caria, Phoenicia, and Babylonia. Then he established his rule over the Bactrians, Indians, and Cilicians, over the Sakians, Paphlagonians, and Magadidians, over a host of other tribes the very names of which defy the memory of the chronicler; and last of all he brought the Hellenes in

Asia beneath his sway, and by a descent on the seaboard C. 1
Cyprus and Egypt also.

5. It is obvious that among this congeries of nations few,
if any, could have spoken the same language as himself, or
understood one another, but none the less Cyrus was able
so to penetrate that vast extent of country by the sheer
terror of his personality that the inhabitants were prostrate
before him: not one of them dared lift hand against him.
And yet he was able, at the same time, to inspire them all
with so deep a desire to please him and win his favour that
all they asked was to be guided by his judgment and his
alone. Thus he knit to himself a complex of nationalities
so vast that it would have taxed a man's endurance merely
to traverse his empire in any one direction, east or west or
south or north, from the palace which was its centre. For
ourselves, considering his title to our admiration proved,
we set ourselves to inquire what his parentage might have
been and his natural parts, and how he was trained and
brought up to attain so high a pitch of excellence in the
government of men. And all we could learn from others
about him or felt we might infer for ourselves we will here
endeavour to set forth.

The father of Cyrus, so runs the story, was Cambyses, a C. 2
king of the Persians, and one of the Perseidae, who look to
Perseus as the founder of their race. His mother, it is
agreed, was Mandane, the daughter of Astyages, king of
the Medes. Of Cyrus himself, even now in the songs and
stories of the East the record lives that nature made him
most fair to look upon, and set in his heart the threefold
love of man, of knowledge, and of honour. He would
endure all labours, he would undergo all dangers, for the
sake of glory. 2. Blest by nature with such gifts of soul and
body, his memory lives to this day in the mindful heart of
ages. It is true that he was brought up according to the
laws and customs of the Persians, and of these laws it must
be noted that while they aim, as laws elsewhere, at the
common weal, their guiding principle is far other than that
which most nations follow. Most states permit their citizens to bring up their own children at their own discretion,
and allow the grown men to regulate their own lives at

C. 2 their own will, and then they lay down certain prohibitions, for example, not to pick and steal, not to break into another man's house, not to strike a man unjustly, not to commit adultery, not to disobey the magistrate, and so forth; and on the transgressor they impose a penalty. 3. But the Persian laws try, as it were, to steal a march on time, to make their citizens from the beginning incapable of setting their hearts on any wickedness or shameful conduct whatsoever. And this is how they set about their object.

In their cities they have an open place or square dedicated to Freedom (Free Square they call it), where stand the palace and other public buildings. From this place all goods for sale are rigidly excluded, and all hawkers and hucksters with their yells and cries and vulgarities. They must go elsewhere, so that their clamour may not mingle with and mar the grace and orderliness of the educated classes. 4. This square, where the public buildings stand, is divided into four quarters which are assigned as follows: one for the boys, another for the youths, a third for the grown men, and the last for those who are past the age of military service. The law requires all the citizens to present themselves at certain times and seasons in their appointed places. The lads and the grown men must be there at daybreak: the elders may, as a rule, choose their own time, except on certain fixed days, when they too are expected to present themselves like the rest. Moreover, the young men are bound to sleep at night round the public buildings, with their arms at their side; only the married men among them are exempt, and need not be on duty at night unless notice has been given, though even in their case frequent absence is thought unseemly. 5. Over each of these divisions are placed twelve governors, twelve being the number of the Persian tribes. The governors of the boys are chosen from the elders, and those are appointed who are thought best fitted to make the best of their lads: the governors of the youths are selected from the grown men, and on the same principle; and so for the grown men themselves and their own governors; the choice falls on those who will, it is hoped, make them most prompt to

carry out their appointed duties, and fulfil the commands C. 2
imposed by the supreme authority. Finally, the elders
themselves have presidents of their own, chosen to see that
they too perform their duty to the full.

6. We will now describe the services demanded from the
different classes, and thus it will appear how the Persians
endeavour to improve their citizens. The boys go to school
and give their time to learning justice and righteousness:
they will tell you they come for that purpose, and the
phrase is as natural with them as it is for us to speak of
lads learning their letters. The masters spend the chief part
of the day in deciding cases for their pupils: for in this
boy-world, as in the grown-up world without, occasions
of indictment are never far to seek. There will be charges,
we know, of picking and stealing, of violence, of fraud, of
calumny, and so forth. The case is heard and the offender,
if shown to be guilty, is punished. 7. Nor does he escape
who is found to have accused one of his fellows unfairly.
And there is one charge the judges do not hesitate to deal
with, a charge which is the source of much hatred among
grown men, but which they seldom press in the courts, the
charge of ingratitude. The culprit convicted of refusing to
repay a debt of kindness when it was fully in his power
meets with severe chastisement. They reason that the
ungrateful man is the most likely to forget his duty to the
gods, to his parents, to his fatherland, and his friends.
Shamelessness, they hold, treads close on the heels of
ingratitude, and thus ingratitude is the ringleader and chief
instigator to every kind of baseness. 8. Further, the boys
are instructed in temperance and self-restraint, and they
find the utmost help towards the attainment of this virtue
in the self-respecting behaviour of their elders, shown them
day by day. Then they are taught to obey their rulers, and
here again nothing is of greater value than the studied
obedience to authority manifested by their elders everywhere. Continence in meat and drink is another branch of
instruction, and they have no better aid in this than, first,
the example of their elders, who never withdraw to satisfy
these carnal cravings until those in authority dismiss them,
and next, the rule that the boys must take their food, not

C. 2 with their mother but with their master, and not till the
governor gives the sign. They bring from home the staple
of their meal, dry bread with nasturtium for a relish, and
to slake their thirst they bring a drinking-cup, to dip in the
running stream. In addition, they are taught to shoot with
the bow and to fling the javelin.

The lads follow their studies till the age of sixteen or
seventeen, and then they take their places as young men.

9. After that they spend their time as follows. For ten
years they are bound to sleep at night round the public
buildings, as we said before, and this for two reasons, to
guard the community and to practise self-restraint;
because that season of life, the Persians conceive, stands
most in need of care. During the day they present themselves before the governors for service to the state, and,
whenever necessary, they remain in a body round the
public buildings. Moreover, when the king goes out to
hunt, which he will do several times a month, he takes half
the company with him, and each man must carry bow and
arrows, a sheathed dagger, or 'sagaris', slung beside the
quiver, a light shield, and two javelins, one to hurl and the
other to use, if need be, at close quarters. 10. The reason
of this public sanction for the chase is not far to seek: the
king leads just as he does in war, hunting in person at the
head of the field, and making his men follow, because it is
felt that the exercise itself is the best possible training for
the needs of war. It accustoms a man to early rising; it
hardens him to endure heat and cold; it teaches him to
march and to run at the top of his speed; he must perforce
learn to let fly arrow and javelin the moment the quarry is
across his path; and, above all, the edge of his spirit must
needs be sharpened by encountering any of the mightier
beasts: he must deal his stroke when the creature closes,
and stand on guard when it makes its rush: indeed, it
would be hard to find a case in war that has not its parallel
in the chase. 11. But to proceed: the young men set out
with provisions that are ampler, naturally, than the boys'
fare, but otherwise the same. During the chase itself they
would not think of breaking their fast, but if a halt is
called, to beat up the game, or for any hunter's reason,

then they will make, as it were, a dinner of their breakfast, C. 2 and, hunting again on the morrow till dinnertime, they will count the two days as one, because they have only eaten one day's food. This they do in order that, if the like necessity should arise in war, they may be found equal to it. As relish to their bread these young men have whatever they may kill in the chase, or failing that, nasturtium like the boys. And if one should ask how they can enjoy the meal with nasturtium for their only condiment and water for their only drink, let him bethink himself how sweet barley bread and wheaten can taste to the hungry man and water to the thirsty. 12. As for the young men who are left at home, they spend their time in shooting and hurling the javelin, and practising all they learnt as boys, in one long trial of skill. Beside this, public games are open to them and prizes are offered; and the tribe which can claim the greatest number of lads distinguished for skill and courage and faithfulness is given the meed of praise from all the citizens, who honour, not only their present governor, but the teacher who trained them when they were boys. Moreover, these young men are also employed by the magistrates if garrison work needs to be done or if malefactors are to be tracked or robbers run down, or indeed on any errand which calls for strength of limb and fleetness of foot. Such is the life of the youth. But when the ten years are accomplished they are classed as grown men. 13. And from this time forth for five-and-twenty years they live as follows.

First they present themselves, as in youth, before the magistrates for service to the state wherever there is need for strength and sound sense combined. If an expedition be on foot the men of this grade march out, not armed with the bow or the light shield any longer, but equipped with what are called the close-combat arms, a breastplate up to the throat, a buckler on the left arm (just as the Persian warrior appears in pictures), and for the right hand a dagger or a sword. Lastly, it is from this grade that all the magistrates are appointed except the teachers for the boys. But when the five-and-twenty years are over and the men have reached the age of fifty years or more, then they

C. 2 take rank as elders, and the title is deserved. 14. These elders no longer go on military service beyond the frontier; they stay at home and decide all cases, public and private both. Even capital charges are left to their decision, and it is they who choose all the magistrates. If a youth or a grown man breaks the law he is brought into court by the governors of his tribe, who act as suitors in the case, aided by any other citizen who pleases. The cause is heard before the elders and they pronounce judgment; and the man who is condemned is disfranchised for the rest of his days.

15. And now, to complete the picture of the whole Persian polity, I will go back a little. With the help of what has been said before, the account may now be brief: the Persians are said to number something like one hundred and twenty thousand men: and of these no one is by law debarred from honour or office. On the contrary, every Persian is entitled to send his children to the public schools of righteousness and justice. As a fact, all who can afford to bring up their children without working do send them there: those who cannot must forego the privilege. A lad who has passed through a public school has a right to go and take his place among the youths, but those who have not gone through the first course may not join them. In the same way the youths who have fulfilled the duties of their class are entitled eventually to rank with the men, and to share in office and honour: but they must first spend their full time among the youths; if not, they go no further. Finally, those who as grown men have lived without reproach may take their station at last among the elders. Thus these elders form a college, every member of which has passed through the full circle of noble learning; and this is that Persian polity and that Persian training which, in their belief, can win them the flower of excellence. 16. And even to this day signs are left bearing witness to that ancient temperance of theirs and the ancient discipline that preserved it. To this day it is still considered shameful for a Persian to spit in public, or wipe the nose, or show signs of wind, or be seen going apart for his natural needs. And they could not keep to this standard unless they were accustomed to a temperate diet, and were trained to

exercise and toil, so that the humours of the body were C. 2
drawn off in other ways. Hitherto we have spoken of the
Persians as a whole: we will now go back to our starting-
point and recount the deeds of Cyrus from his childhood.

Until he was twelve years old or more, Cyrus was C. 3
brought up in the manner we have described, and showed
himself to be above all his fellows in his aptitude for
learning and in the noble and manly performance of every
duty. But about this time, Astyages sent for his daughter
and her son, desiring greatly to see him because he had
heard how noble and fair he was. So it fell out that
Mandane came to Astyages, bringing her son Cyrus with
her. 2. And as soon as they met, the boy, when he heard
that Astyages was his mother's father, fell on his neck and
kissed him without more ado, like the loving lad nature
had made him, as though he had been brought up at his
grandfather's side from the first and the two of them had
been playmates of old. Then he looked closer and saw that
the king's eyes were stencilled and his cheeks painted, and
that he wore false curls after the fashion of the Medes in
those days (for these adornments, and the purple robes,
the tunics, the necklaces, and the bracelets, they are all
Median first and last, not Persian; the Persian, as you find
him at home even now-a-days, still keeps to his plainer
dress and his plainer style of living.) The boy, seeing his
grandfather's splendour, kept his eyes fixed on him, and
cried, 'Oh, mother, how beautiful my grandfather is!'
Then his mother asked him which he thought the hand-
somer, his father or his grandfather, and he answered at
once, 'My father is the handsomest of all the Persians, but
my grandfather much the handsomest of all the Medes I
ever set eyes on, at home or abroad.' 3. At that Astyages
drew the child to his heart, and gave him a beautiful robe
and bracelets and necklaces in sign of honour, and when
he rode out, the boy must ride beside him on a horse with
a golden bridle, just like King Astyages himself. And Cyrus,
who had a soul as sensitive to beauty as to honour, was
pleased with the splendid robe, and overjoyed at learning
to ride, for a horse is a rare sight in Persia, a mountainous
country, and one little suited to the breed.

C. 3   4. Now Cyrus and his mother sat at meat with the king, and Astyages, wishing the lad to enjoy the feast and not regret his home, plied him with dainties of every sort. At that, so says the story, Cyrus burst out, 'Oh, grandfather, what trouble you must give yourself reaching for all these dishes and tasting all these wonderful foods!' 'Ah, but,' said Astyages, 'is not this a far better meal than you ever had in Persia?' Thereupon, as the tale runs, Cyrus answered, 'Our way, grandfather, is much shorter than yours and much simpler. We are hungry and wish to be fed, and bread and meat bring us where we want to be at once, but you Medes, for all your haste, take so many turns and wind about so much it is a wonder if you ever find your way to the goal that we have reached long ago.' 5. 'Well, my lad,' said his grandfather, 'we are not at all averse to the length of the road: taste the dishes for yourself and see how good they are.' 'One thing I do see,' the boy said, 'and that is that you do not quite like them yourself.' And when Astyages asked him how he felt so sure of that, Cyrus answered, 'Because when you touch an honest bit of bread you never wipe your hands, but if you take one of these fine kickshaws you turn to your napkin at once, as if you were angry to find your fingers soiled.' 6. 'Well and good, my lad, well and good,' said the king, 'only feast away yourself and make good cheer, and we shall send you back to Persia a fine strong fellow.' And with the word he had dishes of meat and game set before his grandson. The boy was taken aback by their profusion, and exclaimed, 'Grandfather, do you give me all this for myself, to do what I like with it?' 'Certainly I do,' said the king. 7. Whereupon, without more ado, the boy Cyrus took first one dish and then another and gave them to the attendants who stood about his grandfather, and with each gift he made a little speech: 'That is for you, for so kindly teaching me to ride;' 'And that is for you, in return for the javelin you gave me, I have got it still;' 'And this is for you, because you wait on my grandfather so prettily;' 'And this is for you, sir, because you honour my mother.' And so on until he had got rid of all the meat he had been given. 8. 'But you do not give a single piece to Sacas, my butler,' quoth the grandfather, 'and I honour him more C. 3 than all the rest.' Now this Sacas, as one may guess, was a handsome fellow, and he had the right to bring before the king all who desired audience, or keep them back if he thought the time unseasonable. But Cyrus, in answer to his grandfather's question retorted eagerly, like a lad who did not know what fear meant, 'And why should you honour him so much, grandfather?' Then Astyages laughed and said, 'Can you not see how prettily he mixes the cup, and with what a grace he serves the wine?' And indeed, these royal cup-bearers are neat-handed at their task, mixing the bowl with infinite elegance, and pouring the wine into the beakers without spilling a drop, and when they hand the goblet they poise it deftly between thumb and finger for the banqueter to take. 9. 'Now, grandfather,' said the boy, 'tell Sacas to give me the bowl, and let me pour out the wine as prettily as he if I can, and win your favour.' So the king bade the butler hand him the bowl, and Cyrus took it and mixed the wine just as he had seen Sacas do, and then, showing the utmost gravity and the greatest deftness and grace, he brought the goblet to his grandfather and offered it with such an air that his mother and Astyages, too, laughed outright, and then Cyrus burst out laughing also, and flung his arms round his grandfather and kissed him, crying, 'Sacas, your day is done! I shall oust you from your office, you may be sure. I shall make just as pretty a cup-bearer as you – and not drink the wine myself!' For it is the fact that the king's butler when he offers the wine is bound to dip a ladle in the cup first, and pour a little into the hollow of his hand and sip it, so that if he has mixed poison in the bowl it will do him no good himself. 10. Accordingly Astyages, to carry on the jest, asked the little lad why he had forgotten to taste the wine though he had imitated Sacas in everything else. And the boy answered, 'Truly, I was afraid there might be poison in the bowl. For when you gave your birthday feast to your friends I could see quite plainly that Sacas had put in poison for you all.' 'And how did you discover that, my boy?' asked the king. 'Because I saw how your wits reeled and how you staggered; and you all

C. 3 began doing what you will not let us children do – you talked at the top of your voices, and none of you understood a single word the others said, and then you began singing in a way to make us laugh, and though you would not listen to the singer you swore that it was right nobly sung, and then each of you boasted of his own strength, and yet as soon as you got up to dance, so far from keeping time to the measure, you could barely keep your legs. And you seemed quite to have forgotten, grandfather, that you were king, and your subjects that you were their sovereign. Then at last I understood that you must be celebrating that "free speech" we hear of: at any rate you were never silent for an instant.' 11. 'Well, but, boy,' said Astyages, 'does your father never lose his head when he drinks?' 'Certainly not,' said the boy. 'What happens then?' asked the king. 'He quenches his thirst,' answered Cyrus, 'and that is all. No harm follows. You see, he has no Sacas to mix his wine for him.' 'But, Cyrus,' put in his mother, 'why are you so unkind to Sacas?' 'Because I do so hate him,' answered the boy. 'Time after time when I have wanted to go to my grandfather this old villain has stopped me. Do please, grandfather, let me manage him for three days.' 'And how would you set about it?' Astyages asked. 'Why,' said the boy, 'I will plant myself in the doorway just as he does, and then when he wants to go in to breakfast I shall say "You cannot have breakfast yet: HE is busy with some people," and when he comes for dinner I will say "No dinner yet: HE is in his bath," and as he grows ravenous I will say "Wait a little: HE is with the ladies of the court," until I have plagued and tormented him as he torments me, keeping me away from you, grandfather, when I want to come.' 12. Thus the boy delighted his elders in the evening, and by day if he saw that his grandfather or his uncle wanted anything, no one could forestall him in getting it; indeed nothing seemed to give him greater pleasure than to please them.

13. Now when Mandane began to think of going back to her husband, Astyages begged her to leave the boy behind. She answered that though she wished to please her father in everything, it would be hard to leave the boy

against his will. 14. Then the old man turned to Cyrus: C. 3
'My boy, if you will stay with us, Sacas shall never stop
you from coming to me: you shall be free to come
whenever you choose, and the oftener you come the better
it will please me. You shall have horses to ride, my own
and as many others as you like, and when you leave us
you shall take them with you. And at dinner you shall go
your own way and follow your own path to your own
goal of temperance just as you think right. And I will make
you a present of all the game in my parks and paradises,
and collect more for you, and as soon as you have learnt
to ride you shall hunt and shoot and hurl the javelin
exactly like a man. And you shall have boys to play with
and anything else you wish for: you have only to ask me
and it shall be yours.' 15. Then his mother questioned the
boy and asked him whether he would rather stay with his
grandfather in Media, or go back home with her: and he
said at once that he would rather stay. And when she went
on to ask him the reason, he answered, so the story says,
'Because at home I am thought to be the best of the lads at
shooting and hurling the javelin, and so I think I am: but
here I know I am the worst at riding, and that you may be
sure, mother, annoys me exceedingly. Now if you leave me
here and I learn to ride, when I am back in Persia you shall
see, I promise you, that I will outdo all our gallant fellows
on foot, and when I come to Media again I will try and
show my grandfather that, for all his splendid cavalry, he
will not have a stouter horseman than his grandson to
fight his battles for him.' 16. Then said his mother, 'But
justice and righteousness, my son, how can you learn them
here when your teachers are at home?' 'Oh,' said Cyrus, 'I
know all about them already.' 'How do you know that
you do?' asked Mandane. 'Because,' answered the boy,
'before I left home my master thought I had learnt enough
to decide the cases, and he set me to try the suits. Yes! and
I remember once,' said he, 'I got a whipping for misjudg-
ment. 17. I will tell you about that case. There were two
boys, a big boy and a little boy, and the big boy's coat was
small and the small boy's coat was huge. So the big boy
stripped the little boy and gave him his own small coat,

C. 3 while he put on the big one himself. Now in giving judgment I decided that it was better for both parties that each should have the coat that fitted him best. But I never got any further in my sentence, because the master thrashed me here, and said that the verdict would have been excellent if I had been appointed to say what fitted and what did not, but I had been called in to decide to whom the coat belonged, and the point to consider was, who had a right to it : Was he who took a thing by violence to keep it, or he who had had it made and bought it for his own ? And the master taught me that what is lawful is just and what is in the teeth of law is based on violence, and therefore, he said, the judge must always see that his verdict tallies with the law. So you see, mother, I have the whole of justice at my fingers' ends already. And if there should be anything more I need to know, why, I have my grandfather beside me, and he will give me lessons.'
18. 'But,' rejoined his mother, 'what everyone takes to be just and righteous at your grandfather's court is not thought to be so in Persia. For instance, your own grandfather has made himself master over all and sundry among the Medes, but with the Persians equality is held to be an essential part of justice : and first and foremost, your father himself must perform his appointed services to the state and receive his appointed dues : and the measure of these is not his own caprice but the law. Have a care then, or you may be scourged to death when you come home to Persia, if you learn in your grandfather's school to love not kingship but tyranny, and hold the tyrant's belief that he and he alone should have more than all the rest.' 'Ah, but, mother,' said the boy, 'my grandfather is better at teaching people to have less than their share, not more. Cannot you see,' he cried, 'how he has taught all the Medes to have less than himself ? So set your mind at rest, mother, my grandfather will never make me, or any one else, an adept in the art of getting too much.'

C. 4   So the boy's tongue ran on. But at last his mother went home, and Cyrus stayed behind and was brought up in Media. He soon made friends with his companions and found his way to their hearts, and soon won their parents

by the charm of his address and the true affection he bore C. 4
their sons, so much so that when they wanted a favour
from the king they bade their children ask Cyrus to arrange
the matter for them. And whatever it might be, the
kindliness of the lad's heart and the eagerness of his
ambition made him set the greatest store on getting it
done. 2. On his side, Astyages could not bring himself to
refuse his grandson's lightest wish. For once, when he was
sick, nothing would induce the boy to leave his side; he
could not keep back his tears, and his terror at the thought
that his grandfather might die was plain for every one to
see. If the old man needed anything during the night Cyrus
was the first to notice it, it was he who sprang up first to
wait upon him, and bring him what he thought would
please him. Thus the old king's heart was his.

3. During these early days, it must be allowed, the boy
was something too much of a talker, in part, may be,
because of his bringing-up. He had been trained by his
master, whenever he sat in judgment, to give a reason for
what he did, and to look for the like reason from others.
And moreover, his curiosity and thirst for knowledge were
such that he must needs inquire from every one he met the
explanation of this, that, and the other; and his own wits
were so lively that he was ever ready with an answer
himself for any question put to him, so that talkativeness
had become, as it were, his second nature. But, just as in
the body when a boy is overgrown, some touch of youth-
fulness is sure to show itself and tell the secret of his age,
so for all the lad's loquacity, the impression left on the
listener was not of arrogance, but of simplicity and warm-
heartedness, and one would gladly have heard his chatter
to the end rather than have sat beside him and found him
dumb.

4. However, as he grew in stature and the years led him
to the time when childhood passes into youth he became
more chary of his words and quieter in his tone: at times,
indeed, he was so shy that he would blush in the presence
of his elders, and there was little sign left of the old
forwardness, the impulsiveness of the puppy who will
jump up on every one, master and stranger alike. Thus he

C. 4 grew more sedate, but his company was still most fascinat-
ing, and little wonder: for whenever it came to a trial of
skill between himself and his comrades he would never
challenge his mates to those feats in which he himself
excelled: he would start precisely one where he felt his
own inferiority, averring that he would outdo them all, –
indeed, he would spring to horse in order to shoot or hurl
the javelin before he had got a firm seat – and then, when
he was worsted, he would be the first to laugh at his own
discomfiture. 5. He had no desire to escape defeat by
giving up the effort, but took glory in the resolution to do
better another time, and thus he soon found himself as
good a horseman as his peers, and presently, such was his
ardour, he surpassed them all, and at last the thinning of
the game in the king's preserves began to show what he
could do. What with the chasing and the shooting and the
spearing, the stock of animals ran so low that Astyages
was hard put to it to collect enough for him. Then Cyrus,
seeing that his grandfather for all his goodwill could never
furnish him with enough, came to him one day and said,
'Grandfather, why should you take so much trouble in
finding game for me? If only you would let me go out to
hunt with my uncle, I could fancy every beast we came
across had been reared for my particular delight!' 6. But
however anxious the lad might be to go out to the chase,
he had somehow lost the old childish art of winning what
he wanted by coaxing: and he hesitated a long time before
approaching the king again. If in the old days he had
quarrelled with Sacas for not letting him in, now he began
to play the part of Sacas against himself, and could not
summon courage to intrude until he thought the right
moment had come: indeed, he implored the real Sacas to
let him know when he might venture. So that the old
butler's heart was won, and he, like the rest of the world,
was completely in love with the young prince.

7. At last when Astyages saw that the lad's heart was
really set on hunting in the open country, he gave him
leave to go out with his uncle, taking care at the same time
to send an escort of mounted veterans at his heels, whose
business it was to keep watch and ward over him in any

dangerous place or against any savage beast. Cyrus plied C. 4 his retinue with questions about the creatures they came across, which must he avoid and which might he hunt? They told him he must be on his guard against bears and wild-boars and lions and leopards: many a man had found himself at too close quarters with these dangerous creatures, and been torn to pieces: but antelopes, they said, and deer and mountain sheep and wild asses were harmless enough. And the huntsman, they added, ought to be as careful about dangerous places as about the beasts themselves: many a time horse and rider had gone headlong down a precipice to death. 8. The lad seemed to take all their lessons to heart at the time: but then he saw a stag leap up, and forgot all the wise cautions he had heard, giving chase forthwith, noticing nothing except the beast ahead of him. His horse, in its furious plunge forward, slipped, and came down on its knees, all but throwing the rider over its head. As luck would have it the boy managed to keep his seat, and the horse recovered its footing. When they reached the flat bottom, Cyrus let fly his javelin, and the stag fell dead, a beautiful big creature. The lad was still radiant with delight when up rode the guards and took him severely to task. Could he not see the danger he had run? They would certainly tell his grandfather, that they would. Cyrus, who had dismounted, stood quite still and listened ruefully, hanging his head while they rated him. But in the middle of it all he heard the view-halloo again: he sprang to his horse as though frenzied — a wild-boar was charging down on them, and he charged to meet it, and drawing his bow with the surest aim possible, struck the beast in the forehead, and laid him low. 9. But now his uncle thought it was high time to scold his nephew himself; the lad's boldness was too much. Only, the more he scolded the more Cyrus begged he would let him take back the spoil as a present for his grandfather. To which appeal, says the story, his uncle made reply: 'But if your grandfather finds out that you have gone in chase yourself, he will not only scold you for going but me for letting you go.' 'Well, let him whip me if he likes,' said the boy, 'when once I have given him my beasts: and you too, uncle,' he

C. 4 went on, 'punish me however you choose, only do not refuse me this.' So Cyaxares was forced to yield : – 'Have it your own way then, you are little less than our king already.' 10. Thus it was that Cyrus was allowed to bring his trophies home, and in due course presented them to his grandfather. 'See, grandfather, here are some animals I have shot for you.' But he did not show his weapons in triumph : he only laid them down with the gore still on them where he hoped his grandfather would see them. It is easy to guess the answer Astyages gave : – 'I must needs accept with pleasure every gift you bring me, only I want none of them at the risk of your own life.' And Cyrus said, 'If you really do not want them yourself, grandfather, will you give them to me ? And I will divide them among the lads.' 'With all my heart,' said the old man, 'take them, or anything else you like ; bestow them where you will, and welcome.' 11. So Cyrus carried off the spoil, and divided it with his comrades, saying all the while, 'What foolery it was, was it not, when we used to hunt in the park ! It was no better than hunting creatures tied by a string. First of all, it was such a little bit of a place, and then what scarecrows the poor beasts were, one halt, and another maimed ! But those real animals on the mountains and the plains – what splendid beasts, so gigantic, so sleek and glossy ! Why, the stags leapt up against the sky as though they had wings, and the wild-boars came rushing to close quarters like warriors in battle ! And thanks to their breadth and bulk one could not help hitting them. Why, even as they lie dead there,' cried he, 'they look finer than those poor walled-up creatures when alive ! But you,' he added, 'could not your fathers let you go out to hunt too ?' 'Gladly enough,' answered they, 'if only the king gave the order.' 12. 'Well,' said Cyrus, 'who will speak to Astyages for us ?' 'Why,' answered they, 'who so fit to persuade him as yourself ?' 'No, by all that's holy, not I !' cried Cyrus. 'I cannot think what has come over me : I cannot speak to my grandfather any more ; I cannot look him straight in the face. If this fit grows on me, I am afraid I shall become no better than an idiot. And yet, when I was a little boy, they tell me, I was sharp enough at talking.' To which the other lads retorted, 'Well, it is a bad business altogether : C. 4 and if you cannot bestir yourself for your friends, if you can do nothing for us in our need, we must turn elsewhere.' 13. When Cyrus heard that he was stung to the quick : he went away in silence and urged himself to put on a bold face, and so went in to his grandfather, not, however, without planning first how he could best bring in the matter. Accordingly he began thus : 'Tell me, grandfather,' said he, 'if one of your slaves were to run away and you caught him, what would you do to him ?' 'What else should I do,' the old man answered, 'but clap irons on him and set him to work in chains ?' 'But if he came back of his own accord, how would you treat him then ?' 'Why, I would give him a whipping, as a warning not to do it again, and then treat him as though nothing had happened.' 'It is high time then,' said the boy, 'that you began getting a birch ready for your grandson : for I am planning to take my comrades and run away on a hunting expedition.' 'Very kind of you to tell me, beforehand,' said Astyages. 'And now listen, I forbid you to set foot outside the palace grounds. A pretty thing,' he added, 'if for the sake of a day's hunting I should let my daughter's lamb get lost.' 14. So Cyrus did as he was ordered and stayed at home, but he spent his days in silence and his brow was clouded. At last Astyages saw how bitterly the lad felt it, and he made up his mind to please him by leading out a hunting-party himself. He held a great muster of horse and foot, and the other lads were not forgotten : he had the beasts driven down into the flat country where the horses could be taken easily, and then the hunt began in splendid style. After the royal fashion – for he was present in person himself – he gave orders that no one was to shoot until Cyrus had hunted to his heart's content. But Cyrus would not hear of any such hindrance to the others : 'Grandfather,' he cried, 'if you wish me to enjoy myself, let my friends hunt with me and each of us try our best.' 15. Thereupon Astyages let them all go, while he stood still and watched the sight, and saw how they raced to attack the quarry and how their ambition burned within them as they followed up the chase and let fly their javelins.

C. 4 But above all he was overjoyed to see how his grandson could not keep silence for sheer delight, calling upon his fellows by name whenever he came up with the quarry, like a noble young hound, baying from pure excitement. It gladdened the old man's heart to hear how gleefully the boy would laugh at one of his comrades and how eagerly he would applaud another without the slightest touch of jealousy. At length it was time to turn, and home they went, laden with their mighty trophies. And ever afterwards, so well pleased was the king with the day's hunting, that whenever it was possible, out he must go with his grandson, all his train behind him, and he never failed to take the boys also, 'to please Cyrus.' Thus did Cyrus spend his early life, sharing in and helping towards the happiness of all, and bringing no sorrow to any man.

16. But when he was about fifteen years of age, it chanced that the young Prince of Assyria, who was about to marry a wife, planned a hunting-party of his own, in honour of the bridal. And, having heard that on the frontiers of Assyria and Media there was much game to be got, untouched and unmolested because of the war, the prince chose these marches for his hunting-ground. But for safety sake he took with him a large escort of cavalry and targeteers, who were to drive the beasts down from their lairs into the cultivated levels below where it was easy to ride. He set out to the place where the Assyrian outposts were planted and a garrison on duty, and there he and his men prepared to take their supper, intending to begin the hunt with the morrow's dawn. 17. And as evening had fallen, it happened that the night-watch, a considerable body of horse and foot, arrived from the city to relieve the garrison on guard. Thus the prince found that he had something like a large army at his call: the two garrisons as well as the troop of horse and foot for the hunt. And then he asked himself whether it would not be the best of plans to drive off booty from the country of the Medes? In this way more lustre would be given to the chase, and there would be great store of beasts for sacrifice. With this intent he rose betimes and led his army out: the foot soldiers he massed together on the frontier, while he

himself, at the head of his cavalry, rode up to the border C. 4
fortresses of the Medes. Here he halted with the strongest
and largest part of his company, to prevent the garrisons
from sallying out, and meanwhile he sent picked men
forward by detachments with orders to raid the country in
every direction, waylay everything they chanced upon, and
drive the spoil back to him.

18. While this was going on news was brought to
Astyages that the enemy was across the border, and he
hastened to the rescue at once, himself at the head of his
own body-guard, and his son with such troopers as were
ready to hand, leaving word for others to follow with all
despatch. But when they were in sight of the Assyrians,
and saw their serried ranks, horse and foot, drawn up in
order, compact and motionless, they came to a halt
themselves. 19. Now Cyrus, seeing that all the rest of the
world was off to the rescue, boot and saddle, must needs
ride out too, and so put on his armour for the first time,
and could scarcely believe it was true, he had longed so
often and so ardently to wear it all. And right beautiful it
was, and right well it fitted the lad, the armour that his
grandsire had had made for him. So he put on the whole
accoutrement, mounted his charger, and galloped to the
front. And Astyages, though he wondered who had sent
the boy, bade him stay beside him, now that he had come.
Cyrus, as he looked at the horsemen facing them, turned
to his grandfather with the question, 'Can those men
yonder be our enemies, grandfather, those who are standing so quietly beside their horses ?' 'Enemies they are for
all that,' said the king. 'And are those enemies too ?' the
boy asked, 'those who are riding over there ?' 'Yes, to be
sure.' 'Well, grandfather,' said the lad, 'a sorry set they
look, and sorry jades they ride to ravage our lands ! It
would be well for some of us to charge them !' 'Not yet,
my boy,' answered his grandfather, 'look at the mass of
horsemen here. If we were to charge the others now, these
friends of theirs would charge us, for our full strength is
not yet on the field.' 'Yes, but,' suggested the boy, 'if you
stay here yourself, ready to receive our supporters, these
fellows will be afraid to stir either, and the cattle-lifters

C. 4 will drop their booty quick enough, as soon as they find they are attacked.'

20. Astyages felt there was much in what the boy said, and thinking all the while what wonderful sense he showed and how wide-awake he was, gave orders for his son to take a squadron of horse and charge the raiders. 'If the main body move to attack,' he added, 'I will charge myself and give them enough to do here.' Accordingly Cyaxares took a detachment of horse and galloped to the field. Cyrus seeing the charge, darted forward himself, and swept to the van, leading it with Cyaxares close at his heels and the rest close behind them. As soon as the plunderers saw them, they left their booty and took to flight. 21. The troopers, with Cyrus at their head, dashed in to cut them off, and some they overtook at once and hewed down then and there; others slipped past, and then they followed in hot pursuit, and caught some of them too. And Cyrus was ever in the front, like a young hound, untrained as yet but bred from a gallant stock, charging a wild-boar recklessly: forward he swept, without eyes or thought for anything but the quarry to be captured and the blow to be struck. But when the Assyrian army saw their friends in trouble they pushed forward, rank on rank, saying to themselves the pursuit would stop when their own movement was seen. 22. But Cyrus never slackened his pace a whit: in a transport of joy he called on his uncle by name as he pressed forward, hanging hot-foot on the fugitives, while Cyaxares still clung to his heels, thinking maybe what his father Astyages would say if he hung back, and the others still followed close behind them, even the faint-hearted changed into heroes for the nonce.

Now Astyages, watching their furious onslaught, and seeing the enemy move steadily forward in close array to meet them, decided to advance without a moment's delay himself, for fear that his son and Cyrus might come to harm, crashing in disorder against the solid battalions of the foe. 23. The Assyrians saw the movement of the king and came to a halt, spears levelled and bows bent, expecting that, when their assailants came within range, they would halt likewise as they had usually done before. For

hitherto, whenever the armies met, they would only charge C. 4
up to a certain distance, and there take flying shots, and so
keep up the skirmish until evening fell. But now the
Assyrians saw their own men borne down on them in rout,
with Cyrus and his comrades at their heels in full career,
while Astyages and his cavalry were already within bow-
shot. It was more than they could face, and they turned
and fled. After them swept the Medes in full pursuit, and
those they caught they mowed down, horse and man, and
those that fell they slew. There was no pause until they
came up with the Assyrian foot. 24. Here at last they drew
rein in fear of some hidden ambuscade, and Astyages led
his army off. The exploit of his cavalry pleased him beyond
measure, but he did not know what he could say to Cyrus.
It was he to whom the engagement was due, and the
victory ; but the boy's daring was on the verge of madness.
Even during the return home his behaviour was strange :
he could not forbear riding round alone to look into the
faces of the slain, and those whose duty it was could
hardly drag him away to lead him to Astyages : indeed, the
youth was glad enough to keep them as a screen between
himself and the king, for he saw that the countenance of
his grandfather grew stern at the sight of him.

25. So matters passed in Media : and more and more the
name of Cyrus was on the lip of every man, in song and
story everywhere, and Astyages, who had always loved
him, was astonished beyond all measure at the lad. Meanwhile his father, Cambyses, rejoiced to hear such tidings
of his son ; but, when he heard that he was already acting
like a man of years, he thought it full time to call him
home again that he might complete his training in the
discipline of his fatherland. The story tells how Cyrus
answered the summons, saying he would rather return
home at once so that his father might not be vexed or his
country blame him. And Astyages, too, thought it his plain
duty to send the boy back, but he must needs give him
horses to take with him, as many as he would care to
choose, and other gifts beside, not only for the love he
bore him but for the high hopes he had that the boy would
one day prove a man of mark, a blessing to his friends,

C. 4 and a terror to his foes. And when the time came for Cyrus to go, the whole world poured out to speed him on his journey — little children and lads of his own age, and grown men and greybeards on their steeds, and Astyages the king. And, so says the chronicle, the eyes of none were dry when they turned home again. 26. Cyrus himself, they tell us, rode away in tears. He heaped gifts on all his comrades, sharing with them what Astyages had given to himself; and at last he took off the splendid Median cloak he wore and gave it to one of them, to tell him, plainer than words could say, how his heart clung to him above the rest. And his friends, they say, took the gifts he gave them, but they brought them all back to Astyages, who sent them to Cyrus again. But once more Cyrus sent them back to Media with this prayer to his grandfather: — 'If you would have me hold up my head when I come back to you again, let my friends keep the gifts I gave them.' And Astyages did as the boy asked.

27. And here, if a tale of boyish love is not out of place, we might tell how, when Cyrus was just about to depart and the last good-byes were being said, each of his kinsmen in the Persian fashion — and to this day the custom holds in Persia — kissed him on the lips as they bade him godspeed. Now there was a certain Mede, as beautiful and brave a man as ever lived, who had been enamoured of Cyrus for many a long day, and, when he saw the kiss, he stayed behind, and after the others had withdrawn he went up to Cyrus and said, 'Me, and me alone, of all your kindred, Cyrus, you refuse to recognise?' And Cyrus answered, 'What, are you my kinsman, too?' 'Yes, assuredly,' the other answered, and the lad rejoined, 'Ah, then, that is why you looked at me so earnestly; and I have seen you look at me like that, I think, more than once before.' 'Yes,' answered the Mede, 'I have often longed to approach you, but as often, heaven knows, my heart failed me.' 'But why should that be,' said Cyrus, 'seeing you are my kinsman?' And with the word, he leant forward and kissed him on the lips. 28. Then the Mede, emboldened by the kiss, took heart and said, 'So in Persia it is really the custom for relatives to kiss?' 'Truly yes,' answered Cyrus,

'when we see each other after a long absence, or when we C. 4
part for a journey.' 'Then the time has come,' said the
other, 'to give me a second kiss, for I must leave you now.'
With that Cyrus kissed him again and so they parted. But
the travellers were not far on their way when suddenly the
Mede came galloping after them, his charger covered with
foam. Cyrus caught sight of him : — 'You have forgotten
something? There is something else you wanted to say?'
'No,' said the Mede, 'it is only such a long, long while
since we met.' 'Such a little, little while you mean, my
kinsman,' answered Cyrus. 'A little while!' repeated the
other. 'How can you say that? Cannot you understand
that the time it takes to wink is a whole eternity if it severs
me from the beauty of your face?'

Then Cyrus burst out laughing in spite of his own tears,
and bade the unfortunate man take heart of grace and be
gone. 'I shall soon be back with you again, and then you
can stare at me to your heart's content, and never wink at
all.'

Thus Cyrus left his grandfather's court and came home C. 5
to Persia, and there, so it is said, he spent one year more
as a boy among the boys. At first the lads were disposed to
laugh at him, thinking he must have learnt luxurious ways
in Media, but when they saw that he could take the simple
Persian food as happily as themselves, and how, whenever
they made good cheer at a festival, far from asking for any
more himself he was ready to give his own share of the
dainties away, when they saw and felt in this and in other
things his inborn nobleness and superiority to themselves,
then the tide turned and once more they were at his feet.

And when this part of his training was over, and the
time was come for him to join the younger men, it was the
same tale once more. Once more he outdid all his fellows,
alike in the fulfilment of his duty, in the endurance of
hardship, in the reverence he showed to age, and the
obedience he paid to authority.

2. Now in the fullness of time Astyages died in Media,
and Cyaxares his son, the brother of Cyrus' mother, took
the kingdom in his stead. By this time the king of Assyria
had subdued all the tribes of Syria, subjugated the king of

C. 5 Arabia, brought the Hyrcanians under his rule, and was holding the Bactrians in siege. Therefore he came to think that, if he could but weaken the power of the Medes, it would be easy for him to extend his empire over all the nations round him, since the Medes were, without doubt, the strongest of them all. 3. Accordingly he sent his messengers to every part of his dominions: to Croesus, king of Lydia, to the king of Cappadocia, to both the Phrygias, to the Paphlagonians and the Indians, to the Carians and the Cilicians. And he bade them spread slanders abroad against the Persians and the Medes, and say moreover that these were great and mighty kingdoms which had come together and made alliance by marriage with one another, and unless a man should be beforehand with them and bring down their power it could not be but that they would fall on each of their neighbours in turn and subdue them one by one. So the nations listened to the messengers and made alliance with the king of Assyria: some were persuaded by what he said and others were won over by gifts and gold, for the riches of the Assyrian were great. 4. Now Cyaxares, the son of Astyages, was aware of these plots and preparations, and he made ready on his side, so far as in him lay, sending word to the Persian state and to Cambyses the king, who had his sister to wife. And he sent to Cyrus also, begging him to come with all speed at the head of any force that might be furnished, if so be the Council of Persia would give him men-at-arms. For by this time Cyrus had accomplished his ten years among the youths and was now enrolled with the grown men. 5. He was right willing to go, and the Council of Elders appointed him to command the force for Media. They bade him choose two hundred men among the Peers, each of them to choose four others from their fellows. Thus was formed a body of a thousand Peers: and each of the thousand had orders to raise thirty men from the commons — ten targeteers, ten slingers, and ten archers — and thus three regiments were levied, 10,000 archers, 10,000 slingers, and 10,000 targeteers, over and above the thousand Peers. The whole force was to be put under the command of Cyrus. 6. As soon as he was appointed, his

first act had been to offer sacrifice, and when the omens C. 5
were favourable he had chosen his two hundred Peers, and
each of them had chosen their four comrades. Then he
called the whole body together, and for the first time spoke
to them as follows : —

7. 'My friends, I have chosen you for this work, but this
is not the first time that I have formed my opinion of your
worth : from my boyhood I have watched your zeal for all
that our country holds to be honourable and your abhor-
rence for all that she counts base. And I wish to tell you
plainly why I have accepted this office myself and why I ask
your help. 8. I have long felt sure that our forefathers were
in their time as good men as we. For their lives were one
long effort towards the self-same deeds of valour as are
held in honour now : and still, for all their worth, I fail to
see what good they gained either for the state or for
themselves. 9. Yet I cannot bring myself to believe that
there is a single virtue practised among mankind merely in
order that the brave and good should fare no better than
the base ones of the earth. Men do not forego the pleasures
of the moment to say good-bye to all joy for evermore – no,
this self-control is a training, so that we may reap the fruits
of a larger joy in the time to come. A man will toil day and
night to make himself an orator, yet oratory is not the one
aim of his existence : his hope is to influence men by his
eloquence and thus achieve some noble end. So too with us,
and those like us, who are drilled in the arts of war : we do
not give our labours in order to fight for ever, endlessly and
hopelessly, we hope that we too one day, when we have
proved our mettle, may win and wear for ourselves and for
our city the threefold ornament of wealth, of happiness, of
honour. 10. And if there should be some who have worked
hard all their lives and suddenly old-age, they find, has
stolen on them unawares, and taken away their powers
before they have gathered in the fruit of all their toil, such
men seem to me like those who desire to be thrifty
husbandmen, and who sow well and plant wisely, but when
the time of harvest comes let the fruit drop back ungar-
nered into the soil whence it sprang. Or as if an athlete
should train himself and reach the heights where victory

C. 5 may be won and at the last forbear to enter the lists – such
an one, I take it, would but meet his deserts if all men cried
out upon him for a fool. 11. Let not such be our fate, my
friends. Our own hearts bear us witness that we, too, from
our boyhood up, have been trained in the school of beauty
and nobleness and honour, and now let us go forward to
meet our foes. They, I know right well, when matched with
us, will prove but novices in war. He is no true warrior,
though he be skilled with the javelin and the bow and ride
on horseback with the best, who, when the call for
endurance comes, is found to fail: toil finds him but a
novice. Nor are they warriors who, when they should wake
and watch, give way to slumber: sleep finds them novices.
Even endurance will not avail, if a man has not learnt to
deal as a man should by friends and foes: such a one is
unschooled in the highest part of his calling. 12. But with
you it is not so: to you the night will be as the day; toil,
your school has taught you, is the guide to happiness;
hunger has been your daily condiment, and water you take
to quench your thirst as the lion laps the stream. And you
have that within your hearts which is the rarest of all
treasures and the most akin to war: of all sweet sounds the
sweetest sound for you is the voice of fame. You are fair
Honour's suitors, and you must needs win your title to her
favour. Therefore you undergo toil and danger gladly.

13. 'Now if I said all this of you, and my heart were not
in my words, I should but cheat myself. For in so far as
you should fail to fulfil my hopes of you, it is on me that
the shame would fall. But I have faith in you, bred of
experience: I trust in your goodwill towards me, and in
our enemy's lack of wit; you will not belie my hopes. Let
us go forth with a light heart; we have no ill-fame to fear:
none can say we covet another man's goods unlawfully.
Our enemy strikes the first blow in an unrighteous cause,
and our friends call us to protect them. What is more
lawful than self-defence? What is nobler than to succour
those we love? 14. And you have another ground of
confidence – in opening this campaign I have not been
forgetful of the gods: you have gone in and out with me,
and you know how in all things, great and small, I strive

to win their blessing. And now,' he added, 'what need of C. 5
further words? I will leave you now to choose your own
men, and when all is ready you will march into Media at
their head. Meanwhile I will return to my father and start
before you, so that I may learn what I can about the enemy
as soon as may be, and thus make all needful preparations,
so that by God's help we may win glory on the field.'

Such were his orders and they set about them at once. C. 6
But Cyrus himself went home and prayed to the gods of
his father's house, to Hestia and Zeus, and to all who had
watched over his race. And when he had done so, he set
out for the war, and his father went with him on the road.
They were no sooner clear of the city, so says the story,
than they met with favourable omens of thunder and
lightning, and after that they went forward without further
divination, for they felt that no man could mistake the
signs from the Ruler of the gods. 2. And as they went on
their way Cyrus' father said to him, 'My son, the gods are
gracious to us, and look with favour on your journey —
they have shown it in the sacrifices, and by their signs from
heaven. You do not need another man to tell you so, for I
was careful to have you taught this art, so that you might
understand the counsels of the gods yourself and have no
need of an interpreter, seeing with your own eyes and
hearing with your own ears and taking the heavenly
meaning for yourself. Thus you need not be at the mercy
of any soothsayers who might have a mind to deceive you,
speaking contrary to the omens vouchsafed from heaven,
nor yet, should you chance to be without a seer, drift in
perplexity and know not how to profit by the heavenly
signs: you yourself through your own learning can understand the warnings of the gods and follow them.'

3. 'Yes, father,' answered Cyrus, 'so far as in me lies, I
bear your words in mind, and pray to the gods continually
that they may show us favour and vouchsafe to counsel
us. I remember,' he went on, 'how once I heard you say
that, as with men, so with the gods, it was but natural if
the prayer of him should prevail who did not turn to flatter
them only in time of need, but was mindful of them above
all in the heyday of his happiness. It was thus indeed, you

C. 6 said, that we ought to deal with our earthly friends.'
4. 'True, my son,' said his father, 'and because of all my teaching, you can now approach the gods in prayer with a lighter heart and a more confident hope that they will grant you what you ask, because your conscience bears you witness that you have never forgotten them.' 'Even so,' said Cyrus, 'and in truth I feel towards them as though they were my friends.' 5. 'And do you remember,' asked his father, 'certain other conclusions on which we were agreed? How we felt there were certain things that the gods had permitted us to attain through learning and study and training? The accomplishment of these is the reward of effort, not of idleness; in these it is only when we have done all that it is our duty to do that we are justified in asking for blessings from the gods.' 6. 'I remember very well,' said Cyrus, 'that you used to talk to me in that way: and indeed I could not but agree with the arguments you gave. You used to say that a man had no right to pray he might win a cavalry charge if he had never learnt to ride, or triumph over master-bowmen if he could not draw a bow, or bring a ship safe home to harbour if he did not know how to steer, or be rewarded with a plenteous harvest if he had not so much as sown grain into the ground, or come home safe from battle if he took no precautions whatsoever. All such prayers as these, you said, were contrary to the very ordinances of heaven, and those who asked for things forbidden could not be surprised if they failed to win them from the gods. In the same way, a petition in the face of law on earth would have no success with men.'

7. 'And do you remember,' said his father, 'how we thought that it would be a noble work enough if a man could train himself really and truly to be beautiful and brave and earn all he needed for his household and himself? That, we said, was a work of which a man might well be proud; but if he went further still, if he had the skill and the science to be the guide and governor of other men, supplying all their wants and making them all they ought to be, that, it seemed to us, would be indeed a marvel.' 8. 'Yes, my father,' answered Cyrus, 'I remember

it very well. I agreed with you that to rule well and nobly C. 6
was the greatest of all works, and I am of the same mind
still,' he went on, 'whenever I think of government in itself.
But when I look on the world at large, when I see of what
poor stuff those men are made who contrive to uphold
their rule and what sort of antagonists we are likely to find
in them, then I can only feel how disgraceful it would be
to cringe before them and not face them myself and try
conclusions with them on the field. All of them, I perceive,'
he added, 'beginning with our own friends here, hold to it
that the ruler should only differ from his subjects by the
splendour of his banquets, the wealth of gold in his coffers,
the length and depth of his slumbers, and his freedom from
trouble and pain. But my views are different: I hold that
the ruler should be marked out from other men, not by
taking life easily, but by his forethought and his wisdom
and his eagerness for work.' 9. 'True, my son,' the father
answered, 'but you know the struggle must in part be
waged not against flesh and blood but against circumstances, and these may not be overcome so easily. You
know, I take it, that if supplies were not forthcoming,
farewell to this government of yours.' 'Yes,' Cyrus
answered, 'and that is why Cyaxares is undertaking to
provide for all of us who join him, whatever our numbers
are.' 'So,' said the father, 'and you really mean, my son,
that you are relying only on these supplies of Cyaxares for
this campaign of yours?' 'Yes,' answered Cyrus. 'And do
you know what they amount to?' 'No,' he said, 'I cannot
say that I do.' 'And yet,' his father went on, 'you are
prepared to rely on what you do not know? Do you forget
that the needs of the morrow must be high, not to speak
of the outlay for the day?' 'Oh, no,' said Cyrus, 'I am well
aware of that.' 'Well,' said the father, 'suppose the cost is
more than Cyaxares can bear, or suppose he actually
meant to deceive you, how would your soldiers fare?' 'Ill
enough, no doubt,' answered he. 'And now tell me, father,
while we are still in friendly country, if you know of any
resources that I could make my own?' 10. 'You want to
kow where you could find resources of your own?'
repeated his father. 'And who is to find that out, if not he

C. 6 who holds the keys of power? We have given you a force
of infantry that you would not exchange, I feel sure, for
one that was more than twice its size: and you will have
the cavalry of Media to support you, the finest in the
world. I conceive there are none of the nations round
about who will not be ready to serve you, whether to win
your favour or because they fear disaster. These are
matters you must look to carefully, in concert with Cyaxares, so that nothing should ever fail you of what you
need, and, if only for habit's sake, you should devise some
means for supplying your revenue. Bear this maxim in
mind before all others – never put off the collecting of
supplies until the day of need, make the season of your
abundance provide against the time of dearth. You will
gain better terms from those on whom you must depend if
you are not thought to be in straits, and, what is more,
you will be free from blame in the eyes of your soldiers.
That in itself will make you more respected; wherever you
desire to help or to hurt, your troops will follow you with
the greater readiness, so long as they have all they need,
and your words, you may be sure, will carry the greater
weight the fuller your display of power for weal or woe.'

11. 'Yes, father,' Cyrus said, 'I feel all you say is true,
and the more because as things now stand none of my
soldiers will thank me for the pay that is promised them.
They are well aware of the terms Cyaxares has offered for
their help: but whatever they get over and above the
covenanted amount they will look upon as a free gift, and
for that they will, in all likelihood, feel most gratitude to
the giver.' 'True,' said the father, 'and really for a man to
have a force with which he could serve his friends and take
vengeance on his foes, and yet neglect the supplies for it,
would be as disgraceful, would it not? as for a farmer to
hold lands and labourers and yet allow fields to lie barren
for lack of tillage.'

'No such neglect,' answered the son, 'shall ever be laid
at my door. Through friendly lands or hostile, trust me, in
this business of supplying my troops with all they need I
will always play my part.'

12. 'Well, my son,' the father resumed, 'and do you

remember certain other points which we agreed must never C. 6
be overlooked?' 'Could I forget them?' answered Cyrus.
'I remember how I came to you for money to pay the
teacher who professed to have taught me generalship, and
you gave it me, but you asked me many questions. "Now,
my boy," you said, "did this teacher you want to pay ever
mention economy among the things a general ought to
understand? Soldiers, no less than servants in a house, are
dependent on supplies." And I was forced to tell the truth
and admit that not a syllable had been mentioned on that
score. Then you asked me if anything had been taught
about health and strength, since a true general is bound to
think of these matters no less than of tactics and strategy.
And when I was forced to say no, you asked me if he had
taught me any of the arts which give the best aid in war.
Once again I had to say no and then you asked whether he
had ever taught me how to kindle enthusiasm in my men.
For in every undertaking, you said, there was all the
difference in the world between energy and lack of spirit. I
shook my head and your examination went on: – Had
this teacher laid no stress on the need for obedience in an
army, or on the best means of securing discipline? 14. And
finally, when it was plain that even this had been utterly
ignored, you exclaimed, "What in the world, then, does
your professor claim to have taught you under the name
of generalship?" To that I could at last give a positive
answer: "He taught me tactics." And then you gave a little
laugh and ran through your list point by point: – "And
pray what will be the use of tactics to an army without
supplies, without health, without discipline, without
knowledge of those arts and inventions that are of use in
war?" And so you made it clear to me that tactics and
manoeuvres and drill were only a small part of all that is
implied in generalship, and when I asked you if you could
teach me the rest of it you bade me betake myself to those
who stood high in repute as great generals, and talk with
them and learn from their lips how each thing should be
done. 15. So I consorted with all I thought to be of
authority in these matters. As regards our present supplies
I was persuaded that what Cyaxares intended to provide

C. 6 was sufficient, and, as for the health of the troops, I was aware that the cities where health was valued appointed medical officers, and the generals who cared for their soldiers took out a medical staff; and so when I found myself in this office I gave my mind to the matter at once: and I flatter myself, father,' he added, 'that I shall have with me an excellent staff of surgeons and physicians.' 16. To which the father made reply, 'Well, my son, but these excellent men are, after all, much the same as the tailors who patch torn garments. When folk are ill, your doctors can patch them up, but your own care for their health ought to go far deeper than that: your prime object should be to save your men from falling ill at all.' 'And pray, father,' asked Cyrus, 'how can I succeed in that?' 'Well,' answered Cambyses, 'I presume if you are to stay long in one place you will do your best to discover a healthy spot for your camp, and if you give your mind to the matter you can hardly fail to find it. Men, we know, are for ever discussing what places are healthy and what are not, and their own complexions and the state of their own bodies is the clearest evidence. But you will not content yourself with choosing a site, you will remember the care you take yourself for your own health.' 17. 'Well,' said Cyrus, 'my first rule is to avoid over-feeding as most oppressive to the system, and my next to work off all that enters the body: that seems the best way to keep health and gain strength.' 'My son,' Cambyses answered, 'these are the principles you must apply to others.' 'What!' said Cyrus; 'do you think it will be possible for the soldiers to diet and train themselves?' 'Not only possible,' said the father, 'but essential. For surely an army, if it is to fulfil its function at all, must always be engaged in hurting the foe or helping itself. A single man is hard enough to support in idleness, a household is harder still, an army hardest of all. There are more mouths to be filled, less wealth to start with, and greater waste; and therefore an army should never be unemployed.' 18. 'If I take your meaning,' answered Cyrus, 'you think an idle general as useless as an idle farmer. And here and now I answer for the working general, and promise on his behalf that with God's help he will show you that his

troops have all they need and their bodies are all they ought C. 6
to be. And I think,' he added, 'I know a way by which an
officer might do much towards training his men in the
various branches of war. Let him propose competitions of
every kind and offer prizes; the standard of skill will rise,
and he will soon have a body of troops ready to his hand
for any service he requires.' 'Nothing could be better,'
answered the father. 'Do this, and you may be sure you will
watch your regiments at their manoeuvres with as much
delight as if they were a chorus in the dance.'

19. 'And then,' continued Cyrus, 'to rouse enthusiasm
in the men, there can be nothing, I take it, like the power
of kindling hope?' 'True,' answered his father, 'but that
alone would be as though a huntsman were for ever
rousing his pack with the view-halloo. At first, of course,
the hounds will answer eagerly enough, but after they have
been cheated once or twice they will end by refusing the
call even when the quarry is really in sight. And so it is
with hope. Let a man rouse false expectations often
enough, and in the end, even when hope is at the door, he
may cry the good news in vain. Rather ought he to refrain
from speaking positively himself when he cannot know
precisely; his agents may step in and do it in his place;
but he should reserve his own appeal for the supreme
crises of supreme danger, and not dissipate his credit.'

'By heaven, a most admirable suggestion!' cried Cyrus,
'and one much more to my mind! 20. As for enforcing
obedience, I hope I have had some little training in that
already: you began my education yourself when I was a
child by teaching me to obey you, and then you handed
me over to masters who did as you had done, and
afterwards, when we were lads, my fellows and myself,
there was nothing on which the governors laid more stress.
Our laws themselves, I think, enforce this double lesson:
– "Rule thou and be thou ruled." And when I come to
study the secret of it all, I seem to see that the real incentive
to obedience lies in the praise and honour that it wins
against the discredit and the chastisement which fall on
the disobedient.' 21. 'That, my son,' said the father, 'is the
road to the obedience of compulsion. But there is a shorter

C. 6 way to a nobler goal, the obedience of the will. When the interests of mankind are at stake, they will obey with joy the man whom they believe to be wiser than themselves. You may prove this on all sides: you may see how the sick man will beg the doctor to tell him what he ought to do, how a whole ship's company will listen to the pilot, how travellers will cling to the one who knows the way better, as they believe, than they do themselves. But if men think that obedience will lead them to disaster, then nothing, neither penalties, nor persuasion, nor gifts, will avail to rouse them. For no man accepts a bribe to his own destruction.' 22. 'You would have me understand,' said Cyrus, 'that the best way to secure obedience is to be thought wiser than those we rule?' 'Yes,' said Cambyses, 'that is my belief.'

'And what is the quickest way,' asked Cyrus, 'to win that reputation?'

'None quicker, my lad, than this: wherever you wish to seem wise, be wise. Examine as many cases as you like, and you will find that what I say is true. If you wished to be thought a good farmer, a good horseman, a good physician, a good flute-player, or anything else whatever, without really being so, just imagine what a world of devices you would need to invent, merely to keep up the outward show! And suppose you did get a following to praise you and cry you up, suppose you did burden yourself with all kinds of paraphernalia for your profession, what would come of it all? You succeed at first in a very pretty piece of deception, and then by and by the test comes, and the impostor stands revealed.'

23. 'But,' said Cyrus, 'how can a man really and truly attain to the wisdom that will serve his turn?'

'Well, my son, it is plain that where learning is the road to wisdom, learn you must, as you learnt your battalion-drill, but when it comes to matters which are not to be learnt by mortal men, nor foreseen by mortal minds, there you can only become wiser than others by communicating with the gods through the art of divination. But, always, wherever you know that a thing ought to be done, see that

it is done, and done with care; for care, not carelessness, C. 6
is the mark of the wise man.'

24. 'And now,' said Cyrus, 'to win the affection of those
we rule – and there is nothing, I take it, of greater
importance – surely the path to follow lies open to all who
desire the love of their friends. We must, I mean, show
that we do them good.' 'Yes, my child, but to do good
really at all seasons to those we wish to help is not always
possible: only one way is ever open, and that is the way of
sympathy; to rejoice with the happy in the day of good
things, to share their sorrow when ill befalls them, to lend
a hand in all their difficulties, to fear disaster for them,
and guard against it by foresight – these, rather than actual
benefits, are the true signs of comradeship. 25. And so in
war: if the campaign is in summer the general must show
himself greedy for his share of the sun and the heat, and in
winter for the cold and the frost, and in all labours for toil
and fatigue. This will help to make him beloved of his
followers.' 'You mean, father,' said Cyrus, 'that a commander should always be stouter-hearted in everything
than those whom he commands.' 'Yes, my son, that is my
meaning,' said he; 'only be well assured of this: the
princely leader and the private soldier may be alike in
body, but their sufferings are not the same: the pains of
the leader are always lightened by the glory that is his and
by the very consciousness that all his acts are done in the
public eye.'

26. 'But now, father, suppose the time has come, and
you are satisfied that your troops are well supplied, sound
in wind and limb, well able to endure fatigue, skilled in
the arts of war, covetous of honour, eager to show their
mettle, anxious to follow, would you not think it well to
try the chance of battle without delay?' 'By all means,'
said the father, 'if you are likely to gain by the move: but
if not, for my own part, the more I felt persuaded of my
own superiority and the power of my troops, the more I
should be inclined to stand on my guard, just as we put
our greatest treasures in the safest place we have.' 27. 'But
how can a man make sure that he will gain?' 'Ah, there
you come,' said the father, 'to a most weighty matter. This

C. 6 is no easy task, I can tell you. If your general is to succeed he must prove himself an arch-plotter, a king of craft, full of deceits and stratagems, a cheat, a thief, and a robber, defrauding and over-reaching his opponent at every turn.'

'Heavens!' said Cyrus, and burst out laughing, 'is this the kind of man you want your son to be!' 'I want him to be,' said the father, 'as just and upright and law-abiding as any man who ever lived.' 28. 'But how comes it,' said his son, 'that the lessons you taught us in boyhood and youth were exactly opposed to what you teach me now?' 'Ah,' said the father, 'those lessons were for friends and fellow-citizens, and for them they still hold good, but for your enemies – do you not remember that you were also taught to do much harm?'

'No, father,' he answered, 'I should say certainly not.'

'Then why were you taught to shoot? Or to hurl the javelin? Or to trap wild-boars? Or to snare stags with cords and caltrops? And why did you never meet the lion or the bear or the leopard in fair fight on equal terms, but were always trying to steal some advantage over them? Can you deny that all that was craft and deceit and fraud and greed?'

29. 'Why, of course,' answered the young man, 'in dealing with animals, but with human beings it was different; if I was ever suspected of a wish to cheat another, I was punished, I know, with many stripes.'

'True,' said the father, 'and for the matter of that we did not permit you to draw bow or hurl javelin against human beings; we taught you merely to aim at a mark. But why did we teach you that? Not so that you might injure your friends, either then or now, but that in war you might have the skill to make the bodies of living men your targets. So also we taught you the arts of deceit and craft and greed and covetousness, not among men it is true, but among beasts; we did not mean you ever to turn these accomplishments against your friends, but in war we wished you to be something better than raw recruits.'

30. 'But, father,' Cyrus answered, 'if to do men good and to do men harm were both of them things we ought

to learn, surely it would have been better to teach them in C. 6
actual practice?'

31. Then the father said, 'My son, we are told that in
the days of our forefathers there was such a teacher once.
This man did actually teach his boys righteousness in the
way you suggest, to lie and not to lie, to cheat and not to
cheat, to calumniate and not to calumniate, to be grasping
and not grasping. He drew the distinction between our
duty to friends and our duty to enemies; and he went
further still; he taught men that it was just and right to
deceive even a friend for his own good, or steal his
property. 32. And with this he must needs teach his pupils
to practise on one another what he taught them, just as the
people of Hellas, we are told, teach lads in the wrestling-
school to fence and to feint, and train them by their practice with one another. Now some of his scholars showed
such excellent aptitudes for deception and overreaching,
and perhaps no lack of taste for common money-making,
that they did not even spare their friends, but used their
arts on them. 33. And so an unwritten law was framed by
which we still abide, bidding us teach our children as we
teach our servants, simply and solely not to lie, and not to
cheat, and not to covet, and if they did otherwise to punish
them, hoping to make them humane and law-abiding
citizens. 34. But when they came to manhood, as you have
come, then, it seemed, the risk was over, and it would be
time to teach them what is lawful against our enemies. For
at your age we do not believe you will break out into
savagery against your fellows with whom you have been
knit together since childhood in ties of friendship and
respect. In the same way we do not talk to the young
about the mysteries of love, for if lightness were added to
desire, their passion might sweep them beyond all bounds.'

35. 'Then in heaven's name, father,' said Cyrus, 'remember that your son is but a backward scholar and a late
learner in this lore of selfishness, and teach me all you can
that may help me to over-reach the foe.'

'Well,' said the father, 'you must plot and you must
plan, whatever the size of his force and your own, to catch
his men in disorder when yours are all arrayed, unarmed

C. 6 when yours are armed, asleep when yours are awake, or
you must wait till he is visible to you and you invisible to
him, or till he is labouring over heavy ground and you are
in your fortress and can give him welcome there.'

36. 'But how,' asked Cyrus, 'can I catch him in all these
blunders ?'

'Simply because both you and he are bound to be often
in some such case; both of you must take your meals
sometime; both of you must sleep; your men must scatter
in the morning to satisfy the needs of nature, and, for
better for worse, whatever the roads are like, you will be
forced to make use of them. All these necessities you must
lay to heart, and wherever you are the weaker, there you
must be most on your guard, and wherever your foe is
most assailable, there you must press the attack.'

37. Then Cyrus asked, 'And are these the only cases
where one can apply the great principle of greed, or are
there others ?'

'Oh, yes, there are many more; indeed in these simple
cases any general will be sure to keep good watch, knowing
how necessary it is. But your true cheat and prince of
swindlers is he who can lure the enemy on and throw him
off his guard, suffer himself to be pursued and get the
pursuers into disorder, lead the foe into difficult ground
and then attack him there. 38. Indeed, as an ardent stu-
dent, you must not confine yourself to the lessons you have
learnt; you must show yourself a creator and discoverer,
you must invent stratagems against the foe; just as a real
musician is not content with the mere elements of his art,
but sets himself to compose new themes. And if in music it
is the novel melody, the flower-like freshness, that wins
popularity, still more in military matters it is the newest
contrivance that stands the highest, for the simple reason
that such will give you the best chance of outwitting your
opponent. 39. And yet, my son, I must say that if you did
no more than apply against human beings the devices you
learnt to use against the smallest game, you would have
made considerable progress in this art of over-reaching. Do
you not think so yourself ? Why, to snare birds you would
get up by night in the depth of winter and tramp off in the

cold; your nets were laid before the creatures were astir, C. 6
and your tracks completely covered and you actually had
birds of your own, trained to serve you and decoy their
kith and kin, while you yourself lay in some hiding-place,
seeing yet unseen, and you had learnt by long practice to
jerk in the net before the birds could fly away. 40. Or you
might be out after hares, and for a hare you had two
breeds of dogs, one to track her out by scent, because she
feeds in the dusk and takes to her form by day, and
another to cut off her escape and run her down, because
she is so swift. And even if she escaped these, she did not
escape you; you had all her runs by heart and knew all
her hiding-places, and there you would spread your nets,
so that they were scarcely to be seen, and the very haste of
her flight would fling her into the snare. And to make sure
of her you had men placed on the spot to keep a look-out,
and pounce on her at once. And there were you at her
heels, shouting and scaring her out of her wits, so that she
was caught from sheer terror, and there lay your men, as
you had taught them, silent and motionless in their ambuscade. 41. I say, therefore, that if you chose to act like this
against human beings, you would soon have no enemies
left to fight, or I am much mistaken. And even if, as well
may be, the necessity should arise for you to do battle on
equal terms in open field, even so, my son, there will still
be power in those arts which you have studied so long and
which teach you to out-villain villainy. And among them I
include all that has served to train the bodies and fire the
courage of your men, all that has made them adepts in
every craft of war. One thing you must ever bear in mind:
if you wish your men to follow you, remember that they
expect you to plan for them. 42. Hence you must never
know a careless mood: if it be night, you must consider
what your troops shall do when it is day; if day, how the
night had best be spent. 43. For the rest, you do not need
me to tell you now how you should draw up your troops
or conduct your march by day or night, along broad roads
or narrow lanes, over hills or level ground, or how you
should encamp and post your pickets, or advance into
battle or retreat before the foe, or march past a hostile

C. 6 city, or attack a fortress or retire from it, or cross a river or pass through a defile, or guard against a charge of cavalry or an attack from lancers or archers, or what you should do if the enemy comes into sight when you are marching in column and how you are to take up position against him, or how deploy into action if you are in line and he takes you in flank or rear, and how you are to learn all you can about his movements, while keeping your own as secret as may be; these are matters on which you need no further words of mine; all that I know about them you have heard a hundred times, and I am sure you have not neglected any other authority on whom you thought you could rely. You know all their theories, and you must apply them now, I take it, according to circumstances and your need. 44. But,' he added, 'there is one lesson that I would fain impress on you, and it is the greatest of them all. Observe the sacrifices and pay heed to the omens; when they are against you, never risk your army or yourself, for you must remember that men undertake enterprises on the strength of probability alone and without any real knowledge as to what will bring them happiness. 45. You may learn this from all life and all history. How often have cities allowed themselves to be persuaded into war, and that by advisers who were thought the wisest of men, and then been utterly destroyed by those whom they attacked! How often have statesmen helped to raise a city or a leader to power, and then suffered the worst at the hands of those whom they exalted! And many who could have treated others as friends and equals, giving and receiving kindnesses, have chosen to use them as slaves, and then paid the penalty at their hands; and many, not content to enjoy their own share of good, have been swept on by the craving to master all, and thereby lost everything that they once possessed; and many have won the very wealth they prayed for and through it have found destruction. 46. So little does human wisdom know how to choose the best, helpless as a man who could but draw lots to see what he should do. But the gods, my son, who live for ever, they know all things, the things that have been and the things that are and the things

that are to be, and all that shall come from these ; and to C. 6
us mortals who ask their counsel and whom they love they
will show signs, to tell us what we should do and what we
should leave undone. Nor must we think it strange if the
gods will not vouchsafe their wisdom to all men equally ;
no compulsion is laid on them to care for men, unless it be
their will.'

BOOK II

C. 1 Thus they talked together, and thus they journeyed on until they reached the frontier, and there a good omen met them: an eagle swept into view on the right, and went before them as though to lead the way, and they prayed the gods and heroes of the land to show them favour and grant them safe entry, and then they crossed the boundary. And when they were across, they prayed once more that the gods of Media might receive them graciously, and when they had done this they embraced each other, as father and son will, and Cambyses turned back to his own city, but Cyrus went forward again, to his uncle Cyaxares in the land of Media. 2. And when his journey was done and he was face to face with him and they had greeted each other as kinsmen may, then Cyaxares asked the prince how great an armament he had brought with him? And Cyrus answered, 'I have 30,000 with me, men who have served with you before as mercenaries; and more are coming on behind, fresh troops, from the Peers of Persia.'

'How many of those?' asked Cyaxares. 3. And Cyrus answered, 'Their numbers will not please you, but remember these Peers of ours, though they are few, find it easy to rule the rest of the Persians, who are many. But now,' he added, 'have you any need of us at all? Perhaps it was only a false alarm that troubled you, and the enemy are not advancing?'

'Indeed they are,' said the other, 'and in full force.'

4. 'How do you know?' asked Cyrus.

'Because,' said he, 'many deserters come to us, and all of them, in one fashion or another tell the same tale.'

'Then we must give battle?' said Cyrus.

'Needs must,' Cyaxares replied.

'Well,' answered Cyrus, 'but you have not told me yet how great their power is, or our own either. I want to hear, if you can tell me, so that we may make our plans.'

'Listen, then,' said Cyaxares. 5. 'Croesus the Lydian is coming, we hear, with 10,000 horse and more than 40,000 archers and targeteers. Artamas the governor of Greater Phrygia is bringing, they say, 8,000 horse and lancers and targeteers also, 40,000 strong. Then there is Aribaius the king of Cappadocia with 6,000 horse and 30,000 archers and targeteers. And Aragdus the Arabian with 10,000 horse, a hundred chariots, and innumerable slingers. As for the Hellenes who dwell in Asia, it is not clear as yet whether they will send a following or not. But the Phrygians from the Hellespont, we are told, are mustering in the Caystrian plain under Gabaidus, 6,000 horse and 40,000 targeteers. Word has been sent to the Carians, Cilicians, and Paphlagonians, but it is said they will not rise; the Lord of Assyria and Babylon will himself, I believe, bring not less than 20,000 horse, and I make no doubt as many as 200 chariots, and thousands upon thousands of men on foot; such at least has been his custom whenever he invaded us before.'

6. Cyrus answered: 'Then you reckon the numbers of the enemy to be, in all, something like 60,000 horse and 200,000 archers and targeteers. And what do you take your own to be?'

'Well,' he answered, 'we ourselves can furnish over 10,000 horse and perhaps, considering the state of the country, as many as 60,000 archers and targeteers. And from our neighbours, the Armenians,' he added, 'we look to get 4,000 horse and 20,000 foot.'

'I see,' said Cyrus, 'you reckon our cavalry at less than a third of the enemy's, and our infantry at less than half.'

7. 'Ah,' said Cyaxares, 'and perhaps you feel that the force you are bringing from Persia is very small?'

'We will consider that later on,' answered Cyrus, 'and see then if we require more men or not. Tell me first the methods of fighting that the different troops adopt.'

'They are much the same for all,' answered Cyaxares,

C. 1 'that is to say, their men and ours alike are armed with bows and javelins.'

'Well,' replied Cyrus, 'if such arms are used, skirmishing at long range must be the order of the day.' 'True,' said the other. 8. 'And in that case,' went on Cyrus, 'the victory is in the hands of the larger force; for even if the same numbers fall on either side, the few would be exhausted long before the many.' 'If that be so,' cried Cyaxares, 'there is nothing left for us but to send to Persia, and make them see that if disaster falls on Media it will fall on Persia next, and beg them for a larger force.' 'Ah, but,' said Cyrus, 'you must remember that even if every single Persian were to come at once, we could not outnumber our enemies.' 9. 'But,' said the other, 'can you see anything else to be done?' 'For my part,' answered Cyrus, 'if I could have my way, I would arm every Persian who is coming here in precisely the same fashion as our Peers at home, that is to say, with a corslet for the breast, a shield for the left arm, and a sword or battle-axe for the right hand. If you will give us these, you will make it quite safe for us to close with the enemy, and our foes will find that flight is far pleasanter than defence. But we Persians,' he added, 'will deal with those who do stand firm, leaving the fugitives to you and to your cavalry, who must give them no time to rally and no time to escape.'

10. That was the counsel of Cyrus, and Cyaxares approved it. He thought no more of sending for a larger force, but set about preparing the equipment he had been asked for, and all was in readiness just about the time when the Peers arrived from Persia at the head of their own troops. 11. Then, so says the story, Cyrus called the Peers together and spoke to them as follows: 'Men of Persia, my friends and comrades, when I looked at you first and saw the arms you bore and how you were all on fire to meet the enemy, hand to hand, and when I remembered that your squires are only equipped for fighting on the outskirts of the field, I confess my mind misgave me. Few and forlorn they will be, I said to myself, swallowed up in a host of enemies; no good can come of it. But to-day you are here, and your men behind you, stalwart and

stout of limb, and to-morrow they shall have armour like C. 1
our own. None could find fault with their thews and
sinews, and as for their spirit, it is for us to see it does not
fail. A leader must not only have a stout heart himself; he
must see to it that his followers are as valiant as he.'

12. Thus Cyrus spoke, and the Peers were well satisfied
at his words, feeling that on the day of battle they would
have more to help them in the struggle. 13. And one of
them said, 'Perhaps it will seem strange if I ask Cyrus to
speak in our stead to our fellow-combatants when they
receive their arms, and yet I know well that the words of
him who has the greatest power for weal or woe sink
deepest into the listener's heart. His very gifts, though they
should be less than the gifts of equals, are valued more.
These new comrades of ours,' he went on, 'would far
rather be addressed by Cyrus himself than by us, and now
that they are to take their place among the Peers their title
will seem to them far more secure if it is given them by the
king's own son and our general-in-chief. Not that we have
not still our own duties left. We are bound to do our best
in every way to rouse the spirit of our men. Shall we not
gain ourselves by all they gain in valour?'

14. So it came about that Cyrus had the new armour
placed before him and summoned a general meeting of the
Persian soldiery, and spoke to them as follows:

15. 'Men of Persia, born and bred in the same land as
ourselves, whose limbs are as stout and strong as our own,
your hearts should be as brave. I know they are; and yet
at home in the land of our fathers you did not share our
rights; not that we drove you out ourselves, but you were
banished by the compulsion that lay upon you to find your
livelihood for yourselves. Now from this day forward,
with heaven's help, it shall be my care to provide it for
you; and now, if so you will, you have it in your power to
take the armour that we wear ourselves, face the same
perils and win the same honours, if so be you make any
glorious deed your own. 16. In former days you were
trained, like ourselves, in the use of bow and javelin, and
if you were at all inferior to us in skill, that was not to be
wondered at; you had not the same leisure for practice as

C. 1 we; but now in this new accoutrement we shall have no pre-eminence at all. Each of us will wear a corslet fitted to his breast and carry a shield on his left arm of the type to which we are all accustomed, and in his right hand a sabre or a battle-axe. With these we shall smite the enemy before us, and need have no fear that we shall miss the mark. 17. How can we differ from one another with these arms? There can be no difference except in daring. And daring you may foster in your hearts as much as we in ours. What greater right have we than you to love victory and follow after her, victory who wins for us and preserves to us all things that are beautiful and good? Why should you, any more than we, be found lacking in that power which takes the goods of weaklings and bestows them on the strong?'

18. He ended: 'Now you have heard all. There lie your weapons; let him who chooses take them up and write his name with the brigadier in the same roll as ours. And if a man prefers to remain a mercenary, let him do so; he carries the arms of a servant.'

19. Thus spoke Cyrus; and the Persians, every man of them, felt they would be ashamed for the rest of their days, and deservedly, if they drew back now, when they were offered equal honour in return for equal toil. One and all they inscribed their names and took up the new arms.

20. And now in the interval, before the enemy were actually at hand, but while rumour said they were advancing, Cyrus took on himself a three-fold task: to bring the physical strength of his men to the highest pitch, to teach them tactics, and to rouse their spirit for martial deeds. 21. He asked Cyaxares for a body of assistants whose duty it should be to provide each of his soldiers with all they could possibly need, thus leaving the men themselves free for the art of war. He had learnt, he thought, that success, in whatever sphere, was only to be won by refusing to attempt a multitude of tasks and concentrating the mind on one.

Thus in the military training itself he gave up the practice with bow and javelin, leaving his men to perfect themselves in the use of sabre, shield, and corslet, accustoming them from the very first to the thought that they must close with

the enemy, or confess themselves worthless as fellow- C. 1
combatants; a harsh conclusion for those who knew that
they were only protected in order to fight on behalf of
their protectors. 22. And further, being convinced that
wherever the feeling of emulation can be roused, there the
eagerness to excel is greatest, he instituted competitions
for everything in which he thought his soldiers should be
trained. The private soldier was challenged to prove himself prompt to obey, anxious to work, eager for danger,
and yet ever mindful of discipline, an expert in the science
of war, an artist in the conduct of his arms, and a lover of
honour in all things. The petty officer commanding a
squad of five was not only to equal the leading private, he
must also do what he could to bring his men to the same
perfection; the captain of ten must do the same for his ten,
and the company's captain for the company, while the
commander of the whole regiment, himself above
reproach, must take the utmost care with the officers under
him so that they in their turn should see that their
subordinates were perfect in all their duties. 23. For prizes,
Cyrus announced that the brigadier in command of the
finest regiment should be raised to the rank of general, the
captain of the finest company should be made a brigadier,
the captain of the finest squad of ten captain of a company,
and the captain of the best five a captain of ten, while the
best soldiers from the ranks should become captains of five
themselves. Every one of these officers had the privilege of
being served by those beneath him, and various other
honours also, suited to their several grades, while ampler
hopes were offered for any nobler exploits. 24. Finally
prizes were announced to be won by a regiment or a
company or a squad taken as a whole, by those who
proved themselves most loyal to their leaders and most
zealous in the practice of their duty. These prizes, of
course, were such as to be suitable for men taken in the
mass.

Such were the orders of the Persian leader, and such the
exercises of the Persian troops. 25. For their quarters, he
arranged that a separate shelter should be assigned to
every brigadier, and that it should be large enough for the

C. 1 whole regiment he commanded; a regiment consisting of
100 men. Thus they were encamped by regiments, and in
the mere fact of common quarters there was this advantage, Cyrus thought, for the coming struggle, that the men
saw they were all treated alike, and therefore no one could
pretend that he was slighted, and no one sink to the
confession that he was a worse man than his neighbours
when it came to facing the foe. Moreover the life in
common would help the men to know each other, and it is
only by such knowledge, as a rule, that a common conscience is engendered; those who live apart, unknowing
and unknown, seem far more apt for mischief, like those
who skulk in the dark. 26. Cyrus thought the common life
would lead to the happiest results in the discipline of the
regiments. By this system all the officers – brigadiers,
company-captains, captains of the squads – could keep
their men in as perfect order as if they were marching
before them in single file. 27. Such precision in the ranks
would do most to guard against disorder and re-establish
order if ever it were broken; just as when timbers and
stones have to be fitted together it is easy enough to put
them in place, wherever they chance to lie, provided only
that they are marked so as to leave no doubt where each
belongs. 28. And finally, he felt, there was the fact that
those who live together are the less likely to desert one
another; even the wild animals, Cyrus knew, who are
reared together suffer terribly from loneliness when they
are severed from each other.

29. There was a further matter, to which he gave much
care; he wished no man to take his meal at morning or at
night till he had sweated for it. He would lead the men out
to hunt, or invent games for them, or if there was work to
be done, he would so conduct it that they did not leave it
without sweat. He believed this regimen gave them zest for
their food, was good for their health, and increased their
powers of toil; and the toil itself was a blessed means for
making the men more gentle towards each other; just as
horses that work together grow gentle, and will stand
quietly side by side. Moreover the knowledge of having

gone through a common training would increase tenfold C. 1
the courage with which they met the foe.

30. Cyrus had his own quarters built to hold all the
guests he might think it well to entertain, and, as a rule, he
would invite such of the brigadiers as the occasion seemed
to call for, but sometimes he would send for the company-
captains and the officers in command of the smaller
squads, and even the private soldiers were summoned to
his board, and from time to time a squad of five, or of ten,
or an entire company, or even a whole regiment, or he
would give a special invitation by way of honour to any
one whom he knew had undertaken some work he had at
heart himself. In every case there was no distinction
whatever between the meats for himself and for his guests.
31. Further he always insisted that the army servants
should share and share alike with the soldiers in everything, for he held that those who did such service for the
army were as much to be honoured as heralds or ambassadors. They were bound, he said, to be loyal and intelligent, alive to all a soldier's needs, active, swift,
unhesitating, and withal cool and imperturbable. Nor was
that all ; he was convinced that they ought also to possess
those qualities which are thought to be peculiar to what
we call 'the better classes,' and yet never despise their
work, but feel that everything their commander laid upon
them must be fit for them to do.

It was the constant aim of Cyrus whenever he and his C. 2
soldiers messed together, that the talk should be lively and
full of grace, and at the same time do the listeners good.
Thus one day he brought the conversation round to the
following theme : —

'Do you think, gentlemen,' said he, 'that our new
comrades appear somewhat deficient in certain respects
simply because they have not been educated in the same
fashion as ourselves ? Or will they show themselves our
equals in daily life and on the field of battle when the time
comes to meet the foe ?'

2. Hystaspas took up the challenge : — 'What sort of
warriors they will prove I do not pretend to know, but this
I do say, in private life some of them are cross-grained

C. 2 fellows enough. Only the other day,' he went on, 'Cyaxares sent a present of sacrificial meat to every regiment. There was flesh enough for three courses apiece or more, and the attendant had handed round the first, beginning with myself. So when he came in again, I told him to begin at the other end of the board, and serve the company in that order. 3. But I was greeted by a yell from the centre: one of these men who was sitting there bawled out, "Equality indeed! There's not much of it here, if we who sit in the middle are never served first at all!" It nettled me that they should fancy themselves treated worse than we, so I called him up at once and made him sit beside me. And I am bound to say he obeyed that order with the most exemplary alacrity. But when the dish came round to us, we found, not unnaturally, since we were the last to be served, that only a few scraps were left. At this my man fell into the deepest dudgeon, and made no attempt to conceal it, muttering to himself, "Just like my ill-luck! To be invited here just now and never before!" 4. I tried to comfort him. "Never mind," I said, "presently the servant will begin again with us, and then you will help yourself first and you can take the biggest piece." Just then the third course, and, as it proved, the last, came round, and so the poor fellow took his helping, but as he did so it struck him that the piece he had chosen first was too small, and he put it back, meaning to pick out another. But the carver, thinking he had changed his mind and did not want any more, passed on to the next man before he had time to secure his second slice. 5. At this our friend took his loss so hard that he only made matters worse: his third course was clean gone, and now in his rage at his bad luck he somehow managed to overset the gravy, which was all that remained to him. The captain next to us seeing how matters stood rubbed his hands with glee and went into peals of laughter. And,' said Hystaspas, 'I took refuge in a fit of coughing myself, for really I could not have controlled my laughter. There, Cyrus,' said he, 'that is a specimen of our new comrades, as nearly as I can draw his portrait.'

6. The description, as may be guessed, was greeted with shouts of laughter, and then another brigadier took up the

word: 'Well, Cyrus,' said he, 'our friend here has certainly C. 2
met with an absolute boor: my own experience is somewhat different. You remember the admonitions you gave
us when you dismissed the regiments, and how you bade
each of us instruct his own men in the lessons we had
learnt from you. Well, I, like the rest of us, went off at
once and set about instructing one of the companies under
me. I posted the captain in front with a fine young fellow
behind him, and after them the others in the order I
thought best; I took my stand facing them all, and waited,
with my eyes fixed on the captain, until I thought the right
moment had come, and then I gave the order to advance.
7. And what must my fine fellow do but get in front of the
captain and march off ahead of the whole troop. I cried
out, "You, sir, what are you doing?" "Advancing as you
ordered." "I never ordered you to advance alone," I
retorted, "the order was given to the whole company." At
which he turned right round and addressed the ranks:
"Don't you hear the officer abusing you? The orders are
for all to advance!" Whereupon the rest of them marched
right past their captain and up to me. 8. Of course the
captain called them back, and they began to grumble and
growl: "Which of the two are we to obey? One tells us to
advance, the other won't let us move."

'Well, I had to take the whole matter very quietly and
begin again from the beginning, posting the company as
they were, and explaining that no one in the rear was to
move until the front rank man led off: all they had to do
was to follow the man in front. 9. As I was speaking, up
came a friend of mine; he was going off to Persia, and had
come to ask me for a letter I had written home. So I turned
to the captain who happened to know where I had left the
letter lying, and bade him fetch it for me. Off he ran, and
off ran my young fellow at his heels, breast-plate, battle-
axe, and all. The rest of the company thought they were
bound to follow suit, joined in the race, and brought my
letter back in style. That is how my company, you see,
carries out your instructions to the full.'

10. He paused, and the listeners laughed to their hearts'

C. 2 content, as well they might, over the triumphant entry of
the letter under its armed escort. Then Cyrus spoke:

'Now heaven be praised! A fine set they are, these new
friends of ours, a most rare race! So grateful are they for
any little act of courtesy, you may win a hundred hearts
by a dish of meat! And so docile, some of them, they must
needs obey an order before they have understood it! For
my part I can only pray to be blest with an army like them
all.'

11. Thus he joined in the mirth, but he turned the
laughter to the praise of his new recruits.

Then one of the company, a brigadier called Aglaïtadas,
a somewhat sour-tempered man, turned to him and said:

'Cyrus, do you really think the tales they tell are true?'

'Certainly,' he answered, 'why should they say what is
false?'

'Why,' repeated the other, 'simply to raise a laugh, and
make a brag like the impostors that they are.' 12. But
Cyrus cut him short, 'Hush! hush! You must not use such
ugly names. Let me tell you what an impostor is. He is a
man who claims to be wealthier or braver than he is in
fact, and who undertakes what he can never carry out, and
all this for the sake of gain. But he who contrives mirth for
his friends, not for his own profit, or his hearers' loss, or
to injure any man, surely, if we must needs give him a
name, we ought to call him a man of taste and breeding
and a messenger of wit.'

13. Such was the defence of Cyrus in behalf of the
merrymakers. And the officer who had begun the jest
turned to Aglaïtadas and said:

'Just think, my dear sir, if we had tried to make you
weep! What fault you would have found with us! Suppose
we had been like the ballad-singers and story-tellers who
put in lamentable tales in the hope of reducing their
audience to tears! What would you have said about us
then? Why, even now, when you know we only wish to
amuse you, not to make you suffer, you must needs hold
us up to shame.'

14. 'And is not the shame justified?' Aglaïtadas replied.
'The man who sets himself to make his fellows laugh does

far less for them than he who makes them weep. If you C. 2
will but think, you will admit that what I say is true. It is
through tears our fathers teach self-control unto their sons,
and our tutors sound learning to their scholars, and the
laws themselves lead the grown man to righteousness by
putting him to sit in the place of penitence. But your mirth-
makers, can you say they benefit the body or edify the
soul? Can smiles make a man a better master or a better
citizen? Can he learn economy or statesmanship from a
grin?'

15. But Hystaspas answered back:

'Take my advice, Aglaïtadas, pluck up heart and spend
this precious gift of yours upon our enemies: make them
sit in the seat of the sorrowful, and fling away on us, your
friends, that vile and worthless laughter. You must have
an ample store of it in reserve: it cannot be said you have
squandered it on yourself, or ever wasted a smile on friend
or foreigner if you could help it. So you have no excuse to
be niggardly now, and cannot refuse us a smile.'

'I see,' said Aglaïtadas, 'you are trying to get a laugh out
of me, are you not?'

But the brigadier interposed, 'Then he is a fool for his
pains, my friend: one might strike fire out of you, perhaps,
but not a laugh, not a laugh.'

16. At this sally all the others shouted with glee, and
even Aglaïtadas could not help himself: he smiled.

And Cyrus, seeing the sombre face light up, said:

'Brigadier, you are very wrong to corrupt so virtuous a
man, luring him to laughter, and that too when he is the
sworn foe of gaiety.'

So they talked and jested. 17. And then Chrysantas
began on another theme.

18. 'Cyrus,' he said, 'and gentlemen all, I cannot help
seeing that within our ranks are men of every kind, some
better and some worse, and yet if anything is won every
man will claim an equal share. Now to my mind nothing
is more unfair than that the base man and the good should
be held of equal account.'

'Perhaps it would be best, gentlemen,' said Cyrus in
answer, 'to bring the matter before the army in council

C. 2 and put it to them, whether, if God grant us success, we should let all share and share alike, or distribute the rewards and honours in proportion to the deserts of each.'

19. 'But why,' asked Chrysantas, 'why discuss the point? Why not simply issue a general order that you intend to do this? Was not that enough in the case of the competitions?'

'Doubtless,' Cyrus answered, 'but this case is different. The troops, I take it, will feel that all they win by their services on the campaign should belong to them in common: but they hold that the actual command of the expedition was mine by right even before we left home, so that I was fully entitled, on their view, to appoint umpires and judges at my own will.'

20. 'And do you really expect,' asked Chrysantas, 'that the mass of the army will pass a resolution giving up the right of all to an equal share in order that the best men should receive the most?'

'Yes, I do,' said Cyrus, 'partly because we shall be there to argue for that course, but chiefly because it would seem too base to deny that he who works the hardest and does most for the common good deserves the highest recompense. Even the worst of men must admit that the brave should gain the most.'

21. It was, however, as much for the sake of the Peers themselves as for any other reason that Cyrus wished the resolution to be passed. They would prove all the better men, he thought, if they too were to be judged by their deeds and rewarded accordingly. And this was the right moment, he felt, to raise the question and put it to the vote, now when the Peers were disposed to resent being put on a level with the common people. In the end it was agreed by all the company that the question should be raised, and that every one who claimed to call himself a man was bound to argue in its favour.

22. And on that one of the brigadiers smiled to himself and said: 'I know at least one son of the soil who will be ready to agree that the principle of share and share alike should not be followed everywhere.'

'And who is he?' another asked.

'Well,' said the first, 'he is a member of our quarters, I C. 2
can tell you that, and he is always hunting after the lion's
share of every single thing.'

'What? Of everything?' said a third. 'Of work as well?'
'Oh, no!' said the first, 'you have caught me there. I was
wrong to say so much, I must confess. When it comes to
work, I must admit, he is quite ready to go short: he will
give up his own share of that, without a murmur, to any
man whatever.'

23. 'For my part, gentlemen,' said Cyrus, 'I hold that all
such idlers ought to be turned out of the army, that is, if
we are ever to cultivate obedience and energy in our men.
The bulk of our soldiers, I take it, are of the type to follow
a given lead: they will seek after nobleness and valour if
their leaders are valiant and noble, but after baseness if
these are base. 24. And we know that only too often the
worthless will find more friends than the good. Vice,
passing lightly along her path of pleasure, wins the hearts
of thousands with her gifts; but Virtue, toiling up the steep
ascent, has little skill to snare the souls of men and draw
them after her, when all the while their comrades are
calling to them on the easy downward way. 25. It is true
there are degrees, and where the evil springs only from
sloth and lethargy, I look on the creatures as mere drones,
only injuring the hive by what they cost: but there are
others, backward in toil and forward in greed, and these
are the captains in villainy: for not seldom can they show
that rascality has its advantages. Such as they must be
removed, cut out from among us, root and branch.
26. And I would not have you fill their places from our
fellow-citizens alone, but, just as you choose your horses
from the best stocks, wherever you find them, not limiting
yourselves to the national breed, so you have all mankind
before you, and you should choose those, and those only,
who will increase your power and add to your honour. Let
me clinch my argument by examples: no chariot can travel
fast if the horses in the team are slow, or run straight if
they will not be ruled; no house can stand firm if the
household is evil: better empty walls than traitors who
will bring it to the ground.

C. 2   27. 'And be sure, my friends,' he added, 'the removal of the bad means a benefit beyond the sheer relief that they are taken away and will trouble us no more: those who are left and were ripe for contagion are purified, and those who were worthy will cleave to virtue all the closer when they see the dishonour that falls on wickedness.'

28. So Cyrus spoke, and his words won the praise of all his friends, and they set themselves to do as he advised.

But after that Cyrus began to jest again. His eye fell on a certain captain who had chosen for his comrade at the feast a great hairy lad, a veritable monster of ugliness, and Cyrus called to the captain by name: 'How now, Sambulas? Have you adopted the Hellenic fashion too? And will you roam the world together, you and the lad who sits beside you, because there is none so fair as he?' 'By heaven,' answered Sambulas, 'you are not far wrong. It is bliss to me to feast my eyes on him.' 29. At that all the guests turned and looked on the young man's face, but when they saw how ugly it was, they could not help laughing outright. 'Heavens, Sambulas, tell us the valiant deed that knit your souls together! How has he drawn you to himself?' 30. 'Listen then,' he answered, 'and I will tell you the whole truth. Every time I call him, morning, noon, or night, he comes to me; never yet has he excused himself, never been too busy to attend; and he comes at a run, he does not walk. Whatever I have bidden him do, he has always done it, and at the top of his speed. He has made all the petty captains under him the very models of industry; he shows them, not by word but deed, what they ought to be.' 31. 'And so,' said another, 'for all these virtues you give him, I take it, the kiss of kinship?' But the ugly lad broke out: 'Not he! He has no great love for work. And to kiss me, if it came to that, would mean more effort than all his exercises.'

C. 3   So the hours passed in the general's tent, from grave to gay, till at last the third libation was poured out, and the company bent in prayer to the gods – 'Grant us all that is good' – and so broke up, and went away to sleep.

But the next day Cyrus assembled the soldiers in full conclave, and spoke to them: 2. 'My men,' he said, 'my

friends, the day of struggle is at hand, and the enemy are C. 3
near. The prizes of victory, if victory is to be ours — and
we must believe it will be ours, we must make it ours — the
prizes of victory will be nothing short of the enemy himself
and all that he possesses. And if the victory should be his,
then, in like manner, all the goods of the vanquished must
lie at the victor's feet. 3. Therefore I would have you take
this to your hearts: wherever those who have joined
together for war remember that unless each and every one
of them play his part with zeal nothing good can follow;
there we may look for glorious success. For there nothing
that ought to be done will be left undone. But if each man
thinks "My neighbour will toil and fight, even though my
own heart should fail and my own arm fall slack," then,
believe me, disaster is at the door for each and all alike,
and no man shall escape. 4. Such is the ordinance of God:
those who will not work out their own salvation he gives
into the hands of other men to bear rule over them. And
now I call on any man here,' he added, 'to stand up and
say whether he believes that virtue will best be nourished
among us if he who bears the greatest toil and takes the
heaviest risk shall receive the highest honours. Or whether
we should hold that cowardice makes no difference in the
end, seeing that we all must share alike?'

5. Thereupon Chrysantas of the Peers rose up. He was a
man of understanding, but his bodily presence was weak.
And now he spoke thus:

'I do not imagine, Cyrus, that you put this question with
any belief that cowards ought really to receive the same
share as the brave. No, you wished to make trial of us and
see whether any man would dare to claim an equal part in
all that his fellows win by their nobleness, though he never
struck a single valiant stroke himself. 6. I myself,' he
continued, 'am neither fleet of foot nor stout of limb, and
for aught I can do with my body, I perceive that on the
day of trial neither the first place nor the second can be
mine, no, nor yet the hundredth, nor even, it may be, the
thousandth. But this I know right well, that if our mighty
men put forth all their strength, I too shall receive such
portion of our blessings as I may deserve. But if the

C. 3 cowards sit at ease and the good and brave are out of heart, then I fear that I shall get a portion, a larger than I care to think, of something that is no blessing but a curse.'

7. So spoke Chrysantas, and then Pheraulas stood up. He was a man of the people, but well known to Cyrus in the old days at home and well-beloved by him: no mean figure to look at, and in soul like a man of noble birth. Now he spoke as follows:

8. 'Cyrus, friends, and Persians, I hold to the belief that on this day we all start equal in that race where valour is the goal. I speak of what I see: we are trained on the same fare; we are held worthy of the same comradeship; we contend for the same rewards. All of us alike are told to obey our leaders, and he who obeys most frankly never fails to meet with honour at the hands of Cyrus. Valour is no longer the privilege of one class alone: it has become the fairest prize that can fall to the lot of any man. 9. And to-day a battle is before us where no man need teach us how to fight: we have the trick of it by nature, as a bull knows how to use his horns, or a horse his hoofs, or a dog his teeth, or a wild boar his tusks. The animals know well enough,' he added, 'when and where to guard themselves: they need no master to tell them that. 10. I myself, when I was a little lad, I knew by instinct how to shield myself from the blow I saw descending: if I had nothing else, I had my two fists, and used them with all my force against my foe: no one taught me how to do it, on the contrary they beat me if they saw me clench my fists. And a knife, I remember, I never could resist: I clutched the thing whenever I caught sight of it: not a soul showed me how to hold it, only nature herself, I do aver. I did it, not because I was taught to do it, but in spite of being forbidden, like many another thing to which nature drove me, in spite of my father and mother both. Yes, and I was never tired of hacking and hewing with my knife whenever I got the chance: it did not seem merely natural, like walking or running, it was positive joy. 11. Well, to-day we are to fight in this same simple fashion: energy, rather than skill, is called for, and glorious it will be to match ourselves against our friends, the Peers of Persia. And let

us remember that the same prizes are offered to us all, but C. 3
the stakes differ: our friends give up a life of honour, the
sweetest life there can be, but we escape from years of toil
and ignominy, and there can be no life worse than that.
12. And what fires me most of all, my friends, and sends
me into the lists most gladly, is the thought that Cyrus will
be our judge: one who will give no partial verdict. I call
the gods to witness when I say that he loves a valiant man
as he loves his own soul: I have seen him give such an one
more than he ever keeps for himself. 13. And now,' he
added, 'I know that our friends here pride themselves upon
their breeding and what it has done for them. They have
been brought up to endure hunger and thirst, cold and
nakedness, and yet they are aware that we too have been
trained in the self-same school and by a better master than
they: we were taught by Necessity, and there is no teacher
so good, and none so strict. 14. How did our friends here
learn their endurance? By bearing arms, weapons of war,
tools that the wit of the whole human race has made as
light as well could be: but Necessity drove us, my fellows
and myself, to stagger under burthens so heavy that to-
day, if I may speak for myself, these weapons of mine seem
rather wings to lift me than weights to bear. 15. I for one
am ready, Cyrus, ready to enter the lists, and, however I
prove, I will ask from you no more than I deserve: I would
have you believe this. And you,' he added, turning to his
fellows, 'you, men of the people, I would have you plunge
into the battle and match yourselves with these gentlemen-
warriors: the fine fellows must meet us now, for this is the
people's day.'

16. That was what Pheraulas said, and many rose to
follow him and support his views. And it was resolved that
each man should be honoured according to his deserts and
that Cyrus should be the judge. So the matter ended, and
all was well.

17. Now Cyrus gave a banquet and a certain brigadier
was the chief guest, and his regiment with him. Cyrus had
marked the officer one day when he was drilling his men;
he had drawn up the ranks in two divisions, opposite each
other, ready for the charge. They were all wearing corslets

C. 3 and carried light shields, but half were equipped with stout staves of fennel, and half were ordered to snatch up clods of earth and do what they could with these. 18. When all were ready, the officer gave the signal and the artillery began, not without effect: the missiles fell fast on shields and corslets, on thighs and greaves. But when they came to close quarters the men of the staves had their turn: they struck at thighs and hands and legs, or, if the adversary stooped and twisted, they belaboured back and shoulders, till they put the foe to utter rout, delivering their blows with shouts of laughter and the glee of boys. Then there was an exchange of weapons, and the other side had their revenge: they took the staves in their turn, and once more the staff triumphed over the clod. 19. Cyrus was full of admiration, partly at the inventiveness of the commander, partly at the discipline of the men; it was good to see the active exercise, and the gaiety of heart, and good to know that the upshot of the battle favoured those who fought in the Persian style. In every way he was pleased, and then and there he bade them all to dinner. But at the feast many of the guests wore bandages, some on their hands, others on their legs, and Cyrus saw it and asked what had befallen them. They told him they had been bruised by the clods. 20. 'At close quarters?' said he, 'or at long range?' 'At long range,' they answered, and all the club-bearers agreed that when it came to close quarters, they had the finest sport. But here those who had been carbonaded by that weapon broke in and protested loudly that it was anything but sport to be clubbed at short range, and in proof thereof they showed the weals on hand and neck and face. Thus they laughed at one another as soldiers will; and on the next day the whole plain was studded with combats of this type, and whenever the army had nothing more serious in hand, this sport was their delight.

21. Another day Cyrus noticed a brigadier who was marching his regiment up from the river back to their quarters. They were advancing in single file on his left, and at the proper moment he ordered the second company to wheel round and draw up to the front alongside the first, and then the third, and then the fourth; and when the

company-captains were all abreast, he passed the word C. 3 along, 'Companies in twos,' and the captains-of-ten came into line; and then at the right moment he gave the order, 'Companies in fours,' and the captains-of-five wheeled round and came abreast, and when they reached the tent doors he called a halt, made them fall into single file once more, and marched the first company in first, and then the second at its heels, and the third and fourth behind them, and as he introduced them, he seated them at the table, keeping the order of their entry. What Cyrus commended was the quiet method of instruction and the care the officer showed, and it was for that he invited him and all his regiment to dinner in the royal tent.

22. Now it chanced that another brigadier was among the guests, and he spoke up and said to Cyrus: 'But will you never ask my men to dinner too? Day after day, morning and evening, whenever we come in for a meal we do just the same as they, and when the meal is over the hindmost man of the last company leads out his men with their fighting-order reversed, and the next company follows, led by their hindmost man, and then the third, and then the fourth: so that all of them, if they have to retire before an enemy, will know how to fall back in good order. And as soon as we are drawn up on the parade-ground we set off marching east, and I lead off with all the divisions behind me, in their regular order, waiting for my word. By-and-by we march west, and then the hindmost man of the last division leads the way, but they must still look to me for commands, though I am marching last: and thus they learn to obey with equal promptitude whether I am at the head or in the rear.'

23. 'Do you mean to tell me,' said Cyrus, 'that this is a regular rule of yours?'

'Truly yes,' he answered, 'as regular as our meals, heaven help us!'

'Then I hereby invite you all to dinner, and for three good reasons; you practise your drill in both forms, you do this morning and evening both, and by your marching and counter-marching you train your bodies and benefit

C. 3 your souls. And since you do it all twice over every day, it is only fair to give you dinner twice.'

24. 'Not twice in one day, I beg you!' said the officer, 'unless you can furnish us with a second stomach apiece.'

And so the conversation ended for the time. But the next day Cyrus was as good as his word. He had all the regiment to dinner; and the day after he invited them again: and when the other regiments knew of it they fell to doing as they did.

C. 4 Now it chanced one day as Cyrus was holding a review, a messenger came from Cyaxares to tell him that an embassy from India had just arrived, and to bid him return with all despatch.

'And I bring with me,' said the messenger, 'a suit of splendid apparel sent from Cyaxares himself: my lord wishes you to appear in all possible splendour, for the Indians will be there to see you.'

2. At that Cyrus commanded the brigadier of the first regiment to draw up to the front with his men behind him on the left in single file, and to pass the order on to the second, and so throughout the army. Officers and men were quick to obey; so that in a trice the whole force on the field was drawn up, one hundred deep and three hundred abreast, with their officers at the head. 3. When they were in position Cyrus bade them follow his lead and off they went at a good round pace. However the road leading to the royal quarters was too narrow to let them pass with so wide a front and Cyrus sent word along the line that the first detachment, one thousand strong, should follow as they were, and then the second, and so on to the last, and as he gave the command he led on without a pause and all the detachments followed in due order, one behind the other. 4. But to prevent mistakes he sent two gallopers up to the entrance with orders to explain what should be done in case the men were at a loss. And when they reached the gates, Cyrus told the leading brigadier to draw up his regiment round the palace, twelve deep, the front rank facing the building, and this command he was to pass on to the second, and the second to the third, and so on till the last. 5. And while they saw to this he went in

to Cyaxares himself, wearing his simple Persian dress C. 4 without a trace of pomp. Cyaxares was well pleased at his celerity, but troubled by the plainness of his attire, and said to him, 'What is the meaning of this, Cyrus? How could you show yourself in this guise to the Indians? I wished you to appear in splendour: it would have done me honour for my sister's son to be seen in great magnificence.'

6. But Cyrus made answer: 'Should I have done you more honour if I had put on a purple robe, and bracelets for my arms, and a necklace about my neck, and so presented myself at your call after long delay? Or as now, when to show you respect I obey you with this despatch and bring you so large and fine a force, although I wear no ornament but the dust and sweat of speed, and make no display unless it be to show you these men who are as obedient to you as I am myself.' Such were the words of Cyrus, and Cyaxares felt that they were just, and so sent for the Indian ambassadors forthwith. 7. And when they entered they gave this message: — The king of the Indians bade them ask what was the cause of strife between the Assyrians and the Medes, 'And when we have heard you,' they said, 'our king bids us betake ourselves to the Assyrian and put the same question to him, and in the end we are to tell you both that the king of the Indians, when he has enquired into the justice of the case, will uphold the cause of him who has been wronged.'

8. To this Cyaxares replied:

'Take them from me this answer: we do the Assyrian no wrong nor any injustice whatsoever. And now go and make inquiry of him, if you are so minded, and see what answer he will give.'

Then Cyrus, who was standing by, asked Cyaxares, 'May I too say what is in my mind?' 'Say on,' answered Cyaxares. Then Cyrus turned to the ambassadors: 'Tell your master,' he said, 'unless Cyaxares is otherwise minded, that we are ready to do this: if the Assyrian lays any injustice to our charge we choose the king of the Indians himself to be our judge, and he shall decide between us.'

C. 4   9. With that the embassy departed. And when they had
gone out Cyrus turned to his uncle and began, 'Cyaxares,
when I came to you I had scant wealth of my own and of
the little I brought with me only a fragment is left. I have
spent it all on my soldiers. You may wonder at this,' he
added, 'when it is you who have supported them, but,
believe me, the money has not been wasted: it has all been
spent on gifts and rewards to the soldiers who have
deserved it. 10. And I am sure,' he added, 'if we require
good workers and good comrades in any task whatever, it
is better and pleasanter to encourage them by kind
speeches and kindly acts than to drive them by pains and
penalties. And if it is for war that we need such trusty
helpers, we can only win the men we want by every charm
of word and grace of deed. For our true ally must be a
friend and not a foe, one who can never envy the prosperity
of his leader nor betray him in the day of disaster. 11. Such
is my conviction, and such being so, I do not hide from
myself the need of money. But to look to you for everything, when I know that you spend so much already,
would be monstrous in my eyes. I only ask that we should
take counsel together so as to prevent the failure of your
funds. I am well aware that if you won great wealth, I
should be able to help myself at need, especially if I used it
for your own advantage. 12. Now I think you told me the
other day that the king of Armenia has begun to despise
you, because he hears we have an enemy, and therefore he
will neither send you troops nor pay the tribute which is
due.' 13. 'Yes,' answered Cyaxares, 'such are his tricks.
And I cannot decide whether to march on him at once and
try to subdue him by force, or let the matter be for the
time, for fear of adding to the enemies we have.' Then
Cyrus asked, 'Are his dwellings very strongly fortified, or
could they be attacked?' And Cyaxares answered, 'The
actual fortifications are not very strong: I took good care
of that. But he has the hill-country to which he can retire,
and there for the moment lie secure, knowing that he
himself is safely out of reach, with everything that he can
convoy thither; unless we are prepared to carry on a siege,
as my father actually did.'

14. Thereupon Cyrus said, 'Now if you were willing to C. 4
send me with a moderate force of cavalry – I will not ask
for many men – I believe, heaven helping me, I could
compel him to send the troops and the tribute. And I even
hope that in the future he may become a firmer friend than
he is now.' 15. And Cyaxares said: 'I think myself they
are more likely to listen to you than to me. I have been
told that his sons were your companions in the chase when
you were lads, and possibly old habits will return and they
will come over to you. Once they were in our power,
everything could be done as we desire.' 'Then,' said Cyrus,
'this plan of ours had better be kept secret, had it not?'
'No doubt,' answered Cyaxares. 'In that way they would
be more likely to fall into our hands, and if we attack them
they would be taken unprepared.'

16. 'Listen then,' said Cyrus, 'and see what you think of
this. I have often hunted the marches between your country
and Armenia with all my men, and sometimes I have taken
horsemen with me from our comrades here.' 'I see,' said
Cyaxares, 'and if you chose to do the like again it would
seem only natural, but if your force was obviously larger
than usual, suspicion would arise at once.' 17. 'But it is
possible,' said Cyrus, 'to frame a pretext which would find
credit with us and with them too, if any rumour reached
them. We might give out that I intend to hold a splendid
hunt and I might ask you openly for a troop of horse.'

'Admirable!' said Cyaxares. 'And I shall refuse to give
you more than a certain number, my reason being that I
wish to visit the outposts on the Syrian side. And as a
matter of fact,' he added, 'I do wish to see them and put
them in as strong a state as possible. Then, as soon as you
have started with your men, and marched, let us say, for a
couple of days, I could send you a good round number of
horse and foot from my own detachment. And when you
have them at your back, you could advance at once, and I
will follow with the rest of my men as near you as I may,
close enough to appear in time of need.'

18. Accordingly Cyaxares proceeded to muster horse
and foot for his own march, and sent provision-waggons
forward to meet him on the road. Meanwhile Cyrus

C. 4 offered sacrifice for the success of his expedition and found
an opportunity to ask Cyaxares for a troop of his junior
cavalry. But Cyaxares would only spare a few, though
many wished to go. Soon afterwards he started for the
outposts himself with all his horse and foot, and then
Cyrus found the omens favourable for his enterprise, and
led his soldiers out as though he meant to hunt. 19. He
was scarcely on his way when a hare started up at their
feet, and an eagle, flying on the right, saw the creature as
it fled, swooped down and struck it, bore it aloft in its
talons on a cliff hard by, and did its will upon it there. The
omen pleased Cyrus well, and he bowed in worship to
Zeus the King, and said to his compay, 'This shall be a
right noble hunt, my friends, if God so will.'

20. When he came to the borders he began the hunt in
his usual way, the mass of horse and foot going on ahead
in rows like reapers, beating out the game, with picked
men posted at intervals to receive the animals and give
them chase. And thus they took great numbers of boars
and stags and antelopes and wild-asses: even to this day
wild-asses are plentiful in those parts. 21. But when the
chase was over, Cyrus had touched the frontier of the
Armenian land, and there he made the evening meal. The
next day he hunted till he reached the mountains which
were his goal. And there he halted again and made the
evening meal. At this point he knew that the army from
Cyaxares was advancing, and he sent secretly to them and
bade them keep about eight miles off, and take their
evening meal where they were, since that would make for
secrecy. And when their meal was over he told them to
send their officer to him, and after supper he called his
own brigadiers together and addressed them thus:

22. 'My friends, in old days the Armenian was a faithful
ally and subject of Cyaxares, but now when he sees an
enemy against us, he assumes contempt: he neither sends
the troops nor pays the tribute. He is the game we have
come to catch, if catch we can. And this, I think, is the
way. You, Chrysantas,' said he, 'will sleep for a few hours,
and then take half the Persians with you, make for the hill
country and seize the heights which we hear are his places

of refuge when alarmed. I will give you guides. 23. The C. 4
hills, they tell us, are covered with trees and scrub, so that
we may hope you will escape unseen: still you might send
a handful of scouts ahead of you, disguised as a band of
robbers. If they should come across any Armenians they
can either make them prisoners and prevent them from
spreading the news, or at least scare them out of the way,
so that they will not realise the whole of your force, and
only take measures against a pack of thieves. 24. That is
your task, Chrysantas, and now for mine. At break of day
I shall take half the foot and all the cavalry and march
along the level straight to the king's residence. If he resists,
we must fight, if he retreats along the plain we must run
him down, if he makes for the mountains, why then,' said
Cyrus, 'it will be your business to see that none of your
visitors escape. 25. Think of it as a hunt: we down below
are the beaters rounding up the game, and you are the men
at the nets: only bear in mind that the earths must all be
stopped before the game is up, and the men at the traps
must be hidden, or they will turn back the flying quarry.
26. One last word, Chrysantas: you must not behave now
as I have known you do in your passion for the chase: you
must not sit up the whole night long without a wink of
sleep, you must let all your men have the modicum of rest
that they cannot do without. 27. Nor must you − just
because you scour the hills in the hunt without a guide,
following the lead of the quarry and that alone, checking
and changing course wherever it leads you − you must not
now plunge into the wildest paths: you must tell your
guides to take you by the easiest road unless it is much the
longest. 28. In war, they say, the easiest way is the
quickest. And once more, because you can race up a
mountain yourself you are not to lead on your men at the
double; suit your pace to the strength of all. 29. Indeed, it
were no bad thing if some of your best and bravest were
to fall behind here and there and cheer the laggards on:
and it would quicken the pace of all, when the column had
gone ahead, to see them racing back to their places past
the marching files.'

30. Chrysantas listened, and his heart beat high at the

C. 4 trust reposed in him. He took the guides, and gave the
necessary orders for those who were to march with him,
and then he lay down to rest. And when all his men had
had the sleep he thought sufficient he set out for the hills.
31. Day dawned, and Cyrus sent a messenger to the
Armenian with these words: 'Cyrus bids you see to it that
you bring your tribute and your troops without delay.'
'And if he asks you where Cyrus is, tell the truth and say I
am on the frontier. And if he asks whether I am advancing
myself, tell the truth again and say that you do not know.
And if he enquires how many we are, bid him send some
one with you to find out.'

32. Having so charged the messenger he sent him on
forthwith, holding this to be more courteous than to attack
without warning. Then he drew up his troops himself in
the order best suited for marching, and, if necessary, for
fighting, and so set forth. The soldiers had orders that not
a soul was to be wronged, and if they met any Armenians
they were to bid them have no fear, but open a market
wherever they wished, and sell meat or drink as they chose.

BOOK III

THUS Cyrus made his preparations. But the Armenian,
when he heard what the messenger had to say, was terror-
stricken: he knew the wrong he had done in neglecting the
tribute and withholding the troops, and, above all, he was
afraid it would be discovered that he was beginning to put
his palace in a fit state for defence. 2. Therefore, with
much trepidation, he began to collect his own forces, and
at the same time he sent his younger son Sabaris into the
hills with the women, his own wife, and the wife of his
elder son and his daughters, taking the best of their
ornaments and furniture with them and an escort to be
their guide. Meanwhile he despatched a party to discover
what Cyrus was doing, and organised all the Armenian
contingents as they came in. But it was not long before
other messengers arrived, saying that Cyrus himself was
actually at hand. 3. Then his courage forsook him; he
dared not come to blows and he withdrew. As soon as the
recruits saw this they took to their heels, each man bent
on getting his own property safely out of the way. When
Cyrus saw the plains full of them, racing and riding
everywhere, he sent out messengers privately to explain
that he had no quarrel with any who stayed quietly in their
homes, but if he caught a man in flight, he warned them
he would treat him as an enemy. Thus the greater part
were persuaded to remain, though there were some who
retreated with the king.

4. But when the escort with the women came on the
Persians in the mountains, they fled with cries of terror,
and many of them were taken prisoners. In the end the

C. 1 young prince himself was captured, and the wife of the king, and his daughters, and his daughter-in-law, and all the goods they had with them. And when the king learnt what had happened, scarcely knowing where to turn, he fled to the summit of a certain hill. 5. Cyrus, when he saw it, surrounded the spot with his troops and sent word to Chrysantas, bidding him leave a force to guard the mountains and come down to him. So the mass of the army was collected under Cyrus, and then he sent a herald to the king with this enquiry :

'Son of Armenia, will you wait here and fight with hunger and thirst, or will you come down into the plain and fight it out with us ?' But the Armenian answered that he wished to fight with neither. 6. Cyrus sent again and asked, 'Why do you sit there, then, and refuse to come down ?' 'Because I know not what to do,' answered the other. 'It is simple enough,' said Cyrus, 'come down and take your trial.' 'And who shall try me ?' asked the king. 'He,' answered Cyrus, 'to whom God has given the power to treat you as he lists, without a trial at all.'

Thereupon the Armenian came down, yielding to necessity, and Cyrus took him and all that he had and placed him in the centre of the camp, for all his forces were now at hand.

7. Meanwhile Tigranes, the elder son of the king, was on his way home from a far country. In old days he had hunted with Cyrus and been his friend, and now, when he heard what had hapopened, he came forward just as he was; but when he saw his father and his mother, his brother and sisters, and his own wife all held as prisoners, he could not keep back the tears. 8. But Cyrus gave him no sign of friendship or courtesy, and only said, 'You have come in time, you may be present now to hear your father tried.' With that he summoned the leaders of the Pesians and the Medes, and any Armenian of rank and dignity who was there, nor would he send away the women as they sat in their covered carriages, but let them listen too. 9. When all was ready he began : 'Son of Armenia, I would counsel you, in the first place, to speak the truth, so that at least you may stand free from what deserves the utmost

hate: beyond all else, be assured, manifest lying checks the C. 1
sympathy between man and man. Moreover,' said he,
'your own sons, your daughters, and your wife are well
aware of all that you have done, and so are your own
Armenians who are here: if they perceive that you say
what is not true, they must surely feel that out of your
own lips you condemn yourself to suffer the uttermost
penalty when I learn the truth.' 'Nay,' answered the king,
'ask me whatever you will, and I will answer truly, come
what come may.' 10. 'Answer then,' said Cyrus, 'did you
once make war upon Astyages, my mother's father, and
his Medes?' 'I did,' he answered. 'And were you conquered
by him, and did you agree to pay tribute and furnish
troops whenever he required, and promise not to fortify
your dwellings?' 'Even so,' he said. 'Why is it, then, that
to-day you have neither brought the tribute nor sent the
troops, and are building forts?' 'I set my heart on liberty:
it seemed to me so fair a thing to be free myself and to
leave freedom to my sons.' 11. 'And fair and good it is,'
said Cyrus, 'to fight for freedom and choose death rather
than slavery, but if a man is worsted in war or enslaved by
any other means and then attempts to rid himself of his
lord, tell me yourself, would you honour such a man as
upright and a doer of noble deeds, or would you, if you
got him in your power, chastise him as a malefactor?' 'I
would chastise him,' he answered, 'since you drive me to
the truth.' 12. 'Then answer me now, point by point,' said
Cyrus. 'If you have an officer and he does wrong, do you
suffer him to remain in office, or do you set up another in
his stead?' 'I set up another.' 'And if he have great riches,
do you leave him all his wealth, or do you make him a
beggar?' 'I take away from him all that he has.' 'And if
you found him deserting to your enemies, what would you
do?' 'I would kill him,' he said: 'why should I perish with
a lie on my lips rather than speak the truth and die?'

13. But at this his son rent his garments and dashed the
tiara from his brows, and the women lifted up their voices
in wailing and tore their cheeks, as though their father was
dead already, and they themselves undone.

But Cyrus bade them keep silence, and spoke again. 'Son

C. 1 of Armenia, we have heard your own judgment in this
case, and now tell us, what ought we to do ?' But the king
sat silent and perplexed, wondering whether he should bid
Cyrus put him to death, or act in the teeth of the rule that
he had laid down for himself. 14. Then his son Tigranes
turned to Cyrus and said, 'Tell me, Cyrus, since my father
sits in doubt, may I give counsel in his place and say what
I think best for you ?'

Now Cyrus remembered that, in the old hunting days,
he had noticed a certain man of wisdom who went about
with Tigranes and was much admired by him, and he was
curious to know what the youth would say. So he readily
agreed and bade him speak his mind.

15. 'In my view, then,' said Tigranes, 'if you approve of
all that my father has said or done, certainly you ought to
do as he did, but if you think he has done wrong, then you
must not copy him.'

'But surely,' said Cyrus, 'the best way to avoid copying
the wrongdoer is to practise what is right ?'

'True enough,' answered the prince.

'Then on your own reasoning, I am bound to punish
your father, if it is right to punish wrong.'

'But would you wish your vengeance to do you harm
instead of good ?'

'Nay,' said Cyrus, 'for then my vengeance would fall
upon myself.'

16. 'Even so,' said Tigranes, 'and you will do yourself
the greatest harm if you put your own subjects to death
just when they are most valuable to you.'

'Can they have any value,' asked Cyrus, 'when they are
detected doing wrong ?'

'Yes,' answered Tigranes, 'if that is when they turn to
good and learn sobriety. For it is my belief, Cyrus, that
without this virtue all others are in vain. What good will
you get from a strong man or a brave if he lack sobriety,
be he never so good a horseman, never so rich, never so
powerful in the state ? But with sobriety every friend is a
friend in need and every servant a blessing.'

17. 'I take your meaning,' answered Cyrus ; 'your father,

you would have me think, has been changed in this one C. 1
day from a fool into a wise and sober-minded man?'

'Exactly,' said the prince.

'Then you would call sober-mindedness a condition of
our nature, such as pain, not a matter of reason that can
be learnt? For certainly, if he who is to be sober-minded
must learn wisdom first, he could not be converted from
folly in a day.'

18. 'Nay, but, Cyrus,' said the prince, 'surely you yourself have known one man at least who out of sheer folly
has set himself to fight a stronger man than he, and on the
day of defeat his senselessness has been cured. And surely
you have known a city ere now that has marshalled her
battalions against a rival state, but with defeat she changes
suddenly and is willing to obey and not resist?'

19. 'But what defeat,' said Cyrus, 'can you find in your
father's case to make you so sure that he has come to a
sober mind?'

'A defeat,' answered the young man, 'of which he is well
aware in the secret chambers of his soul. He set his heart
on liberty, and he has found himself a slave as never
before: he had designs that needed stealth and speed and
force, and not one of them has he been able to carry
through. With you he knows that design and fulfilment
went hand in hand; when you wished to outwit him,
outwit him you did, as though he had been blind and deaf
and dazed; when stealth was needed, your stealth was
such that the fortresses he thought his own you turned
into traps for him; and your speed was such that you were
upon him from miles away with all your armament before
he found time to muster the forces at his command.'

20. 'So you think,' said Cyrus, 'that merely to learn
another is stronger than himself is defeat enough to bring
a man to his senses?'

'I do,' answered Tigranes, 'and far more truly than mere
defeat in battle. For he who is conquered by force may
fancy that if he trains he can renew the war, and captured
cities dream that with the help of allies they will fight again
one day, but if we meet with men who are better than
ourselves and whom we recognise to be so, we are ready

C. 1 to obey them of our own free will.' 21. 'You imagine then,' said Cyrus, 'that the bully and the tyrant cannot recognise the man of self-restraint, nor the thief the honest man, nor the liar the truth-speaker, nor the unjust man the upright? Has not your own father lied even now and broken his word with us, although he knew that we had faithfully observed every jot and tittle of the compact Astyages made?' 22. 'Ah, but,' replied the prince, 'I do not pretend that the bare knowledge alone will bring a man to his senses, it cannot cure him unless he pays the penalty as my father pays it to-day.' 'But,' answered Cyrus, 'your father has suffered nothing at all so far: although he fears, I know, that the worst suffering may be his.' 23. 'Do you suppose then,' asked Tigranes, 'that anything can enslave a man more utterly than fear? Do you not know that even the men who are beaten with the iron rod of war, the heaviest rod in all the world, may still be ready to fight again, while the victims of terror cannot be brought to look their conquerors in the face, even when they try to comfort them?' 'Then, you maintain,' said Cyrus, 'that fear will subdue a man more than suffering?' 24. 'Yes,' he answered, 'and you of all men know that what I say is true: you know the despondency men feel in dread of banishment, or on the eve of battle facing defeat, or sailing the sea in peril of shipwreck – they cannot touch their food or take their rest because of their alarm: while it may often be that the exiles themselves, the conquered, or the enslaved, can eat and sleep better than men who have not known adversity. 25. Think of those panic-stricken creatures who through fear of capture and death have died before their day, have hurled themselves from cliffs, hanged themselves, or set the knife to their throats; so cruelly can fear, the prince of horrors, bind and subjugate the souls of men. And what, think you, does my father feel at this moment? He, whose fears are not for himself alone, but for us all, for his wife, and for his children.' 26. And Cyrus said, 'To-day and at this time, it may be with him as you say: but still I think that the same man may well be insolent in good fortune and cringing in defeat: let such an one go free again, and he will return to his arrogance

and trouble us once more.' 27. 'I do not deny it, Cyrus,' C. 1
said the prince. 'Our offences are such that you may well
mistrust us : but you have it in your power to set garrisons
in our land and hold our strong places and take what
pledges you think best. And even so,' he added, 'you will
not find that we fret against our chains, for we shall
remember we have only ourselves to blame. Whereas, if
you hand over the government to some who have not
offended, they may either think that you mistrust them,
and thus, although you are their benefactor, you cannot
be their friend, or else in your anxiety not to rouse their
enmity you may leave no check on their insolence, and in
the end you will need to sober them even more than us.'
28. 'Nay, but by all the gods,' cried Cyrus, 'little joy
should I ever take in those who served me from necessity
alone. Only if I recognise some touch of friendship, or
goodwill in the help it is their duty to render, I could find
it easier to forgive them all their faults than to accept the
full discharge of service paid upon compulsion by those
who hate me.'

Then Tigranes answered, 'You speak of friendship, but
can you ever find elsewhere so great a friendship as you
may find with us ?' 'Surely I can,' he answered, 'and with
those who have never been my enemies, if I choose to be
their benefactor as you would have me yours.' 29. 'But to-
day and now, can you find another man in all the world
whom you could benefit as you can benefit my father ? Say
you let a man live who has never done you wrong, will he
be grateful for the boon ? Say he need not lose his children
and his wife, will he love you for that more than one who
knows he well deserved the loss ? Say he may not sit upon
the throne of Armenia, will he suffer from that as we shall
suffer ? And is it not clear that the one who feels the pain
of forfeiture the most will be the one most grateful for the
granting of the gift ? 30. And if you have it at all at heart
to leave matters settled here, think for yourself, and see
where tranquillity will lie when your back is turned. Will
it be with the new dynasty, or with the old familiar house ?
And if you want as large a force as possible at your
command, where will you find a man better fitted to test

C. 1 the muster-roll than the general who has used it time and again? If you need money, who will provide the ways and means better than he who knows and can command all the resources of the country? I warn you as a friend,' he added, 'that if you throw us aside you will do yourself more harm than ever my father could have done.'

31. Such were the pleadings of the prince, and Cyrus, as he listened, was overjoyed, for he felt he would accomplish to the full all he had promised Cyaxares; his own words came back to him, 'I hope to make the Armenian a better friend than before.'

Thereupon he turned to the king and said, 'Son of Armenia, if I were indeed to hearken unto you and yours in this, tell me, how large an army would you send me and how much money for the war?'

32. And the king replied, 'The simplest answer I can make and the most straightforward is to tell you what my power is, and then you may take the men you choose, and leave the rest to garrison the country. And so with the money: it is only fair that you should know the whole of our wealth, and with that knowledge to guide you, you will take what you like and leave what you like.' 33. And Cyrus said, 'Tell me then, and tell me true: how great is your power and your wealth?' Whereupon the Armenian replied: 'Our cavalry is 8000 strong and our infantry 40,000; and our wealth,' said he, 'if I include the treasures which my father left, amounts in silver to more than 3000 talents.'

34. And Cyrus, without more ado, said at once, 'Of your whole armament you shall give me half, not more, since your neighbours the Chaldaeans are at war with you: but for the tribute, instead of the fifty talents which you paid before, you shall hand over twice as much to Cyaxares because you made default: and you will lend me another hundred for myself, and I hereby promise you, if God be bountiful, I will requite you for the loan with things of higher worth, or I will pay the money back in full, if I can; and if I cannot, you may blame me for want of ability, but not for want of will.' 35. But the Armenian cried, 'By all the gods, Cyrus, speak not so, or you will put

me out of heart. I beg you to look on all I have as yours, C. 1
what you leave behind as well as what you take away.'

'So be it then,' answered Cyrus, 'and to ransom your
wife, how much money would you give?' 'All that I have,'
said he. 'And for your sons?' 'For them too, all that I
have.' 'Good,' answered Cyrus, 'but is not that already
twice as much as you possess? 36. And you, Tigranes,'
said he, 'at what price would you redeem your bride?'
Now the youth was but newly wedded, and his wife was
beyond all things dear to him. 'I would give my life,' said
he, 'to save her from salvery.' 37. 'Take her then,' said
Cyrus, 'she is yours. For I hold that she has never yet been
made a prisoner, seeing that her husband never deserted
us. And you, son of Armenia,' said he, turning to the king,
'you shall take home your wife and children, and pay no
ransom for them, so that they shall not feel they come to
you from slavery. But now,' he added, 'you shall stay and
sup with us, and afterwards you shall go wherever you
wish.'

And so the Armenians stayed. 38. But when the company broke up after the evening meal, Cyrus asked
Tigranes, 'Tell me, where is that friend of yours who used
to hunt with us, and whom, as it seemed to me, you
admired so much?' 'Do you not know,' he said, 'that my
father put him to death?' 'And why?' said Cyrus, 'what
fault did he find in him?' 'He thought he corrupted me,'
said the youth; 'and yet, I tell you, Cyrus, he was so gentle
and so brave, so beautiful in soul, that when he came to
die, he called me to him and said, "Do not be angry with
your father, Tigranes, for putting me to death. What he
does is not done from malice but from ignorance; and the
sins of ignorance, I hold, are unintentional."'

39. And at that Cyrus could not but say: 'Poor soul! I
grieve for him.' But the king spoke in his own defence:
'Remember this, Cyrus, that the man who finds another
with his wife kills him not simply because he believes that
he has turned the woman to folly, but because he has
robbed him of her love. Even so I was jealous of that man
who seemed to put himself between my son and me and
steal away his reverence.' 40. 'May the gods be merciful to

C. 1 us !' said Cyrus, 'you did wrong, but your fault was human. And you, Tigranes,' said he, turning to the son, 'you must forgive your father.'

And so they talked in all friendliness and kindliness, as befitted that time of reconciliation; and then the father and son mounted their carriages, with their dear ones beside them, and drove away rejoicing.

41. But when they were home again, they all spoke of Cyrus, one praising his wisdom, another his endurance, a third the gentleness of his nature, and a fourth his stature and his beauty. Then Tigranes turned to his wife and asked, 'Did Cyrus seem so beautiful in your eyes ?' But she answered, 'Ah, my lord, he was not the man I saw.' 'Who was it then ?' asked Tigranes. 'He,' she answered, 'who offered his own life to free me from slavery.'

And so they took their delight together, as lovers will, after all their sufferings.

42. But on the morrow the king of Armenia sent gifts of hospitality to Cyrus and all his army, and bade his own contingent make ready to march on the third day, and himself brought Cyrus twice the sum which he had named. But Cyrus would take no more than he had fixed, and gave the rest back to the king, only asking whether he or his son was to lead the force. And the father answered that it should be as Cyrus chose, but the son said, 'I will not leave you, Cyrus, if I must carry the baggage to follow you.' 43. And Cyrus laughed and said, 'What will you take to let us tell your wife that you have become a baggage-bearer ?' 'She will not need to be told,' he answered, 'I mean to bring her with me, and she can see for herself all that her husband does.' 'Then it is high time,' said Cyrus, 'that you got your own baggage together now.' 'We will come,' said he, 'be sure of that, in good time, with whatever baggage my father gives.'

So the soldiers were the guests of Armenia for the day, and rested for that night.

C. 2 But on the day following Cyrus took Tigranes and the best of the Median cavalry, with chosen followers of his own, and scoured the whole country to decide where he should build a fort. He halted on the top of a mountain-

pass and asked Tigranes where the heights lay down which C. 2
the Chaldaeans swept when they came to plunder.
Tigranes showed him. Then Cyrus asked him if the mountains were quite uninhabited. 'No, indeed,' said the prince,
'there are always men on the look-out, who signal to the
others if they catch sight of anything.' 'And what do they
do,' he asked, 'when they see the signal?' 'They rush to
the rescue,' he said, 'as quickly as they can.' 2. Cyrus
listened and looked, and he could see that large tracts lay
desolate and untilled because of the war. That day they
came back to camp and took their supper and slept. 3. But
the next morning Tigranes presented himself with all his
baggage in order and ready for the march, 4000 cavalry at
his back, 10,000 bowmen, and as many targeteers. While
they were marching up, Cyrus offered sacrifice, and finding
that the victims were favourable, he called the leaders of
the Persians together and the chief captains of the Medes
and spoke to them thus:

4. 'My friends, there lie the Chaldaean hills. If we could
seize them and set a garrison to hold the pass, we should
compel them both, Chaldaeans and Armenians alike, to
behave themselves discreetly. The victims are favourable;
and to help a man in such a work as this there is no ally
half so good as speed. If we scale the heights before the
enemy have time to gather, we may take the position out
of hand without a blow, and at most we shall only find a
handful of weak and scattered forces to oppose us.
5. Steady speed is all I ask for, and surely I could ask for
nothing easier or less dangerous. To arms then! The Medes
will march on our left, half the Armenians on our right,
and the rest in the van to lead the way, the cavalry in our
rear, to cheer us on and push us forward and let none of
us give way.'

6. With that Cyrus led the advance, the army in column
behind him. As soon as the Chaldaeans saw them sweeping
up from the plain, they signalled to their fellows till the
heights re-echoed with answering shouts, and the tribes-
men gathered on every side. Then Cyrus sent word along
his lines, 'Soldiers of Persia, they are signalling to us to

C. 2 make haste. If only we reach the top before them, all they can do will be in vain.'

7. Now the Chaldaeans were said to be the most warlike of all the tribes in that country, and each of them was armed with a shield and a brace of javelins. They fight for pay wherever they are needed, partly because they are warriors born, but partly through poverty; for their country is mountainous, and the fertile part of it small. 8. As Cyrus and his force drew near the head of the pass, Tigranes, who was marching at his side, said:

'Do you know, Cyrus, that before long we shall be in the thick of the fight ourselves? Our Armenians will never stand the charge.' Cyrus answered that he was well aware of that, and immediately sent word that the Persians should be ready to give chase at once, 'as soon as we see the Armenians decoying the enemy by feigning flight and drawing them within our reach.'

9. Thus they marched up with the Armenians in the van: and the Chaldaeans who had collected waited till they were almost on them, and then charged with a tremendous shout, as their custom was, and the Armenians, as was ever theirs, turned and ran. 10. But in the midst of the pursuit the Chaldaeans met new opponents streaming up the pass, armed with short swords, and some of them were cut to pieces at once before they could withdraw, while others were taken prisoners and the rest fled, and in a few moments the heights were won. From the top of the pass Cyrus and his staff looked down and saw below them the Chaldaean villages with fugitives pouring from the nearest houses. 11. Soon the rest of the army came up, and Cyrus ordered them all to take the morning meal. When it was over, and he had ascertained that the look-out was really in a strong position, and well supplied with water, he set about fortifying a post without more ado, and he bade Tigranes send to his father and bid him come at once with all the carpenters and stonemasons he could fetch, and while a messenger went off to the king Cyrus did all he could with what he had at hand.

12. Meanwhile they brought up the prisoners, all of them bound in chains and some wounded. But Cyrus when

he saw their plight ordered the chains to be struck off, and C. 2
sent for surgeons to dress their wounds, and then he told
them that he came neither to destroy them nor to war
against them, but to make peace between them and the
Armenians. 'I know,' he said, 'before your pass was taken
you did not wish for peace. Your own land was in safety
and you could harry the Armenians: but you can see for
yourselves how things stand to-day. 13. Accordingly I will
let you all go back to your homes in freedom, and I will
allow you and your fellows to take counsel together and
choose whether you will have us for your enemies or your
friends. If you decide on war, you had better not come
here again without your weapons, but if you choose peace,
come unarmed and welcome: it shall be my care to see
that all is well with you, if you are my friends.'

14. And when the Chaldaeans heard that, they poured
out praises and thanks, and then they turned homewards
and departed.

Meanwhile the king, receiving the call of Cyrus, and
hearing the business that was in hand, had gathered his
workmen together and took what he thought necessary
and came with all speed. 15. And when he caught sight of
Cyrus, he cried: 'Ah, my lord, blind mortals that we are!
How little can we see of the future, and how much we
take in hand to do! I set myself to win freedom and I made
myself a slave, and now, when we were captured and said
to ourselves that we were utterly undone, suddenly we find
a safety we never had before. Those who troubled us are
taken now, even as I would have them. 16. Be well assured,
Cyrus,' he added, 'that I would have paid the sum you had
from me over and over again simply to dislodge the
Chaldaeans from these heights. The things of worth you
promised me when you took the money have been paid in
full already, and we discover that we are not your credi-
tors, but deep in your debt for many kindnesses; and we
shall be ashamed not to return them, or we should be base
indeed, for try as we may, we shall never be able to requite
in full so great a benefactor.'

17. Such thanks the Armenian gave.

Then the Chaldaeans came back, begging Cyrus to make

C. 2 peace with them. And Cyrus asked them : 'Am I right in
thinking that you desire peace to-day because you believe
it will be safer for you than war, now that we hold these
heights ?'

And the Chaldaeans said that so it was. 18. 'Well and
good,' said he. 'And what if other benefits were gained by
peace ?' 'We should be all the better pleased,' said they. 'Is
there any other reason,' he asked, 'for your present poverty, except your lack of fertile soil ?' They said that there
was one. 'Well then,' Cyrus went on, 'would you be willing
to pay the same dues as the Armenians, if you were
allowed to cultivate as much of their land as you desired ?'
And the Chaldaeans said they would, if only they could
rely on being fairly treated. 19. 'Now,' said Cyrus, turning
to the Armenian king, 'would you like that land of yours
which is now lying idle to be tilled and made productive,
supposing the workers paid you the customary dues ?' 'I
would, indeed,' said the king, 'so much so that I am ready
to pay a large sum for it. It would mean a great increase to
my revenue.' 20. 'And you Chaldaeans,' said Cyrus, with
your splendid mountains, would you let the Armenians use
them for pasture if the graziers paid you what was fair ?'
'Surely yes,' said the Chaldaeans, 'it would mean much
profit and no pains.'

'Son of Armenia,' said Cyrus, 'would you take this land
for grazing, if by paying a small sum to the Chaldaeans
you got a far greater return yourself ?'

'Right willingly,' said he, 'if I thought my flocks could
feed in safety.'

'And would they not be safe enough,' suggested Cyrus,
'if this pass were held for you ?' To which the king agreed.
21. But the Chaldaeans cried, 'Heaven help us ! We could
not till our own fields in safety, not to speak of theirs, if
the Armenians held the pass.' 'True,' answered Cyrus, 'but
how would it be if the pass were held for you ?' 'Ah, then,'
said they, 'all would be well enough.' 'Heaven help us !'
cried the Armenian in his turn, 'all might be well enough
for them, but it would be ill for us if these neighbours of
ours recovered the post, especially now that it is fortified.'
22. Then Cyrus said, 'See, then, this is what I will do : I

will hand over the pass to neither of you : we Persians will C. 2
guard it ourselves, and if either of you injure the other, we
will step in and side with the sufferers.'

23. Then both parties applauded the decision, and said
that only thus could they establish a lasting peace, and on
these terms they exchanged pledges, and a covenant was
made that both nations alike were to be free and independ-
ent, but with common rights of marriage, and tillage, and
pasturage, and help in time of war if either were attacked.
24. Thus the matter was concluded, and to this day the
treaty holds between the Chaldaeans and Armenia.

Peace was no sooner made than both parties began
building what they now considered their common fortress,
working side by side and bringing up all that was needed.
25. And when evening fell, Cyrus summoned them all as
fellow-guests to his board, saying that they were friends
already. At the supper as they sat together, one of the
Chaldaeans said to Cyrus that the mass of his nation
would feel they had received all they could desire, 'But
there are men among us,' he added, 'who live as freeboot-
ers : they do not know how to labour in the field, and they
could not learn, accustomed as they are from youth up to
get their livelihood either by plundering for themselves or
serving as mercenaries, often under the king of India, for
he is a man of much wealth, but sometimes under
Astyages.' 26. Then Cyrus said : 'Why should they not
take service with me ? I undertake to give them at least as
much as they ever got elsewhere.' The Chaldaeans readily
agreed with him, and prophesied that he would have many
volunteers.

27. So this matter was settled to the mind of all. But
Cyrus, on hearing that the Chaldaeans were in the habit of
going to India, remembered how Indian ambassadors had
come to the Medes to spy out their affairs, and how they
had gone on to their enemies – doubtless to do the same
there – and he felt a wish that they should hear something
of what he had achieved himself. 28. So he said to the
company : 'Son of Armenia, and men of the Chaldaeans, I
have something to ask you. Tell me, if I were to send
ambassadors to India, would you send some of your own

C. 2 folk with them to show them the way, and support them in gaining for us all that I desire? I still need more money if I am to pay all the wages, as I wish, in full, and give rewards and make presents to such of my soldiers as deserve them. It is for such things I need all the money I can get, for I believe them to be essential. It would be pleasanter for me not to draw on you, because I look on you already as my friends, but I should be glad to take from the Indian as much as he will give me. My messenger – the one for whom I ask guides and coadjutors – will go to the king and say: "Son of India, my master has sent me to you, bidding me say that he has need of more money. He is expecting another army from Persia," and indeed I do expect one,' Cyrus added. 'Then my messenger will proceed, "If you can send my master all that you have at hand he will do his best, if God grant him success, that you should feel your kindness has not been ill-advised." 30. That is what my emissary will say: and you must give such instructions to yours as you think fit yourselves. If I get money from the king, I shall have abundance at my disposal: if I fail, at least we shall owe him no gratitude, and as far as he is concerned we may look to our own interests alone.'

31. So Cyrus spoke, convinced that the ambassadors from Armenia and Chaldaea would speak of him as he desired all men might do. And then, as the hour was come, they broke up the meeting and took their rest.

C. 3   But on the next day Cyrus despatched his messenger with the instructions, and the Armenians and Chaldaeans sent their own ambassadors, choosing the men they thought would help Cyrus most and speak of his exploits in the most fitting terms. Cyrus put a strong garrison in the fort and stored it with supplies, and left an officer in command, a Mede, whose appointment, he thought, would gratify Cyaxares, and then he turned homewards, taking with him not only the troops he had brought, but the force the Armenians had furnished, and a picked body of Chaldaeans who considered themselves stronger than all the rest together. 2. And as he came down from the hills into the cultivated land, not one of the Armenians,

man or woman, stayed indoors: with one accord they all C. 3
went out to meet him, rejoicing that peace was made, and
bringing him offerings from their best, driving before them
the animals they valued most. The king himself was not
ill-pleased at this, for he thought that Cyrus would take
delight in the honour the people showed him. Last of all
came the queen herself, with her daughters and her
younger son, bearing many gifts, and among them the
golden treasure that Cyrus had refused before. 3. But when
he saw it he said: 'Nay, you must not make me a
mercenary and a benefactor for pay; take this treasure
back and hie you home, but do not give it to your lord
that he may bury it again; spend it on your son, and send
him forth gloriously equipped for war, and with the
residue buy for yourself and for your husband and your
children such precious things as shall endure, and bring
joy and beauty into all your days. As for burying, let us
only bury our bodies on the day when each must die.'

4. With that he rode away, the king and all his people
escorting him, like a guard of honour, calling him their
saviour, their benefactor, and their hero, and heaping
praises on him until he had left the land. And the king sent
with him a larger army than ever he had sent before, seeing
that now he had peace at home. 5. Thus Cyrus took his
departure, having gained not only the actual money he
took away with him, but a far ampler store of wealth, won
by his own graciousness, on which he could draw in time
of need.

For the first night he encamped on the borders of
Armenia, but the next day he sent the army and the money
to Cyaxares, who was close at hand, as he had promised
to be, while he himself took his pleasure in hunting
wherever he could find the game, in company with
Tigranes and the flower of the Persian force.

6. And when he came back to Media he gave gifts of
money to his chief officers, sufficient for each to reward
their own subordinates, for he held to it that, if every one
made his own division worthy of praise, all would be well
with the army as a whole. He himself secured anything
that he thought of value for the campaign, and divided it

C. 3 among the most meritorious, convinced that every gain to the army was an adornment to himself.

7. At every distribution he would take occasion to address the officers and all whom he chose to honour in some such words as these: 'My friends, the god of mirth must be with us to-day: we have found a source of plenty, and we have the wherewithal to honour whom we wish and as they may deserve. 8. Let us call to mind, all of us, the only way in which these blessings can be won. We shall find it is by toil, and watchfulness, and speed, and the resolve never to yield to our foes. After this pattern must we prove ourselves to be men, knowing that all high delights and all great joys are only gained by obedience and hardihood, and through pains endured and dangers confronted in their proper season.'

9. But presently, when Cyrus saw that his men were strong enough for all the work of war, and bold enough to meet their enemies with scorn, expert and skilful in the use of the weapons each man bore, and all of them perfect in obedience and discipline, the desire grew in his heart to be up and doing and achieve something against the foe. He knew well how often a general has found delay ruin his fairest armament. 10. He noticed, moreover, that in the eagerness of rivalry and the strain of competition many of the soldiers grew jealous of each other; and for this, if for no other reason, he desired to lead them into the enemy's country without delay, feeling that common dangers awaken comradeship among those who are fighting in a common cause, and then all such bickerings cease, and no man is galled by the splendour of his comrade's arms, or the passion of his desire for glory: envy is swallowed up in praise, and each competitor greets his rivals with delight as fellow-workers for the common good.

11. Therefore Cyrus ordered his whole force to assemble under arms, and drew them up in battle-array, using all his skill to make the display a wonder of beauty and perfection. Then he summoned his chief officers, his generals, his brigadiers, and his company-captains. These men were not bound to be always in the ranks, and some were always free to wait on the commander-in-chief or carry

orders along the lines without leaving the troops unoffi- C. 3
cered: for the captains-of-twelve and the captains-of-six
stepped into the gaps, and absolute order was preserved.
12. So Cyrus assembled his staff and led them along the
lines, pointing out the merits of the combined forces and
the special strength of each, and thus he kindled in their
hearts the passion for achievement, and then he bade them
return to their regiments and repeat the lessons he had
taught them, trying to implant in their own men the same
desire for action, so that one and all might sally out in the
best of heart; and the next morning they were to present
themselves at Cyaxares' gates. 13. So the officers went
away and did as he commanded, and the next morning at
daybreak they assembled at the trysting-place, and Cyrus
met them and came before Cyaxares and said to him:

'I know well that what I am about to say must often
have been in your own mind, but you have shrunk from
suggesting it yourself lest it might seem that you were
weary of supporting us. 14. Therefore since you must keep
silence, let me speak for both of us. We are all agreed that
since our preparations are complete we should not wait
until the enemy invades your territory before we give him
battle, nor loiter here in a friendly land, but attack him on
his own ground with what speed we may. 15. For while
we linger here, we injure your property in spite of ourselves, but once on the enemy's soil we can damage his,
and that with the best will in the world. 16. As things are,
you must maintain us, and the cost is great; but once
launched on foreign service, we can maintain ourselves,
and at our foe's expense. 17. Possibly, if it were more
dangerous to go forward than to stay here, the more
cautious might seem the wiser plan. But whether we stay
or whether we go, the enemy's numbers will be the same,
and so will ours, whether we receive them here or join
battle with them there. 18. Moreover, the spirit of our
soldiers will be all the higher and all the bolder if they feel
that they are marching against the foe and not cowering
before him; and his alarm will be all the greater when he
hears that we are not crouching at home in terror but
coming out to meet him as soon as we have heard of his

C. 3 advance, eager to close at once, not holding back until our
territory suffers, but prompt to seize the moment and
ravage his own land first. 19. Indeed,' he added, 'if we do
no more than quicken our own courage and his fears, I
would reckon it a substantial gain, and count it so much
the less danger for us and so much the more for him. My
father never tires of telling me what I have heard you say
yourself, and what all the world admits, that battles are
decided more by the character of the troops than by their
bodily strength.'

20. He ended, and Cyaxares answered:

'Cyrus, both you and all my Persian friends may feel
sure that I find it no trouble to maintain you; do not
imagine such a thing; but I agree with you that the time is
ripe for an advance on the enemy's land.'

'Then,' said Cyrus, 'since we are all of one mind, let us
make our final preparations, and, if heaven will, let us set
forth without delay.'

21. So they bade the soldiers prepare for the start, and
Cyrus offered sacrifices to Zeus the Lord and to the other
gods in due order, and prayed, 'Look on us with favour,
and be gracious to us; guide our army, stand beside us in
the battle, aid us in council, help us in action, be the
comrades of the brave.' Also he called upon the Heroes of
Media, who dwell in the land and guard it. 22. Then,
when the signs were favourable and his army was mustered
on the frontier, he felt that the moment had come, and
with all good omens to support him, he invaded the
enemy's land. And so soon as he had crossed the border
he offered libations to the Earth and victims to the gods,
and sought to win the favour of the Heroes who guard
Assyria. And having so done, once more he sacrificed to
Zeus, the god of his fathers, and was careful to reverence
every other god who came before his mind.

23. But when these duties were fulfilled, there was no
further pause. He pushed his infantry on at once, a short
day's march, and then encamped, while the cavalry made
a swift descent and captured much spoil of every kind. For
the future they had only to shift their camp from time to
time, and they found supplies in abundance, and could

ravage the enemy's land at their ease while waiting his C. 3 approach. 24. Presently news came of his advance : he was said to be barely ten days off, and at that Cyrus went to Cyaxares and said : 'The hour has come, and we must face the enemy. Let it not seem to friend or foe that we fear the encounter : let us show them that we enjoy the fight.'

25. Cyaxares agreed, and they moved forward in good order, marching each day as far as appeared desirable. They were careful to take their evening meal by daylight, and at night they lit no fires in the camp : they made them in front of it, so that in case of attack they might see their assailants, while they themselves remained unseen. And often they lit other fires in their rear as well, to deceive the enemy ; so that at times the Assyrian scouts actually fell in with the advance-guard, having fancied from the distance of the fires that they were still some way from the encampment.

26. Meanwhile the Assyrians and their allies, as the two armies came into touch, halted, and threw up an entrenchment, just as all barbarian leaders do to-day, whenever they encamp, finding no difficulty in the work because of the vast numbers at their command, and knowing that cavalry may easily be thrown into confusion and become unmanageable, especially if they are barbarians. 27. The horses must be tethered at their stalls, and in case of attack a dozen difficulties arise : the soldier must loose his steed in the dark, bridle and saddle him, put on his own armour, mount, and then gallop through the camp, and this last it is quite impossible to do. Therefore the Assyrians, like all barbarians, throw up entrenchments round their position, and the mere fact of being inside a fastness leaves them, they consider, the choice of fighting at any moment they think fit. 28. So the two armies drew nearer and nearer, and when they were about four miles apart, the Assyrians proceeded to encamp in the manner described : their position was completely surrounded by a trench, but also perfectly visible, while Cyrus took all the cover he could find, screening himself behind villages and hillocks, in the conviction that the more sudden the disclosure of a hostile force the greater will be the enemy's alarm.

C. 3 29. During the first night neither army did more than post the customary guards before they went to sleep, and on the next day the king of Assyria, and Crœsus, and their officers, still kept the troops within their lines. But Cyrus and Cyaxares drew up their men, prepared to fight if the enemy advanced.

Ere long it was plain that they would not venture out that day, and Cyaxares summoned Cyrus and his staff and said:

30. 'I think, gentlemen, it would be well for us to march up to the breastworks in our present order, and show them that we wish to fight. If we do so,' he added, 'and they refuse our challenge, it will increase the confidence of our own men, and the mere sight of our boldness will add to the enemy's alarm.'

31. So it seemed to Cyaxares, but Cyrus protested: 'In the name of heaven, Cyaxares, let us do no such thing. By such an advance we should only reveal our numbers to them: they would watch us at their ease, conscious that they are safe from any danger, and when we retire without doing them any harm they will have another look at us and despise us because of our inferiority in numbers, and to-morrow they will come out much emboldened. 32. At present,' he added, 'they know that we are here, but they have not seen us, and you may be sure they do not despise us; they are asking what all this means, and they never cease discussing the problem; of that I am convinced. They ought not to see us until they sally out, and in that moment we ought to come to grips with them, thankful to have caught them as we have so long desired.'

33. So Cyrus spoke, and Cyaxares and the others were convinced, and waited. In the evening they took their meal, and posted their pickets and lit watch-fires in front of their outposts, and so turned to sleep. 34. But early the next morning Cyrus put a garland on his head and went out to offer sacrifice, and sent word to all the Peers of Persia to join him, wearing garlands like himself. And when the rite was over, he called them together and said: 'Gentlemen, the soothsayers tell us, and I agree, that the gods announce by the signs in the victims that the battle is at hand, and

they assure us of victory, they promise us salvation. 35. I C. 3 should be ashamed to admonish you at such a season, or tell you how to bear yourselves: I do not forget that we have all been brought up in the same school, you have learnt the same lessons as I, and practised them day by day, and you might well instruct others. But you may not have noticed one point, and for this I would ask a hearing. 36. Our new comrades, the men we desire to make our peers — it may be well to remind them of the terms on which Cyaxares has kept us and of our daily discipline, the goal for which we asked their help, and the race in which they promised to be our friendly rivals. 37. Remind them also that this day will test the worth of every man. With learners late in life, we cannot wonder if now and then a prompter should be needed: it is much to be thankful for if they show themselves good men and true with the help of a reminder. 38. Moreover, while you help them you will be putting your own powers to the test. He who can give another strength at such a crisis may well have confidence in his own, whereas one who keeps his ideal to himself and is content with that, ought to remember that he is only half a man. 39. There is another reason,' he added, 'why I do not speak to them myself, but ask you to do so. I want them to try to please you: you are nearer to them than I, each of you to the men of his own division: and be well assured that if you show yourselves stout-hearted you will be teaching them courage, and others too, by deeds as well as words.'

40. With that Cyrus dismissed them, and bade them break their fast and make libation, and then take their places in the ranks, still wearing their garlands on their heads. And as they went away he summoned the leaders of the rearguard and gave them his instructions:

41. 'Men of Persia, you have been made Peers and chosen for special duties, because we think you equal to the best in other matters, and wiser than most in virtue of your age. The post that you hold is every whit as honourable as theirs who form the front: from your position in the rear you can single out the gallant fighters, and your praise will make them outdo themselves in valour, while if

C. 3 any man should be tempted to give way, your eyes will be upon him and you will not suffer it. 42. Victory will mean even more to you than to the others, because of your age and the weight of your equipment. If the men in front call on you to follow, answer readily, and let them see that you can hold your own with them, shout back to them, and bid them lead on quicker still. And now,' said he, 'go back and take your breakfast, and then join your ranks with the rest, wearing your garlands on your heads.'

43. Thus Cyrus and his men made their preparations, and meanwhile the Assyrians on their side took their breakfast, and then sallied forth boldly and drew up in gallant order. It was the king himself who marshalled them, driving past in his chariot and encouraging his troops.

44. 'Men of Assyria,' he said, 'to-day you must show your valour. To-day you fight for your lives and your land, the land where you were born and the homes where you were bred, and for your wives and your children, and all the blessings that are yours. If you win, you will possess them all in safety as before, but if you lose, you must surrender them into the hands of your enemies. 45. Abide therefore, and do battle as though you were enamoured of victory. It would be folly for her lovers to turn their backs to the foe, sightless, handless, helpless, and a fool is he who flies because he longs to live, for he must know that safety comes to those who conquer, but death to those who flee; and fools are they whose hearts are set on riches, but whose spirits are ready to admit defeat. It is the victor who preserves his own possessions and wins the property of those whom he overcomes: the conquered lose themselves and all they call their own.'

46. Thus spoke the king of Assyria.

But meanwhile Cyaxares sent to Cyrus saying that the moment for attack had come. 'Although,' he added, 'there are as yet but few of them outside the trenches, by the time we have advanced there will be quite enough. Let us not wait until they outnumber us, but charge at once while we are satisfied we can master them easily.'

47. But Cyrus answered him, 'Unless those we conquer

are more than half their number, they are sure to say that C. 3 we attacked when they were few, because we were afraid of their full force, and in their hearts they will not feel that they are beaten; and we shall have to fight another battle, when perhaps they will make a better plan than they have made to-day, delivering themselves into our hands one by one, to fight with as we choose.'

48. So the messengers took back his reply, but meanwhile Chrysantas and certain other Peers came to Cyrus bringing Assyrian deserters with them, and Cyrus, as a general would, questioned the fugitives about the enemy's doings, and they told him that the Assyrians were marching out in force and that the king himself had crossed the trenches and was marshalling his troops, addressing them in stirring words, as all the listeners said. 49. Then Chrysantas turned to Cyrus:

'What if you also were to summon our men, while there is yet time, and inspire them with your words?'

50. But Cyrus answered:

'Do not be disturbed by the thought of the Assyrian's exhortations; there are no words so fine that they can turn cowards into brave men on the day of hearing, nor make good archers out of bad, nor doughty spearmen, nor skilful riders, no, nor even teach men to use their arms and legs if they have not learnt before.'

51. 'But,' replied Chrysantas, 'could you not make the brave men braver still, and the good better?'

'What!' cried Cyrus, 'can one solitary speech fill the hearer's soul on the selfsame day with honour and uprightness, guard him from all that is base, spur him to undergo, as he ought, for the sake of glory every toil and every danger, implant in him the faith that it is better to die sword in hand than to escape by flight? 52. If such thoughts are ever to be engraved in the hearts of men and there abide, we must begin with the laws, and frame them so that the righteous can count on a life of honour and liberty, while the bad have to face humiliation, suffering, and pain, and a life that is no life at all. 53. And then we ought to have tutors and governors to instruct and teach and train our citizens until the belief is engendered in their

C. 3 souls that the righteous and the honourable are the happiest of all men born, and the bad and the infamous the most miserable. This is what our men must feel if they are to show that their schooling can triumph over their terror of the foe. 54. Surely, if in the moment of onset, amid the clash of arms, at a time when lessons long learnt seem suddenly wiped away, it were possible for any speaker, by stringing a few fine sentiments together, to manufacture warriors out of hand, why, it would be the easiest thing in all the world to teach men the highest virtue man can know. 55. For my own part,' he added, 'I would not trust our new comrades yonder, whom we have trained ourselves, to stand firm this day unless they saw you at their side, to be examples unto them and to remind them if they forget. As for men who are utterly undisciplined, I should be astonished if any speech, however splendid, did one whit more to encourage valour in their hearts than a song well sung could do to make a musician of a man who had no music in his soul.'

56. But while they were speaking, Cyaxares sent again, saying that Cyrus did ill to loiter instead of advancing against the enemy with all speed. And Cyrus sent back word there and then by the messengers :

'Tell Cyaxares once more, that even now there are not as many before us as we need. And tell him this so that all may hear. But add that, if it so please him, I will advance at once.'

57. So saying and with one prayer to the gods, he led his troops into battle.

Once the advance began he quickened the pace, and his men followed in perfect order, steadily, swiftly, joyously, brimful of emulation, hardened by toil, trained by their long discipline, every man in the front a leader, and all of them alert. They had laid to heart the lesson of many a day that it was always safest and easiest to meet enemies at close quarters, especially archers, javelin-men, and cavalry. 58. While they were still out of range Cyrus sent the watchword along the lines, 'Zeus our help and Zeus our leader.' And as soon as it was returned to him, he sounded the first notes of the battle-paean, and the men took up the

hymn devoutly, in one mighty chorus. For at such times C. 3
those who fear the gods have less fear of their fellow-men.
59. And when the chant was over, the Peers of Persia went
forward side by side, radiant, high-bred, disciplined, a
band of gallant comrades; they looked into each other's
eyes, they called each other by name, with many a cheery
cry, 'Forward, friends, forward, gallant gentlemen!' And
the rear-ranks heard the call, and sent back a ringing cheer,
bidding the van lead on. The whole army of Cyrus was
brimming with courage and zeal and strength and hardihood and comradeship and self-control; more terrible, I
imagine, to an opponent than aught else could be. 60. On
the Assyrian side, those in the van who fought from the
chariots, as soon as the mass of the Persian force drew
near, leapt back and drove to their own main body; but
the archers, javelin-men, and slingers, let fly long before
they were in range. 61. And as the Persians steadily
advanced, stepping over the spent missiles, Cyrus called to
his men:

'Forward now, bravest of the brave! Show us what your
pace can be!'

They caught the word and passed it on, and in their
eagerness and passion for the fray some of the leaders
broke into a run, and the whole phalanx followed at their
heels. 62. Cyrus himself gave up the regular march and
dashed forward at their head, shouting:

'Brave men to the front! Who follows me? Who will lay
the first Assyrian low?'

And the men behind took up the shout till it rang
through the field like a battle-cry: 'Who follows? Brave
men to the front!' 63. Thus the Persians closed. But the
enemy could not hold their ground; they turned and fled
to their entrenchments. 64. The Persians swept after them,
many a warrior falling as they crowded in at the gates or
tumbled into the trenches. For in the rout some of the
chariots were carried into the fosse, and the Persians
sprang down after them and slew man and horse where
they fell. 65. Then the Median troopers, seeing how matters stood, charged the Assyrian cavalry, who swerved and
broke before them, chased and slaughtered, horse and

C. 3 rider, by their conquerors. 66. Meanwhile the Assyrians within the camp, though they stood upon the breastworks, had neither wit nor power to draw bow or fling spear against the destroyers, dazed as they were by their panic and the horror of the sight. Then came the tidings that the Persians had cut their way through to the gates, and at that they fled from the breastworks. 67. The women, seeing the rout in the camp, fell to wailing and lamentations, running hither and thither in utter dismay, young maidens, and mothers with children in their arms, rending their garments and tearing their cheeks and crying on all they met, 'Leave us not, save us, save your children and yourselves!' 68. Then the princes gathered their trustiest men and stood at the gates, fighting on the breastworks themselves, and urging their troops to make a stand. 69. Cyrus, seeing this, and fearing that if his handful of Persians forced their way into the camp they would be overborne by numbers, gave the order to fall back out of range. 70. Then was shown the perfect discipline of the Peers; at once they obeyed the order and passed it on at once. And when they all were out of range they halted and reformed their ranks, better than any chorus could have done, every man of them knowing exactly where he ought to be.

BOOK IV

CYRUS waited, with his troops as they were, long enough C. 1
to show that he was ready to do battle again if the enemy
would come out; but as they did not stir he drew the
soldiers off as far as he thought well, and there encamped.
He had guards posted and scouts sent forward, and then
he gathered his warriors round him and spoke to them as
follows:

2. 'Men of Persia, first and foremost I thank the gods of
heaven with all my soul and strength; and I know you
render thanks with me, for we have won salvation and
victory, and it is meet and right to thank the gods for all
that comes to us. But in the next place I must praise you,
one and all; it is through you all that this glorious work
has been accomplished, and when I have learnt what each
man's part has been from those whose place it is to tell
me, I will do my best to give each man his due, in word
and deed. 3. But I need none to tell me the exploits of your
brigadier Chrysantas; he was next to me in the battle and
I could see that he bore himself as I believe you all have
done. Moreover, at the very moment when I called on him
to retire, he had just raised his sword to strike an Assyrian
down, but he heard my voice, and at once he dropped his
hand and did my bidding. He sent the word along the lines
and led his division out of range before the enemy could
see that he meant to withdraw or could lay one arrow to
the string or let one javelin fly. Thus he brought himself
and his men safely out of action, because he had learnt to
obey. 4. But some of you, I see, are wounded, and when I
hear at what moment they received their wounds I will

C. 1 pronounce my opinion on their deserts. Chrysantas I know already to be a true soldier and a man of sense, able to command because he is able to obey, and here and now I put him at the head of a thousand troops, nor shall I forget him on the day when God may please to give me other blessings. 5. There is one reminder I would make to all. Never let slip the lesson of this day's encounter, and judge for yourselves whether it is cowardice or courage that saves a man in war, whether the fighters or the shirkers have the better chance, and what the joy is that victory can yield. To-day of all days you can decide, for you have made the trial and the result is fresh. 6. With such thoughts as these in your hearts you will grow braver and better still. And now you may rest in the consciousness that you are dear to God and have done your duty bravely and steadily, and so take your meal and make your libations and sing the paean and be ready for the watchword.'

So saying, Cyrus mounted his horse and galloped on to Cyaxares, and the two rejoiced together as victors will. And then, after a glance at matters there and an inquiry if aught were needed, he rode back to his own detachment. Then the evening meal was taken and the watches were posted and Cyrus slept with his men.

8. Meanwhile the Assyrians, finding that their king was among the slain and almost all his nobles with him, fell into utter despair, and many of them deserted during the night. And at this fear crept over Croesus and the allies; they saw dangers on every side, and heaviest of all was the knowledge that the leading nation, the head of the whole expedition, had received a mortal blow. Nothing remained but to abandon the encampment under cover of night. 9. Day broke, and the camp was seen to be deserted, and Cyrus, without more ado, led his Persians within the entrenchments, where they found the stores that the enemy had left: herds of sheep and goats and kine, and long rows of waggons laden with good things. Cyaxares and his Medes followed, and all arms took their breakfast in the camp. 10. But when the meal was over, Cyrus summoned his brigadiers and said to them:

'Think what blessings we are flinging away now, spurn-

ing, as it were, the very gifts of heaven ! So at least it seems C. 1
to me. The enemy have given us the slip, as you see with
your own eyes. Is it likely that men who forsook the shelter
of their own fortress will ever face us in fair field on level
ground ? Will those who shrank from us before they put
our prowess to the test ever withstand us now when we
have overthrown and shattered them ? They have lost their
best and bravest, and will the cowards dare to give us
battle ?'

11. At that one of his officers cried, 'Why not pursue at
once, if such triumphs are before us ?'

And Cyrus answered, 'Because we have not the horses.
The stoutest of our enemies, those whom we must seize or
slay, are mounted on steeds that could sweep past us like
the wind. God helping us, we can put them to flight, but
we cannot overtake them.'

12. 'Then,' said they, 'why not go and lay the matter
before Cyaxares ?'

And he answered, 'If so, you must all go with me, that
Cyaxares may see it is the wish of all.'

So they all went together and spoke as they thought
best. 13. Now Cyaxares felt, no doubt, a certain jealousy
that the Persians should be the first to broach the matter,
but he may also have felt that it was really wiser to run no
further risks for the present ; he had, moreover, abandoned
himself to feasting and merrymaking, and he saw that
most of his Medes were in like case. Whatever the reason,
this was the answer he gave :

14. 'My good nephew, I have always heard and always
seen that you Persians of all men think it your duty never
to be insatiate in the pursuit of any pleasure ; and I myself
believe that the greater the joy the more important is self-
restraint. Now what greater joy could there be than the
good fortune which waits on us to-day ? 15. When fortune
comes to us, if we guard her with discretion, we may live
to grow old in peace, but if we are insatiate, if we use and
abuse our pleasures, chasing first one and then another,
we may well fear lest that fate be ours which, the proverb
tells us, falls on those mariners who cannot forgo their
voyages in the pursuit of wealth, and one day the deep sea

C. 1 swallows them. Thus has many a warrior achieved one victory only to clutch at another and lose the first. 16. If indeed, our enemies who have fled were weaker than we, it might be safe enough to pursue them. But now, bethink you, how small a portion of them we have fought and conquered; the mass have had no part in the battle, and they, if we do not force them to fight, will take themselves off through sheer cowardice and sloth. As yet they know nothing of our powers or their own, but if they learn that to fly is as dangerous as to hold their ground, we run the risk of driving them to be brave in spite of themselves. 17. You may be sure they are just as anxious to save their wives and children as you can be to capture them. Take a lesson from hunting: the wild sow when she is sighted will scamper away with her young, though she be feeding with the herd; but if you attack her little ones she will never fly, even if she is all alone; she will turn on the hunters. 18. Yesterday the enemy shut themselves up in a fort, and then handed themselves over to us to choose how many we cared to fight. But if we meet them in open country, and they learn how to divide their forces and take us in front and flank and rear, I wonder how many pairs of eyes and hands each man of us would need! Finally,' he added, 'I have no great wish myself to disturb my Medes in their enjoyment, and drive them out to further dangers.'

19. Then Cyrus took him up: 'Nay, I would not have you put pressure on any man; only let those who are willing follow me, and perhaps we shall come back with something for all of you to enjoy. The mass of the enemy we should not think of pursuing; indeed, how could we overtake them? But if we cut off any stragglers, we could clap hands on them and bring them back to you. 20. Remember,' he added, 'when you sent for us, we came a long way to do you service: is it not fair that you should do us a kindness in return, and let us have something to take back with us for ourselves, and not stand here agape at all your treasures?'

21. At that Cyaxares answered, 'Ah, if any will follow you of their own free will, I can but be most grateful.'

'Send some one with me then,' said Cyrus, 'from these C. 1 trusty men of yours, to carry your commands.'

'Take whomever you like,' he answered, 'and begone.'

22. Now, as it chanced, among the officers present was the Mede who had claimed kinship with Cyrus long ago and won a kiss thereby. Cyrus pointed to him and said, 'That man will do for me.' 'He shall go with you then,' Cyaxares replied. And turning to the officer, 'Tell your fellows,' he said, 'that he who lists may follow Cyrus.' 23. Thus Cyrus chose his man and went forth. And when they were outside he said, 'To-day you can show me if you spoke truth long ago when you told me that the sight of me was your joy.'

'If you say that,' said the Mede, 'I will never leave you.'

'And will you not do your best,' added Cyrus, 'to bring me others too?' 'By the gods in heaven,' cried the Mede, 'that will I, until you say in your turn that to see me is your joy.' Thereupon, with the authority of Cyaxares to support him, the officer went to the Medes and delivered the message with all diligence, adding that he for one would never forsake Cyrus, the bravest, noblest, and best of men, and a hero whose lineage was divine.

While Cyrus was busied with these matters, by some C. 2 strange chance two ambassadors arrived from the Hyrcanians. These people are neighbours of the Assyrians, and being few in number, they were held in subjection. But they seemed then, as they seem now, to live on horseback. Hence the Assyrians used them as the Lacedaemonians employ the Skirites, for every toil and every danger, without sparing them. In fact, at that very moment they had ordered them to furnish a rear-guard of a thousand men and more, so as to bear the brunt of any rear attack. 2. The Hyrcanians, as they were to be the hindmost, had put their waggons and families in the rear, for, like most of the tribes in Asia, they take their entire households with them on the march. 3. But when they thought of the sorry treatment they got from the Assyrians and when they saw the king fallen, the army worsted and a prey to panic, the allies disheartened and ready to desert, they judged it a fine moment to revolt themselves, if only the Medes and

C. 2 Persians would make common cause with them. So they sent an embassy to Cyrus, for after the late battle there was no name like his. 4. They told him what good cause they had to hate the Assyrians, and how if he was willing to attack them now, they themselves would be his allies and show him the way. At the same time they gave a full account of the enemy's doings, being eager to get Cyrus on the road. 5. 'Do you think,' said Cyrus, 'we could overtake the Assyrians before they reach their fortresses? We look on it as a great misfortune,' he added, 'that they ever slipped through our fingers and escaped.' (This he said, wishing to give his hearers as high an opinion as possible of himself and his friends.) 6. 'You could certainly catch them,' they answered, 'and that to-morrow, ere the day is old, if you gird up your loins: they move heavily because of their numbers and their train of waggons, and to-day, since they did not sleep last night, they have only gone a little way ahead, and are now encamped for the evening.'

7. 'Can you give us any guarantee,' said Cyrus, 'that what you say is true?'

'We will give you hostages,' they said; 'we will ride off at once and bring them back this very night. Only do you on your side call the gods to witness and give us the pledge of your own right hand, that we may give our people the assurance we have received from you ourselves.'

8. Thereupon Cyrus gave them his pledge that if they would make good what they promised he would treat them as his true friends and faithful followers, of no less account than the Persians and the Medes. And to this day one may see Hyrcanians treated with trust and holding office on an equal footing with Persians and Medes of high distinction.

9. Now Cyrus and his men took their supper and then while it was still daylight he led his army out, having made the two Hyrcanians wait so that they might go with them. The Persians, of course, were with him to a man, and Tigranes was there, with his own contingent, and the Median volunteers, who had joined for various reasons. 10. Some had been friends of Cyrus in boyhood, others had hunted with him and learnt to admire his character,

others were grateful, feeling he had lifted a load of fear C. 2
from them, others were flushed with hope, nothing doubt-
ing that great things were reserved for the man who had
proved so brave and so fortunate already. Others remembered the time when he was brought up in Media, and
were glad to return the kindnesses that he had shown
them; many could recall the favours the boy had won for
them from his grandfather through his sheer goodness of
heart; and many, now that they had seen the Hyrcanians
and heard say they were leading them to untold treasures,
went out from simple love of gain. 11. So they sallied
forth, the entire body of the Persians and all the Medes,
except those who were quartered with Cyaxares: these
stayed behind, and their men with them. But all the rest
went out with radiant faces and eager hearts, not following
him from constraint, but offering willing service in their
gratitude. 12. So, as soon as they were well afield, Cyrus
went to the Medes and thanked them, praying that the
gods in their mercy might guide them all, and that he
himself might have power given him to reward their zeal.
He ended by saying that the infantry would lead the van,
while they would follow with the cavalry, and whenever
the column halted on the march they were to send him
gallopers to receive his orders. 13. Then he bade the
Hyrcanians lead the way, but they exclaimed, 'What? Are
you not going to wait until we bring the hostages? Then
you could begin the march with pledges from us in return
for yours.'

But he answered, as the story says, 'If I am not mistaken,
we hold the pledges now, in our own hearts and our own
right hands. We believe that if you are true to us we can
do you service, and if you play us false, you will not have
us at your mercy; God willing, we shall hold you at ours.
Nevertheless,' he added, 'since you tell us your own folk
follow in the Assyrian rear, point them out to us as soon
as you set eyes on them, that we may spare their lives.'

14. When the Hyrcanians heard this they led the way as
he ordered, marvelling at his strength of soul. Their own
fear of the Assyrians, the Lydians, and their allies, had
altogether gone; their dread now was lest Cyrus should

C. 2 regard themselves as mere dust in the balance, and count
it of no importance whether they stayed with him or not.

15. As night closed in on their march, the legend runs
that a strange light shone out, far off in the sky, upon
Cyrus and his host, filling them with awe of the heavenly
powers and courage to meet the foe. Marching as they did,
their loins girt and their pace swift, they covered a long
stretch of road in little time, and with the half light of the
morning they were close to the Hyrcanian rearguard.
16. As soon as the guides saw it, they told Cyrus that these
were their own men: they knew this, they added, from the
number of their fires, and the fact that they were in the
rear. 17. Thereupon Cyrus sent one of the guides to them,
bidding them come out at once, if they were friendly, with
their right hands raised. And he sent one of his own men
also to say, 'According as you make your approach, so
shall we Persians comport ourselves.'

Thus one of the two messengers stayed with Cyrus while
the other rode up to his fellows. 18. Cyrus halted his army
to watch what the tribe would do, and Tigranes and the
Median officers rode along the ranks to ask for orders.
Cyrus explained that the troops nearest to them were the
Hyrcanians, and that one of the ambassadors had gone,
and a Persian with him, to bid them come out at once, if
they were friendly, with their right hands raised. 'If they
do so,' he added, 'you must welcome them as they come,
each of you at your post, and take them by the hand and
encourage them, but if they draw sword or try to escape,
you must make an example of them: not a man of them
must be left.'

Such were his orders. 19. However, as soon as the
Hyrcanians heard the message, they were overjoyed:
springing to their steeds they galloped up to Cyrus, holding
out their right hands as he had bidden. Then the Medes
and Persians gave them the right hand of fellowship in
return, and bade them be of courage. 20. And Cyrus
spoke:

'Sons of the Hyrcanians, we have shown our trust in
you already, and you must trust us in return. And now tell
me, how far from here do the Assyrian headquarters lie,

and their main body?' 'About four miles hence,' they C. 2 answered.

21. 'Forward then, my men,' said Cyrus, 'Persians, Medes, and Hyrcanians. I have learnt already, you see, to call you friends and comrades. All of you must remember that the moment has come when, if hand falters or heart fails, we meet with utter disaster: our enemies know why we are here. But if we summon our strength and charge home, you shall see them caught like a pack of runaway slaves, some on their knees, others in full flight, and the rest unable to do even so much for themselves. They are beaten already, and they will see their conquerors fall on them before they dream of an approach, before their ranks are formed or their preparations made, and the sight will paralyse them. 22. If we wish to sleep and eat and live in peace and happiness from this time forth, let us not give them leisure to take counsel or arrange defence, or so much as see that we are men, and not a storm of shields and battle-axes and flashing swords, sweeping on them in one rain of blows. 23. You Hyrcanians must go in front of us as a screen, that we may lie hid behind you as long as may be. And as soon as I close with them, you must give me, each of you, a squadron of horse, to use in case of need while I am waiting at the camp. 24. I would advise the older men among you and the officers, to ride in close order, so that your ranks should not be broken, if you come across a compact body of the foe; let the younger men give chase, and do the killing: our safest plan to-day is to leave as few of the enemy alive as possible. 25. And if we conquer,' he added, 'we must beware of what has overset the fortune of many a conqueror ere now, I mean the lust for plunder. The man who plunders is no longer a man, he is a machine for porterage, and all who list may treat him as a slave. 26. One thing we must bear in mind: nothing can bring such gain as victory; at one clutch the victor seizes all, men and women, and wealth, and territory. Therefore make it your one object to secure the victory; if he is conquered, the greatest plunderer is caught. One more word – remember, even in the heat of pursuit to rejoin me while it is still daylight, for when

C. 2 darkness has fallen we will not admit a soul within the lines.'

27. With these words he sent them off to their appointed stations, bidding them repeat his instructions on the way to their own lieutenants, who were posted in front to receive the orders, and make each of them pass down the word to his own file of ten. Thereupon the advance began, the Hyrcanians leading off, Cyrus holding the centre himself, marching with his Persians, and the cavalry in the usual way, drawn up on either flank.

28. As the day broke the enemy saw them for the first time: some simply stared at what was happening, others began to realise the truth, calling and shouting to each other, unfastening their horses, getting their goods together, tearing what they needed off the beasts of burden, and others arming themselves, harnessing their steeds, leaping to horse, others helping the women into their carriages, or seizing their valuables, some caught in the act of burying them, others, and by far the greatest number, in sheer headlong flight. Many and divers were their shifts, as one may well conceive, save only that not one man stood at bay: they perished without a blow. 29. Now Croesus, king of Lydia, seeing that it was summer-time, had sent his women on during the night, so that they might travel more pleasantly in the cool, and he himself had followed with his cavalry to escort them. 30. The Lord of Hellespontine Phrygia, it is said, had done the same. And these two, when they heard what was happening from the fugitives who overtook them, fled for their lives with the rest. 31. But it was otherwise with the kings of Cappadocia and Arabia; they had not gone far, and they stood their ground, but they had not even time to put on their corslets, and were cut down by the Hyrcanians. Indeed, the mass of those who fell were Assyrians and Arabians, for, being in their own country, they had taken no precautions on the march. 32. The victorious Medes and the Hyrcanians had their hands full with the chase, and meanwhile Cyrus made the cavalry who were left with him ride all round the camp and cut down any man who left it with weapons in his hands. Then he sent a herald to

those who remained, bidding the horsemen and targeteers C. 2
and archers come out on foot, with their weapons tied in
bundles, and deliver them up to him, leaving their horses
in their stalls : he who disobeyed should lose his head, and
a cordon of Persian troops stood round with their swords
drawn. 33. At that the weapons were brought out at once,
and flung down, and Cyrus had the whole pile burnt.

34. Meanwhile he did not forget that his own troops
had come without food or drink, that nothing could be
done without provisions, and that to obtain these in the
quickest way, it was necessary on every campaign to have
some one to see that quarters were prepared and supplies
ready for the men on their return. 35. It occurred to him it
was more than likely that such officers, of all others, would
be left behind in the Assyrian camp, because they would
have been delayed by the packing.

Accordingly, he sent out a proclamation that all the
stewards should present themselves before him, and if
there was no such officer left, the oldest man in every tent
must take his place ; any one failing to obey would suffer
the severest penalties. The stewards, following the example
of their masters, obeyed at once. And when they came
before him he ordered those who had more than two
months' rations in their quarters to sit down on the
ground, and then those who had provisions for one month.
36. Thereupon very few were left standing. 37. Having
thus got the information he needed, he spoke to them as
follows :

'Gentlemen, if any of you dislike hard blows and desire
gentle treatment at our hands, make it your business to
provide twice as much meat and drink in every tent as you
have been wont to do, with all things that are needed for a
fine repast. The victors, whoever they are, will be here
anon, and will expect an overflowing board. You may rest
assured it will not be against your interests to give them a
welcome they can approve.'

38. At that the stewards went off at once and set to
work with all zeal to carry out their instructions. Then
Cyrus summoned his own officers and said to them :

'My friends, it is clear that we have it in our power, now

C. 2 that our allies' backs are turned, to help ourselves to breakfast, and take our choice of the most delicate dishes and the rarest wines. But I scarcely think this would do us so much good as to show that we study the interest of our friends: the best of cheer will not give us half the strength we could draw from the zeal of loyal allies whose gratitude we had won. 39. If we forget those who are toiling for us now, pursuing our foes, slaying them, and fighting wherever they resist, if they see that we sit down to enjoy ourselves and devour our meal before we know how it goes with them, I fear we shall cut a sorry figure in their eyes, and our strength will turn to weakness through lack of friends. The true banquet for us is to study the wants of those who have run the risk and done the work, to see that they have all they need when they come home, a banquet that will give us richer delight than any gorging of the belly. 40. And remember, that even if the thought of them were not enough to shame us from it, in no case is this a moment for gluttony and drunkenness: the thing we set our minds to do is not yet done: everything is full of danger still, and calls for carefulness. We have enemies in this camp ten times more numerous than ourselves, and they are all at large: we need both to guard against them and to guard them, so that we may have servants to furnish us with supplies. Our cavalry are not yet back, and we must ask ourselves where they are and whether they mean to stay with us when they return. 41. Therefore, gentlemen, I would say, for the present let us above all be careful to avoid the food and drink that leads to slumber and stupefaction. 42. And there is another matter: this camp contains vast treasures, and I am well aware we have it in our power to pick and choose as much as we like for ourselves out of what belongs by right to all who helped in its capture. But it does not seem to me that grasping will be so lucrative as proving ourselves just toward our allies, and so binding them the closer. 43. I go further: I say that we should leave the distribution of the spoil to the Medes, the Hyrcanians, and Tigranes, and count it gain if they allot us the smaller share, for then they will be all the more willing to stay with us. 44. Selfishness now could only

secure us riches for the moment, while to let these vanities C. 2
go in order to obtain the very fount of wealth, that, I take
it, will ensure for us and all whom we call ours a far more
enduring gain. 45. Was it not,' he continued, 'for this very
reason that we trained ourselves at home to master the
belly and its appetites, so that, if ever the need arose, we
might turn our education to account? And where, I ask,
shall we find a nobler opportunity than this, to show what
we have learnt?'

46. Such were his words and Hystaspas the Persian rose
to support him, saying:

'Truly, Cyrus, it would be a monstrous thing if we could
go fasting when we hunt, and keep from food so often and
so long merely to lay some poor beast low, worth next to
nothing, maybe, and yet, when a world of wealth is our
quarry, let ourselves be baulked by one of those temp-
tations which flee before the noble and rule the bad. Such
conduct, me thinks, would be little worthy of our race.'

47. So Hystaspas spoke, and the rest approved him, one
and all. Then Cyrus said:

'Come now, since we are all of one mind, each of you
give me five of the trustiest fellows in his company, and let
them go the rounds, and see how the supplies are furnished; let them praise the active servants, and where they
see neglect, chastise them more severely than their own
masters could.'

Thus they dealt with these matters.

But it was not long before some of the Medes returned: C. 3
one set had overtaken the waggons that had gone ahead,
seized them and turned them back, and were now driving
them to the camp, laden with all that an army could
require, and others had captured the covered carriages in
which the women rode, the wives of the Assyrian grandees
or their concubines, whom they had taken with them
because of their beauty. 2. Indeed, to this day the tribes of
Asia never go on a campaign without their most precious
property: they say they can fight better in the presence of
their beloved, feeling they must defend their treasures,
heart and soul. It may be so, but it may also be that the
desire for pleasure is the cause.

C. 3   3. And when Cyrus saw the feats of arms that the Medes and the Hyrcanians had performed, he came near reproaching himself and those that were with him; the others, he felt, had risen with the time, had shown their strength and won their prizes, while he and his had stayed behind like sluggards. Indeed it was a sight to watch the victors riding home, driving their spoil before them, pointing it out with some display to Cyrus, and then dashing off again at once in search of more, according to the instructions they had received.

But though he ate out his heart with envy Cyrus was careful to set all their booty apart; and then he summoned his own officers again, and standing where they could all hear what he had to propose, he spoke as follows:

4. 'My friends, you would all agree, I take it, that if the spoils displayed to us now were our own to keep, wealth would be showered on every Persian in the land, and we ourselves, no doubt, through whom it was won, would receive the most. But what I do not see is how we are to get possession of such prizes unless we have cavalry of our own. 5. Consider the facts,' he continued, 'we Persians have weapons with which, we hope, we can rout an enemy at close quarters: but when we do rout them, what sort of horsemen or archers or light-armed troops could ever be caught and killed, if we can only pursue them on foot? Why should they ever be afraid to dash up and harry us, when they know full well that they run no greater risk at our hands than if we were stumps in their orchards? 6. And if this be so, it is plain that the cavalry now with us consider every gain to be as much theirs as ours, and possibly even more, God wot! 7. At present things must be so: there is no help for it. But suppose we were to provide ourselves with as good a force as our friends, it must be pretty evident to all of us, I think, that we could then deal with the enemy by ourselves precisely as we do now with their help, and then perhaps we should find that they would carry their heads less high. It would be of less importance to us whether they chose to stay or go, we should be sufficient for ourselves without them. 8. So far then I expect that no one will disagree: if we could get a

body of Persian cavalry it would make all the difference to C. 3
us; but no doubt you feel the question is, how are we to
get it? Well, let us consider first, suppose we decide to
raise the force, exactly what we have to start with and
what we need. 9. We certainly have hundreds of horses
now captured in this camp, with their bridles and all their
gear. Besides these, we have all the accoutrements for a
mounted force, breastplates to protect the trunk, and light
spears to be flung or wielded at close quarters. What else
do we need? It is plain we need men. 10. But that is just
what we have already at our own command. For nothing
is so much ours as our own selves. Only, some will say, we
have not the necessary skill. No, of course not, and none
of those who have it now had it either before they learnt
to get it. Ah, you object, but they learnt when they were
boys. 11. Maybe; but are boys more capable of learning
what they are taught than grown men? Which are the
better at heavy physical tasks, boys or men? 12. Besides,
we, of all pupils, have advantages that neither boys nor
other men possess: we have not to be taught the use of the
bow as boys have, we are skilled in that already; nor yet
the use of the javelin, we are versed in that; our time has
not been taken up like other men's with toiling on the land
or labouring at some craft or managing household matters; we have not only had leisure for war, it has been our
life. 13. Moreover, one cannot say of riding as of so many
warlike exercises that it is useful but disagreeable. To ride
a-horseback is surely pleasanter than to trudge a-foot?
And as for speed – how pleasant to join a friend betimes
whenever you wish, or come up with your quarry be it
man or beast! And then, the ease and satisfaction of it!
Whatever weapon the rider carries his horse must help to
bear the load: "wear arms" and "bear arms," – they are
the same thing on horseback. 14. But now, to meet the
worst we can apprehend: suppose, before we are adepts,
we are called upon to run some risk, and then find that we
are neither infantry nor thoroughgoing cavalry? This may
be a danger, but we can guard against it. We have it
always in our power to turn into infantry again at a

C. 3 moment's notice. I do not propose that by learning to ride we should unlearn the arts of men on foot.'

15. Thus spoke Cyrus, and Chrysantas rose to support him, saying:

'For my part I cannot say I so much desire to be a horseman as flatter myself that once I can ride I shall be a sort of flying man. 16. At present when I race I am quite content if, with a fair start, I can beat one of my rivals by the head, or when I sight my game I am happy if, by laying legs to the ground, I can get close enough to let fly javelin or arrow before he is clean out of range. But when once I am a horseman I shall be able to overhaul my man as far as I can see him, or come up with the beasts I chase and knock them over myself or else spear them as though they stood stock still, for when hunter and hunted are both of them racing, if they are only side by side, it is as good as though neither of them moved. 17. And the creature I have always envied,' he continued, 'the centaur – if only he had the intelligence and forethought of a man, the adroit skill and the cunning hand, with the swiftness and strength of a horse, so as to overtake all that fled before him, and overthrow all that resisted – why, all these powers I shall collect and gather in my own person when once I am a rider. 18. Forethought I intend to keep with my human wits, my hands can wield my weapons, and my horse's legs will follow up the foe, and my horse's rush overthrow him. Only I shall not be tied and fettered to my steed, flesh of his flesh, and blood of his blood, like the old centaur. 19. And that I count a great improvement on the breed, far better than being united to the animal, body and soul. The old centaur, I imagine, must have been for ever in difficulties; as a horse, he could not use the wonderful inventions of man, and as a man, he could not enjoy the proper pleasures of a horse. 20. But I, if I learn to ride, once set me astride my horse, and I will do all that the centaur can, and yet, when I dismount, I can dress myself as a human being, and dine, and sleep in my bed, like the rest of my kind: in short, I shall be a jointed centaur that can be taken to pieces and put together again. 21. And I shall gain another point or so over the original beast: he,

we know, had only two eyes to see with and two ears to C. 3
hear with, but I shall watch with four eyes and with four
ears I shall listen. You know, they tell us a horse can often
see quicker than any man, and hear a sound before his
master, and give him warning in some way. Have the
goodness, therefore,' he added, 'to write my name down
among those who want to ride.'

22. 'And ours too,' they all cried, 'ours too, in heaven's
name !'

Then Cyrus spoke : 'Gentlemen, since we are all so well
agreed, suppose we make it a rule that every one who
receives a horse from me shall be considered to disgrace
himself if he is seen trudging afoot, be his journey long or
short ?'

23. Thus Cyrus put the question, and one and all
assented ; and hence it is that even to this day the custom
is retained, and no Persian of the gentle class would
willingly be seen anywhere on foot.

In this debate their time was spent, and when it was past C. 4
midday the Median cavalry and the Hyrcanians came
galloping home, bringing in men and horses from the
enemy, for they had spared all who surrendered their arms.
2. As they rode up the first inquiry of Cyrus was whether
all of them were safe, and when they answered yes, he
asked what they had achieved. And they told their exploits
in detail, and how bravely they had borne themselves,
magnifying it all. 3. Cyrus heard their story through with
a pleasant smile, and praised them for their work. 'I can
see for myself,' he said, 'that you have done gallant deeds.
You seem to have grown taller and fairer and more terrible
to look on than when we saw you last.'

4. Then he made them tell him how far they had gone,
and whether they found the country inhabited. They said
they had ridden a long way, and that the whole country
was inhabited, and full of sheep and goats and cattle and
horses, and rich in corn and every good thing.

5. 'Then there are two matters,' he said, 'to which we
must attend ; first we must become masters of those who
own all this, and next we must ensure that they do not run
away. A well-populated country is a rich possession, but a

C. 4 deserted land will soon become a desert. 6. You have put the defenders to the sword, I know, and rightly — for that is the only safe road to victory; but you have brought in as prisoners those who laid down their arms. Now if we let these men go, I maintain we should do the very best thing for ourselves. 7. We gain two points; first, we need neither be on our guard against them nor mount guard over them nor find them victuals (and we do not propose to starve them, I presume), and in the next place, their release means more prisoners to-morrow. 8. For if we dominate the country all the inhabitants are ours, and if they see that these men are still alive and at large they will be more disposed to stay where they are, and prefer obedience to battle. That is my own view, but if any one sees a better course, let him point it out.'

9. However, all his hearers approved the plan proposed. Thus it came to pass that Cyrus summoned the prisoners and said to them:

10. 'Gentlemen, you owe it to your own obedience this day that your lives are safe; and for the future if you continue in this conduct, no evil whatsoever shall befall you; true, you will not have the same ruler as before, but you will dwell in the same houses, you will cultivate the same land, you will live with your wives and govern your children as you do now. Moreover you will not have us to fight with, nor any one else. 11. On the contrary, if any wrong is done you, it is we who will fight on your behalf. And to prevent any one from ordering you to take the field, you will bring your arms to us and hand them over. Those who do this can count on peace and the faithful fulfilment of all our promises; those who will not, must expect war, and that at once. 12. Further, if any man of you comes to us and shows a friendly spirit, giving us information and helping us in any way, we will treat him, not as a servant, but as a friend and benefactor. This,' he added, 'we wish you to understand yourselves and make known among your fellows. 13. And if it should appear that you yourselves are willing to comply but others hinder you, lead us against them, and you shall be their masters, not they yours.'

Such were his words; and they made obeisance and C. 4
promised to do as he bade.

And when they were gone, Cyrus turned to the Medes C. 5
and the men of Armenia, and said, 'It is high time,
gentlemen, that we should dine, one and all of us; food
and drink are prepared for you, the best we had skill to
find. Send us, if you will, the half of the bread that has
been baked; there is ample, I know, for both of us; but do
not send any relish with it, nor any drink, we have quite
enough at hand. 2. And do you,' he added, turning to the
Hyrcanians, 'conduct our friends to their quarters, the
officers to the largest tents – you know where they are –
and the rest where you think best. For yourselves, you may
dine where you like; your quarters are intact, and you will
find everything there prepared for you exactly as it is for
the others. 3. All of you alike must understand that during
the night we Persians will guard the camp outside, but you
must keep an eye over what goes on within; and see that
your arms are ready to hand; our messmates are not our
friends as yet.'

4. So the Medes and Tigranes with his men washed
away the stains of battle, and put on the apparel that was
laid out for them, and fell to dinner, and the horses had
their provender too. They sent half the bread to the
Persians but no relish with it and no wine, thinking that
Cyrus and his men possessed a store, because he had said
they had enough and to spare. But Cyrus meant the relish
of hunger, and the draught from the running river. 5. Thus
he regaled his Persians, and when the darkness fell he sent
them out by fives and tens and ordered them to lie in
ambush around the camp, so as to form a double guard,
against attack from without, and absconders from within;
any one attempting to make off with treasures would be
caught in the act. And so it befell; for many tried to
escape, and all of them were seized. 6. As for the treasures,
Cyrus allowed the captors to keep them, but he had the
absconders beheaded out of hand, so that for the future a
thief by night was hardly to be found. Thus the Persians
passed their time. 7. But the Medes drank and feasted and
made music and took their fill of good cheer and all

C. 5 delights; there was plenty to serve their purpose, and work enough for those who did not sleep.

8. Cyaxares, the king of the Medes, on the very night when Cyrus set forth, drank himself drunk in company with the officers in his own quarters to celebrate their good fortune. Hearing uproar all about him, he thought that the rest of the Medes must have stayed behind in the camp, except perhaps a few, but the fact was that their domestics, finding the masters gone, had fallen to drinking in fine style and were making a din to their hearts' content, the more so that they had procured wine and dainties from the Assyrian camp. 9. But when it was broad day and no one knocked at the palace gate except the guests of last night's revel, and when Cyaxares heard that the camp was deserted – the Medes gone, the cavalry gone – and when he went out and saw for himself that it was so, then he fumed with indignation against Cyrus and his own men, to think that they had gone off and left him in the lurch. It is said that without more ado, savage and mad with anger as he was, he ordered one of his staff to take his troopers and ride at once to Cyrus and his men, and there deliver this message:

10. 'I should never have dreamed that Cyrus could have acted towards me with such scant respect, or, if he could have thought of it, that the Medes could have borne to desert me in this way. And now, whether Cyrus will or no, I command the Medes to present themselves before me without delay.'

11. Such was the message. But he who was to take it said, 'And how shall I find them, my lord?'

'Why,' said Cyaxares, 'as Cyrus and his men found those they went to seek.'

'I only asked,' continued the messenger, 'because I was told that some Hyrcanians who had revolted from the enemy came here, and went off with him to act as guides.'

12. When Cyaxares heard that, he was the more enraged to think that Cyrus had never told him, and the more urgent to have his Medes removed from him at once, and he summoned them home under fiercer threats than ever;

threatening the officer as well if he failed to deliver the C. 5
message in full force.

13. So the emissary set off with his troops, about one
hundred strong, fervently regretting that he had not gone
with Cyrus himself. On the way they took a turning which
led them wrong, and they did not reach the Persians until
they had chanced upon some of the Assyrians in retreat
and forced them to be their guides, and so at last arrived,
sighting the watch-fires about midnight. 14. But though
they had got to the camp, the pickets, acting on the orders
of Cyrus, would not let them in till dawn. With the first
faint gleam of morning Cyrus summoned the Persian
Priests, who are called Magians, and bade them choose the
offerings due to the gods for the blessings they had
vouchsafed. 15. And while they were about this, Cyrus
called the Peers together and said to them :

'Gentlemen, God has put before us many blessings, but
at present we Persians are a scant company to keep them.
If we fail to guard what we have toiled for, it will soon fall
back into other hands, and if we leave some of our number
to watch our gains, it will soon be seen that we have no
strength in us. 16. I propose therefore that one of you
should go home and bid them despatch an army forthwith,
if they desire Persia to win the empire of Asia and the
fruits thereof. 17. Do you,' said he, turning to one of the
Peers, 'do you, who are the eldest, go and repeat these
words, and tell them that it shall be my care to provide for
the soldiers they send me as soon as they are here. And as
to what we have won – you have seen it yourself – keep
nothing back, and ask my father how much I ought to
send home for an offering to the gods, if I wish to act in
honour and according to the law, and ask the magistrates
how much is due to the commonwealth. And let them send
commissioners to watch all that we do and answer all that
we ask. So, sir,' he ended, 'you will get your baggage
together, and take your company with you as an escort.
Fare you well.'

18. With that he turned to the Medes and at the same
moment the messenger from Cyaxares presented himself,
and in the midst of the whole assembly announced the

C. 5 anger of the king against Cyrus, and his threats against the
Medes, and so bade the latter return home at once, even if
Cyrus wished them to stay. 19. The Medes listened, but
were silent; for they were sore bested; they could hardly
disobey the summons, and yet they were afraid to go back
after his threats, being all too well acquainted with the
savage temper of their lord. 20. But Cyrus spoke:

'Herald,' said he, 'and sons of the Medes, I am not
surprised that Cyaxares, who saw the host of the enemy
so lately, and knows so little of what we have done now,
should tremble for us and himself. But when he learns how
many have fallen, and that all have been dispersed, his
fears will vanish, and he will recognise that he is not
deserted on this day of all days when his friends are
destroying his foes. 21. Can we deserve blame for doing
him a service? And that not even without his own consent? I am acting as I am, only after having gained his
leave to take you out; it is not as though you had come to
me in your own eagerness, and begged me to let you go,
and so were here now; he himself ordered you out, those
of you who did not find it a burthen. Therefore, I feel sure,
his anger will melt in the sunshine of success, and, when
his fears are gone, it will vanish too. 22. For the moment
then,' he added, turning to the messenger, 'you must
recruit yourself; you have had a heavy task; and for
ourselves,' said he, turning to the Persians, 'since we are
waiting for an enemy who will either offer us battle or
render us submission, we must draw up in our finest style;
the spectacle, perhaps, will bring us more than we could
dare to hope. And do you,' he said, taking the Hyrcanian
chieftain aside, 'after you have told your officers to arm
their men, come back and wait with me a moment.'

23. So the Hyrcanian went and returned. Then Cyrus
said to him, 'Son of Hyrcania, it gives me pleasure to see
that you show not only friendliness, but sagacity. It is clear
that our interests are the same; the Assyrians are my foes
as well as yours, only they hate you now even more bitterly
than they hate me. 24. We must consult together and see
that not one of our present allies turns his back on us, and
we must do what we can to acquire more. You heard the

Mede summon the cavalry to return, and if they go, we C. 5 shall be left with nothing but infantry. 25. This is what we must do, you and I; we must make this messenger, who is sent to recall them, desirous to stay here himself. You must find him quarters where he will have a merry time and everything heart can wish, and I will offer him work which he will like far better than going back. And do you talk to him yourself, and dilate on all the wonders we expect for our friends if things go well. And when you have done this, come back again and tell me.'

26. So the chieftain took the Mede away to his own quarters, and meanwhile the messenger from Persia presented himself equipped for the journey, and Cyrus bade him tell the Persians all that had happened, as it has been set out in this story, and then he gave him a letter to Cyaxares. 'I would like to read you the very words,' he added, 'so that what you say yourself may agree with it, in case you have questions asked you.'

27. The letter ran as follows: — 'Cyrus to Cyaxares, greeting. We do not admit that we have deserted you; for no one is deserted when he is being made the master of his enemies. Nor do we consider that we put you in jeopardy by our departure; on the contrary, the greater the distance between us the greater the security we claim to have won for you. 28. It is not the friend at a man's elbow who serves him and puts him out of danger, but he who drives his enemies farthest and furthest away. 29. And I pray you to remember what I have done for you, and you for me, before you blame me. I brought you allies, not limiting myself to those you asked for, but pressing in every man that I could find; you allowed me while we were on friendly soil only to take those whom I could persuade to follow me, and now that I am in hostile territory you insist that they must all return; you do not leave it to their own choice. 30. Yesterday I felt that I owed both you and them a debt of gratitude, but to-day you drive me to forget your share, you make me wish to repay those, and those only, who followed me. 31. Not that I could bring myself to return you like for like; even now I am sending to Persia for more troops, and instructing all the men who come

C. 5 that, if you need them before we return, they must hold
themselves at your service absolutely, to act not as they
wish, but as you may care to use them. 32. In conclusion,
I would advise you, though I am younger than yourself,
not to take back with one hand what you give with the
other, or else you will win hatred instead of gratitude; nor
to use threats if you wish men to come to you speedily;
nor to speak of being deserted when you threaten an army,
unless you would teach them to despise you. 33. For
ourselves, we will do our best to rejoin you as soon as we
have concluded certain matters which we believe will prove
a common blessing to yourself and us. Farewell.'

34. 'Deliver this,' said Cyrus, 'to Cyaxares, and whatever questions he puts to you, answer in accordance with
it. My injunctions to you about the Persians agree exactly
with what is written here.' With that he gave him the letter
and sent him off, bidding him remember that speed was of
importance.

35. Then he turned to review his troops, who were
already fully armed, Medes, Hyrcanians, the men Tigranes
had brought, and the whole body of the Persians. And
already some of the neighbouring folk were coming up, to
bring in their horses or hand over their arms. 36. The
javelins were then piled in a heap as before and burnt at
his command, after his troops had taken what they needed
for themselves, but he bade the owners stay with their
horses until they received fresh orders. This done, Cyrus
called together the officers of the Hyrcanians and of the
cavalry, and spoke as follows:

37. 'My friends and allies, you must not be surprised
that I summon you so often. Our circumstances are so
novel that much still needs adjustment, and we must expect
difficulty until everything has found its place. 38. At
present we have a mass of spoil, and prisoners set to guard
it. But we do not ourselves know what belongs to each of
us, nor could the guards say who the owners are: and thus
it is impossible for them to be exact in their duties, since
scarcely any of them know what these duties may be.
39. To amend this, you must divide the spoil. There will
be no difficulty where a man has won a tent that is fully

supplied with meat and drink, and servants to boot, C. 5
bedding, apparel, and everything to make it a comfortable
home; he has only to understand that this is now his
private property, and he must look after it himself. But
where the quarters are not furnished so well, there you
must make it your business to supply what is lacking.
40. There will be more than enough for this; of that I am
sure; the enemy had a stock of everything quite out of
proportion to our scanty numbers. Moreover, certain
treasurers have come to me, men who were in the service
of the king of Assyria and other potentates, and according
to what they tell me, they have a supply of gold coin, the
produce of certain tributes they can name. 41. You will
send out a proclamation that this deposit must be delivered
up to you in your quarters; you must terrify those who
fail to execute the order, and then you must distribute the
money; the mounted men should have two shares apiece
to the foot-soldier's one; and you should keep the surplus,
so that in case of need you may have wherewith to make
your purchases. 42. With regard to the camp-market,
proclamation must be made at once, forbidding any injustice; the hucksters must be allowed to sell the goods they
have brought, and when these are disposed of they may
bring more, so that the camp may be duly supplied.'

43. So the proclamations were issued forthwith. But the
Medes and the Hyrcanians asked Cyrus:

'How are we to distribute the spoil alone, without your
men and yourself?'

44. But Cyrus met question by question: 'Do you really
think, gentlemen, that we must all preside over every
detail, each and all of us together? Can I never act for
you, nor you for me? I could scarcely conceive a surer way
of creating trouble, or of reducing results. See,' said he, 'I
will take a case in point. 45. We Persians guarded this
booty for you, and you believe that we guarded it well:
now it is for you to distribute it, and we will trust you to
be fair. 46. And there is another benefit that I should be
glad to obtain for us all. You see what a number of horses
we have got already, and more are being brought in. If
they are left riderless we shall get no profit out of them;

C. 5 we shall only have the burden of looking after them. But if we set riders on them, we shall be quit of the trouble and add to our strength. 47. Now if you have other men in view, men whom you would choose before us to share the brunt of danger with you, by all means give these horses to them. But if you would rather have us to fight at your side than any others, bestow them upon us. 48. To-day when you dashed ahead to meet danger all alone, great was our fear lest you might come to harm, and bitter our shame to think that where you were we were not. But if once we have horses, we can follow at your heels. 49. And if it is clear that we do more good so mounted, shoulder to shoulder with yourselves, we shall not fail in zeal; or if it appears better to support you on foot, why, to dismount is but the work of a moment, and you will have your infantry marching by your side at once, and we will find men to hold our horses for us.'

50. To which they answered:

'In truth, Cyrus, we have not men for these horses ourselves, and even if we had them we should not do anything against your wish. Take them, we beg you, and use them as you think best.'

51. 'I will,' said he, 'and gladly, and may good fortune bless us all, you in your division of the spoil and us in our horsemanship. In the first place,' he added, 'you will set apart for the gods whatever our priests prescribe, and after that you must select for Cyaxares what you think will please him most.'

52. At that they laughed, and said they must choose him a bevy of fair women. 'So let it be,' said Cyrus, 'fair women, and anything else you please. And when you have chosen his share, the Hyrcanians must see to it that our friends among the Medes who followed us of their own free will shall have no cause to find fault with their own portion. 53. And the Medes on their side must show honour to the first allies we have won, and make them feel their decision was wise when they chose us for their friends. And be sure to give a share of everything to the messenger who came from Cyaxares and to his retinue; persuade him to stay on with us, say that I would like it,

and that he could tell Cyaxares all the better how matters C. 5
stood. 54. As for my Persians,' he added, 'we shall be quite
content with what is left over, after you are all provided
for; we are not used to luxury, we were brought up in a
very simple fashion, and I think you would laugh at us if
you saw us tricked out in grand attire, just as I am sure
you will when you see us seated on our horses, or, rather,
rolling off them.'

55. So they dispersed to make the distribution, in great
mirth over the thought of the riding; and then Cyrus called
his own officers and bade them take the horses and their
gear, and the grooms with them, number them all, and
then distribute them by lot in equal shares for each
division. 56. Finally he sent out another proclamation,
saying that if there was any slave among the Syrians,
Assyrians, or Arabians who was a Mede, a Persian, a
Bactrian, a Carian, a Cilician, or a Hellene, or a member
of any other nation, and who had been forcibly enrolled,
he was to come forward and declare himself. 57. And
when they heard the herald, many came forward gladly,
and out of their number Cyrus selected the strongest and
fairest, and told them they were now free, and would be
required to bear arms, with which he would furnish them,
and as to necessaries, he would see himself that they were
not stinted. 58. With that he brought them to the officers
and had them enrolled forthwith, saying they were to be
armed with shields and light swords, so as to follow the
troopers, and were to receive supplies exactly as if they
were his own Persians. The Persian officers themselves,
wearing corslets and carrying lances, were for the future
to appear on horseback, he himself setting the example,
and each one was to appoint another of the Peers to lead
the infantry for him.

While they were concerned with these matters, an old C. 6
Assyrian prince, Gobryas by name, presented himself
before Cyrus, mounted on horseback and with a mounted
retinue behind him, all of them armed as cavalry. The
Persian officers who were appointed to receive the
weapons bade them hand over their lances and have them
burnt with the rest, but Gobryas said he wished to see

C. 6 Cyrus first. At that the adjutants led him in, but they made
his escort stay where they were. 2. When the old man came
before Cyrus, he addressed him at once, saying:

'My lord, I am an Assyrian by birth; I have a strong
fortress in my territory, and I rule over a wide domain; I
have cavalry at my command, two thousand three hundred
of them, all of which I offered to the king of Assyria; and
if ever he had a friend, that friend was I. But he has fallen
at your hands, the gallant heart, and his son, who is my
bitterest foe, reigns in his stead. Therefore I have come to
you, a suppliant at your feet. I am ready to be your slave
and your ally, and I implore you to be my avenger. You
yourself will be as a son to me, for I have no male chldren
now. 3. He whom I had, my only son, he was beautiful
and brave, my lord, and loved me and honoured me as a
father rejoices to be loved. And this vile king – his father,
my old master, had sent for my son, meaning to give him
his own daughter in marriage; and I let my boy go, with
high hopes and a proud heart, thinking that when I saw
him again the king's daughter would be his bride. And the
prince, who is now king, invited him to the chase, and
bade him do his best, for he thought himself far the finer
horseman of the two. So they hunted together, side by
side, as though they were friends, and suddenly a bear
appeared, and the two of them gave chase, and the king's
son let fly his javelin, but alas! he missed his aim, and then
my son threw – oh, that he never had! – and laid the
creature low. 4. The prince was stung to the quick, though
for the moment he kept his rancour hidden. But, soon after
that, they roused a lion, and then he missed a second time
– no unusual thing for him, I imagine – but my son's spear
went home, and he brought the beast down, and cried,
"See, I have shot but twice, and killed each time!" And at
this the monster could not contain his jealousy; he
snatched a spear from one of his followers and ran my son
through the body, my only son, my darling, and took his
life. 5. And I, unhappy that I am, I, who thought to
welcome a bridegroom, carried home a corpse. I, who am
old, buried my boy with the first down on his chin, my
brave boy, my well-beloved. And his assassin acted as

though it were an enemy that he had done to death. He C. 6
never showed one sign of remorse, he never paid one
tribute of honour to the dead, in atonement for his cruel
deed. Yet his own father pitied me, and showed that he
could share the burden of my grief. 6. Had he lived, my
old master, I would never have come to you to do him
harm; many a kindness have I received from him, and
many a service have I done him. But now that his kingdom
has descended to my boy's murderer — I could never be
loyal to that man, and he, I know, could never regard me
as a friend. He knows too well how I feel towards him,
and how, after my former splendour, I pass my days in
mourning, growing old in loneliness and grief. 7. If you
can receive me, if you can give me some hope of vengeance
for my dear son, I think I should grow young again, I
should not feel ashamed to live, and when I came to die I
should not die in utter wretchedness.'

8. So he spoke, and Cyrus answered:

'Gobryas, if your heart be set towards us as you say, I
receive you as my suppliant, and I promise, God helping
me, to avenge your son. But tell me,' he added, 'if we do
this for you, and if we suffer you to keep your stronghold,
your land, your arms, and the power which you had, how
will you serve us in return?'

9. And the old man answered:

'My stronghold shall be yours, to live in as often as you
come to me; the tribute which I used to pay to Assyria
shall be paid to you; and whenever you march out to war,
I will march at your side with the men from my own land.
Moreover, I have a daughter, a well-beloved maiden, ripe
for marriage; once I thought of bringing her up to be the
bride of the man who is now king; but she besought me
herself, with tears, not to give her to her brother's murderer, and I have no mind to oppose her. And now I will
put her in your hands, to deal with as I shall deal with
you.'

10. So it came to pass that Cyrus said, 'On the faith that
you have spoken truly and with true intent, I take your
hand and I give you mine; let the gods be witness.'

And when this was done, Cyrus bade the old man depart

C. 6 in peace, without surrendering his arms, and then he asked
him how far away he lived, 'Since,' said he, 'I am minded
to visit you.' And Gobryas answered, 'If you set off early
to-morrow, the next day you may lodge with us.' 11. With
that he took his own departure, leaving a guide for Cyrus.

Then the Medes presented themselves; they had set
apart for the gods what the Persian Priests thought right,
and had left it in their hands, and they had chosen for
Cyrus the finest of all the tents, and a lady from Susa, of
whom the story says that in all Asia there was never a
woman half so fair as she, and two singing-girls with her,
the most skilful among the musicians. The second choice
was for Cyaxares, and for themselves they had taken their
fill of all they could need on the campaign, since there was
abundance of everything. 12. The Hyrcanians had all they
wanted too, and they made the messenger from Cyaxares
share and share alike with them. The tents which were left
over they delivered to Cyrus for his Persians; and the
coined money they said should be divided as soon as it
was all collected, and divided it was.

BOOK V

S<small>UCH</small> were the deeds they did and such the words they C. 1
spoke. Then Cyrus bade them set a guard over the share
chosen for Cyaxares, selecting those whom he knew were
most attached to their lord, 'And what you have given me,'
he added, 'I accept with pleasure, but I hold it at the
service of those among you who would enjoy it the most.'

At that one of the Medes who was passionately fond of
music said, 'In truth, Cyrus, yesterday evening I listened to
the singing-girls who are yours to-day, and if you could
give me one of them, I would far rather be serving on this
campaign than sitting at home.'

And Cyrus said, 'Most gladly I will give her; she is
yours. And I believe I am more grateful to you for asking
than you can be to me for giving; I am so thirsty to gratify
you all.'

So this suitor carried off his prize. 2. And then Cyrus
called to his side Araspas the Mede, who had been his
comrade in boyhood. It was he to whom Cyrus gave the
Median cloak he was wearing when he went back to Persia
from his grandfather's court. Now he summoned him, and
asked him to take care of the tent and the lady from Susa.
3. She was the wife of Abradatas, a Susian, and when the
Assyrian camp was captured it happened that her husband
was away: his master had sent him on an embassy to
Bactria to conclude an alliance there, for he was the friend
and host of the Bactrian king. And now Cyrus asked
Araspas to guard the captive lady until her husband could
take her back himself. 4. To that Araspas replied, 'Have
you seen the lady whom you bid me guard?'

'No, indeed,' said Cyrus, 'certainly I have not.'

C. 1   'But I have,' rejoined the other, 'I saw her when we chose her for you. When we came into the tent, we did not make her out at first, for she was seated on the ground with all her maidens round her, and she was clad in the same attire as her slaves, but when we looked at them all to discover the mistress, we soon saw that one outshone the others, although she was veiled and kept her eyes on the ground. 5. And when we bade her rise, all her women rose with her, and then we saw that she was marked out from them all by her height, and her noble bearing, and her grace, and the beauty that shone through her mean apparel. And, under her veil, we could see the big tear-drops trickling down her garments to her feet. 6. At that sight the eldest of us said, "Take comfort, lady, we know that your husband was beautiful and brave, but we have chosen you a man to-day who is no whit inferior to him in face or form or mind or power; Cyrus, we believe, is more to be admired than any soul on earth, and you shall be his from this day forward." But when the lady heard that, she rent the veil that covered her head and gave a pitiful cry, while her maidens lifted up their voice and wept with their mistress. 7. And thus we could see her face, and her neck, and her arms, and I tell you, Cyrus,' he added, 'I myself, and all who looked on her, felt that there never was, and never had been, in broad Asia a mortal woman half so fair as she. Nay, but you must see her for yourself.'

8. 'Say, rather, I must not,' answered Cyrus, 'if she be such as you describe.'

'And why not ?' asked the young man.

'Because,' said he, 'if the mere report of her beauty could persuade me to go and gaze on her to-day, when I have not a moment to spare, I fear she would win me back again and perhaps I should neglect all I have to do, and sit and gaze at her for ever.'

9. At that the young man laughed outright and said:

'So you think, Cyrus, that the beauty of any human creature can compel a man to do wrong against his will ? Surely if that were the nature of beauty, all men would feel its force alike. 10. See how fire burns all men equally; it is the nature of it so to do; but these flowers of beauty, one man loves them, and another loves them not, nor does C. 1 every man love the same. For love is voluntary, and each man loves what he chooses to love. The brother is not enamoured of his own sister, nor the father of his own daughter; some other man must be the lover. Reverence and law are strong enough to break the heart of passion. 11. But if a law were passed saying, "Eat not, and thou shalt not starve; Drink not, and thou shalt not thirst; Let not cold bite thee in winter nor heat inflame thee in summer," I say there is no law that could compel us to obey; for it is our nature to be swayed by these forces. But love is voluntary; each man loves to himself alone, and according as he chooses, just as he chooses his cloak or his sandals.'

12. 'Then,' said Cyrus, 'if love be voluntary, why cannot a man cease to love when he wishes? I have seen men in love,' said he, 'who have wept for very agony, who were the very slaves of those they loved, though before the fever took them they thought slavery the worst of evils. I have seen them make gifts of what they ill could spare, I have seen them praying, yes, praying, to be rid of their passion, as though it were any other malady, and yet unable to shake it off; they were bound hand and foot by a chain of something stronger than iron. There they stood at the beck and call of their idols, and that without rhyme or reason; and yet, poor slaves, they make no attempt to run away, in spite of all they suffer; on the contrary, they mount guard over their tyrants, for fear these should escape.'

13. But the young man spoke in answer: 'True,' he said, 'there are such men, but they are worthless scamps, and that is why, though they are always praying to die and be put out of their misery and though ten thousand avenues lie open by which to escape from life, they never take one of them. These are the very men who are prepared to steal and purloin the goods of others, and yet you know yourself, when they do it, you are the first to say stealing is not done under compulsion, and you blame the thief and the robber; you do not pity him, you punish him. 14. In the same way, beautiful creatures do not compel others to love them or pursue them when it is wrong, but

C. 1 these good-for-nothing scoundrels have no self-control, and then they lay the blame on love. But the nobler type of man, the true gentleman, beautiful and brave, though he desire gold and splendid horses and lovely women, can still abstain from each and all alike, and lay no finger on them against the law of honour. 15. Take my own case,' he added, 'I have seen this lady myself, and passing fair I found her, and yet here I stand before you, and am still your trooper and can still perform my duty.'

16. 'I do not deny it,' said Cyrus; 'probably you came away in time. Love takes a little while to seize and carry off his victim. A man may touch fire for a moment and not be burnt; a log will not kindle all at once; and yet for all that, I am not disposed to play with fire or look on beauty. You yourself, my friend, if you will follow my advice, will not let your own eyes linger there too long; burning fuel will only burn those who touch it, but beauty can fire the beholder from afar, until he is all aflame with love.'

17. Oh, fear me not, Cyrus,' answered he; 'if I looked till the end of time I could not be made to do what ill befits a man.'

'A fair answer,' said Cyrus. 'Guard her then, as I bid you, and be careful of her. This lady may be of service to us all one day.'

18. With these words they parted. But afterwards, after the young man saw from day to day how marvellously fair the woman was, and how noble and gracious in herself, after he took care of her, and fancied that she was not insensible to what he did, after she set herself, through her attendants, to care for his wants and see that all things were ready for him when he came in, and that he should lack for nothing if ever he were sick, after all this, love entered his heart and took possession, and it may be there was nothing surprising in his fate. So at least it was.

19. Meanwhile Cyrus, who was anxious that the Medes and the allies should stay with him of their own free choice, called a meeting of their leading men, and when they were come together he spoke as follows:

20. 'Sons of the Medes and gentlemen all, I am well aware it was not from need of money that you went out

with me, nor yet in order to serve Cyaxares; you came for C. 1
my sake. You marched with me by night, you ran into
danger at my side, simply to do me honour. 21. Unless I
were a miscreant, I could not but be grateful for such
kindness. But I must confess that at present I lack the
ability to make a fit requital. This I am not ashamed to tell
you, but I would feel ashamed to add, "If you will stay
with me, I will be sure to repay you," for that would look
as though I spoke to bribe you into remaining. Therefore I
will not say that; I will say instead, "Even if you listen to
Cyaxares and go back to-day, I will still act so that you
shall praise me, I will not forget you in the day of my good
fortune." 22. For myself, I will never go back; I cannot,
for I must confirm my oath to the Hyrcanians and the
pledge I gave them; they are my friends and I shall never
be found a traitor to them. Moreover, I am bound to
Gobryas, who has offered us the use of his castle, his
territory, and his power; and I would not have him repent
that he came to me. 23. Last of all, and more than all,
when the great gods have showered such blessings on us, I
fear them and I reverence them too much to turn my back
on all they have given us. This, then, is what I myself must
do; it is for you to decide as you think best, and you will
acquaint me with your decision.'

24. So he spoke, and the first to answer was the Mede
who had claimed kinship with Cyrus in the old days.

'Listen to me,' he said, 'O king! For king I take you to
be by right of nature; even as the king of the hive among
the bees, whom all the bees obey and take for their leader
of their own free will; where he stays they stay also, not
one of them departs, and where he goes, not one of them
fails to follow; so deep a desire is in them to be ruled by
him. 25. Even thus, I believe, do our men feel towards you.
Do you remember the day you left us to go home to
Persia? Was there one of us, young or old, who did not
follow you until Astyages turned us back? And later, when
you returned to bring us aid, did we not see for ourselves
how your friends poured after you? And again, when
you had set your heart on this expedition, we know that
the Medes flocked to your standard with one consent.

C. 1 26. Today we have learnt to feel that even in an enemy's country we may be of good heart if you are with us, but, without you, we should be afraid even to return to our homes. The rest may speak for themselves, and tell you how they will act, but for myself, Cyrus, and for those under me, I say we will stand by you; we shall not grow weary of gazing at you, and we will continue to endure your benefits.'

27. Thereupon Tigranes spoke:

'Do not wonder, Cyrus, if I am silent now. The soul within me is ready, not to offer counsel, but to do your bidding.' 28. And the Hyrcanian chieftain said, 'For my part, if you Medes turn back to-day I shall say it was the work of some evil genius, who could not brook the fulfilment of your happiness. For no human heart could think of retiring when the foe is in flight, refusing to receive his sword when he surrenders it, rejecting him when he offers himself and all that he calls his own; above all, when we have a prince of men for our leader, one who, I swear it by the holy gods, takes delight to do us service, not to enrich himself.'

29. Thereupon the Medes cried with one consent:

'It was you, Cyrus, who led us out, and it is you who must lead us home again, when the right moment comes.'

And when Cyrus heard that, he prayed aloud:

'O most mighty Zeus, I supplicate thee, suffer me to outdo these friends of mine in courtesy and kindly dealing.'

30. Upon that he gave his orders. The rest of the army were to place their outposts and see to their own concerns, while the Persians took the tents allotted them, and divided them among their cavalry and infantry, to suit the needs of either arm. Then they arranged for the stewards to wait on them in future, bring them all they needed, and keep their horses groomed, so that they themselves might be free for the work of war. Thus they spent that day.

C. 2 But on the morrow they set out for their march to Gobryas. Cyrus rode on horseback at the head of his new Persian cavalry, two thousand strong, with as many more behind them, carrying their shields and swords, and the rest of the army followed in due order. The cavalry were told to make their new attendants understand that they would be punished if they were caught falling behind the C. 2 rear-guard, or riding in advance of the column, or straggling on either flank. 2. Towards evening of the second day the army found themselves before the castle of Gobryas, and they saw that the place was exceedingly strong and that all preparations had been made for the stoutest possible defence. They noticed also that great herds of cattle and endless flocks of sheep and goats had been driven up under the shelter of the castle walls. 3. Then Gobryas sent word to Cyrus, bidding him ride round and see where the place was easiest of approach, and meanwhile send his trustiest Persians to enter the fortress and bring him word what they found within. 4. Cyrus, who really wished to see if the citadel admitted of attack in case Gobryas proved false, rode all round the walls, and found they were too strong at every point. Presently the messengers who had gone in brought back word that there were supplies enough to last a whole generation and still not fail the garrison. 5. While Cyrus was wondering what this could mean, Gobryas himself came out, and all his men behind him, carrying wine and corn and barley, and driving oxen and goats and swine, enough to feast the entire host. 6. And his stewards fell to distributing the stores at once, and serving up a banquet. Then Gobryas invited Cyrus to enter the castle now that all the garrison had left it, using every precaution he might think wise; and Cyrus took him at his word, and sent in scouts and a strong detachment before he entered the place himself. Once within, he had the gates thrown open and sent for all his own friends and officers. 7. And when they joined him, Gobryas had beakers of gold brought out, and pitchers, and goblets, and costly ornaments, and golden coins without end, and all manner of beautiful things, and last of all he sent for his own daughter, tall and fair, a marvel of beauty and stateliness, still wearing mourning for her brother. And her father said to Cyrus, 'All these riches I bestow on you for a gift, and I put my daughter in your hands, to deal with as you think best. We are your suppliants; I but three days gone for my son, and she this day for her brother; we beseech you to avenge him.'

8. And Cyrus made answer:

C. 2   'I gave you my promise before that if you kept faith with me I would avenge you, so far as in me lay, and to-day I see the debt is due, and the promise I made to you I repeat to your daughter; God helping me, I will perform it. As for these costly gifts,' he added, 'I accept them, and I give them for a dowry to your daughter, and to him who may win her hand in marriage. One gift only I will take with me when I go, one only, but that is a thing so precious that if I changed it for all the wealth of Babylon or the whole world itself I could not go on my way with half so blithe a heart.'

9. And Gobryas wondered what this rare thing could be, half suspecting it might be his daughter. 'What is it, my lord?' said he. And Cyrus answered, 'I will tell you. A man may hate injustice and impiety and lies, but if no one offers him vast wealth or unbridled power or impregnable fortresses or lovely children, he dies before he can show what manner of man he is. 10. But you have placed everything in my hands to-day, this mighty fortress, treasures of every kind, your own power, and a daughter most worthy to be won. And thus you have shown all men that I could not sin against my friend and my host, nor act unrighteously for the sake of wealth, nor break my plighted word of my own free will. 11. This is your gift, and, so long as I am a just man and known to be such, receiving the praise of my fellow-men, I will never forget it; I will strive to repay you with every honour I can give. 12. Doubt not,' he added, 'but that you will find a husband worthy of your daughter. I have many a good man and true among my friends, and one of them will win her hand; but I could not say whether he will have less wealth, or more, than what you offer me. Only of one thing you may be certain; there are those among them who will not admire you one whit the more because of the splendour of your gifts; they will only envy me and supplicate the gods that one day it may be given to them to show that they too are loyal to their friends, that they too will never yield to their foes while life is in them, unless some god strike them down; that they too would never sacrifice virtue and fair renown for all the wealth you proffer and all the treasure

of Syria and Assyria to boot. Such is the nature, believe C. 2
me, of some who are seated here.'

13. And Gobryas smiled. 'By heaven, I wish you would
point them out to me, and I would beg you to give me one
of them to be my son-in-law.' And Cyrus said, 'You will
not need to learn their names from me; follow us, and you
will be able to point them out yourself.'

14. With these words he rose, clasped the hand of
Gobryas, and went out, all his men behind him. And
though Gobryas pressed him to stay and sup in the citadel,
he would not, but took his supper in the camp and
constrained Gobryas to take his meal with them. 15. And
there, lying on a couch of leaves, he put this question to
him, 'Tell me, Gobryas, who has the largest store of
coverlets, yourself, or each of us?' And the Assyrian
answered, 'You, I know, have more than I, more coverlets,
more couches, and a far larger dwelling-place, for your
home is earth and heaven, and every nook may be a couch,
and for your coverlets you need not count the fleeces of
your flocks, but the brushwood, and the herbage of hill
and plain.'

16. Nevertheless, when the meal began, it must be said
that Gobryas, seeing the poverty of what was set before
him, thought at first that his own men were far more
open-handed than the Persians. 17. But his mood changed
as he watched the grace and decorum of the company;
and saw that not a single Persian who had been schooled
would ever gape, or snatch at the viands, or let himself be
so absorbed in eating that he could attend to nothing else;
these men prided themselves on showing their good sense
and their intelligence while they took their food, just as a
perfect rider sits his horse with absolute composure, and
can look and listen and talk to some purpose while he puts
him through his paces. To be excited or flustered by meat
and drink was in their eyes something altogether swinish
and bestial. 18. Nor did Gobryas fail to notice that they
only asked questions which were pleasant to answer, and
only jested in a manner to please; all their mirth was as
far from impertinence and malice as it was from vulgarity
and unseemliness. 19. And what struck him most was their

C. 2 evident feeling that on a campaign, since the danger was the same for all, no one was entitled to a larger share than any of his comrades; on the contrary, it was thought the perfection of the feast to perfect the condition of those who were to share the fighting. 20. And thus when he rose to return home, the story runs that he said:

'I begin to understand, Cyrus, how it is that while we have more goblets and more gold, more apparel and more wealth than you, yet we ourselves are not worth as much. We are always trying to increase what we possess, but you seem to set your hearts on perfecting your own souls.'

21. But Cyrus only answered:

'My friend, be here without fail to-morrow, and bring all your cavalry in full armour, so that we may see your power, and then lead us through your country and show us who are hostile and who are friendly.'

22. Thus they parted for the time and each saw to his own concerns.

But when the day dawned Gobryas appeared with his cavalry and led the way. And Cyrus, as a born general would, not only supervised the march, but watched for any chance to weaken the enemy and add to his own strength. 23. With this in view, he summoned the Hrycanian chief and Gobryas himself; for they were the two he thought most likely to give him the information that he needed.

'My friends,' said he, 'I think I shall not err if I trust to your fidelity and consult you about the campaign. You, even more than I, are bound to see that the Assyrians do not overpower us. For myself, if I fail, there may well be some loophole of escape. But for you, if the king conquers, I see nothing but enmity on every side. 24. For, although he is my enemy, he bears me no malice, he only feels that it is against his interest for me to be powerful and therefore he attacks me. But you he hates with a bitter hatred, believing he is wronged by you.'

To this his companions answered that he must finish what he had to say; they were well aware of the facts, and had the deepest interest in the turn events might take.

25. Thereupon Cyrus put his questions: 'Does the king

suppose that you alone are his enemies, or do you know C. 2
of others who hate him too?' 'Certainly we do,' replied
the Hyrcanian, 'the Cadousians are his bitterest foes, and
they are both numerous and warlike. Then there are the
Sakians, our neighbours, who have suffered severely at his
hands, for he tried to subdue them as he subdued us.'

26. 'Then you think,' said Cyrus, 'that they would be
glad to attack him in our company?' 'Much more than
glad,' answered they; 'if they could manage to join us.'
'And what stands in their way?' asked he. 'The Assyrians
themselves,' said they, 'the very people among whom you
are marching now.' 27. At that Cyrus turned to Gobryas:

'And what of this lad who is now on the throne? Did
you not charge him with unbridled insolence?'

'Even so,' replied Gobryas, 'and I think he gave me
cause.' 'Tell me,' said Cyrus, 'were you the only man he
treated thus, or did others suffer too?'

28. 'Many others,' said Gobryas, 'but some of them
were weak, and why should I weary you with the insults
they endured? I will tell you of a young man whose father
was a much greater personage than I, and who was
himself, like my own son, a friend and comrade of the
prince. One day at a drinking-bout this monster had the
youth seized and mutilated, and why? Some say simply
because a paramour of his own had praised the boy's
beauty and said his bride was a woman to be envied. The
king himself now asserts it was because he had tried to
seduce his paramour. That young man, eunuch as he is, is
now at the head of his province, for his father is dead.'

29. 'Well,' rejoined Cyrus, 'I take it, you believe he
would welcome us, if he thought we came to help him?' 'I
am more than sure of that,' said Gobryas, 'but it is not so
easy to set eyes on him.' 'And why?' asked Cyrus. 'Because
if we are to join him at all, we must march right past
Babylon itself.' 30. 'And where is the difficulty in that?'
said Cyrus. 'Heaven help us!' cried Gobryas. 'The city has
only to open her gates, and she can send out an army ten
thousand times as large as yours. That is why,' he added,
'the Assyrians are less prompt than they were at bringing
in their weapons and their horses, because those who have

C. 2 seen your army think it so very small, and their report has got about. So that in my opinion it would be better to advance with the utmost care.'

31. Cyrus listened and replied.

'You do well, Gobryas, my friend, in urging as much care as possible. But I cannot myself see a safer route for us than the direct advance on Babylon, if Babylon is the centre of the enemy's strength. They are numerous, you say, and if they are in good heart, we shall soon know it. 32. Now, if they cannot find us and imagine that we have disappeared from fear of them, you may take it as certain that they will be quit of the terror we have inspired. Courage will spring up in its place, and grow the greater the longer we lie hid. But if we march straight on them, we shall find them still mourning for the dead whom we have slain, still nursing the wounds we have inflicted, still trembling at the daring of our troops, still mindful of their own discomfiture and flight. 33. Gobryas,' he added, 'be assured of this; men in the mass, when aflame with courage, are irresistible, but when their hearts fail them, the more numerous they are the worse the panic that seizes them. 34. It comes upon them magnified by a thousand lies, blanched by a thousand pallors, it gathers head from a thousand terror-stricken looks, until it grows so great that no orator can allay it by his words, no general arouse the old courage by a charge, or revive the old confidence by retreat; the more their leader cheers them on, the worse do the soldiers take their case to be. 35. Now by all means let us see exactly how things stand with us. If from henceforward victory must fall to those who can reckon the largest numbers, your fears for us are justified, and we are indeed in fearful danger; but if the old rule still holds, and battles are decided by the qualities of those who fight, then, I say, take heart and you will never fail. You will find far more stomach for the fight among our ranks than theirs. 36. And to hearten you the more, take note of this: our enemies are far fewer now than when we worsted them, far weaker than when they fled from us, while we are stronger because we are conquerors, and greater because fortune has been ours; yes, and actually more

numerous because you and yours have joined us, for I C. 2
would not have you hold your men too low, now that they
are side by side with us. In the company of conquerors,
Gobryas, the hearts of the followers beat high. 37. Nor
should you forget,' he added, 'that the enemy is well able
to see us as it is, and the sight of us will certainly not be
more alarming if we wait for him where we are than if we
advance against him. That is my opinion, and now you
must lead us straight for Babylon.'

And so the march continued, and on the fourth day they C. 3
found themselves at the limit of the territory over which
Gobryas ruled. Since they were now in the enemy's country
Cyrus changed the disposition of his men, taking the
infantry immediately under his own command, with sufficient cavalry to support them, and sending the rest of the
mounted troops to scour the land. Their orders were to
cut down every one with arms in his hands, and drive in
the rest, with all the cattle they could find. The Persians
were ordered to take part in this raid, and though many
came home with nothing for their trouble but a toss from
their horses, others brought back a goodly store of booty.

2. When the spoil was all brought in, Cyrus summoned
the officers of the Medes and the Hyrcanians, as well as
his own Peers, and spoke as follows :

'My friends, Gobryas has entertained us nobly ; he has
showered good things upon us. What say you then ? After
we have set aside the customary portion for the gods and
a fair share for the army, shall we not give all the rest of
the spoil to him ? Would it not be a noble thing, a sign and
symbol at the outset that we desire to outdo in well-doing
those who do good to us ?'

3. At that all his hearers with one consent applauded,
and a certain officer rose and said :

'By all means, Cyrus, let us do so. I myself cannot but
feel that Gobryas must have thought us almost beggars
because we were not laden with coins of gold and did not
drink from golden goblets. But if we do this, he will
understand that men may be free and liberal without the
help of gold.'

4. 'Come then,' said Cyrus, 'let us pay the priests our

C. 3 debt to heaven, select what the army requires, and then summon Gobryas and give the rest to him.'

So they took what they needed and gave all the rest to Gobryas.

5. Forthwith Cyrus pressed on towards Babylon, his troops in battle order. But as the Assyrians did not come out to meet them, he bade Gobryas ride forward and deliver this message:

'If the king will come out to fight for his land, I, Gobryas, will fight for him, but, if he will not defend his own country, we must yield to the conquerors.'

6. So Gobryas rode forward, just far enough to deliver the message in safety. And the king sent a messenger to answer him:

'Thy master says to thee: "It repents me, Gobryas, not that I slew thy son but that I stayed my hand from slaying thee. And now if ye will do battle, come again on the thirtieth day from hence. We have no leisure now, our preparations are still on foot."'

7. And Gobryas made answer:

'It repents thee: may that repentance never cease! I have begun to make thee suffer, since the day repentance took hold on thee.'

8. Then Gobryas brought back the words of the king to Cyrus, and Cyrus led his army off, and then he summoned Gobryas and said to him:

'Surely you told me that you thought the man who was made an eunuch by the king would be upon our side?' 'And I am sure he will,' answered Gobryas, 'for we have spoken freely to each other many a time, he and I.' 9. 'Then,' said Cyrus, 'you must go to him when you think the right moment has come: and you must so act at first that only he and you may know what he intends, and when you are closeted with him, if you find he really wishes to be a friend, you must contrive that his friendship remain a secret: for in war a man can scarcely do his friends more good than by a semblance of hostility, or his enemies more harm than under the guise of friendship.' 10. 'Aye,' answered Gobryas, 'and I know that Gadatas would pay a great price to punish the king of Assyria. But

it is for us to consider what he can best do.' 11. 'Tell me C. 3
now,' rejoined Cyrus, 'you spoke of an outpost, built
against the Hyrcanians and the Sakians, which was to
protect Assyria in time of war, – could the eunuch be
admitted there by the commandant if he came with a force
at his back?' 'Certainly he could,' said Gobryas, 'if he
were as free from suspicion as he is to-day.' 12. 'And free
he would be,' Cyrus went on, 'if I were to attack his
strongholds as though in earnest, and he were to repel me
in force. I might capture some of his men, and he some of
my soldiers, or some messengers sent by me to those you
say are the enemies of Assyria, and these prisoners would
let it be known that they were on their way to fetch an
army with scaling-ladders to attack this fortress, and the
eunuch, hearing their story, would pretend that he came
to warn the commandant in time. 13. 'Undoubtedly,' said
Gobryas, 'if things went thus, the commandant would
admit him; he would even beg him to stay there until you
withdrew.'

'And then,' Cyrus continued, 'once inside the walls, he
could put the place in our hands?' 14. 'We may suppose
so,' said Gobryas. 'He would be there to settle matters
within, and you would be redoubling the pressure from
without.'

'Then be off at once,' said Cyrus, 'and do your best to
teach him his part, and when you have arranged affairs,
come back to me; and as for pledges of good faith, you
could offer him none better than those you received from
us yourself.'

15. Then Gobryas made haste and was gone, and the
eunuch welcomed him gladly; he agreed to everything,
and helped to arrange all that was needed. Presently
Gobryas brought back word that he thought the eunuch
had everything in readiness, and so, without more ado,
Cyrus made his feigned attack on the following day, and
was beaten off. 16. But on the other hand there was a
fortress, indicated by Gadatas himself, that Cyrus took.
The messengers Cyrus had sent out, telling them exactly
where to go, fell into the hands of Gadatas: some were
allowed to escape – their business was to fetch the troops

C. 3 and carry the scaling-ladders – but the rest were narrowly examined in the presence of many witnesses, and when Gadatas heard the object of their journey he got his equipment together and set out in the night at full speed to take the news. 17. In the end he made his way into the fortress, trusted and welcomed as a deliverer, and for a time he helped the commandant to the best of his ability. But as soon as Cyrus appeared he seized the place, aided by the Persian prisoners he had taken. 18. This done, and having set things in order within the fortress, Gadatas went out to Cyrus, bowed before him according to the custom of his land, and said, 'Cyrus, may joy be yours!'

19. 'Joy is mine already,' answered he, 'for you, God helping you, have brought it to me. You must know,' he added, 'that I set great store by this fortress, and rejoice to leave it in the hands of my allies here. And for yourself, Gadatas,' he added, 'if the Assyrian has robbed you of the ability to beget children, remember he has not stolen your power to win friends; you have made us yours, I tell you, by this deed, and we will stand by you as faithfully as sons and grandsons of your own.'

20. So Cyrus spoke. And at that instant the Hyrcanian chief, who had only just learnt what had happened, came running up to him, and seizing him by the hand cried out:

'O Cyrus, you godsend to your friends! How often you make me thank the gods for bringing me to you!'

21. 'Off with you, then,' said Cyrus, 'and occupy this fortress for which you bless me so. Take it and make the best use of it you can, for your own nation, and for all our allies, and above all for Gadatas, our friend, who won it and surrenders it to us.'

22. 'Then,' said the chieftain, 'as soon as the Cadousians arrive and the Sakians and my countrymen, we must, must we not? call a council of them all, so that we may consult together, and see how best to turn it to account.'

23. Cyrus thought the proposal good, and when they met together it was decided to garrison the post with a common force, chosen from all who were concerned that it should remain friendly and be an outer bulwark to overawe the Assyrians. 24. This heightened the enthusiasm

of them all, Cadousians, Sakians, and Hyrcanians, and C. 3
their levies rose high, until the Cadousians sent in 20,000
light infantry and 4,000 cavalry, and the Sakians 11,000
bowmen, 10,000 on foot and 1,000 mounted, while the
Hyrcanians were free to despatch all their reserves of
infantry and make up their horsemen to a couple of
thousand strong, whereas previously the larger portion of
their cavalry had been left at home to support the
Cadousians and Sakians against Assyria.

25. And while Cyrus was kept in the fortress, organising
and arranging everything, many of the Assyrians from the
country round brought in their horses and handed over
their arms, being by this time in great dread of their
neighbours.

26. Soon after this Gadatas came to Cyrus and told him
that messengers had come to say that the king of Assyria,
learning what had happened to the fortress, was beside
himself with anger, and was preparing to attack his
territory. 'If you, Cyrus,' said he, 'will let me go now, I
will try to save my fortresses: the rest is of less account.'
27. Cyrus said, 'If you go now, when will you reach
home?' And Gadatas answered, 'On the third day from
this I can sup in my own house.' 'Do you think,' asked
Cyrus, 'that you will find the Assyrian already there?' 'I
am sure of it,' he answered, 'for he will make haste while
he thinks you are still far off.' 28. 'And I,' said Cyrus,
'when could I be there with my army?' But to this Gadatas
made answer, 'The army you have now, my lord, is very
large, and you could not reach my home in less than six
days or seven.' 'Well,' Cyrus replied, 'be off yourself:
make all speed, and I will follow as best I can.'

29. So Gadatas was gone, and Cyrus called together all
the officers of the allies, and a great and goodly company
they seemed, noble gentlemen, beautiful and brave. And
Cyrus stood up among them all and said:

30. 'My allies and my friends, Gadatas has done deeds
that we all feel worthy of high reward, and that too before
ever he had received any benefit from us. The Assyrians,
we hear, have now invaded his territory, to take vengeance
for the monstrous injury they consider he has done them,

C. 3 and moreover, they doubtless argue that if those who revolt to us escape scot-free, while those who stand by them are cut to pieces, ere long they will not have a single supporter on their side. 31. To-day, gentlemen, we may do a gallant deed, if we rescue Gadatas, our friend and benefactor; and truly it is only just and right thus to repay gift for gift, and boon for boon. Moreover, as it seems to me, what we accomplish will be much to our own interest. 32. If all men see that we are ready to give blow for blow and sting for sting, while we outdo our benefactors in generous deeds, it is only natural that multitudes will long to be our friends, and no man care to be our foe. 33. Whereas, if it be thought that we left Gadatas in the lurch, how in heaven's name shall we persuade another to show us any kindness? How shall we dare to think well of ourselves again? How shall one of us look Gadatas in the face, when all of us, so many and so strong, showed ourselves less generous than he, one single man and in so sore a plight?'

34. Thus Cyrus spoke, and all of them assented right willingly, and said it must be done.

'Come then,' concluded Cyrus, 'since you are all of one mind with me, let each of us choose an escort for our waggons and beasts of burden. 35. Let us leave them behind us, and put Gobryas at their head. He is acquainted with the roads, and for the rest he is a man of skill. But we ourselves will push on with our stoutest men and our strongest horses, taking provision for three days and no more: the lighter and cheaper our gear the more gaily shall we break our fast and take our supper and sleep on the road. 36. And now,' said he, 'let us arrange the order of the march. You, Chrysantas, must lead the van with your cuirassiers, since the road is broad and smooth, and you must put your brigadiers in the first line, each regiment marching in file, for if we keep close order we shall travel all the quicker and be all the safer. 37. I put the cuirassiers in the front,' he added, 'because they are our heaviest troops, and if the heaviest are leading, the lighter cannot find it hard to follow: whereas where the swiftest lead and the march is at night, it is no wonder if the column

fall to pieces: the vanguard is always running away. C. 3
38. And behind the cuirassiers,' he went on, 'Artabazas is
to follow with the Persian targeteers and the bowmen, and
behind them Andamyas the Mede with the Median infantry, and then Embas and the Armenian infantry, and then
Artouchas with the Hyrcanians, and then Thambradas
with the Sakian foot, and finally Datamas with the
Cadousians. 39. All these officers will put their brigadiers
in the first line, their targeteers on the right, and their
bowmen on the left of their own squares: this is the order
in which they will be of most use. 40. All the baggage-
bearers are to follow in the rear: and their officers must
see that they get everything together before they sleep, and
present themselves betimes in the morning, with all their
gear, and always keep good order on the march. 41. In
support of the baggage-train,' he added, 'there will be,
first, Madatas the Persian with the Persian cavalry, and he
too must put his brigadiers in the front, each regiment
following in single file, as with the infantry. 42. Behind
them Rambacas the Mede and his cavalry, in the same
order, and then you, Tigranes, and yours, and after you
the other cavalry leaders with the men they brought. The
Sakians will follow you, and last of all will come the
Cadousians, who were the last to join us, and you,
Alkeunas, who are to command them, for the present you
will take complete control of the rear, and allow no one to
fall behind your men. 43. All of you alike, officers, and all
who respect yourselves, must be most careful to march in
silence. At night the ears, and not the eyes, are the channels
of information and the guides for action, and at night any
confusion is a far more serious matter than by day, and far
more difficult to put right. For this reason silence must be
studied and order absolutely maintained. 44. Whenever
you mean to rise before daybreak, you must make the
night-watches as short and as numerous as possible, so
that no one may suffer on the march because of his long
vigil before it; and when the hour for the start arrives the
horn must be blown. 45. Gentlemen, I expect you all to
present yourselves on the road to Babylon with everything

C. 3 you require, and as each detachment starts, let them pass down the word for those in the rear to follow.'

46. So the officers went to their quarters, and as they went they talked of Cyrus, and what a marvellous memory he had, always naming each officer as he assigned him his post. 47. The fact was Cyrus took special pains over this: it struck him as odd that a mere mechanic could know the names of all his tools, and a physician the names of all his instruments, but a general be such a simpleton that he could not name his own officers, the very tools he had to depend on each time he wanted to seize a point or fortify a post or infuse courage or inspire terror. Moreover it seemed to him only courteous to address a man by name when he wished to honour him. 48. And he was sure that the man who feels he is personally known to his commander is more eager to be seen performing some noble feat of arms, and more careful to refrain from all that is unseemly and base. 49. Cyrus thought it would be quite foolish for him to give his orders in the style of certain householders: 'Somebody fetch the water, some one split the wood.' 50. After a command of that kind, every one looks at every one else, and no one carries it out, every one is to blame, and no one is ashamed or afraid, because there are so many beside himself. Therefore Cyrus always named the officers whenever he gave an order.

51. That, then, was his view of the matter. The army now took supper and posted their guards and got their necessaries together and went to rest. 52. And at midnight the horn was blown. Cyrus had told Chrysantas he would wait for him at a point on the road in advance of the troops, and therefore he went on in front himself with his own staff, and waited till Chrysantas appeared shortly afterwards at the head of his cuirassiers. 53. Then Cyrus put the guides under his command, and told him to march on, but to go slowly until he received a message, for all the troops were not yet on the road. This done, Cyrus took his stand on the line of march, and as each division came up, hurried it forward to its place, sending messengers meanwhile to summon those who were still behind. 54. When all had started, he despatched gallopers to Chrysantas to

tell him that the whole army was now under way, and that C. 4
he might lead on as quick as he could. 55. Then he
galloped to the front himself, reined up, and quietly
watched the ranks defile before him. Whenever a division
advanced silently and in good order, he would ride up and
ask their names and pay them compliments; and if he saw
any sign of confusion he would inquire the reason and
restore tranquillity. 56. One point remains to add in
describing his care that night: he sent forward a small but
picked body of infantry, active fellows all of them, in
advance of the whole army. They were to keep Chrysantas
in sight, and he was not to lose sight of them; they were
to use their ears and all their wits, and report at once to
Chrysantas if they thought there was any need. They had
an officer to direct their movements, announce anything of
importance, and not trouble about trifles.

57. Thus they pressed forward through the night, and
when day broke Cyrus ordered the mass of the cavalry to
the front, the Cadousians alone remaining with their own
infantry, who brought up the rear, and who were as much
in need as others of cavalry support. But the rest of the
horsemen he sent ahead because it was ahead that the
enemy lay, and in case of resistance he was anxious to
oppose them in battle-order, while if they fled he wished
no time to be lost in following up the pursuit. 58. It was
always arranged who were to give chase and who were to
stay with himself: he never allowed the whole army to be
broken up. 59. Thus Cyrus conducted the advance, but it
is not to be thought that he kept to one particular spot; he
was always galloping backwards and forwards, first at one
point and then at another, supervising everything and
supplying any defect as it arose. Thus Cyrus and his men
marched forward.

Now there was a certain officer in the cavalry with C. 4
Gadatas, a man of power and influence, who, when he
saw that his master had revolted from Assyria, thought to
himself, 'If anything should happen to him, I myself could
get from the king all that he possessed.'

Accordingly he sent forward a man he could trust, with
instructions that, if he found the Assyrian army already in

C. 4 the territory of Gadatas, he was to tell the king that he could capture Gadatas and all who were with him, if he thought fit to make an ambuscade. 2. And the messenger was also to say what force Gadatas had at his command and to announce that Cyrus was not with him. Moreover, the officer stated the road by which Gadatas was coming. Finally, to win the greater confidence, he sent word to his own dependants and bade them deliver up to the king of Assyria the castle which he himself commanded in the province, with all that it contained: he would come himself, he added, if possible, after he had slain Gadatas, and, even if he failed in that, he would always stand by the king.

3. Now the emissary rode as hard as he could and came before the king and told his errand, and, hearing it, the king at once took over the castle and formed an ambuscade, with a large body of horse and many chariots, in a dense group of villages that lay upon the road. 4. Gadatas, when he came near the spot, sent scouts ahead to explore, and the king, as soon as he sighted them, ordered two or three of his chariots and a handful of horsemen to dash away as though in flight, giving the impression that they were few in number and panic-stricken. At this the scouting party swept after them, signalling to Gadatas, who also fell into the trap and gave himself up to the chase.

The Assyrians waited till the quarry was within their grasp and then sprang out from their ambuscade. 5. The men, with Gadatas, seeing what had happened, turned back and fled, as one might expect, with the Assyrians at their heels, while the officer who had planned it all stabbed Gadatas himself. He struck him in the shoulder, but the blow was not mortal. Thereupon the traitor fled to the pursuers, and when they found out who he was he galloped on with them, his horse at full stretch, side by side with the king. 6. Naturally the men with the slower horses were overtaken by the better mounted, and the fugitives, already wearied by their long journey, were at the last extremity when suddenly they caught sight of Cyrus advancing at the head of his army, and were swept into safety, as glad

and thankful, we may well believe, as ship-wrecked mari- C. 4
ners into port.

7. The first feeling of Cyrus was sheer astonishment, but
he soon saw how matters stood. The whole force of the
Assyrian cavalry was rolling on him, and he met it with
his own army in perfect order, till the enemy, realising
what had happened, turned and fled. Then Cyrus ordered
his pursuing party to charge, while he followed more
slowly at the pace he thought the safest. 8. The enemy
were utterly routed: many of the chariots were taken,
some had lost their charioteers, others were seized in the
sudden change of front, others surrounded by the Persian
cavalry. Right and left the conquerors cut down their foes,
and among them fell the officer who had dealt the blow at
Gadatas. 9. But of the Assyrian infantry, those who were
besieging the fortress of Gadatas escaped to the stronghold
that had revolted from him, or managed to reach an
important city belonging to the king, where he himself, his
horsemen, and his chariots had taken refuge.

10. After this exploit Cyrus went on to the territory of
Gadatas, and as soon as he had given orders to those who
guarded the prisoners, he went himself to visit the eunuch
and see how it was with him after his wound. Gadatas
came out to meet him, his wound already bandaged. And
Cyrus was gladdened and said, 'I came myself to see how
it was with you.' 11. 'And I,' said Gadatas, 'heaven be my
witness, I came out to see how a man would look who had
a soul like yours. I cannot tell what need you had of me,
or what promise you ever gave me, to make you do as you
have done. I had shown you no kindness for your private
self: it was because you thought I had been of some little
service to your friends, that you came to help me thus, and
help me you did, from death to life. Left to myself I was
lost. 12. By heaven above, I swear it, Cyrus, if I had been
a father as I was born to be, God knows whether I could
have found in the son of my loins so true a friend as you. I
know of sons – this king of ours is such an one, who has
caused his own father ten thousand times more trouble
than ever he causes you.'

13. And Cyrus made answer:

C. 4   'You have overlooked a much more wonderful thing,
Gadatas, to turn and wonder at me.'

'Nay,' said Gadatas, 'what could that be ?'

'That all these Persians,' he answered, 'are so zealous in
your behalf, and all these Medes and Hyrcanians, and
every one of our allies, Armenians, Sakians, Cadousians.'

14. Then Gadatas prayed aloud :

'O Father Zeus, may the gods heap blessings on them
also, but above all on him who has made them what they
are ! And now, Cyrus, that I may entertain as they deserve
these men you praise, take the gifts I bring you as their
host, the best I have it in my power to bring.'

And with the word he brought out stores of every kind,
enough for all to offer sacrifice who listed ; and the whole
army was entertained in a manner worthy of their feat and
their success.

15. Meanwhile the Cadousians had been always in the
rear, unable to share in the pursuit, and they longed to
achieve some exploit of their own. So their chieftain, with
never a word to Cyrus, led them forth alone, and raided
the country towards Babylon. But, as soon as his cavalry
were scattered the Assyrians came out from their city of
refuge in regular battle-order. 16. When they saw that the
Cadousians were unsupported they attacked them, killing
the leader himself and numbers of his men, capturing
many of their horses and retaking the spoil they were in
the act of driving away. The king pursued as far as he
thought safe, and then turned back, and the Cadousians at
last found safety in their own camp, though even the
vanguard only reached it late in the afternoon. 17. When
Cyrus saw what had happened he went out to meet them,
succouring every wounded man and sending him off to
Gadatas at once, to have his wounds dressed, while he
helped to house the others in their quarters, and saw that
they had all they needed, his Peers aiding him, for at such
times noble natures will give help with all their hearts.
18. Still it was plain to see that he was sorely vexed, and
when the hour for dinner came, and the others went away,
he was still there on the ground with the attendants and
the surgeons ; not a soul would he leave uncared for if

anything could be done: he either saw to it himself or sent C. 4
for the proper aid.

19. So for that night they rested. But with daybreak
Cyrus sent out a herald and summoned a gathering of all
the officers and the whole Cadousian army, and spoke as
follows:

'My friends and allies, what has happened is only
natural; for it is human nature to err, and I cannot find it
astonishing. Still we may gain at least one advantage from
what has occurred, if we learn that we must never cut off
from our main body a detachment weaker than the force
of the enemy. 20. I do not say that one is never to march
anywhere, if necessary, with an even smaller fraction than
the Cadousians had; but, before doing so you must
communicate with some one able to bring up reinforce-
ments, and then, though you may be trapped yourself, it is
at least probable that your friends behind you may foil the
foilers, and divert them from your own party: there are
fifty ways in which one can embarrass the enemy and save
one's friends. Thus separation need not mean isolation,
and union with the main force may still be kept, whereas
if you sally forth without telling your plan, you are no
better off than if you were alone in the field. 21. However,
God willing, we shall take our revenge for this ere long;
indeed, as soon as you have breakfasted, I will lead you
out to the scene of yesterday's skirmish, and there we will
bury those who fell, and show our enemies that the very
field where they thought themselves victorious is held by
those who are stronger than they: they shall never look
again with joy upon the spot where they slew our comrades. Or else, if they refuse to come out and meet us, we
will burn their villages and harry all their land, so that in
lieu of rejoicing at the sight of what they did to us, they
shall gnash their teeth at the spectacle of their own
disasters. 22. Go now,' said he, 'the rest of you, and take
your breakfast forthwith, but let the Cadousians first elect
a leader in accordance with their own laws, one who will
guide them well and wisely, by the grace of God, and with
our human help, if they should need it. And when you

C. 4 have chosen your leader, and had your breakfast, send him hither to me.'

23. So they did as Cyrus bade them, and when he led the army out, he stationed their new general close to his own person, and told him to keep his detachment there, 'So that you and I,' said he, 'may rekindle the courage in their souls.'

In this order they marched out, and thus they buried the Cadousian dead and ravaged the country. Which done, they went back to the province of Gadatas, laden with supplies taken from the foe.

24. Now Cyrus felt that those who had come over to his side and who dwelt in the neighbourhood of Babylon would be sure to suffer unless he were constantly there himself, and so he bade all the prisoners he set free take a message to the king, and he himself despatched a herald to say that he would leave all the tillers of the soil unmolested and unhurt if the Assyrian would let those who had come over to him continue their work in peace. 25. 'And remember,' he added, 'that even if you try to hinder my friends, it is only a few whom you could stop, whereas there is a vast territory of yours that I could allow to be cultivated. As for the crops,' he added, 'if we have war, it will be the conqueror, I make no doubt, who will reap them, but if we have peace, it will be you. If, however, any of my people take up arms against you, or any of yours against me, we must, of course, each of us, defend ourselves as best we can.'

26. With this message Cyrus despatched the herald, and when the Assyrians heard it, they urged the king to accept the proposal, and so limit the war as much as possible. 27. And he, whether influenced by his own people or because he desired it himself, consented to the terms. So an agreement was drawn up, proclaiming peace to the tillers of the soil and war to all who carried arms.

28. Thus Cyrus arranged matters for the husbandmen, and he asked his own supporters among the drovers to bring their herds, if they liked, into his dominions and leave them there, while he treated the enemy's cattle as booty wherever he could, so that his allies found attraction

in the campaign. For the risk was no greater if they took C. 4
what they needed, while the knowledge that they were
living at the enemy's expense certainly seemed to lighten
the labour of the war.

29. When the time came for Cyrus to go back, and the
final preparations were being made, Gadatas brought him
gifts of every kind, the produce of a vast estate, and among
the cattle a drove of horses, taken from cavalry of his own,
whom he distrusted owing to the late conspiracy. 30. And
when he brought them he said, 'Cyrus, this day I give you
these for your own, and I would pray you to make such
use of them as you think best, but I would have you
remember that all else which I call mine is yours as well.
For there is no son of mine, nor can there ever be, sprung
from my own loins, to whom I may leave my wealth:
when I die myself, my house must perish with me, my
family and my name. 31. And I must suffer this, Cyrus, I
swear to you by the great gods above us, who see all things
and hear all things, though never by word or deed did I
commit injustice or foulness of any kind.'

But here the words died on his lips; he burst into tears
over his sorrows, and could say no more. 32. Cyrus was
touched with pity at his suffering and said to him:

'Let me accept the horses, for in that I can help you, if I
set loyal riders on them, men of a better mind, methinks,
than those who had them before, and I myself can satisfy
a wish that has long been mine, to bring my Persian
cavalry up to ten thousand men. But take back, I pray you,
all these other riches, and guard them safely against the
time when you may find me able to vie with you in gifts. If
I left you now so hugely in your debt, heaven help me if I
could hold up my head again for very shame.'

33. Thereto Gadatas made answer, 'In all things I trust
you, and will trust you, for I see your heart. But consider
whether I am competent to guard all this myself. 34. While
I was at peace with the king, the inheritance I had from
my father was, it may be, the fairest in all the land: it was
near that mighty Babylon, and all the good things that can
be gathered from a great city fell into our laps, and yet
from all the trouble of it, the noise and the bustle, we

C. 4 could be free at once by turning our backs and coming home here. But now that we are at war, the moment you have left us we are sure to be attacked, ourselves and all our wealth, and methinks we shall have a sorry life of it, our enemies at our elbow and far stronger than ourselves. 35. I seem to hear some one say, why did you not think of this before you revolted? But I answer, Cyrus, because the soul within me was stung beyond endurance by my wrongs; I could not sit and ponder the safest course, I was always brooding over one idea, always in travail of one dream, praying for the day of vengeance on the miscreant, the enemy of God and man, whose hatred never rested, once aroused, once he suspected a man, not of doing wrong, but of being better than himself. 36. And because he is a villain, he will always find, I know, worse villains than himself to aid him, but if one day a nobler rival should appear — have no concern, Cyrus, you will never need to do battle with such an one, yonder fiend would deal with him and never cease to plot against him until he had dragged him in the dust, only because he was the better man. And to work me trouble and disaster, he and his wicked tools will, I fear me, have strength enough and to spare.'

37. Cyrus thought there was much in what he said, and he answered forthwith:

'Tell me, Gadatas, did we not put a stout garrison in your fortress, so as to make it safe for you whenever you needed it, and are you not taking the field with us now, so that, if the gods be on our side as they are to-day, that scoundrel may fear you, not you him? Go now, bring with you all you have that is sweet to look on and to love, and then join our march: you shall be, I am persuaded, of the utmost service to me, and I, so far as in me lies, will give you help for help.'

38. When Gadatas heard that, he breathed again, and he said:

'Could I really be in time to make my preparations and be back before you leave? I would fain take my mother with me on the march.'

'Assuredly,' said Cyrus, 'you will be in time: for I will C. 4
wait until you say that all is ready.'

39. So it came to pass that Gadatas went his way, and
with the aid of Cyrus put a strong garrison in his fortress,
and got together the wealth of his broad estates. And
moreover he brought with him in his own retinue servants
he could trust and in whom he took delight, as well as
many others in whom he put no trust at all, and these he
compelled to bring their wives with them, and their sisters,
that so they might be bound to his service.

40. Thus Gadatas went with Cyrus, and Cyrus kept him
ever at his side, to show him the roads and the places for
water and fodder and food, and lead them where there
was most abundance.

41. At last they came in sight of Babylon once more,
and it seemed to Cyrus that the road they were following
led under the very walls. Therefore he summoned Gobryas
and Gadatas, and asked them if there was not another
way, so that he need not pass so close to the ramparts.
42. 'There are many other ways, my lord,' answered
Gobryas, 'but I thought you would certainly wish to pass
as near the city as possible, and display the size and
splendour of your army to the king. I knew that when
your force was weaker you advanced to his walls, and let
him see us, few as we were, and I am persuaded that if he
has made any preparation for battle now, as he said he
would, when he sees the power you have brought with
you, he will think once more that he is unprepared.'

43. But Cyrus said:

'Does it seem so strange to you, Gobryas, that when I
had a far smaller army I took it right up to the enemy's
walls, and to-day when my force is greater I will not
venture there? 44. You need not think it strange: to march
up is not the same as to march past. Every leader will
march up with his troops disposed in the best order for
battle and a wise leader will draw them off so as to secure
safety rather than speed. 45. But in marching past there is
no means of avoiding long straggling lines of waggons,
long strings of baggage-bearers, and all these must be
screened by the fighting-force so as never to leave the

C. 4 baggage unprotected. 46. But this must mean a thin weak order for the fighting-men, and if the enemy choose to attack at any point with their full force, they can strike with far more weight than any of the troops available to meet them at the moment. 47. Again, the length of line means a long delay in bringing up relief, whereas the enemy have only a handsbreadth to cover as they rush out from the walls or retire. 48. But now, if we leave a distance between ourselves and them as wide as our line is long, not only will they realise our numbers plainly enough, but our veil of glittering armour will make the whole multitude more formidable in their eyes. 49. And, if they do attack us anywhere, we shall be able to foresee their advance a long way off and be quite prepared to give them welcome. But it is far more likely, gentlemen,' he added, 'that they will not make the attempt, with all that ground to cover from the walls, unless they imagine that their whole force is superior to the whole of ours: they know that retreat would be difficult and dangerous.'

50. So Cyrus spoke, and his listeners felt that he was right, and Gobryas led the army by the way that he advised. And as one detachment after another passed the city, Cyrus strengthened the protection for the rear and so withdrew in safety.

51. Marching in this order, he came back at last to his first starting-point, on the frontier between Assyria and Media. Here he dealt with three Assyrian fortresses: one, the weakest, he attacked and took by force, while the garrisons of the other two, what with the eloquence of Gadatas and the terror inspired by Cyrus, were persuaded to surrender.

C. 5   And now that his expedition was completed, Cyrus sent to Cyaxares and urged him to come to the camp in order that they might decide how best to use the forts which they had taken, and perhaps Cyaxares, after reviewing the army, would advise him what the next move ought to be, or, Cyrus added to the messenger, 'if he bids me, say I will come to him and take up my encampment there.' 2. So the emissary went off with the message, and meanwhile Cyrus gave orders that the Assyrian tent chosen for Cyaxares should be furnished as splendidly as possible, and the C. 5 woman brought to her apartment there, and the two singing-girls also, whom they had set aside for him.

3. And while they were busied with these things the envoy went to Cyaxares and delivered his message, and Cyaxares listened and decided it was best for Cyrus and his men to remain on the frontier. The Persians whom Cyrus had sent for had already arrived, forty thousand bowmen and targeteers. 4. To watch these eating up the land was bad enough, and Cyaxares thought he would rather be quit of one horde before he received another. On his side the officer in command of the Persian levy, following the instructions from Cyrus, asked Cyaxares if he had any need of the men, and Cyaxares said he had not. Thereupon, and hearing that Cyrus had arrived, the Persian put himself at the head of his troops and went off at once to join him. 5. Cyaxares himself waited till the next day and then set out with the Median troopers who had stayed behind. And when Cyrus knew of his approach he took his Persian cavalry, who were now a large body of men, and all the Medes, Hyrcanians, and Armenians, and the best-mounted and best-armed among the rest, and so went out to meet Cyaxares and show the power he had won. 6. But when Cyaxares saw so large a following of gallant gentlemen with Cyrus, and with himself so small and mean a retinue, it seemed to him an insult, and mortification filled his heart. And when Cyrus sprang from his horse and came up to give him the kiss of greeting, Cyaxares, though he dismounted, turned away his head and gave him no kiss, while the tears came into his eyes. 7. Whereupon Cyrus told the others to stand aside and rest, and then he took Cyaxares by the hand and led him apart under a grove of palm-trees, and bade the attendants spread Median carpets for them, and made Cyaxares sit down, and then, seating himself beside him, he said:

8. 'Uncle of mine, tell me, in heaven's name, I implore you, why are you angry with me? What bitter sight have you seen to make you feel such bitterness?'

And then Cyaxares answered:

'Listen, Cyrus; I have been reputed royal and of royal

C. 5 lineage as far back as the memory of man can go; my father was a king and a king I myself was thought to be; and now I see myself riding here, meanly and miserably attended, while you come before me in splendour and magnificence, followed by the retinue that once was mine and all your other forces. 9. That would be bitter enough, methinks, from the hand of an enemy, but – O gods above us! – how much more bitter at the hands of those from whom we least deserve it! Far rather would I be swallowed in the earth than live to be seen so low, aye, and to see my own kinsfolk turn against me and make a mock of me. And well I know,' said he, 'that not only you but my own slaves are now stronger and greater than myself: they come out equipt to do me far more mischief than ever I could repay.'

10. But here he stopped, overcome by a passion of weeping, so much so that for very pity Cyrus's own eyes filled with tears. There was silence between them for a while, and then Cyrus said:

'Nay, Cyaxares, what you say is not true, and what you think is not right, if you imagine that because I am here, your Medes have been equipt to do you any harm. 11. I do not wonder that you are pained, and I will not ask if you have cause or not for your anger against them: you would ill brook apologies for them from me. Only it seems to me a grievous error in a ruler to quarrel with all his subjects at once. Widespread terror must needs be followed by widespread hate: anger with all creates unity among all. 12. It was for this reason, take my word for it, that I would not send them back to you without myself, fearing that your wrath might be the cause of what would injure all of us. Through my presence here and by the blessing of heaven, all is safe for you: but that you should regard yourself as wronged by me, – I cannot but feel it bitter, when I am doing all in my power to help my friends, to be accused of plotting against them. 13. However,' he continued, 'let us not accuse each other in this useless way; if possible, let us see exactly in what I have offended. And as between friend and friend, I will lay down the only rule that is just and fair: if I can be shown to have done you

harm, I will confess I am to blame, but if it appears that I C. 5
have never injured you, not even in thought, will you not
acquit me of all injustice towards you?'

'Needs must I,' answered Cyaxares.

14. 'And if I can show that I have done you service, and
been zealous in your cause to the utmost of my power,
may I not claim, instead of rebuke, some little meed of
praise?'

'That were only fair,' said Cyaxares.

15. 'Then,' said Cyrus, 'let us go through all I have
done, point by point, and see what is good in it and what
is evil. 16. Let us begin from the time when I assumed my
generalship, if that is early enough. I think I am right in
saying that it was because you saw your enemies gathering
together against you, and ready to sweep over your land
and you, that you sent to Persia asking for help, and to me
in private, praying me to come, if I could, myself, at the
head of any forces they might send. Was I not obedient to
your word? Did I not come myself with the best and
bravest I could bring?'

17. 'You did indeed,' answered Cyaxares.

'Tell me, then, before we go further, did you see any
wrong in this? Was it not rather a service and a kindly
act?' 'Certainly,' said Cyaxares, 'so far as that went, I saw
nothing but kindliness.' 18. 'Well, after the enemy had
come, and we had to fight the matter out, did you ever see
me shrink from toil or try to escape from danger?' 'That I
never did,' said Cyaxares, 'quite the contrary.'

19. 'And afterwards, when, through the help of heaven,
victory was ours, and the enemy retreated, and I implored
you to let us pursue them together, take vengeance on
them together, win together the fruits of any gallant exploit
we might achieve, can you accuse me then of self-seeking
or self-aggrandisement?'

20. But at that Cyaxares was silent. Then Cyrus spoke
again. 'If you would rather not reply to that, tell me if you
thought yourself injured because, when you considered
pursuit unsafe, I relieved you of the risk, and only begged
you to lend me some of your cavalry? If my offence lay in
asking for that, when I had already offered to work with

C. 5 you, side by side, you must prove it to me; and it will need some eloquence.'

21. He paused, but Cyaxares still kept silence. 'Nay,' said Cyrus, 'if you will not answer that either, tell me at least if my offence lay in what followed, when you said that you did not care to stop your Medes in their merry-making and drive them out into danger, do you think it was wrong in me, without waiting to quarrel on that score, to ask you for what I knew was the lightest boon you could grant and the lightest command you could lay on your soldiers? For I only asked that he who wished it might be allowed to follow me. 22. And thus, when I had won your permission, I had won nothing, unless I could win them too. Therefore I went and tried persuasion, and some listened to me, and with these I set off on my march, holding my commission from your own self. So that, if you look on this act as blameworthy, it would seem that not even the acceptance of your own gifts can be free from blame. 23. It was thus we started, and after we had gone, was there, I ask you, a single deed of mine that was not done in the light of day? Has not the enemy's camp been taken? Have not hundreds of your assailants fallen? And hundreds been deprived of their horses and their arms? Is not the spoiler spoiled? The cattle and the goods of those who harried your land are now in the hands of your friends, they are brought to you, or to your subjects. 24. And, above all and beyond all, you see your own country growing great and powerful and the land of your enemy brought low. Strongholds of his are in your power, and your own that were torn from you in other days by the Syrian domination are now restored to you again. I cannot say I should be glad to learn that any of these things can be bad for you, or short of good, but I am ready to listen, if so it is. 25. Speak, tell me your judgment of it all.'

Then Cyrus paused, and Cyaxares made answer:

'To call what you have done evil, Cyrus, is impossible. But your benefits are of such a kind that the more they multiply upon me, the heavier burden do they bring. 26. I would far rather,' he went on, 'have made your country

great by my own power than see mine exalted in this way C. 5
by you. These deeds of yours are a crown of glory to you ;
but they bring dishonour to me. 27. And for the wealth, I
would rather have made largess of it to yourself than
receive it at your hands in the way you give it now. Goods
so gotten only leave me the poorer. And for my subjects —
I think I would have suffered less if you had injured them
a little than I suffer now when I see how much they owe
you. 28. Perhaps,' he added, 'you find it inhuman of me to
feel thus, but I would ask you to forget me and imagine
that you are in my place and see how it would appear to
you then. Suppose a friend of yours were to take care of
your dogs, dogs that you bred up to guard yourself and
your house, such care that he made them fonder of him
than of yourself, would you be pleased with him for his
attention ? 29. Or take another instance, if that one seems
too slight : suppose a friend of yours were to do so much
for your own followers, men you kept to guard you and
fight for you, that they would rather serve in his train than
yours, would you be grateful to him for his kindness ?
30. Or let me take the tenderest of human ties : suppose a
friend of yours paid court to the wife of your bosom so
that in the end he made her love him more than yourself,
would he rejoice your heart by his courtesy ? Far from it, I
trow ; he who did this, you would say, did you the greatest
wrong in all the world. 31. And now, to come nearest my
own case, suppose some one paid such attention to your
Persians that they learnt to follow him instead of you,
would you reckon that man your friend ? No ; but a worse
enemy than if he had slain a thousand. 32. Or again, say
you spoke in all friendship to a friend and bade him take
what he wished, and straightway he took all he could lay
hands on and carried it off, and so grew rich with your
wealth, and you were left in utter poverty, could you say
that friend was altogether blameless ? 33. And I, Cyrus, I
feel that you have treated me, if not in that way, yet in a
way exactly like it. What you say is true enough : I did
allow you to take what you liked and go, and you took
the whole of my power and went, leaving me desolate, and
to-day you bring the spoil you have won with my forces,

C. 5 and lay it so grandly at my feet – magnificent! And you make my country great through the help of my own might, while I have no part or lot in the performance, but must step in at the end, like a woman, to receive your favours, while in the eyes of all men, not least my faithful subjects yonder, you are the man, and I – I am not fit to wear a crown. 34. Are these, I ask you, Cyrus, are these the deeds of a benefactor? Nay, had you been kind as you are kin, above all else you would have been careful not to rob me of dignity and honour. What advantage is it to me for my lands to be made broad if I myself am dishonoured? When I ruled the Medes, I ruled them not because I was stronger than all of them, but because they themselves thought that our race was in all things better than theirs.'

35. But while he was still speaking Cyrus broke in on his words, crying:

'Uncle of mine, by the heaven above us, if I have ever shown you any kindness, be kind to me now. Do not find fault with me any more, wait, and put me to the test, and learn how I feel towards you, and if you see that what I have done has really brought you good, then, when I embrace you, embrace me in return and call me your benefactor, and if not, you may blame me as you please.'

36. 'Perhaps,' answered Cyaxares, 'you are right. I will do as you wish.'

'Then I may kiss you?' said Cyrus.

'Yes, if it pleases you.' 'And you will not turn aside as you did just now?' 'No, I will not turn aside.' And he kissed him.

37. And when the Medes saw it and the Persians and all the allies – for all were watching to see how matters would shape – joy came into their hearts and gladness lit up their faces. Then Cyrus and Cyaxares mounted their horses and rode back, and the Medes fell in behind Cyaxares, at a nod from Cyrus, and behind Cyrus the Persians, and the others behind them. 38. And when they reached the camp and brought Cyaxares to the splendid tent, those who were appointed made everything ready for him, and while he was waiting for the banquet his Medes presented themselves, some of their own accord, it is true, but most

were sent by Cyrus. 39. And they brought him gifts; one C. 5
came with a beautiful cup-bearer, another with an admirable cook, a third with a baker, a fourth with a musician,
while others brought cups and goblets and beautiful
apparel; almost every one gave something out of the spoils
they had won. 40. So that the mood of Cyaxares changed,
and he seemed to see that Cyrus had not stolen his subjects
from him, and that they made no less account of him than
they used to do.

41. Now when the hour came for the banquet, Cyaxares
sent to Cyrus and begged him to share it: it was so long,
he said, since they had met. But Cyrus answered, 'Bid me
not to the feast, good uncle. Do you not see that all these
soldiers of ours have been raised by us to the pitch of
expectation? And it were ill on my part if I seemed to
neglect them for the sake of my private pleasure. If soldiers
feel themselves neglected even the good become faint-
hearted, and the bad grow insolent. 42. With yourself it is
different, you have come a long journey and you must fall
to without delay, and if your subjects do you honour,
welcome them and give them good cheer, that there may
be confidence between you and them, but I must go and
attend to the matters of which I speak. 43. Early to-
morrow morning,' he added, 'our chief officers will present
themselves at your gate to hear from you what you think
our next step ought to be. You will tell us whether we
ought to pursue the campaign further or whether the time
has now come to disband our army.'

44. Thereupon Cyaxares betook himself to the banquet
and Cyrus called a council of his friends, the shrewdest
and best fitted to act with him, and spoke to them as
follows:

'My friends, thanks to the gods, our first prayers are
granted. Wherever we set foot now we are the masters of
the country: we see our enemies brought low and ourselves
increasing day by day in numbers and in strength. 45. And
if only our present allies would consent to stay with us a
little longer, our achievements could be greater still,
whether force were needed or persuasion. Now it must be
your work as much as mine to make as many of them as

C. 5 possible willing and anxious to remain. 46. Remember that, just as the soldier who overthrows the greatest number in the day of battle is held to be the bravest, so the speaker, when the time has come for persuasion, who brings most men to his side will be thought the most eloquent, the best orator, and the ablest man of action. 47. Do not, however, prepare your speeches as though we asked you to give a rhetorical display: remember that those whom you convince will show it well enough by what they do. 48. I leave you then,' he added, 'to the careful study of your parts: mine is to see, so far as in me lies, that our troops are provided with all they need, before we hold the council of war.'

BOOK VI

So the day ended, and they supped and went to rest. But C. 1 early the next morning all the allies flocked to Cyaxares' gates, and while Cyaxares dressed and adorned himself, hearing that a great multitude were waiting, Cyrus gave audience to the suitors his own friends had brought. First came the Cadousians, imploring him to stay, and then the Hyrcanians, and after them the Sakians, and then some one presented Gobryas, and Hystaspas brought in Gadatas the eunuch, whose entreaty was still the same. 2. At that Cyrus, who knew already that for many a day Gadatas had been half-dead with fear lest the army should be disbanded, laughed outright and said, 'Ah, Gadatas, you cannot conceal it: you have been bribed by my friend Hystaspas to take this view.'

3. But Gadatas lifted up his hands to heaven and swore most solemnly that Hystaspas had not influenced him.

'Nay,' said he, 'it is because I know myself that, if you depart, I am ruined utterly. And therefore it was that I took it upon me to speak with Hystaspas myself, and ask him if he knew what was in your mind about the disbanding of the army.'

4. And Cyrus said, 'It would be unjust then, I suppose, to lay the blame on Hystaspas.' 'Yes, Cyrus, most unjust,' said Hystaspas, 'for I only said to Gadatas that it would be impossible for you to carry on the campaign, as your father wanted you home, and had sent for you.'

5. 'What?' cried Cyrus, 'you dared to let that be known whether I wished it or not?'

'Certainly I did,' he answered, 'for I can see that you are

C. 1 mad to be home in Persia, the cynosure of every eye, telling
your father how you wrought this and accomplished that.'

'Well,' said Cyrus, 'are you not longing to go home
yourself ?'

'No,' said the other. 'I am not. Nor have I any intention
of going: here I shall stay and be general-in-chief until I
make our friend Gadatas the lord and the Assyrian his
slave.'

6. Thus half in jest and half in earnest they played with
one another, and meanwhile Cyaxares had finished adorn-
ing himself and came forth in great splendour and solemnity, and sat down on a Median throne. And when all
were assembled and silence was proclaimed, Cyaxares
said:

'My friends and allies, perhaps, since I am present and
older than Cyrus, it is suitable that I should address you
first. It appears to me that the moment has come to discuss
one question before all others, the question whether we
ought to go on with the campaign or disband the army. Be
pleased,' he added, 'to state your opinions on the matter.'

7. Then the leader of the Hyrcanians stood up at once
and said:

'Friends and allies, I hardly think that words are needed
when facts themselves show us the path to take. All of us
know that while we stand together we give our enemy
more trouble than we get: but when we stood alone it was
they who dealt with us as they liked best and we liked
least.'

8. Then the Cadousian followed.

'The less we talk,' said he, 'about breaking-up and going
home separately, the better; separation has done us anything but good, it seems to me, even on the march. My
men and I, at any rate, very soon paid the penalty for
private excursions; as I dare say you have not forgotten.'

9. Upon that Artabazus rose, the Mede who had claimed
kinship with Cyrus in the old days.

'Cyaxares,' said he, 'in one respect I differ from those
who have spoken before me: they think we should stay
here in order to go on with the campaign, but I think I was
always on the campaign at home. 10. I was for ever out on

some expedition or other, because our people were being C. 1
harried, or our fortresses threatened, and a world of
trouble I had, what with fears within and fighting without,
and all too at my own expense. As it is now, I occupy the
enemy's forts, my fear of them is gone, I make good cheer
on their own good things, and I drink their own good
wine. Since home means fighting and service here means
feasting, I am not in favour myself,' said he, 'of breaking
up the company.'

11. Then Gobryas spoke.

'Friends,' said he, 'I have trusted Cyrus' word and had
no fault to find with him: what he promises that he
performs: but if he leaves the country now, the Assyrian
will be reprieved, he will never be punished for the wrongs
he tried to inflict on you and did inflict on me: I shall be
punished instead, because I have been your friend.'

12. At that Cyrus rose at last and said:

'Gentlemen, I am well aware that the disbanding of our
forces must mean the decrease of our own power and the
increase of theirs. If some of them have given up their
weapons, they will soon procure others; if some have lost
their horses, the loss will soon be made good; if some have
fallen in battle, others, younger and stronger, will take
their place. We need not be surprised if they are soon in a
condition to cause us trouble again. 13. Why, then, did I
ask Cyaxares to put the question to debate? Because, I
answer, I am afraid of the future. I see opponents against
us whom we cannot fight, if we conduct the campaign as
we are doing now. 14. Winter is advancing against us, and
though we may have shelter for ourselves we have nothing,
heaven knows, for our horses and our servants and the
great mass of our soldiery, without whom we cannot even
think of a campaign. As to provisions, up to the limits of
our advance and because of that advance they have been
exhausted; and beyond that line, owing to the terror we
inspire, the inhabitants will have stowed their supplies
away in strong places where they can enjoy them and we
cannot get them. 15. Where is the warrior, stout of heart
and strong of will, who can wage war with cold and
hunger? If our style of soldiering is to be only what it has

C. 1 been, I say we ought to disband at once of our own accord, and not wait to be driven from the field against our will by sheer lack of means. If we do wish to go forward, this is what we must do: we must detach from the enemy all the fortresses we can and secure all we can for our own: if this is done, the larger supply will be in the hands of those who can stow away the larger store, and the weaker will suffer siege. 16. At present we are like mariners on the ocean: they may sail on for ever, but the seas they have crossed are no more theirs than those that are still unsailed. But if we hold the fortresses, the enemy will find they are living in a hostile land, while we have halcyon weather. 17. Some of you may dread the thought of garrison duty far from home; if so, dispel your doubts. We Persians, who must, as it is, be exiles for the time, will undertake the positions that are nearest to the foe, while it will be for you to occupy the land on the marches between Assyria and yourselves and put it under tillage. 18. For, if we can hold his inner line, your peace will not be disturbed in the outlying parts: he will scarcely neglect the danger at his door to attack you out in the distance.'

19. At this the whole assembly rose to express their eagerness and assent, and Cyaxares stood up with them. And both Gadatas and Gobryas offered to fortify a post if the allies wished, and thus provide two cities of refuge to start with.

20. Finally Cyrus, thus assured of the general consent to his proposals, said, 'If we really wish to carry out what we have set ourselves, we must prepare battering-rams and siege engines, and get together mechanics and builders for our own castles.' 21. Thereupon Cyaxares at once undertook to provide an engine at his own expense, Gadatas and Gobryas made themselves responsible for a second, Tigranes for a third, and Cyrus himself promised he would try to furnish two. 22. That done, every one set to work to find engineers and artisans and to collect material for the machines; and superintendents were appointed from those best qualified for the work.

23. Now Cyrus was aware that all this would take some time, and therefore he encamped his troops in the

healthiest spot he could find and the easiest to supply, C. 1
strengthening, wherever necessary, the natural defences of
the place, so that the detachment left in charge for the time
should always be in complete security, even though he
might be absent himself with the main body of his force.
24. Nor was this all; he questioned those who knew the
country best, and, learning where he would be rewarded
for his pains, he would lead his men out to forage, and
thus procure as large supplies as possible, keep his soldiers
in the best of health and strength, and fix their drill in their
minds.

25. So Cyrus spent his days, and meanwhile the deserters
from Babylon and the prisoners who were captured all
told the same story: they said that the king had gone off
to Lydia, taking with him store of gold and silver, and
riches and treasures of every kind. 26. The mass of the
soldiers were convinced that he was storing his goods
away from fear, but Cyrus knew that he must have gone
to raise, if possible, an opponent who could face them,
and therefore he pushed his preparations forward vigor-
ously, feeling that another battle must be fought. He filled
up the Persian cavalry to its full complement, getting the
horses partly from the prisoners, partly from his own
friends. There were two gifts he would never refuse, horses
and good weapons. 27. He also procured chariots, taking
them from the enemy or wherever he could find them. The
old Trojan type of charioteering, still in use to this day
among the Cyrenaeans, he abolished; before his time the
Medes, the Syrians, the Arabians, and all Asiatics generally, used their chariots in the same way as the Cyrenaeans
do now. 28. The fault of the system to his mind was that
the very flower of the army, if the picked men were in the
chariots, could only act at long range and so contribute
little after all to the victory. Three hundred chariots meant
twelve hundred horses and three hundred fighting-men,
beside the charioteers, who would naturally be men above
the common, in whom the warriors could place confidence: and that meant another three hundred debarred
from injuring the enemy in any kind of way. 29. Such was
the system he abolished in favour of the war-chariot

C. 1 proper, with strong wheels to resist the shock of collision, and long axles, on the principle that a broad base is the firmer, while the driver's seat was changed into what might be called a turret, stoutly built of timber and reaching up to the elbow, leaving the driver room to manage the horses above the rim. The drivers themselves were all fully armed, only their eyes uncovered. 30. He had iron scythes about two feet long attached to the axles on either side, and others, under the tree, pointing to the ground, for use in a charge. Such was the type of chariot invented by Cyrus, and it is still in use to-day among the subjects of the Great King. Beside the chariots he had a large number of camels, collected from his friends or captured from the enemy. 31. Moreover, he decided to send a spy into Lydia to ascertain the movements of the king, and he thought that the right man for this purpose was Araspas, the officer in charge of the fair lady from Susa. Matters had gone ill with Araspas: he had fallen passionately in love with his prisoner, and been led to entreat her to be his paramour. 32. She had refused, faithful to her husband who was far away, for she loved him dearly, but she forbore to accuse Araspas to Cyrus, being unwilling to set friend at strife with friend. 33. But when at length Araspas, thinking it would help him in his desires, began to threaten her, saying that if she would not yield he would have his will of her by force, then in her dread of violence she could keep the matter hid no longer, and she sent her eunuch to Cyrus with orders to tell him everything. 34. And when Cyrus heard it he smiled over the man who had boasted that he was superior to love, and sent Artabazus back with the eunuch to tell Araspas that he must use no violence against such a woman, but if he could persuade her, he might do so. 35. But Artabazus, when he saw Araspas, rebuked him sternly, saying that the woman was a sacred trust, and his conduct disgraceful, impious, and wicked, till Araspas burst into tears of misery and shame, and was half dead at thought of what Cyrus would do. 36. Learning this, Cyrus sent for him, saw him alone, and said to him face to face:

'Araspas, I know that you are afraid of me and in an agony of shame. Be comforted; we are told that the gods

themselves are made subject to desire, and I could tell you   C. 1
what love has forced some men to undergo, men who
seemed most lofty and most wise. Did I not pass sentence
on myself, when I confessed I was too weak to consort
with loveliness and remain unmoved? Indeed it is I who
am most to blame in the matter, for I shut you up myself
with this irresistible power.'

37. But Araspas broke in on his words:

'Ah, Cyrus, you are ever the same, gentle and com-
passionate to human weaknesses. But all the rest of the
world has no pity on me; they drown me in wretchedness.
As soon as the tattlers got wind of my misfortune, all my
enemies exulted, and my friends came to me, advising me
to make away with myself for fear of you, because my
iniquity was so great.'

38. Then Cyrus said, 'Now listen: this opinion about
you may be the means by which you can do me a great
kindness and your comrades a great service.' 'Oh, that it
were possible,' said Araspas, 'for me ever to be of service
to you!' 39. 'Well,' said the other, 'if you went to the
enemy, feigning that you had fled from me, I think they
would believe you.' 'I am sure they would,' said Araspas,
'I know even my own friends would think that of course I
ran away.' 40. 'Then you will come back to us,' Cyrus
went on, 'with full information about the enemy's affairs;
for, if I am right in my expectation, they will trust you and
let you see all their plans, so that you need miss nothing of
what we wish to know.' 'I will be off this moment,' said
Araspas; 'it will be my best credential to have it thought I
was just in time to escape punishment from you.'

41. 'Then you can really bring yourself to leave the
beautiful Pantheia?'

'Yes, Cyrus,' he answered, 'I can; for I see now that we
have two souls. This is the lesson of philosophy that I have
learnt from the wicked sophist Love. If we had but a single
soul, how could she be at once evil and good? How could
she be enamoured at once of nobleness and baseness, or at
once desire and not desire one deed and the same? No, it
is clear that we have two souls, and when the beautiful
soul prevails, all fair things are wrought, and when the evil

C. 1 soul has the mastery, she lays her hand to shame and wickedness. But to-day my good soul conquers, because she has you to help her.'

42. 'Well,' said Cyrus, 'if you have decided on going, it is thus you had better go. Thus you will win their confidence, and then you must tell them what we are doing, but in such a way as to hinder their own designs. It would hinder them, for example, if you said that we were preparing an attack on their territory at a point not yet decided; for this would check the concentration of their forces, each leader being most concerned for the safety of his own home. 43. Stay with them,' he added, 'till the last moment possible: what they do when they are close at hand is just what is most important for us to know. Advise them how to dispose their forces in the way that really seems the best, for then, after you are gone and although it may be known that you are aware of their order, they will be forced to keep to it, they will not dare to change it, and should they do so at the last moment they will be thrown into confusion.'

44. Thereupon Araspas took his leave, called together his trustiest attendants, said what he thought necessary for the occasion, and departed.

45. Now Pantheia, when she heard that Araspas had fled, sent a messenger to Cyrus, saying:

'Grieve not, Cyrus, that Araspas has gone to join the foe: I will bring you a far trustier friend than he, if you will let me send for my husband, and I know he will bring with him all the power that he has. It is true that the old king was my husband's friend, but he who reigns now tried to tear us two asunder, and my husband knows him for a tyrant and a miscreant, and would gladly be quit of him and take service with such a man as you.'

46. When Cyrus heard that, he bade Pantheia send word to her husband, and she did so. Now when Abradatas saw the tokens from his wife, and learnt how matters stood, he was full of joy, and set out for Cyrus' camp immediately, with a thousand horsemen in his train. And when he came to the Persian outposts he sent to Cyrus saying who he was, and Cyrus gave orders that he should be taken to

Pantheia forthwith. 47. So husband and wife met again C. 1
after hope had well-nigh vanished, and were in each other's
arms once more. And then Pantheia spoke of Cyrus, his
nobleness, his honour, and the compassion he had shown
her, and Abradatas cried:

'Tell me, tell me, how can I repay him all I owe him in
your name and mine!' And she answered:

'So deal with him, my husband, as he has dealt with
you.'

48. Thus Abradatas went to Cyrus, and took him by the
hand, and said:

'Cyrus, in return for the kindness you have shown us, I
can say no more than this: I give myself to you, I will be
your friend, your servant, and your ally: whatever you
desire, I will help you to win, your fellow-worker always,
so far as in me lies.'

49. Then Cyrus answered:

'And I will take your gift: but for the moment you must
leave me, and sup with your wife: another day you will let
me play the host, and give you lodging with your friends
and mine.'

50. Afterwards Abradatas perceived how much Cyrus
had at heart the scythe-bearing chariots and the cavalry
and the war-horses with their armour, and he resolved to
equip a hundred chariots for him out of his own cavalry
force. 51. These he proposed to lead himself in a chariot
of his own, four-poled and drawn by eight horses, all the
eight protected by chest-plates of bronze. 52. So Abradatas
set to work, and this four-poled chariot of his gave Cyrus
the idea of making a car with eight poles, drawn by eight
yoke of oxen, to carry the lowest compartment of the
battering engines, which stood, with its wheels, about
twenty-seven feet from the ground. 53. Cyrus felt that if
he had a series of such towers brought into the field at a
fair pace they would be of immense service to him, and
inflict as much damage on the enemy. The towers were
built with galleries and parapets, and each of them could
carry twenty men. 54. When the whole was put together
he tested it and found that the eight yoke of oxen could
draw the whole tower with the men more easily than one

C. 1 yoke by itself could manage the ordinary weight of baggage, which came to about five-and-twenty talents apiece, whereas the tower, built of planks about as thick as the boards for a stage, weighed less than fifteen for each yoke. 55. Thus, having satisfied himself that the attempt was perfectly possibly, he arranged to take the towers into action, believing that in war selfishness meant salvation, justice, and happiness.

C. 2 About this time ambassadors came to Cyrus from India with gifts of courtesy and a message from their king, saying:

'I send you greeting, Cyrus, and I rejoice that you told me of your needs. I desire to be your friend and I offer you gifts; and if you have need of anything more, I bid you say the word, and it shall be yours. I have told my men to do whatever you command.'

2. Then Cyrus answered:

'This, then, is my bidding: the rest of you shall stay where you have pitched your tents; you shall guard your treasures and live as you choose: but three of you shall go to the enemy and make believe that you have come to him about an alliance with your king, and thus you shall learn how matters stand, and all they say and all they do, and so bring me word again with speed. And if you serve me well in this, I shall owe you even more than I could owe you for these gifts. There are some spies who are no better than slaves, and have no skill to find out anything more than is known already, but there are men of another sort, men of your stamp, who can discover plans that are not yet disclosed.'

3. The Indians listened gladly, and for the moment made themselves at home as the guests of Cyrus: but the next day they got ready and set off on their journey, promising to find out as much as they could of the enemy's secrets and bring him word again with all possible speed.

4. Meanwhile Cyrus continued his preparations for the war on a magnificent scale, like one who meant to accomplish no small achievement. Not only did he carry out all the resolutions of the allies, but he breathed a spirit of emulation into his own friends and followers, till each

strove to outshine his fellows in arms and accoutrements, C. 2
in horsemanship and spearmanship and archery, in endurance of toil and danger. 5. Cyrus would lead them out to
the chase, and show especial honour to those who distinguished themselves in any way: he would whet the
ambition of the officers by praising all who did their best
to improve their men, and by gratifying them in every way
he could. 6. At every sacrifice and festival he instituted
games and contests in all martial exercises, and lavished
prizes on the victors, till the whole army was filled with
enthusiasm and confidence. 7. By this time Cyrus had
almost everything in readiness for the campaign, except
the battering-machines. The Persian cavalry was made up
to its full number of ten thousand men, and the scythed
chariots were complete, a hundred of his own, and a
hundred that Abradatas of Susa had provided. 8. Beside
these there were a hundred of the old Median chariots
which Cyrus had persuaded Cyaxares to remodel on his
own type, giving up the Trojan and Lydian style. The
camels were ready also, each animal carrying a couple of
mounted archers.

The bulk of the great army felt almost as though they
had already conquered, and the enemy's power was held
of no account.

9. While matters were thus, the Indians whom Cyrus
had sent out returned with their report. Croesus had been
chosen leader and general-in-chief; a resolution had been
passed, calling on all the allied kings to bring up their
entire forces, raise enormous sums for the war, and spend
them in hiring mercenaries where they could and making
presents where they must. 10. Large numbers of Thracians,
armed with the short sword, had already been enrolled,
and a body of Egyptians were coming by sea, amounting —
so said the Indians — to 120,000 men, armed with long
shields reaching to their feet, huge spears (such as they
carry to this day), and sabres. Beside these, an army was
expected from Cyprus, and there were already on the spot
all the Cilicians, the men of both the Phrygias, of Lycaonia,
Paphlagonia, and Cappadocia, the Arabians, the Phoeni-
cians, and all the Assyrians under the king of Babylon.

C. 2 Moreover, the Ionians, and Aeolians, and indeed nearly all the Hellenic colonists on the coast were compelled to follow in the train of Croesus. 11. Croesus himself had already sent to Lacedaemon to propose an alliance with the Spartans. The armament was mustering on the banks of the Pactolus, and they were to push forward presently to Thymbrara (the place which is still the mustering-ground for all the Asiatic subjects of the Great King west of Syria), and orders had been issued to open a market there. This report agreed with the accounts given by the prisoners, for Cyrus was always at pains to have men captured from whom he could get some information, and he would also send out spies disguised as runaway slaves.

12. Such were the tidings, and when the army heard the news there was much anxiety and concern, as one may well suppose. The men went about their work with an unusual quietness, their faces clouded over, or gathered in knots and clusters everywhere, anxiously asking each other the news and discussing the report. 13. When Cyrus saw that fear was in the camp, he called a meeting of his generals, and indeed of all whose dejection might injure the cause and whose confidence assist it. Moreover, he sent word that any of the attendants, or any of the rank and file, who wished to hear what he had to say, would be allowed to come and listen. When they met, he spoke as follows:

14. 'My friends and allies, I make no secret of the reason I have called you here. It was because I saw that some of you, when the reports of the enemy reached us, looked like men who were panic-stricken. But I must say I am astonished that any of you should feel alarm because the enemy is mustering his forces, and not be reassured by remembering that our own is far larger than it was when we conquered him before, and far better provided, under heaven, with all we need. 15. I ask you how you would have felt, you who are afraid now, if you had been told that a force exactly like our own was marching upon us, if you had heard that men who had conquered us already were coming now, carrying in their hearts the victory they had won, if you knew that those who made short work

then of all our bows and javelins were advancing again, C. 2 and others with them, ten thousand times as many? 16. Suppose you heard that the very men who had routed our infantry once were coming no now equipt as before, but this time on horseback, scorning arms and javelins, each man armed with one stout spear, ready to charge home? 17. Suppose you heard of chariots, made on a new pattern, not to be kept motionless, standing, as hitherto, with their backs turned to the foe as if for flight, but with the horses shielded by armour, and the drivers sheltered by wooden walls and protected by breastplates and helmets, and the axles fitted with iron scythes so that they can charge straight into the ranks of the foe? 18. And suppose you heard that they have camels to ride on, each one of which would scare a hundred horses, and that they will bring up towers from which to help their own friends, and overwhelm us with volleys of darts so that we cannot fight them on level ground? 19. If this were what you had heard of the enemy, I ask you, once again, you who are now so fearful, what would you have done? You who turn pale when told that Croesus has been chosen commander-in-chief, Croesus who proved himself so much more cowardly than the Syrians, that when they were worsted in battle and fled, instead of helping them, his own allies, he took to his heels himself. 20. We are told, moreover, that the enemy himself does not feel equal to facing you alone, he is hiring others to fight for him better than he could for himself. I can only say, gentlemen, that if any individual considers our position as I describe it alarming or unfavourable, he had better leave us. Let him join our opponents, he will do us far more service there than here.'

21. When Cyrus had ended, Chrysantas the Persian stood up and said:

'Cyrus, you must not wonder if the faces of some were clouded when they heard the news. The cloud was a sign of annoyance, not of fear. Just as if,' he went on, 'a company were expecting breakfast immediately, and then were told there was some business that must be got through first, I do not suppose any of them would be particularly pleased. Here we were, saying to ourselves

C. 2 that our fortunes were made, and now we are informed there is still something to be done, and of course our countenances fell, not because we were afraid, but because we could have wished it all over and done with. 22. However, since it now appears that Syria is not to be the only prize – though there is much to be got in Syria, flocks and herds and corn and palm-trees yielding fruit – but Lydia as well, Lydia, the land of wine and oil and fig-trees, Lydia, to whose shores the sea brings more good things than eyes can feast on, I say that once we realise this we shall mope no longer, our spirits will rise apace, and we shall hasten to lay our hands on the Lydian wealth without delay.'

So he spoke, and the allies were well pleased at his words and gave him loud applause.

23. 'Truly, gentlemen,' said Cyrus, 'as Chrysantas says, I think we ought to march without delay, if only to be beforehand with our foes, and reach their magazines before they do themselves; and besides, the quicker we are, the fewer resources we shall find with them. 24. That is how I put the matter, but if any one sees a safer or an easier way, let him instruct us.'

But many speakers followed, all urging an immediate march, without one speech in opposition, and so Cyrus took up the word again and said:

25. 'My friends and allies, God helping us, our hearts, our bodies, and our weapons have now been long prepared: all that remains is to get together what we need for ourselves and our animals on a march of at least twenty days. I reckon that the journey itself must take more than fifteen, and not a vestige of food shall we find from end to end. It has all been made away with, partly by ourselves, partly by our foes, so far as they could. 26. We must collect enough corn, without which one can neither fight nor live: and as for wine, every man must carry just so much as will accustom him to drink water: the greater part of the country will be absolutely devoid of wine, and the largest supply we could take with us would not hold out. 27. But to avoid too sudden a change and the sickness that might follow, this is what we must do. We must begin

by taking water with our food: we can do this without C. 2
any great change in our habits. 28. For every one who eats
porridge has the oatmeal mixed with water, and every one
who eats bread has the wheat soaked in water, and all
boiled meat is prepared with water. We shall not miss the
wine if we drink a little after the meal is done. 29. Then
we must gradually lessen the amount, until we find that,
without knowing it, we have become water-drinkers.
Gradual change enables every creature to go through a
complete conversion; and this is taught us by God, who
leads us little by little out of winter until we can bear the
blazing heat of summer, and out of heat back again into
the depths of winter. So should we follow God, and take
one step after another until we reach our goal. 30. What
you might spend on heavy rugs and coverlets spend rather
on food: any superfluity there will not be wasted: and you
will not sleep less soundly for lack of bedclothes; if you
do, I give you leave to blame me. But with clothing the
case is different: a man can hardly have too much of that
in sickness or in health. 31. And for seasoning you should
take what is sharp and dry and salted, for such meats are
more appetising and more satisfying. And since we may
come into districts as yet unravaged where we may find
growing corn, we ought to take handmills for grinding:
these are the lightest machines for the purpose. 32. Nor
must we forget to supply ourselves with medicines – they
are small in bulk and, if need arises, invaluable. And we
ought to have a large supply of straps – I wonder what is
not fastened by a strap to man or horse? But straps wear
out and get broken and then things are at a standstill
unless there are spare ones to be had. 33. Some of you
have learnt to shave spears, so that it would be as well not
to forget a plane, and also to carry a rasp, for the man
who sharpens a spearhead will sharpen his spirit too. He
will feel ashamed to whet the edge and be a coward. And
we must take plenty of timber for chariots and waggons;
there is bound to be many a breakdown on the road.
34. Also we shall need the most necessary tools for repairs,
since smiths and carpenters are not to be found at every
turn, but there are few who cannot patch up a makeshift

C. 2 for the time. Then there should be a mattock and a shovel apiece for every waggon, and on every beast of burden a billhook and an axe, always useful to the owner and sometimes a boon to all. 35. The provisions must be seen to by the officers of the fighting-line; they must inspect the men under their command and see that nothing is omitted which any man requires; the omission would be felt by us all. Those of you who are in command of the baggage-train will inspect what I have ordered for the animals and insist upon every man being provided who is not already supplied. 36. You, gentlemen, who are in command of the road-makers, you have the lists of the soldiers I have disqualified from serving as javelin-men, bowmen, or slingers, and you will make the old javelin-men march with axes for felling timber, the bowmen with mattocks, and the slingers with shovels. They will advance by squads in front of the waggons so that if there is any road-making to be done you may set to work at once, and in case of need I may know where to get the men I want. 37. I mean also to take a corps of smiths, carpenters, and cobblers, men of military age, provided with the proper tools, to supply any possible need. These men will not be in the fighting-line, but they will have a place assigned them where they can be hired by any one who likes. 38. If any huckster wishes to follow the army with his wares, he may do so, but if caught selling anything during the fifteen days for which provisions have been ordered, he will be deprived of all his goods : after the fifteen days are done he may sell what he likes. Any merchant who offers us a well-stocked market will receive recompense and honour from the allies and myself. 39. And if any one needs an advance of money for trading, he must send me guarantors who will undertake that he will march with the army, and then he can draw on our funds. These are the general orders : and I will ask any of you who think that anything has been omitted to point it out to me. 40. You will now go back to your quarters and make preparations, and while you do so I will offer sacrifice for our journey and when the signs are favourable we will give the signal. At that you must present yourselves, with everything I have ordered, at the

appointed place, under your own officers. 41. And you, C. 2
gentlemen,' said he, turning to the officers, 'when your
divisions are all in line, you will come to me in a body to
receive your final orders.'

With these instructions the army went to make their C. 3
preparations while Cyrus offered sacrifice.

As soon as the victims were favourable, he set out with
his force.

On the first day they encamped as near by as possible,
so that anything left behind could easily be fetched and
any omission readily supplied. 2. Cyaxares stayed in
Media with a third of the Median troops in order not to
leave their own country undefended. Cyrus himself pushed
forward with all possible speed, keeping his cavalry in the
van and constantly sending explorers and scouts ahead to
some look-out. Behind the cavalry came the baggage, and
on the plains he had long strings of waggons and beasts of
burden, and the main army behind them, so that if any of
the baggage-train fell back, the officers who caught them
up would see that they did not lose their places in the
march. 3. But where the road was narrower the fighting-
men marched on either side with the baggage in the middle,
and in case of any block it was the business of the soldiers
on the spot to attend to the matter. As a rule, the different
regiments would be marching alongside their own baggage, orders having been given that all members of the
train should advance by regiments unless absolutely pre-
vented. 4. To help matters the brigadier's own body-
servant led the way with an ensign known to his men, so
that each regiment marched together, the men doing their
best to keep up with their comrades. Thus there was no
need to search for each other, everything was to hand,
there was greater security, and the soldiers could get what
they wanted more quickly.

5. After some days the scouts ahead thought they could
see people in the plain collecting fodder and timber, and
then they made out beasts of burden, some grazing and
others already laden, and as they scanned the distance they
felt sure they could distinguish something that was either
smoke rising or clouds of dust; and from all this they

C. 3 concluded that the enemy's army was not far off.
6. Whereupon their commander despatched a messenger
with the news to Cyrus, who sent back word that the
scouts should stay where they were, on their look-out, and
tell him if they saw anything more, while he ordered a
squadron of cavalry to ride forward, and intercept, if they
could, some of the men on the plain and so discover the
actual state of affairs. 7. While the detachment carried out
this order Cyrus halted the rest of his army to make such
dispositions as he thought necessary before coming to close
quarters. His first order was for the troops to take their
breakfast: after breakfast they were to fall in and wait for
the word of command. 8. When breakfast was over he
sent for all the officers from the cavalry, the infantry, and
the chariot brigade, and for the commanders of the battering engines and the baggage train, and they came to him.
9. Meanwhile the troop of horse had dashed into the plain,
cut off some of the men, and now brought them in captive.
The prisoners, on being questioned by Cyrus, said they
belonged to the camp and had gone out to forage or cut
wood and so had passed beyond their own pickets, for,
owing to the size of their army, everything was scarce.

10. 'How far is your army from here?' asked Cyrus.
'About seven miles,' said they. 'Was there any talk about
us down there?' said he. 'We should think there was,' they
answered; 'it was all over the camp that you were coming.'
'Ah,' said Cyrus, 'I suppose they were glad to hear we
were coming so soon?' (putting this question for his
officers to hear the answer). 'That they were not,' said the
prisoners, 'they were anything but glad; they were miserable.' 11. 'And what are they doing now?' asked Cyrus.
'Forming their line of battle,' answered they; 'yesterday
and the day before they did the same.'

'And their commander?' said Cyrus, 'who is he?' 'Croesus himself,' said they, 'and with him a Greek, and also
another man, a Mede, who is said to be a deserter from
you.'

'Ah,' cried Cyrus, 'is that so? Most mighty Zeus, may I
deal with him as I wish!'

12. Then he had the prisoners led away and turned to

speak to his officers, but at this moment another scout C. 3 appeared, saying that a large force of cavalry was in the plain. 'We think,' he added, 'that they are trying to get a sight of our army. For about thirty of them are riding ahead at a good round pace and they seem to be coming straight for our little company, perhaps to capture our look-out if they can, for there are only ten of us there.'

13. At that Cyrus sent off a detachment from his own bodyguard, bidding them gallop up to the place, unseen by the enemy, and stay there motionless. 'Wait,' he said, 'until our own ten must leave the spot and then dash out on the thirty as they come up the hill. And to prevent any injury from the larger body, do you, Hystaspas,' said he, turning to the latter, 'ride out with a thousand horse, and let them see you suddenly, face to face. But remember not to pursue them out of sight, come back as soon as you have secured our post. And if any of your opponents ride up with their right hands raised, welcome them as friends.'

14. Accordingly Hystaspas went off and got under arms, while the bodyguard galloped to the spot. But before they reached the scouts, some one met them with his squires, the man who had been sent out as a spy, the guardian of the lady from Susa, Araspas himself. 15. When the news reached Cyrus, he sprang up from his seat, went to meet him himself, and clasped his hand, but the others, who of course knew nothing, were utterly dumbfounded, until Cyrus said:

'Gentlemen, the best of our friends has come back to us. It is high time that all men should know what he has done. It was not through any baseness, or any weakness, or any fear of me, that he left us; it was because I sent him to be my messenger, to learn the enemy's doings and bring us word. 16. Araspas, I have not forgotten what I promised you, I will repay you, we will all repay you. For, gentlemen, it is only just that all of you should pay him honour. Good and true I call him who risked himself for our good, and took upon himself a reproach that was heavy to bear.'

17. At that all crowded round Araspas and took him by the hand and made him welcome. Then Cyrus spoke again:

C. 3　　'Enough, my friends, Araspas has news for us, and it is time to hear it. Tell us your tale, Araspas, keep back nothing of the truth, and do not make out the power of the enemy less than it really is. It is far better that we should find it smaller than we looked for rather than strong beyond our expectations.' 18. 'Well,' began Araspas, 'in order to learn their numbers, I managed to be present at the marshalling of their troops.' 'Then you can tell us,' said Cyrus, 'not only their numbers but their disposition in the field.' 'That I can,' answered Araspas, 'and also how they propose to fight.' 'Good,' said Cyrus, 'but first let us hear their numbers in brief.' 19. 'Well,' he answered, 'they are drawn up thirty deep, infantry and cavalry alike, all except the Egyptians, and they cover about five miles; for I was at great pains,' he added, 'to find out how much ground they occupied.'

20. 'And the Egyptians?' Cyrus asked, 'how are they drawn up? I noticed you said, "all except the Egyptians."'

'The Egyptians,' he answered, 'are drawn up in companies of ten thousand, under their own officers, a hundred deep, and a hundred broad: that, they insisted, was their usual formation at home. Croesus, however, was very loth to let them have their own way in this: he wished to outflank you as much as possible.' 'Why?' Cyrus asked, 'what was his object?' 'To encircle you, I imagine, with his wings.' 'He had better take care,' said Cyrus, 'or his circle may find itself in the centre. 21. But now you have told us what we most needed to know, and you, gentlemen,' said he to the officers, 'on leaving this meeting, you will look to your weapons and your harness. It often happens that the lack of some little thing makes man or horse or chariot useless. Tomorrow morning early, while I am offering sacrifice, do you take your breakfast and give your steeds their provender, so that when the moment comes to strike you may not be found wanting. And then you, Araspas, must hold the right wing in the position it has now, and the rest of you who command a thousand men must do the same with your divisions: it is no time to be changing horses when the race is being run; and you will send word to the brigadiers and captains under you to

draw up the phalanx with each company two deep.' (Now C. 3
a company consisted of four-and-twenty men.)

22. Then one of the officers, a captain of ten thousand,
said:

'Do you think, Cyrus, that with so shallow a depth we
can stand against their tremendous phalanx?'

'But do you suppose,' rejoined he, 'that any phalanx so
deep that the rear-ranks cannot close with the enemy could
do much either for friend or foe? 23. I myself,' he added,
'would rather this heavy infantry of theirs were drawn up,
not a hundred, but ten thousand deep: we should have all
the fewer to fight. Whereas with the depth that I propose,
I believe we shall not waste a man: every part of our army
will work with every other. 24. I will post the javelin-men
behind the cuirassiers, and the archers behind them: it
would be absurd to place in the van troops who admit that
they are not made for hand-to-hand fighting; but with the
cuirassiers thrown in front of them they will stand firm
enough, and harass the enemy over the heads of our own
men with their arrows and their darts. And every stroke
that falls on the enemy means so much relief to our friends.
25. In the very rear of all I will post our reserve. A house
is useless without a foundation as well as a roof, and our
phalanx will be no use unless it has a rear-guard and a
van, and both of them good. 26. You,' he added, 'will
draw up the ranks to suit these orders, and you who
command the targeteers will follow with your companies
in the same depth, and you who command the archers will
follow the targeteers. 27. Gentlemen of the reserve, you
will hold your men in the rear, and pass the word down to
your own subordinates to watch the men in front, cheer
on those who do their duty, threaten him who plays the
coward, and if any man show signs of treachery, see that
he dies the death. It is for those in the van to hearten those
behind them by word and deed: it is for you, the reserve,
to make the cowards dread you more than the foe. 28. You
know your work, and you will do it. Euphratas,' he added,
turning to the officer in command of the artillery, 'see that
the waggons with the towers keep as close to the phalanx
as possible. 29. And you, Daouchus, bring up the whole of

C. 3 your baggage-train under cover of the towers and make your squires punish severely any man who breaks the line. 30. You, Carouchas, keep the women's carriages close behind the baggage-train. This long line of followers should give an impression of vast numbers, allow our own men opportunity for ambuscades, and force the enemy, if he try to surround us, to widen his circuit, and the wider he makes it the weaker he will be. 31. That, then, is your business; and you, gentlemen, Artaozus and Artagersas, each of you take your thousand foot and guard the baggage. 32. And you, Pharnouchus and Asiadatas, neither of you must lead your thousand horse into the fighting-line, you must get them under arms by themselves behind the carriages: and then come to me with the other officers as fully-equipt as if you were to be the first to fight. 33. You, sir, who command the camel-corps will take up your post behind the carriages and look for further orders to Artagersas. 34. Officers of the war-chariots, you will draw lots among yourselves, and he on whom the lot falls will bring his hundred chariots in front of the fighting-line, while the other two centuries will support our flanks on the right and left.'

35. Such were the dispositions made by Cyrus; but Abradatas, the lord of Susa, cried:

'Cyrus, let me, I pray you, volunteer for the post in front.'

36. And Cyrus, struck with admiration for the man, took him by the hand, and turning to the Persians in command of the other centuries said:

'Perhaps, gentlemen, you will allow this?'

But they answered that it was hard to resign the post of honour, and so they all drew lots, and the lot fell on Abradatas, and his post was face to face with the Egyptians. Then the officers left the council and carried out the orders given, and took their evening meal and posted the pickets and went to rest.

C. 4 But early on the morrow Cyrus offered sacrifice, and meanwhile the rest of the army took their breakfast, and after the libation they armed themselves, a great and goodly company in bright tunics and splendid breastplates

and shining helmets. All the horses had frontlets and C. 4
chest-plates, the chargers had armour on their shoulders,
and the chariot-horses on their flanks; so that the whole
army flashed with bronze, and shone like a flower with
scarlet. 2. The eight-horse chariot of Abradatas was a
marvel of beauty and richness; and just as he was about
to put on the linen corslet of his native land, Pantheia
came, bringing him a golden breastplate and a helmet of
gold, and armlets and broad bracelets for his wrists, and a
full flowing purple tunic, and a hyacinth-coloured helmet-
plume. All these she had made for him in secret, taking the
measure of his armour without his knowledge. 3. And
when he saw them, he gazed in wonder and said:

'Dear wife, and did you destroy your own jewels to
make this armour for me?'

But she said, 'No, my lord, at least not the richest of
them all, for you shall be my loveliest jewel, when others
see you as I see you now.'

As she spoke, she put the armour on him, but then,
though she tried to hide it, the tears rolled down her
cheeks.

4. And truly, when Abradatas was arrayed in the new
panoply, he, who had been fair enough to look upon
before, was now a sight of splendour, noble and beautiful
and free, as indeed his nature was. 5. He took the reins
from the charioteer, and was about to set foot on the car,
when Pantheia bade the bystanders withdraw, and said to
him, 'My own lord, little need to tell you what you know
already, yet this I say, if any woman loved her husband
more than her own soul, I am of her company. Why should
I try to speak? Our lives say more than any words of mine.
6. And yet, feeling for you what you know, I swear to you
by the love between us that I would rather go down to the
grave beside you after a hero's death than live on with you
in shame. I have thought you worthy of the highest, and
believed myself worthy to follow you. 7. And I bear in
mind the great gratitude we owe to Cyrus, who, when I
was his captive, chosen for his spoil, was too high-minded
to treat me as a slave, or dishonour me as a free woman;
he took me and saved me for you, as though I had been

C. 4 his brother's wife. 8. And when Araspas, my warder, turned from him, I promised, if he would let me send for you, I would bring him a friend in the other's place, far nobler and more faithful.'

9. And as Pantheia spoke, Abradatas listened with rapture to her words, and when she ended, he laid his hand upon her head, and looking up to heaven he prayed aloud:

'O most mighty Zeus, make me worthy to be Pantheia's husband, and the friend of Cyrus who showed us honour!'

10. Then he opened the driver's seat and mounted the car, and the driver shut the door, and Pantheia could not take him in her arms again, so she bent and kissed the chariot-box. Then the car rolled forward and she followed unseen till Abradatas turned and saw her and cried, 'Be strong, Pantheia, be of a good heart! Farewell, and hie thee home!'

11. Thereupon her chamberlains and her maidens took her and brought her back to her own carriage, and laid her down and drew the awning. But no man, of all who were there that day, splendid as Abradatas was in his chariot, had eyes to look on him until Pantheia had gone.

12. Meanwhile Cyrus had found the victims favourable, and his army was already drawn up in the order he had fixed. He had scouts posted ahead, one behind the other, and then he called his officers together for his final words:

13. 'Gentlemen, my friends and allies, the sacred signs from heaven are as they were the day the gods gave us victory before, and I would call to your minds thoughts to bring you gladness and confidence for the fight. 14. You are far better trained than your enemies, you have lived together and worked together far longer than they, you have won victories together. What they have shared with one another has been defeat, and those who have not fought us yet feel they have traitors to right and left of them, while our recruits know that they enter battle in company with men who help their allies. 15. Those who trust each other will stand firm and fight without flinching, but when confidence has gone no man thinks of anything but flight. 16. Forward then, gentlemen, against the foe; drive our scythed chariots against their defenceless cars, let

our armed cavalry charge their unprotected horse, and C. 4 charge them home. 17. The mass of their infantry you have met before; and as for the Egyptians, they are armed in much the same way as they are marshalled; they carry shields too big to let them stir or see, they are drawn up a hundred deep, which will prevent all but the merest handful fighting. 18. If they count on forcing us back by their weight, they must first withstand our steel and the charge of our cavalry. And if any of them do hold firm, how can they fight at once against cavalry, infantry, and turrets of artillery? For our men on the towers will be there to help us, they will smite the enemy till he flies instead of fighting. 19. If you think there is anything wanting, tell me now; God helping us, we will lack nothing. And if any man wishes to say anything, let him speak now; if not, go to the altar and there pray to the gods to whom we have sacrificed, and then fall in. 20. Let each man say to his own men what I have said to him, let him show the men he rules that he is fit to rule, let them see the fearlessness in his face, his bearing, and his words.'

BOOK VII

C. 1 So they prayed to the gods and went to their places, and the squires brought food and drink to Cyrus and his staff as they stood round the sacrifice. And he took his breakfast where he stood, after making the due offering, sharing what he had with all who needed it, and he poured out the libation and prayed, and then drank, and his men with him.

Then he supplicated Zeus, the god of his fathers, to be his leader and helper in the fight, and so he mounted his horse and bade those about him follow. 2. All his squires were equipped as he was, with scarlet tunics, breastplates of bronze, and brazen helmets plumed with white, short swords, and a lance of cornel-wood apiece. Their horses had frontlets, chest-plates, and armour for their shoulders, all of bronze, and the shoulder-pieces served as leg-guards for the riders. In one thing only the arms of Cyrus differed from the rest; theirs was covered with a golden varnish and his flashed like a mirror. 3. As he sat on his steed, gazing into the distance, where he meant to go, a peal of thunder rang out on the right, and he cried, 'We will follow thee, O Zeus most high!'

So he set forth with Chrysantas on his right at the head of cavalry and Arsamas on the left with infantry. 4. And the word went down the lines, 'Eyes on the standard and steady marching.'

The standard was a golden eagle, with outspread wings, borne aloft on a long spear-shaft, and to this day such is the standard of the Persian king.

Before they came in full sight of the Assyrians Cyrus halted the army thrice. 5. And when they had gone about two miles or more, they began to see the enemy advancing. C. 1 As soon as both armies were in full view of each other, and the Assyrians could see how much they outflanked the Persians on either side, Croesus halted, in order to prepare an encircling movement, and pushed out a column on the right wing and the left, so that the Persian forces might be attacked on every side at once.

6. Cyrus saw it, but gave no sign of stopping; he led straight on as before. Meanwhile he noticed that the turning-point where the Assyrians had pushed out on either flank was at an immense distance from their centre, and he said to Chrysantas:

'Do you see where they have fixed their angle?' 'Yes, I do,' answered Chrysantas, 'and I am surprised at it: it seems to me they are drawing their wings too far away from their centre.' 'Just so,' said Cyrus, 'and from ours too.' 7. 'Why are they doing that?' asked the other. 'Clearly,' said Cyrus, 'they are afraid we shall attack, if their wings are in touch with us while their centre is stil some way off.' 'But,' went on Chrysantas, 'how can they support each other at such a distance?' 'Doubtless,' said Cyrus, 'as soon as their wings are opposite our flanks, they will wheel round, and then advance at once on every side, and so set us fighting everywhere at once.' 8. 'Well,' said Chrysantas, 'do you think the movement wise?' 'Yes,' said Cyrus, 'it is good enough in view of what they can see, but, in view of what they cannot, it is worse for them than if they had advanced in a single column. Do you,' he said, turning to Arsamas, 'advance with your infantry, slowly, taking your pace from me, and do you, Chrysantas, march beside him with your cavalry, step for step. I will make for their angle myself, where I propose to join battle, first riding round the army to see how things are with all our men. 9. When I reach the point, and we are on the verge of action, I will raise the paean and then you must quicken your pace. You will know when we have closed with the enemy, the din will be loud enough. At the same moment Abradatas will dash out upon them: such will be his orders; your duty is to follow, keeping as close to the chariots as possible. Thus we shall fall on the enemy at the

C. 1 height of his confusion. And, God helping me, I shall be
with you also, cutting my way through the rout by the
quickest road I can.'

10. So he spoke, and sent the watchword down the lines,
'Zeus our saviour, and Zeus our leader,' and went forward. As he passed between the chariots and the cuirassiers, he would say to some, 'My men, the look on your
faces rejoices my heart,' and to others, 'You understand,
gentlemen, that this battle is not for the victory of a day,
but for all that we have won ere now, and for all our
happiness to come.' 11. And to others, 'My friends, we
can never reproach the gods again: to-day they have put
all blessings in our hands. 12. Let us show ourselves good
men and true.' Or else, 'Gentlemen, can we invite each
other to a more glorious feast than this? This day all
gallant hearts are bidden; this day they may feast their
friends.' 13. Or again, 'You know, I think, the prizes in
this game: the victors pursue and smite and slay, and win
wealth and fame and freedom and empire: the cowards
lose them all. He who loves his own soul let him fight
beside me: for I will have no disgrace.' 14. But if he met
soldiers who had fought for him before, he only said, 'To
you, gentlemen, what need I say? You know the brave
man's part in battle, and the craven's.' 15. And when he
came to Abradatas, he halted, and Abradatas gave the
reins to his charioteer and came up to him, and others
gathered round from the infantry and the chariots, and
Cyrus said:

'God has rewarded you, Abradatas, according to your
prayer, you and yours. You hold the first rank among our
friends. And you will not forget, when the moment for
action comes, that those who watch you will be Persians,
and those who follow you, and they will not let you bear
the brunt alone.'

16. And Abradatas answered:

'Even so, Cyrus; and with us here, methinks, all looks
well enough: but the state of our flanks troubles me: the
enemy's wings are strong and stretch far: he has chariots
there, and every kind of arm as well, while we have
nothing else with which to oppose him. So that for myself,'

said he, 'if I had not won by lot the post I hold, I should C. 1
feel ashamed to be here in the safest place of all.'

17. 'Nay,' answered Cyrus, 'if it is well with you, have
no concern for the rest. God willing, I mean to relieve our
flanks. But you yourself, I conjure you, do not attack until
you see the rout of those detachments that you fear.'

So much of boasting did Cyrus allow himself on the eve
of action, though he was the last man to boast at other
times.

'When you see them routed,' he said, 'you may take it
that I am there, and then make your rush, for that is the
moment when you will find the enemy weakest and your
own men strongest. 18. And while there is time, Abradatas, be sure to drive along your front and prepare your
men for the charge, kindle their courage by your looks, lift
up their hearts by your hopes. Breathe a spirit of emulation
into them, to make them prove themselves the flower of
the chariot-force. Be assured if things go well with us all
men will say nothing is so profitable as valour.'

19. Accordingly Abradatas mounted his chariot and
drove along the lines to do as Cyrus bade.

Meanwhile Cyrus went on to the left where Hystaspas
was posted with half the Persian cavalry, and he called to
him and said :

'Hystaspas, here is work to test your pace ! If we are
quick enough in cutting off their heads, none of us will be
slaughtered first.'

20. And Hystaspas answered with a laugh :

'Leave it to us ! We'll see to the men opposite. But set
some one to deal with the fellows on our flank : it would
be a pity for them to be idle.'

And Cyrus answered, 'I am going to them myself. But
remember, Hystaspas, to which ever of us God grants the
victory, so long as a single foeman is on the field, attack
we must, again and again, until the last has yielded.'

21. With that he passed on, and as he came to the flank
he went up to the officer in command of the chariots and
said to him :

'Good, I intend to support you myself. And when you
hear me fall on the wing, at that instant do your best to

C. 1 charge straight through your opponents; you will be far
safer once outside their ranks than if you are caught half-
way.'

22. Then he went on to the rear and the carriages, where
the two detachments were stationed, a thousand horse and
a thousand foot, and told Artagersas and Pharnouchus,
their leaders, to keep the men where they were.

'But when,' he added, 'you see me close with the enemy
on our right, then set upon those in front of you; take
them in flank, where they are weakest, while you advance
in line, at your full strength. Their lines, as you see, are
closed by cavalry; hurl your camels at these, and you may
be sure, even before the fighting begins, they will cut a
comic figure.'

23. Thus, with all his dispositions made, Cyrus rode
round the head of his right. By this time Croesus, believing
that the centre, where he himself was marching, must be
nearer the enemy than the distant wings, had the signal
raised for them to stop their advance, halt, and wheel
round where they were. When they were in position
opposite the Persian force, he signalled for them to charge,
and thus three columns came against Cyrus, one facing his
front and one on either flank. 24. A tremor ran through
the whole army; it was completely enclosed, like a little
brick laid within a large, with the forces of the enemy all
round it, on every side except the rear, cavalry and heavy
infantry, targeteers, archers, and chariots. 25. None the
less, the instant Cyrus gave the word they swung round to
confront the foe. There was deep silence through the ranks
as they realised what they had to face, and then Cyrus,
when the moment came, began the battle-hymn and it
thundered through the host. 26. And as it died away the
war-cry rang out unto the God of Battles, and Cyrus
swooped forward at the head of his cavalry, straight for
the enemy's flank, and closed with them then and there,
while the infantry behind him followed, swift and steady,
wave on wave, sweeping out on either side, far out-
flanking their opponents, for they attacked in line and the
foe were in column, to the great gain of Cyrus. A short
struggle, and the ranks broke and fled before him head-

long. 27. Artagersas, seeing that Cyrus had got to work, C. 1 made his own charge on the left, hurling his camels forward as Cyrus had advised. Even at a distance the horses could not face the camels: they seemed to go mad with fear, and galloped off in terror, rearing and falling foul of one another: such is the strange effect of camels upon horses. 28. So that Artagersas, his own troops well in hand, had easy work with the enemy's bewildered masses. At the same moment the war-chariots dashed in, right and left, so that many, flying from the chariots, were cut down by the troopers, and many, flying from these, were caught by the chariots. 29. And now Abradatas could wait no longer. 'Follow me, my friends,' he shouted, and drove straight at the enemy, lashing his good steeds forward till their flanks were bloody with the goad, the other charioteers racing hard behind him. The enemy's chariots fled before them instantly, some not even waiting to take up their fighting-men. 30. But Abradatas drove on through them, straight into the main body of the Egyptians, his rush shared by his comrades on either hand. And then, what has often been shown elsewhere was shown here, namely, that of all strong formations the strongest is a band of friends. His brothers-in-arms and his mess-mates charged with him, but the others, when they saw that the solid ranks of the Egyptians stood firm, swung round and pursued the flying chariots. 31. Meanwhile Abradatas and his companions could make no further way: there was not a gap through the Egyptian lines on either hand, and they could but charge the single soldiers where they stood, overthrow them by the sheer weight of horse and car, and crush them and their arms beneath the hoofs and wheels. And where the scythes caught them, men and weapons were cut to shreds. 32. In the midst of indescribable confusion, the chariots rocking among the weltering mounds, Abradatas was thrown out and some of his comrades with him. There they stood, and fought like men, and there they were cut down and died. The Persians, pouring in after them, dealt slaughter and destruction where Abradatas and his men had charged and shaken the ranks, but elsewhere the Egyptians, who were still

C. 1 unscathed, and they were many, moved steadily on to meet them.

33. There followed a desperate struggle with lance and spear and sword, and still the Egyptians had the advantage, because of their numbers and their weapons. Their spears were immensely stout and long, such as they carry to this day, and the huge shield not only gave more protection than corslet and buckler, but aided the thrust of the fighter, slung as it was from the shoulder.

34. Shield locked into shield, they thrust their way forward : and the Persians could not drive them back, with their light bucklers borne on the forearm only. Step by step they gave ground, dealing blow for blow, till they came under cover of their own artillery. Then at last a second shower of blows fell on the Egyptians, while the reserves would allow no flight of the archers or the javelin-men : at the sword's point they made them do their duty.

35. Thick was the slaughter, and loud the din of clashing weapons and whirring darts, and shouting warriors, cheering each other and calling on the gods.

36. At this moment Cyrus appeared, cutting his way through his own opponents. To see the Persians thrust from their position was misery to him, but he knew he could check the enemy's advance most quickly by galloping round to their rear, and thither he dashed, bidding his troops follow, and there they fell on them and smote them as they were gazing ahead, and there they mowed them down.

37. The Egyptians, seeing what had happened, cried out that the enemy had taken them in the rear, and wheeled round under a storm of blows. At this the confusion reached its height, cavalry and infantry struggling all together. An Egyptian fell under Cyrus' horse, and as the hoofs struck him he stabbed the creature in the belly. The charger reared at the blow and Cyrus was thrown.

38. Then was seen what it is for a leader to be loved by his men. With a terrible cry the men dashed forward, conquering thrust with thrust and blow with blow. One of his squires leapt down and set Cyrus on his own charger.

39. And as Cyrus sprang on the horse he saw the Egyptians

worsted everywhere. For by now Hystaspas was on the C. 1
ground with his cavalry, and Chrysantas also. Still Cyrus
would not allow them to charge the Egyptian phalanx:
the archers and javelin-men were to play on them from
outside. Then he made his way along the lines to the
artillery, and there he mounted one of the towers to take a
survey of the field, and see if any of the foe still held their
ground and kept up the fight. 40. But he saw the plain one
chaos of flying horses and men and chariots, pursuers and
pursued, conquerors and conquered, and nowhere any
who still stood firm, save only the Egyptians. These, in
sore straits as they were, formed themselves into a circle
behind a ring of steel, and sat down under cover of their
enormous shields. They no longer attempted to act, but
they suffered, and suffered heavily. 41. Cyrus, in admiration and pity, unwilling that men so brave should be done
to death, drew off his soldiers who were fighting round
them, and would not let another man lift sword.

Then he sent them a herald asking if they wished to be
cut to pieces for the sake of those who had betrayed them,
or save their lives and keep their reputation for gallantry?
And they answered, 'Is it possible that we can be saved
and yet keep our reputation untarnished?' 42. And Cyrus
said, 'Surely yes, for we ourselves have seen that you alone
have held your ground and been ready to fight.' 'But even
so,' said the Egyptians, 'how can we act in honour if we
save ourselves?'

'By betraying none of those at whose side you fought,'
answered Cyrus: 'only surrender your arms to us, and
become our friends, the friends of men who chose to save
you when they might have destroyed you.' 43. 'And if we
become your friends,' said they, 'how will you treat us?'
'As you treat us,' answered he, 'and the treatment shall be
good.'

'And what will that good treatment be?' they asked
once more. 'This,' said Cyrus: 'better pay than you have
had, so long as the war lasts, and when peace comes, if
you choose to stay with me, lands and cities and women
and servants.' 44. Then they asked him if he would excuse
them from one duty, service against Croesus. Croesus,

C. 1 they said, was the only leader who knew them; for the
rest, they were content to agree. And so they came to
terms, and took and gave pledges of good faith. 45. Thus
it came about that their descendants are to this day faithful
subjects of the king, and Cyrus gave them cities, some in
the interior, which are still called the cities of the Egyptians, beside Larissa and Kyllene and Kyme on the coast,
still held by their descendants.

When this matter was arranged darkness had already
fallen, and Cyrus drew off his army and encamped at
Thymbrara.

46. In this engagement the Egyptians alone among the
enemy won themselves renown, and of the troops under
Cyrus the Persian cavalry was held to have done the best,
so much so that to this day they are still armed in the
manner that Cyrus devised. 47. High praise also was given
to the scythe-bearing chariots, and this engine of war is
still employed by the reigning king. 48. As for the camels,
all they did was to scare the horses; their riders could take
no part in the slaughter, and were never touched themselves by the enemy's cavalry. For not a horse would come
near the camels. 49. It was a useful arm, certainly, but no
gallant gentleman would dream of breeding camels for his
own use or learning to fight on camel-back. And so they
returned to their old position among the baggage-train.

C. 2 Then Cyrus and his men took their evening meal and
posted their pickets and went to rest. But Croesus and his
army fled in haste to Sardis, and the other tribes hurried
away homewards under cover of night as fast and as far as
they could. 2. When day broke Cyrus marched straight for
Sardis, and when he came before the citadel he set up his
engines as though for the assault and got out his ladders.
3. But the following night he sent a scaling party of
Persians and Chaldaeans to climb the fortifications at the
steepest point. The guide was a Persian who had served as
a slave to one of the garrison in the citadel, and who knew
a way down to the river by which one could get up. 4. As
soon as it became clear that the heights had been taken, all
the Lydians without exception fled from the walls and hid
wherever they could. At daybreak Cyrus entered the city

and gave orders that not a man was to leave the ranks. C. 2
5. Croesus, who had shut himself up inside his palace,
cried out on Cyrus, and Cyrus left a guard round the
building while he himself went to inspect the captured
citadel. Here he found the Persians keeping guard in
perfect order, but the Chaldaean quarters were deserted,
for the men had rushed down to pillage the town. Instantly
he summoned their officers, and bade them leave his army
at once. 6. 'I could never endure,' he said, 'to have
undisciplined fellows seizing the best of everything. You
knew well enough,' he added, 'all that was in store for
you. I meant to make all who served with me the envy of
their fellows; but now,' he said, 'you cannot be surprised
if you encounter some one stronger than yourselves on
your way home.'

7. Fear fell on the Chaldaeans at this, and they entreated
him to lay aside his anger and vowed they would give back
all the booty they had taken. He answered that he had no
need of it himself. 'But if,' he added, 'you wish to appease
me, you will hand it over to those who stayed and guarded
the citadel. For if my soldiers see that discipline means
reward, all will be well with us.'

8. So the Chaldaeans did as he bade them, and the
faithful and obedient received all manner of good things.

Then Cyrus made his troops encamp in the most convenient quarter of the town, and told them to stay at their
posts and take their breakfast there. 9. That done, he gave
orders that Croesus should be brought to him, and when
he came into his presence, Croesus cried:

'Hail, Cyrus, my lord and master! Fate has given you
that title from now henceforward, and thus must I salute
you.'

10. 'All hail to you likewise,' answered Cyrus: 'we are
both of us men. And tell me now,' he continued, 'would
you be willing to advise me as a friend?' 'I should be more
than glad,' said Croesus, 'to do you any good. It would
mean good for myself, I know.' 11. 'Listen, then,'
answered Cyrus: 'I see that my soldiers have endured
much toil and encountered many dangers, and now they
are persuaded that they have taken the wealthiest city in

C. 2 all Asia, after Babylon. I would not have them cheated of their recompense, seeing that if they win nothing by their labour, I know not how I can keep them obedient to me for long. Yet I am unwilling to give them this city over to plunder. I believe it would be utterly destroyed, and moreover I know full well that in plunder the worst villains win the most.'

12. To this Croesus answered, 'Suffer me then to tell what Lydians I please that I have won your promise that the city shall not be sacked, nor their women and children made away with. 13. I promise you in return that my men will bring you willingly everything that is costly and beautiful in Sardis. If I can announce such terms, I am certain there is not one treasure belonging to man or woman that will not be yours to-morrow. Further, on this day year, the city will overflow once more with wealth and beauty. But if you sack it, you will destroy the crafts in its ruin, and they, we know, are the well-springs of all loveliness. 14. Howbeit, you need not decide at once, wait and see what is brought to you. Send first,' he added, 'to my own treasuries, and let your guards take some of my own men with them.'

To all this Cyrus consented, and then he said:

15. 'And now, O Croesus, tell me one thing more. How did matters go between you and the oracle at Delphi? It is said that you did much reverence to Apollo and obeyed him in all things.'

16. 'I could wish it had been so,' said Croesus, 'but, truth to say, from the beginning I have acted in all things against him.' 'How can that be?' said Cyrus. 'Explain it to me: for your words seem strange indeed.' 17. 'Because,' he answered, 'in the first place, instead of asking the god for all I wanted I must needs put him to the test, to see if he could speak the truth. This,' he added, 'no man of honour could endure, let be the godhead. Those who are doubted cannot love their doubters. 18. And yet he stood the test; for though the things I did were strange, and I was many leagues from Delphi, he knew them all. And so I resolved to consult him about children. 19. At first he would not so much as answer me, but I sent him many an

offering, some of gold and some of silver, and I propitiated C. 2
him, as I deemed, by countless sacrifices, and at last he
answered me when I asked him what I must do that sons
might be born to me. He said they should be born. 20. And
so they were; in that he uttered no lie, but they brought
me no joy. One of them was dumb his whole life long, and
the noblest perished in the flower of his youth. And I,
crushed by these sorrows, sent again to the god and asked
him how I could live in happiness for the rest of my days,
and he answered :

'Know thyself, O Croesus, and happiness shall be thine.'

And when I heard the oracle, I was comforted. 21. I said
to myself, the god has laid the lightest of tasks upon me,
and promised me happiness in return. Some of his neighbours a man may know and others not: but every one can
know himself. 22. So I thought, and in truth so long as I
was at peace I had no fault to find with my lot after my
son's death ; but when the Assyrian persuaded me to march
against you I encountered every danger. Yet I was saved, I
came to no harm. Once again, therefore, I have no charge
to bring against the god : when I *knew myself* incapable of
warring against you, he came to my help and saved mine
and me. 23. But afterwards, intoxicated by my wealth,
cajoled by those who begged me to be their leader, tempted
by the gifts they showered on me, flattered by all who said
that if I would but lead them they would obey me to a
man, and that I would be the greatest ruler in all the
world, and that all their kings had met together and chosen
me for their champion in the war, I undertook the generalship as though I were born to be the monarch of the
world, for I did not *know myself*. 24. I thought myself able
to fight against you, you who are sprung from the seed of
the gods, born of a royal line, trained in valour and virtue
from your youth, while I – I believe that the first of my
ancestors to reign won his freedom and his crown on the
self-same day. For this dull ignorance of mine I see I am
justly punished. 25. But now at last, O Cyrus,' he cried,
'now I *know myself*. And tell me, do you think the god
will still speak truth ? Do you think that, knowing myself,

C. 2   I can be happy now? I ask you, because you of all men have it in your power to answer best. Happiness is yours to give.'

26. Cyrus answered, 'Give me time to deliberate, Croesus. I bear in mind your former happiness and I pity you. I give you back at once your wife and your daughters (for they tell me you have daughters), and your friends and your attendants; they are yours once more. And yours it is to sit at your own table as you used to live. But battles and wars I must put out of your power.'

27. 'Now by the gods above us,' cried Croesus, 'you need take no further thought about your answer: if you will do for me what you say, I shall live the life that all men called the happiest of lives, and I knew that they were right.' 28. 'And who,' said Cyrus, 'who was it that lived that life of happiness?' 'My own wife,' said Croesus; 'she shared all my good things with me, my luxuries, my softest joys; but in the cares on which those joys were based, in war and battle and strife, she had no part or lot. Methinks, you will provide for me as I provided for her whom I loved beyond all others in the world, and I must needs send to Apollo again, and send thank-offerings.'

29. And as Cyrus listened he marvelled at the man's contentedness of soul, and for the future wherever he went he took Croesus with him, either because he thought he might be useful or perhaps because he felt it was safer so.

C. 3   So for that night they rested. But the next day Cyrus called his friends and his generals together and told some to make an inventory of the treasures and others to receive all the wealth that Croesus brought in. First they were to set aside for the gods all that the Persian priests thought fit, and then store the rest in coffers, weigh them, and pack them on waggons, distributing the waggons by lot to take with them on the march, so that they could receive their proper share at any convenient time. 2. So they set about the work.

Then Cyrus called some of his squires and said:

'Tell me, have any of you seen Abradatas? I wonder that he who used to come to me so often is nowhere to be found.'

3. Then one of the squires made answer, 'My lord, he is C. 3 dead: he fell in the battle, charging straight into the Egyptian ranks: the rest, all but his own companions, swerved before their close array. 4. And now,' he added, 'we hear that his wife has found his body and laid it in her own car, and has brought it here to the banks of the Pactolus. 5. Her chamberlains and her attendants are digging a grave for the dead man upon a hill, and she, they say, has put her fairest raiment on him and her jewels, and she is seated on the ground with his head upon her knees.'

6. Then Cyrus smote his hand upon his thigh and leapt up and sprang to horse, galloping to the place of sorrow, with a thousand troopers at his back. 7. He bade Gadatas and Gobryas take what jewels they could find to honour the dear friend and brave warrior who had fallen, and follow with all speed: and he bade the keepers of the herds, the cattle, and the horses drive up their flocks wherever they heard he was, that he might sacrifice on the grave.

8. But when he saw Pantheia seated on the ground and the dead man lying there, the tears ran down his cheeks and he cried:

'O noble and loyal spirit, have you gone from us?'

Then he took the dead man by the hand, but the hand came away with his own: it had been hacked by an Egyptian blade. 9. And when he saw that, his sorrow grew, and Pantheia sobbed aloud and took the hand from Cyrus and kissed it and laid it in its place, as best she could, and said:

10. 'It is all like that, Cyrus. But why should you see it?' And presently she said, 'All this, I know, he suffered for my sake, and for yours too, Cyrus, perhaps as much. I was a fool: I urged him so to bear himself as became a faithful friend of yours, and he, I know, he never thought once of his own safety, but only of what he might do to show his gratitude. Now he has fallen, without a stain upon his valour: and I, who urged him, I live on to sit beside his grave.'

11. And Cyrus wept silently for a while, and then he said:

C. 3   'Lady, his end was the noblest and the fairest that could
be: he died in the hour of victory. Take these gifts that I
have brought and adorn him.'

For now Gobryas and Gadatas appeared with store of
jewels and rich apparel. 'He shall not lack for honour,'
Cyrus said; 'many hands will raise his monument: it shall
be a royal one; and we will offer such sacrifice as befits a
hero. 12. And you, lady,' he added, 'you shall not be left
desolate. I reverence your chastity and your nobleness, and
I will give you a guardian to lead you whithersoever you
choose, if you will but tell me to whom you wish to go.'

13. And Pantheia answered:

'Be at rest, Cyrus, I will not hide from you to whom I
long to go.'

14. Therewith Cyrus took his leave of her and went,
pitying from his heart the woman who had lost so brave a
husband, and the dead man in his grave, taken from so
sweet a wife, never to see her more. Then Pantheia bade
her chamberlains stand aside 'until,' she said, 'I have wept
over him as I would.' But she made her nurse stay with her
and she said:

'Nurse, when I am dead, cover us with the same cloak.'
And the nurse entreated and besought her, but she could
not move her, and when she saw that she did but vex her
mistress, she sat down and wept in silence. Then Pantheia
took the scimitar, that had been ready for her so long, and
drew it across her throat, and dropped her head upon her
husband's breast and died. And the nurse cried bitterly,
but she covered the two with one cloak as her mistress had
bidden her.

15. And when Cyrus heard what Pantheia had done he
rushed out in horror to see if he could save her. And when
the three chamberlains saw what had happened they drew
their own scimitars and killed themselves, there where she
had bidden them stand. 16, 17. And when Cyrus came to
that place of sorrow, he looked with wonder and reverence
on the woman, and wept for her and went his way and
saw that all due honour was paid to those who lay there
dead, and a mighty sepulchre was raised above them,

mightier, men say, than had been seen in all the world C. 3
before.

After this the Carians, who were always at war and C. 4
strife with one another, because their dwellings were
fortified, sent to Cyrus and asked for aid. Cyrus himself
was unwilling to leave Sardis, where he was having engines
of artillery made and battering-rams to overthrow the
walls of those who would not listen to him. But he sent
Adousius, a Persian, in his place, a man of sound judgment
and a stout soldier and withal a person of winning
presence. He gave him an army; and the Cilicians and
Cypriotes were very ready to serve under him. 2. That was
why Cyrus never sent a Persian satrap to govern either
Cilicia or Cyprus; he was always satisfied with the native
kings: only he exacted tribute and levied troops whenever
he needed them.

3. So Adousius took his army and marched into Caria,
where he was met by the men of both parties, ready to
receive him inside their walls to the detriment of their
opponents. Adousius treated each in exactly the same way,
he told whichever side was pleading that he thought their
case was just, but it was essential that the others should
not realise he was their friend, 'for thus, you perceive, I
shall take them unprepared whenever I attack.'

He insisted they should give him pledges of good faith,
and the Carians had to swear they would receive him
without fraud or guile within their walls and for the
welfare of Cyrus and the Persians; and on his side he was
willing to swear that he would enter without fraud or guile
himself and for the welfare of those who received him.
4. Having imposed these terms on either party without the
knowledge of the other, he fixed on the same night with
both, entered the walls, and had the strongholds of both
parties in his hands. At break of day he took his place in
the midst with his army, and sent for the leading men on
either side. Thus confronted with each other they were
more than a little vexed, and both imagined they had been
cheated. 5. However, Adousius began:

'Gentlemen, I took an oath to you that I would enter
your walls without fraud or guile and for the welfare of

C. 4 those who received me. Now if I am forced to destroy
either of you, I am persuaded I shall have entered to the
detriment of the Carians. But if I give you peace, so that
you can till your lands in safety, I imagine I shall have
come for your welfare. Therefore from this day forwards
you must meet on friendly terms, cultivate your fields
without fear, give your children to each other, and if any
one offends against these laws, Cyrus and ourselves will
be his enemies.'

6. At that the city gates were flung open, the roads were
filled with folk hurrying to one another, the fields were
thronged with labourers. They held high festival together,
and the land was full of peace and joyfulness.

7. Meanwhile messengers came from Cyrus inquiring
whether there was need for more troops or siege-engines,
but Adousius answered, on the contrary his present force
was at Cyrus' service to employ elsewhere if he wished,
and so drew off his army, only leaving a garrison in the
citadels. Thereupon the Carians implored him to remain,
and when he would not, they sent to Cyrus begging him to
make Adousius their satrap.

8. Meanwhile Cyrus had sent Hystaspas with an army
into Phrygia on the Hellespont, and when Adousius came
back he bade him follow, for the Phrygians would be more
ready to obey Hystaspas if they heard that another army
was advancing.

9. Now the Hellenes on the seaboard offered many gifts
and bargained not to receive the Asiatics within their
walls, but only to pay tribute and serve wherever Cyrus
commanded. 10. But the king of Phrygia made preparations to hold his fortresses and not yield, and sent out
orders to that effect. However, when his lieutenants
deserted him and he found himself all alone, he had to put
himself in the hands of Hystaspas, and leave his fate to the
judgment of Cyrus. Then Hystaspas stationed strong Persian garrisons in all the citadels, and departed, taking with
him not only his own troops but many mounted men and
targeteers from Phrygia. 11. And Cyrus sent word to
Adousius to join Hystaspas, put himself at the head of
those who had submitted and allow them to retain their

arms, while those who showed a disposition to resist were C. 4
to be deprived of their horses and their weapons and made
to follow the army as slingers.

12. While his lieutenants were thus employed, Cyrus set
out from Sardis, leaving a large force of infantry to
garrison the place, and taking Croesus with him, and a
long train of waggons laden with riches of every kind.
Croesus presented an accurate inventory of everything in
each waggon, and said, as he delivered the scrolls:

'With these in your possession, Cyrus, you can tell
whether your officers are handing over their freights in full
or not.'

13. And Cyrus answered:

'It was kindly done, Croesus, on your part, to take
thought for this: but I have arranged that the freights
should be in charge of those who are entitled to them, so
that if the men steal, they steal their own property.'

With these words he handed the documents to his
friends and officers to serve as checks on their own
stewards.

14. Cyrus also took Lydians in his train; allowing some
to carry arms, those, namely, who were at pains to keep
their weapons in good order, and their horses and chariots,
and who did their best to please him, but if they gave
themselves ungracious airs, he took away their horses and
bestowed them on the Persians who had served him from
the beginning of the campaign, burnt their weapons, and
forced them to follow the army as slingers. 15. Indeed, as
a rule, he compelled all the subject population who had
been disarmed to practise the use of the sling: it was, he
considered, a weapon for slaves. No doubt there are
occasions when a body of slingers, working with other
detachments, can do excellent service, but, taken alone,
not all the slingers in the world could face a mere handful
armed with steel.

16. Cyrus was marching to Babylon, but on his way he
subdued the Phrygians of Greater Phrygia and the Cappadocians, and reduced the Arabians to subjection. These
successes enabled him to increase his Persian cavalry till it

C. 4 was not far short of forty thousand men, and he had still horses left over to distribute among his allies at large.

At length he came before Babylon with an immense body of cavalry, archers, and javelin-men, beside slingers innumerable.

C. 5 When Cyrus reached the city he surrounded it entirely with his forces, and then rode round the walls himself, attended by his friends and the leading officers of the allies. 2. Having surveyed the fortifications, he prepared to lead off his troops, and at that moment a deserter came to inform him that the Assyrians intended to attack as soon as he began to withdraw, for they had inspected his forces from the walls and considered them very weak. This was not surprising, for the circuit of the city was so enormous that it was impossible to surround it without seriously thinning the lines. 3. When Cyrus heard of their intention, he took up his post in the centre of his troops with his own staff round him and sent orders to the infantry for the wings to double back on either side, marching past the stationary centre of the line, until they met in the rear exactly opposite himself. 4. Thus the men in front were immediately encouraged by the doubling of their depth, and those who retired were equally cheered, for they saw that the others would encounter the enemy first. The two wings being united, the power of the whole force was strengthened, those behind being protected by those in front and those in front supported by those behind. 5. When the phalanx was thus folded back on itself, both the front and the rear ranks were formed of picked men, a disposition that seemed calculated to encourage valour and check flight. On the flanks, the cavalry and the light infantry were drawn nearer and nearer to the commander as the line contracted. 6. When the whole phalanx was in close order, they fell back from the walls, slowly, facing the foe, until they were out of range; then they turned, marched a few paces, and then wheeled round again to the left, and halted, facing the walls, but the further they got the less often they paused, until, feeling themselves secure, they quickened their pace and went off in an uninterrupted march until they reached their quarters.

7. When they were encamped, Cyrus called a council of C. 5
his officers and said, 'My friends and allies, we have
surveyed the city on every side, and for my part I fail to
see any possibility of taking by assault walls so lofty and
so strong: on the other hand, the greater the population
the more quickly must they yield to hunger, unless they
come out to fight. If none of you have any other scheme to
suggest, I propose that we reduce them by blockade.'

8. Then Chrysantas spoke:

'Does not the river flow through the middle of the city,
and is it not at least a quarter of a mile in width?'

'To be sure it is,' answered Gobryas, 'and so deep that
the water would cover two men, one standing on the
other's shoulders; in fact the city is even better protected
by its river than by its walls.'

9. At which Cyrus said, 'Well, Chrysantas, we must
forego what is beyond our power: but let us measure off
at once the work for each of us, set to, and dig a trench as
wide and as deep as we can, that we may need as few
guards as possible.'

10. Thereupon Cyrus took his measurements all round
the city, and, leaving a space on either bank of the river
large enough for a lofty tower, he had a gigantic trench
dug from end to end of the wall, his men heaping up the
earth on their own side. 11. Then he set to work to build
his towers by the river. The foundations were of palm-
trees, a hundred feet long and more – the palm-tree grows
to a greater height than that, and under pressure it will
curve upwards like the spine of an ass beneath a load.
12. He laid these foundations in order to give the
impression that he meant to besiege the town, and was
taking precautions so that the river, even if it found its
way into his trench, should not carry off his towers. Then
he had other towers built along the mound, so as to have
as many guard-posts as possible. 13. Thus his army was
employed, but the men within the walls laughed at his
preparations, knowing they had supplies to last them more
than twenty years. When Cyrus heard that, he divided his
army into twelve, each division to keep guard for one
month in the year. 14. At this the Babylonians laughed

C. 5 louder still, greatly pleased at the idea of being guarded by
Phrygians and Lydians and Arabians and Cappadocians,
all of whom, they thought, would be more friendly to
themselves than to the Persians.

15. However by this time the trenches were dug. And
Cyrus heard that it was a time of high festival in Babylon
when the citizens drink and make merry the whole night
long. As soon as the darkness fell, he set his men to work.
16. The mouths of the trenches were opened, and during
the night the water poured in, so that the river-bed formed
a highway into the heart of the town.

17. When the great stream had taken to its new channel,
Cyrus ordered his Persian officers to bring up their thousands, horse and foot alike, each detachment drawn up
two deep, the allies to follow in their old order. 18. They
lined up immediately, and Cyrus made his own bodyguard
descend into the dry channel first, to see if the bottom was
firm enough for marching. 19. When they said it was, he
called a council of all his generals and spoke as follows:

20. 'My friends, the river has stepped aside for us; he
offers us a passage by his own high-road into Babylon. We
must take heart and enter fearlessly, remembering that
those against whom we are to march this night are the
very men we have conquered before, and that too when
they had their allies to help them, when they were awake,
alert, and sober, armed to the teeth, and in their battle
order. 21. To-night we go against them when some are
asleep and some are drunk, and all are unprepared: and
when they learn that we are within the walls, sheer
astonishment will make them still more helpless than
before. 22. If any of you are troubled by the thought of
volleys from the roofs when the army enters the city, I bid
you lay these fears aside: if our enemies do climb their
roofs we have a god to help us, the god of Fire. Their
porches are easily set aflame, for the doors are made of
palm-wood and varnished with bitumen, the very food of
fire. 23. And we shall come with the pine-torch to kindle
it, and with pitch and tow to feed it. They will be forced
to flee from their homes or be burnt to death. 24. Come,
take your swords in your hand: God helping me, I will

lead you on. Do you,' he said, turning to Gadatas and C. 5
Gobryas, 'show us the streets, you know them ; and once
we are inside, lead us straight to the palace.'

25. 'So we will,' said Gobryas and his men, 'and it
would not surprise us to find the palace-gates unbarred,
for this night the whole city is given over to revelry. Still,
we are sure to find a guard, for one is always stationed
there.'

'Then,' said Cyrus, 'there is no time for lingering ; we
must be off at once and take them unprepared.'

26. Thereupon they entered : and of those they met some
were struck down and slain, and others fled into their
houses, and some raised the hue and cry, but Gobryas and
his friends covered the cry with their shouts, as though
they were revellers themselves. And thus, making their
way by the quickest route, they soon found themselves
before the king's palace. 27. Here the detachment under
Gobryas and Gadatas found the gates closed, but the men
appointed to attack the guards rushed on them as they lay
drinking round a blazing fire, and closed with them then
and there. 28. As the din grew louder and louder, those
within became aware of the tumult, till, the king bidding
them see what it meant, some of them opened the gates
and ran out. 29. Gadatas and his men, seeing the gates
swing wide, darted in, hard on the heels of the others who
fled back again, and they chased them at the sword's point
into the presence of the king.

30. They found him on his feet, with his drawn scimitar
in his hand. By sheer weight of numbers they overpowered
him : and not one of his retinue escaped, they were all cut
down, some flying, others snatching up anything to serve
as a shield and defending themselves as best they could.
31. Cyrus sent squadrons of cavalry down the different
roads with orders to kill all they found in the street, while
those who knew Assyrian were to warn the inhabitants to
stay indoors under pain of death. 32. While they carried
out these orders, Gobryas and Gadatas returned, and first
they gave thanks to the gods and did obeisance because
they had been suffered to take vengeance on their unrighteous king, and then they fell to kissing the hands and feet

C. 5 of Cyrus, shedding tears of joy and gratitude. 33. And when it was day and those who held the heights knew that the city was taken and the king slain, they were persuaded to surrender the citadel themselves. 34. Cyrus took it over forthwith, and sent in a commandant and a garrison, while he delivered the bodies of the fallen to their kinsfolk for burial, and bade his heralds make proclamation that all the citizens must deliver up their arms : wherever weapons were discovered in any house all the inmates would be put to death. So the arms were surrendered, and Cyrus had them placed in the citadel for use in case of need. 35. When all was done he summoned the Persian priests and told them the city was the captive of his spear and bade them set aside the first-fruits of the booty as an offering to the gods and mark out land for sacred demesnes. Then he distributed the houses and the public buildings to those whom he counted his partners in the exploit; and the distribution was on the principle accepted, the best prizes to the bravest men: and if any thought they had not received their deserts they were invited to come and tell him. 36. At the same time he issued a proclamation to the Babylonians, bidding them till the soil and pay the dues and render willing service to those under whose rule they were placed. As for his partners the Persians, and such of his allies as elected to remain with him, he gave them to understand they were to treat as subjects the captives they received.

37. After this Cyrus felt that the time was come to assume the style and manner that became a king: and he wished this to be done with the goodwill and concurrence of his friends and in such a way that, without seeming ungracious, he might appear but seldom in public and always with a certain majesty. Therefore he devised the following scheme. At break of day he took his station at some convenient place, and received all who desired speech with him and then dismissed them. 38. The people, when they heard that he gave audience, thronged to him in multitudes, and in the struggle to gain access there was much jostling and scheming and no little fighting. 39. His attendants did their best to divide the suitors, and intro-

duce them in some order, and whenever any of his personal C. 5
friends appeared, thrusting their way through the crowd,
Cyrus would stretch out his hand and draw them to his
side and say, 'Wait, my friends, until we have finished with
this crowd, and then we can talk at our ease.' So his
friends would wait, but the multitude would pour on,
growing greater and greater, until the evening would fall
before there had been a moment's leisure for his friends.
40. All that Cyrus could do then was to say, 'Perhaps,
gentlemen, it is a little late this evening and time that we
broke up. Be sure to come early to-morrow. I am very
anxious myself to speak with you.' With that his friends
were only too glad to be dismissed, and made off without
more ado. They had done penance enough, fasting and
waiting and standing all day long. 41. So they would get
to rest at last, but the next morning Cyrus was at the same
spot and a much greater concourse of suitors round him
than before, already assembled long before his friends
arrived. Accordingly Cyrus had a cordon of Persian lancers
stationed round him, and gave out that no one except his
personal friends and the generals were to be allowed
access, and as soon as they were admitted he said :

42. 'My friends, we cannot exclaim against the gods as
though they had failed to fulfil our prayers. They have
granted all we asked. But if success means that a man must
forfeit his own leisure and the good company of all his
friends, why, to that kind of happiness I would rather bid
farewell. 43. Yesterday,' he added, 'I make no doubt you
observed yourselves that from early dawn till late evening
I never ceased listening to petitioners, and to-day you see
this crowd before us, larger still than yesterday's, ready
with business for me. 44. If this must be submitted to, I
calculate that what you will get of me and I of you will be
little enough, and what I shall get of myself will simply be
nothing at all. Further,' he added, 'I foresee another absurd
consequence. 45. I, personally, have a feeling towards you
which I need not state, but, of that audience yonder,
scarcely one of them do I know at all, and yet they are all
prepared to thrust themselves in front of you, transact
their business, and get what they want out of me before

C. 5 any of you have a chance. I should have thought it more
suitable myself that men of that class, if they wanted
anything from me, should pay some court to you, my
friends, in the hopes of an introduction. 46. Perhaps you
will ask why I did not so arrange matters from the first,
instead of always appearing in public. Because in war it is
the first business of a commander not to be behindhand in
knowing what ought to be done and seeing that it is done,
and the general who is seldom seen is apt to let things slip.
47. But to-day, when war with its insatiable demands is
over, I feel as if I had some claim myself to rest and
refreshment. I am in some perplexity, however, as to how
I can arrange matters so that all goes well, not only with
you and me, but also with those whom we are bound to
care for. Therefore I seek your advice and counsel, and I
would be glad to learn from any of you the happiest
solution.'

48. Cyrus paused, and up rose Artabazus the Mede,
who had claimed to be his kinsman, and said :

'You did well, Cyrus, to open this matter. Years ago,
when you were still a boy, from the very first I longed to
be your friend, but I saw you did not need me, and so I
shrank from approaching you. 49. Then came a lucky
moment when you did have need of me to be your good
messenger among the Medes with the order from Cyaxares, and I said to myself that if I did the work well, if I
really helped you, I might become your comrade, and have
the right to talk with you as often as I wished. 50. Well,
the work was done, and done so as to win your praise.
After that the Hyrcanians joined us, the first friends we
made, when we were hungry and thirsty for allies, and we
loved them so much we almost carried them about with us
in our arms wherever we went. Then the enemy's camp
was taken, and I scarcely think you had the leisure to
trouble your head with me – oh, I quite forgave you.
51. The next thing was that Gobryas became your friend,
and I had to take my leave, and after him Gadatas, and by
that time it was a real task to get hold of you. Then came
the alliances with the Sakians, and the Cadousians, and no
doubt you had to pay them court ; if they danced attend-

ance on you, you must dance attendance on them. 52. So C. 5
that there I was, back again at my starting-point, and yet
all the whle, as I saw you busy with horses and chariots
and artillery, I consoled myself by thinking, "when he is
done with this he will have a little leisure for me." And
then came the terrible news that the whole world was
gathering in arms against us; I could not deny that these
were important matters, but still I felt certain, if all went
well, a time would come at last when you need not grudge
me your company, and we should be together to my
heart's content, you and I. 53. Now, the day has come;
we have conquered in the great battle; we have taken
Sardis and Babylon; the world is at our feet, and yesterday,
by Mithras! unless I had used my fists a hundred times, I
swear I could never have got near you at all. Well, you
grasped my hand and gave me greeting, and bade me wait
beside you, and there I waited, the cynosure of every eye,
the envy of every man, standing there all day long, without
a scrap to eat or a drop to drink. 54. So now, if any way
can be found by which we who have served you longest
can get the most of you, well and good: but, if not, pray
send me as your messenger once more, and this time I will
tell them they can all leave you, except those who were
your friends of old.'

55. This appeal set them all laughing, Cyrus with the
rest. Then Chrysantas the Persian stood up and spoke as
follows:

'Formerly, Cyrus, it was natural and right that you
should appear in public, for the reasons you have given us
yourself, and also because we were not the folk you had to
pay your court to. We did not need inviting: we were with
you for our own sakes. It was necessary to win over the
masses by every means, if they were to share our toils and
our dangers willingly. 56. But now you have won them,
and not them alone; you have it in your power to gain
others, and the moment has come when you ought to have
a house to yourself. What would your empire profit you if
you alone were left without hearth or home? Man has
nothing more sacred than his home, nothing sweeter,
nothing more truly his. And do you not think,' he added,

C. 5 'that we ourselves would be ashamed if we saw you bearing the hardships of the camp while we sat at home by our own firesides ? Should we not feel we had done you wrong, and taken advantage of you ?'

57. When Chrysantas had spoken thus, many others followed him, and all to the same effect. And so it came about that Cyrus entered the palace, and those in charge brought the treasures from Sardis thither, and handed them over. And Cyrus when he entered sacrificed to Hestia, the goddess of the Hearth, and to Zeus the Lord, and to any other gods named by the Persian priests.

58. This done, he set himself to regulate the matters that remained. Thinking over his position, and the attempt he was making to govern an enormous multitude, preparing at the same time to take up his abode in the greatest of all famous cities, but yet a city that was as hostile to him as a city could be, pondering all this, he concluded that he could not dispense with a bodyguard for himself. 59. He knew well enough that a man can most easily be assassinated at his meals, or in his bath, or in bed, or when he is asleep, and he asked himself who were most to be trusted of those he had about him. A man, he believed, can never be loyal or trustworthy who is likely to love another more than the one who requires his guardianship. 60. He knew that men with children, or wives, or favourites in whom they delight, must needs love them most : while eunuchs, who are deprived of all such dear ones, would surely make most account of him who could enrich them, or help them if they were injured, or crown them with honour. And in the conferring of such benefits he was disposed to think he could outbid the world. 61. Moreover the eunuch, being degraded in the eyes of other men, is driven to seek the assistance of some lord and master. Without some such protection there is not a man in the world who would not think he had the right to over-reach a eunuch : while there was every reason to suppose that the eunuch would be the most faithful of all servants. 62. As for the customary notion that the eunuch must be weak and cowardly, Cyrus was not disposed to accept it. He studied the indications to be observed in animals : a vicious horse, if gelded, will

cease to bite and be restive, but he will charge as gallantly C. 5 as ever; a bull that has been cut will become less fierce and less intractable, but he will not lose his strength, he will be as good as ever for work; castration may cure a dog of deserting his master, but it will not ruin him as a watch-dog or spoil him for the chase. 63. So, too, with men; when cut off from this passion, they become gentler, no doubt, but not less quick to obey, not less daring as horsemen, not less skilful with the javelin, not less eager for honour. 64. In war and in the chase they show plainly enough that the fire of ambition is still burning in their hearts. And they have stood the last test of loyalty in the downfall of their masters. No men have shown more faithfulness than eunuchs when ruin has fallen on their lords. 65. In bodily strength, perhaps, the eunuchs seem to be lacking, but steel is a great leveller, and makes the weak man equal to the strong in war. Holding this in mind, Cyrus resolved that his personal attendants, from his doorkeepers onward, should be eunuchs one and all.

66. This guard, however, he felt was hardly sufficient against the multitude of enemies, and he asked himself whom he could choose among the rest. 67. He remem-bered how his Persians led the sorriest of lives at home owing to their poverty, woring long and hard on the niggard soil, and he felt sure they were the men who would most value the life at his court. 68. Accordingly he selected ten thousand lancers from among them, to keep guard round the palace, night and day, whenever he was at home, and to march beside him whenever he went abroad. 69. Moreover, he felt that Babylon must always have an adequate garrison, whether he was in the country or not, and therefore he stationed a considerable body of troops in the city; and he bade the Babylonians provide their pay, his object being to make the citizens helpless, and therefore humble and submissive. 70. This royal guard that he established there, and the city guard for Babylon, survive to this day unaltered.

Lastly, as he pondered how the whole empire was to be kept together, and possibly another added to it, he felt convinced that his mercenaries did not make up for the

C. 5 smallness of their numbers by their superiority to the subject peoples. Therefore he must keep together those brave warriors, to whom with heaven's help the victory was due, and he must take all care that they did not lose their valour, hardihood, and skill. 71. To avoid the appearance of dictating to them and to bring it about that they should see for themselves it was best to stay with him and remember their valour and their training, he called a council of the Peers and of the leading men who seemed to him most worthy of sharing their dangers and their rewards. 72. And when they were met he began:

'Gentlemen, my friends and allies, we owe the utmost thanks to the gods because they have given us what we believed that we deserved. We are masters to-day of a great country and a good; and those who till it will support us; we have houses of our own, and all the furniture that is in them is ours. 73. For you need not think that what you hold belongs to others. It is an eternal law the wide world over, that when a city is taken in war, the citizens, their persons, and all their property fall into the hands of the conquerors. It is not by injustice, therefore, that you hold what you have taken, rather it is through your own human kindness that the citizens are allowed to keep whatever they do retain.

74. 'Yet I foresee that if we betake ourselves to the life of indolence and luxury, the life of the degenerate who think that labour is the worst of evils and freedom from toil the height of happiness, the day will came, and speedily, when we shall be unworthy of ourselves, and with the loss of honour will come the loss of wealth. 75. Once to have been valiant is not enough; no man can keep his valour unless he watch over it to the end. As the arts decay through neglect, as the body, once healthy and alert, will grow weak through sloth and indolence, even so the powers of the spirit, temperance, self-control, and courage, if we grow slack in training, fall back once more to rottenness and death. 76. We must watch ourselves; we must not surrender to the sweetness of the day. It is a great work, methinks, to found an empire, but a far greater to keep it safe. To seize it may be the fruit of daring and

daring only, but to hold it is impossible without self- C. 5
restraint and self-command and endless care. 77. We must
not forget this; we must train ourselves in virtue from now
henceforward with even greater diligence than before we
won this glory, remembering that the more a man possesses, the more there are to envy him, to plot against him,
and be his enemies, above all when the wealth he wins and
the service he receives are yielded by reluctant hands. But
the gods, we need not doubt, will be upon our side; we
have not triumphed through injustice; we were not the
aggressors, it was we who were attacked and we avenged
ourselves. 78. The gods are with us, I say; but next to that
supreme support there is a defence we must provide out of
our own powers alone; and that is the righteous claim to
rule our subjects because we are better men than they.
Needs must that we share with our slaves in heat and cold
and food and drink and toil and slumber, and we must
strive to prove our superiority even in such things as these,
and first in these. 79. But in the science of war and the art
of it we can admit no share; those whom we mean to
make our labourers and our tributaries can have no part
in that; we will set ourselves to defraud them there; we
know that such exercises are the very tools of freedom and
happiness, given by the gods to mortal men. We have
taken their arms away from our slaves, and we must never
lay our own aside, knowing well that the nearer the sword-
hilt the closer the heart's desire. 80. Does any man ask
himself what profit he has gained from the fulfilment of
his dreams, if he must still endure, still undergo hunger
and thirst and toil and trouble and care? Let him learn the
lesson that a man's enjoyment of all good things is in exact
proportion to the pains he has undergone to gain them.
Toil is the seasoning of delight; without desire and longing, no dish, however costly, could be sweet. 81. Yes, if
some spirit were to set before us what men desire most,
and we were left to add for ourselves that final touch of
sweetness, I say that we could only gain above the poorest
of the poor in so far as we could bring hunger for the
most delicious foods, and thirst for the richest wines,
and weariness to make us woo the deepest slumber.

C. 5 82. Therefore, we must strain every nerve to win and to keep manhood and nobleness; so that we may gain that satisfaction which is the sweetest and the best, and be saved from the bitterest of sorrows; since to fail of good altogether is not so hard as to lose the good that has once been ours. 83. And let us ask ourselves what excuse we could offer for being unworthy of our past. Shall we say it is because we have won an empire? Surely it is hardly fitting that the ruler should be baser than the ruled. Or is it that we seem to be happier to-day than heretofore? Is cowardice, then, an adjunct of happiness? Or is it simply because we have slaves and must punish them if they do wrong? But by what right can a man, who is bad himself, punish others for badness or stupidity? 84. Remember, too, that we have arranged for the maintenance of a whole multitude, to guard our persons and our houses, and it would be shameful for us to depend for safety on the weapons of others and refuse to carry weapons for ourselves. Surely we ought to know that there can be no defence so strong as a man's own gallantry. Courage should be our companion all our days. For if virtue leave us, nothing else whatever can go well with us. 85. What, then, would I have you do? How are we to remember our valour and train our skill? Gentlemen, I have nothing novel to suggest; at home in Persia the Peers spend their days at the public buildings and here we should do the same. Here we are the men of rank and honour, as we are there, and we should hold to the same customs. You must keep your eyes on me and watch whether I am diligent in my duty, and I shall give heed to you, and honour him who trains himself in what is beautiful and brave. 86. And here too let us educate our sons, if sons are born to us. We cannot but become better ourselves if we strive to set the best example we can to our children, and our children could hardly grow up to be unworthy, even if they wished, when they see nothing base before them, and hear nothing shameful, but live in the practice of all that is beautiful and good.'

BOOK VIII

SUCH were the words of Cyrus; and Chrysantas rose up C. 1 after him, saying, 'Gentlemen, this is not the first time I have had occasion to observe that a good ruler differs in no respect from a good father. Even as a father takes thought that blessings may never fail his children, so Cyrus would commend to us the ways by which we can preserve our happiness. And yet, on one point, it seemed to me he had spoken less fully than he might; and I will try to explain it for the benefit of those who have not learnt it. 2. I would have you ask yourselves, was ever a hostile city captured by an undisciplined force? Did ever an undisciplined garrison save a friendly town? When discipline was gone, did ever an army conquer? Is ever disaster nearer than when each soldier thinks about his private safety only? Nay, in peace as in war, can any good be gained if men will not obey their betters? What city could be at rest, lawful, and orderly? What household could be safe? What ship sail home to her haven? 3. And we, to what do we owe our triumph, if not to our obedience? We obeyed; we were ready to follow the call by night and day; we marched behind our leader, ranks that nothing could resist; we left nothing half-done of all we were told to do. If obedience is the one path to win the highest good, remember it is also the one way to preserve it. 4. Now in old days, doubtless, many of us ruled no one else, we were simply ruled. But to-day you find yourselves rulers, one and all of you, some over many and some over few. And just as you would wish your subjects to obey you, so we must obey those who are set over us. Yet there should be this difference between ourselves and slaves; a slave

C. 1 renders unwilling service to his lord, but we, if we claim to be freemen, must do of our own free will that which we see to be the best. And you will find,' he added, 'that even when no single man is ruler, that city which is most careful to obey authority is the last to bow to the will of her enemies. 5. Let us listen to the words of Cyrus. Let us gather round the public buildings and train ourselves, so that we may keep our hold on all we care for, and offer ourselves to Cyrus for his noble ends. Of one thing we may be sure: Cyrus will never put us to any service which can make for his own good and not for ours. Our needs are the same as his, and our foes the same.'

6. When Chrysantas had said his say, many others followed to support him, Persians and allies alike, and it was agreed that the men of rank and honour should be in attendance continually at the palace gates, ready for Cyrus to employ, until he gave them their dismissal. That custom is still in force, and to this day the Asiatics under the Great King wait at the door of their rulers. 7. And the measures that Cyrus instituted to preserve his empire, as set forth in this account, are still the law of the land, maintained by all the kings who followed him. 8. Only as in other matters, so here; with a good ruler, the government is pure; with a bad one, corrupt. Thus it came about that the nobles of Cyrus and all his honourable men waited at his gates, with their weapons and their horses, according to the common consent of the gallant men who had helped to lay the empire at his feet.

9. Then Cyrus turned to other matters, and appointed various overseers: he had receivers of revenue, controllers of finance, ministers of works, guardians of property, superintendents of the household. Moreover, he chose managers for his horses and his dogs, men who could be trusted to keep the creatures in the best condition and ready for use at any moment. 10. But when it came to those who were to be his fellow-guardians for the commonwealth, he would not leave the care and the training of these to others; he regarded that as his own personal task. He knew, if he were ever to fight a battle, he would have to choose his comrades and supporters, the men on

his right hand and his left, from these and these alone; it C. 1
was from them he must appoint his officers for horse and
foot. 11. If he had to send out a general alone it would be
from them that one must be sent: he must depend on them
for satraps and governors over cities and nations; he
would require them for ambassadors, and an embassy was,
he knew, the best means for obtaining what he wanted
without war. 12. He foresaw that nothing could go well if
the agents in his weightiest affairs were not what they
ought to be, while, if they were, everything would prosper.
This charge, therefore, he took on his own shoulders, and
he was persuaded that the training he demanded in others
should also be undergone by himself. No man could rouse
others to noble deeds if he fell short of what he ought to
be himself. 13. The more he pondered the matter, the more
he felt the need of leisure, if he were to deal worthily with
the highest matters. It was, he felt, impossible to neglect
the revenues, in view of the enormous funds necessary for
so vast an empire, yet he foresaw that if he was always to
be occupied with the multitude of his possessions he would
never have time to watch over the safety of the whole.
14. As he pondered how he could compass both objects,
the prosperity of the finances and the leisure he required,
the old military organisation came into his mind. He
remembered how the captains of ten supervised the squads
of ten, and were supervised themselves by the company-
captains, and they by the captains of the thousands, and
these by the captains of ten thousand, and thus even with
hundreds of thousands not a man was left without super-
vision, and when the general wished to employ his troops
one order to the captains of ten thousand was enough.
15. On this principle Cyrus arranged his finances and held
the departments together; in this way, by conferring with
a few officers he could keep the whole system under his
control, and actually have more leisure for himself than
the manager of a single household or the master of a single
ship. Finally, having thus ordered his own affairs, he
taught those about him to adopt the same system.

16. Accordingly, having gained the leisure he needed for
himself and his friends, he could devote himself to his

C. 1 work of training his partners and colleagues. In the first place he dealt with those who, enabled as they were to live on the labour of others, yet failed to present themselves at the palace; he would send for them and seek them out, convinced that attendance would be wholesome for them; they would be unwilling to do anything base or evil in the presence of their king and under the eye of their noblest men; those who were absent were so through self-indulgence or wrong-doing or carelessness. 17. And I will now set forth how he brought them to attend. He would go to one of his most intimate friends and bid him lay hands on the property of the offender, asserting that it was his own. Then of course the truants would appear at once crying out that they had been robbed. 18. But somehow for many days Cyrus could never find leisure to hear their complaints, and when he did listen he took care to defer judgment for many more. 19. This was one way he had of teaching them to attend; another was to assign the lightest and most profitable tasks to those who were punctual, and a third to give nothing whatever to the offenders. 20. But the most effective of all, for those who paid no heed to gentler measures, was to deprive the truant of what he possessed and bestow it on him who would come when he was needed. By this process Cyrus gave up a useless friend and gained a serviceable one. To this day the king sends for and seeks out those who do not present themselves when they should.

21. Such was his method with the truants; with those who came forward he felt, since he was their rightful leader, that he could best incite them to noble deeds by trying to show that he himself had all the virtues that became a man. 22. He believed that men do grow better through written laws, and he held that the good ruler is a living law with eyes that see, inasmuch as he is competent to guide and also to detect the sinner and chastise him. 23. Thus he took pains to show that he was the more assiduous in his service to the gods the higher his fortunes rose. It was at this time that the Persian priests, the Magians, were first established as an order, and always at break of day Cyrus chanted a hymn and sacrificed to such

of the gods as they might name. 24. And the ordinances he C. 1
established survive to this day at the court of the reigning
king. These were the first matters in which the Persians set
themselves to copy their prince; feeling their own fortune
would be the higher if they did reverence to the gods,
following the man who was fortune's favourite and their
own monarch. At the same time, no doubt, they thought
they would please Cyrus by this. 25. On his side Cyrus
looked on the piety of his subjects as a blessing to himself,
reckoning as they do who prefer to sail in the company of
pious men rather than with those who are suspected of
wicked deeds, and he reckoned further that if all his
partners were god-fearing, they would be the less prone to
crime against each other or against himself, for he knew
he was the benefactor of his fellows. 26. And by showing
plainly his own deep desire never to be unfair to friend or
fellow-combatant or ally, but always to fix his eyes on
justice and rectitude, he believed he could induce others to
keep from base actions and walk in the paths of righteousness. 27. And he would bring more modesty, he hoped,
into the hearts of all men if it were plain that he himself
reverenced all the world and would never say a shameful
word to any man or woman or do a shameful deed. 28. He
looked for this because he saw that, apart from kings and
governors who may be supposed to inspire fear, men will
reverence the modest and not the shameless, and modesty
in women will inspire modesty in the men who behold
them. 29. And his people, he thought, would learn to obey
if it were plain that he honoured frank and prompt
obedience even above virtues that made a grander show
and were harder to attain. 30. Such was his belief, and his
practice went with it to the end. His own temperance and
the knowledge of it made others more temperate. When
they saw moderation and self-control in the man who
above all others had licence to be insolent, lesser men were
the more ready to abjure all insolence of their own. 31. But
there was this difference, Cyrus held, between modesty
and self-control: the modest man will do nothing shameful
in the light of day, but the man of self-control nothing
base, not even in secret. 32. Self-restraint, he believed,

C. 1 would best be cultivated if he made men see in himself one who could not be dragged from the pursuit of virtue by the pleasure of the moment, one who chose to toil first for the happy-hearted joys that go hand-in-hand with beauty and nobleness. 33. Thus, being the man he was, he established at his gates a stately company, where the lower gave place to the higher, and they in their turn showed reverence to each other, and courtesy, and perfect harmony. Among them all there was never a cry of anger to be heard, nor a burst of insolent laughter; to look at them was to know that they lived for honour and loveliness.

34. Such was the life at the palace-gates, and to practise his nobles in martial exercises he would lead them out to the hunt whenever he thought it well, holding the chase to be the best training for war and the surest way to excellence in horsemanship. 35. A man learns to keep his seat, no matter what the ground may be, as he follows the flying quarry, learns to hurl and strike on horseback in his eagerness to bring down the game and win applause. 36. And here, above all, was the field in which to inure his colleagues to toil and hardship and cold and heat and hunger and thirst. Thus to this day the Persian monarch and his court spend their leisure in the chase. 37. From all that has been said, it is clear Cyrus was convinced that no one has a right to rule who is not superior to his subjects, and he held that by imposing such exercises as these on those about him, he would lead them to self-control and bring to perfection the art and discipline of war. 38. Accordingly he would put himself at the head of the hunting-parties and take them out himself unless he was bound to stay at home, and, if he was, he would hunt in his parks among the wild creatures he had reared. He would never touch the evening meal himself until he had sweated for it, nor give his horses their corn until they had been exercised, and he would invite his own mace-bearers to join him in the chase. 39. Therefore he excelled in all knightly accomplishments, he and those about him, because of their constant practice. Such was the example he set before his friends. But he also kept his eye on others, and would single out those who worshipped noble deeds,

and reward them with gifts, and high commands, and seats C. 1
at festivals, and every kind of honour. And thus their
hearts were filled with ambition, and every man longed to
outdo his fellows in the eyes of Cyrus.

40. But we seem to learn also that Cyrus thought it
necessary for the ruler not only to surpass his subjects by
his own native worth, but also to charm them through
deception and artifice. At any rate he adopted the Median
dress, and persuaded his comrades to do likewise; he
thought it concealed any bodily defect, enhancing the
beauty and stature of the wearer. 41. The shoe, for
instance, was so devised that a sole could be added without
notice, and the man would seem taller than he really was.
So also Cyrus encouraged the use of ointments to make
the eyes more brilliant and pigments to make the skin look
fairer. 42. And he trained his courtiers never to spit or
blow the nose in public or turn aside to stare at anything;
they were to keep the stately air of persons whom nothing
can surprise. These were all means to one end; to make it
impossible for the subjects to despise their rulers.

43. Thus he moulded the men he considered worthy of
command by his own example, by the training he gave
them, and by the dignity of his own leadership. But the
treatment of those he prepared for slavery was widely
different. Not one of them would he incite to any noble
toil, he would not even let them carry arms, and he was
careful that they should never lack food or drink in any
manly sport. 44. When the beaters drove the wild creatures
into the plain he would allow food to be brought for the
servants, but not for the free men; on a march he would
lead the slaves to the water-springs as he led the beasts of
burden. Or when it was the hour of breakfast he would
wait himself till they had taken a snatch of food and stayed
their wolfish hunger; and the end of it was they called him
their father even as the nobles did, because he cared for
them, but the object of his care was to keep them slaves
for ever.

45. Thus he secured the safety of the Persian empire. He
himself, he felt sure, ran no danger from the masses of the
conquered people; he saw they had no courage, no unity,

C. 1 and no discipline, and, moreover, not one of them could ever come near him, day or night. 46. But there were others whom he knew to be true warriors, who carried arms, and who held by one another, commanders of horse and foot, many of them men of spirit, confident, as he could plainly see, of their own power to rule, men who were in close touch with his own guards, and many of them in constant intercourse with himself; as indeed was essential if he was to make any use of them at all. It was from them that danger was to be feared; and that in a thousand ways. 47. How was he to guard against it? He rejected the idea of disarming them; he thought this unjust, and that it would lead to the dissolution of the empire. To refuse them admission into his presence, to show them his distrust, would be, he considered, a declaration of war. 48. But there was one method, he felt, worth all the rest, an honourable method and one that would secure his safety absolutely; to win their friendship if he could, and make them more devoted to himself than to each other. I will now endeavour to set forth the methods, so far as I conceive them, by which he gained their love.

C. 2   In the first place he never lost an opportunity of showing kindliness wherever he could, convinced that just as it is not easy to love those who hate us, so it is scarcely possible to feel enmity for those who love us and wish us well. 2. So long as he had lacked the power to confer benefits by wealth, all he could do then was to show his personal care for his comrades and his soldiers, to labour in their behalf, manifest his joy in their good fortune and his sympathy in their sorrows, and try to win them in that way. But when the time came for the gifts of wealth, he realised that of all the kindnesses between man and man none come with a more natural grace than the gifts of meat and drink. 3. Accordingly he arranged that his table should be spread every day for many guests in exactly the same way as for himself; and all that was set before him, after he and his guests had dined, he would send out to his absent friends, in token of affection and remembrance. He would include those who had won his approval by their work on guard, or in attendance on himself, or in any

other service, letting them see that no desire to please him C. 2
could ever escape his eyes. 4. He would show the same
honour to any servant he wished to praise; and he had all
the food for them placed at his own board, believing this
would win their fidelity, as it would a dog's. Or, if he
wished some friend of his to be courted by the people, he
would single him out for such gifts; even to this day the
world will pay court to those who have dishes sent them
from the Great King's table, thinking they must be in high
favour at the palace and can get things done for others.
But no doubt there was another reason for the pleasure in
such gifts, and that was the sheer delicious taste of the
royal meats. 5. Nor should that surprise us; for if we
remember to what a pitch of perfection the other crafts are
brought in great communities, we ought to expect the
royal dishes to be wonders of finished art. In a small city
the same man must make beds and chairs and ploughs and
tables, and often build houses as well; and indeed he will
be only too glad if he can find enough employers in all his
trades to keep him. Now it is impossible that a single man
working at a dozen crafts can do them all well; but in the
great cities, owing to the wide demand for each particular
thing, a single craft will suffice for a means of livelihood,
and often enough even a single department of that; there
are shoe-makers who will only make sandals for men and
others only for women. Or one artisan will get his living
merely by stitching shoes, another by cutting them out, a
third by shaping the upper leathers, and a fourth will do
nothing but fit the parts together. Necessarily the man who
spends all his time and trouble on the smallest task will do
that task the best. 6. The arts of the household must follow
the same law. If one and the same servant makes the bed,
spreads the table, kneads the dough, and cooks the various
dishes, the master must take things as they come, there is
no help for it. But when there is work enough for one man
to boil the pot, and another to roast the meat, and a third
to stew the fish, and a fourth to fry it, while some one else
must bake the bread, and not all of it either, for the loaves
must be of different kinds, and it will be quite enough if
the baker can serve up one kind to perfection – it is

C. 2 obvious, I think, that in this way a far higher standard of excellence will be attained in every branch of the work.

7. Thus it is easy to see how Cyrus could outdo all competitors in the grace of hospitality, and I will now explain how he came to triumph in all other services. Far as he excelled mankind in the scale of his revenues, he excelled them even more in the grandeur of his gifts. It was Cyrus who set the fashion; and we are familiar to this day with the open-handedness of Oriental kings. 8. There is no one, indeed, in all the world whose friends are seen to be as wealthy as the friends of the Persian monarch: no one adorns his followers in such splendour of rich attire, no gifts are so well known as his, the bracelets, and the necklaces, and the chargers with the golden bridles. For in that country no one can have such treasures unless the king has given them. 9. And of whom but the Great King could it be said that through the splendour of his presents he could steal the hearts of men and turn them to himself, away from brothers, fathers, sons? Who but he could stretch out an arm and take vengeance on his enemies when yet they were months and months away? Who but Cyrus ever won an empire in war, and when he died was called father by the people he overcame? — a title that proclaims the benefactor and not the robber. 10. Indeed, we are led to think that the offices called 'the king's eyes' and 'the king's ears' came into being through this system of gifts and honours. Cyrus' munificence toward all who told him what it was well for him to know set countless people listening with all their ears and watching with all their eyes for news that might be of service to him. 11. Thus there sprang up a host of 'king's eyes' and 'king's ears,' as they were called, known and reputed to be such. But it is a mistake to suppose that the king has one chosen 'eye.' It is little that one man can see or one man hear, and to hand over the office to one single person would be to bid all others go to sleep. Moreover, his subjects would feel they must be on their guard before the man they knew was 'the king's eye.' The contrary is the case; the king will listen to any man who asserts that he has heard or seen anything that needs attention. 12. Hence the saying that

the king has a thousand eyes and a thousand ears; and C. 2
hence the fear of uttering anything against his interest
since 'he is sure to hear,' or doing anything that might
injure him 'since he may be there to see.' So far, therefore,
from venturing to breathe a syllable against Cyrus, every
man felt that he was under the eye and within the hearing
of a king who was always present. For this universal
feeling towards him I can give no other reason than his
resolve to be a benefactor on a most mighty scale.

13. It is not surprising, no doubt, that being the wealthiest of men, he could outdo the world in the splendour of
his gifts. The remarkable thing was to find a king outstrip
his courtiers in courtesy and kindness. There was nothing,
so the story runs, that could ever shame him more than to
be outdone in courtesy. 14. Indeed, a saying of his is
handed down comparing a good king to a good shepherd
– the shepherd must manage his flock by giving them all
they need, and the king must satisfy the needs of his cities
and his subjects if he is to manage them. We need not
wonder, then, that with such opinions his ambition was to
excel mankind in courtesy and care. 15. There was a noble
illustration of his philosophy in the answer we are told he
gave to Croesus, who had taken him to task, saying his
lavish gifts would bring him to beggary, although he could
lay by more treasures for himself than any man had ever
had before. Cyrus, it is said, asked him in return, 'How
much wealth do you suppose I could have amassed
already, had I collected gold, as you bid me, ever since I
came into my empire?'

16. And Croesus named an enormous sum. Then Cyrus
said, 'Listen, Croesus, here is my friend, Hystaspas, and
you must send with him a man that you can trust.' Then,
turning to Hystaspas, 'Do you,' he said, 'go round to my
friends and tell them that I need money for a certain
enterprise – and that is true, I do need it. Bid each of them
write down the amount he can give me, seal the letter, and
hand it to the messenger of Croesus, who will bring it
here.' 17. Thereupon Cyrus wrote his wishes and put his
seal on the letter, and gave it to Hystaspas to carry round,
only he added a request that they should all welcome

C. 2 Hystaspas as a friend of his. And when the messengers came back, the officer of Croesus carrying the answers, Hystaspas cried, 'Cyrus, my lord, you must know I am a rich man now! I have made my fortune, thanks to your letter! They have loaded me with gifts.' 18. And Cyrus said, 'There, Croesus, that is treasure number one; and now run through the rest, and count what sums I have in hand, in case I need them.' And Croesus counted, and found, so the story tells us, that the sum was far larger than the amount he had said would have been lying in the treasury if only Cyrus had made a hoard. 19. At this discovery Cyrus said, so we are told, 'You see, Croesus, I have my treasures too. Only you advise me to collect them and hide them, and be envied and hated because of them, and set mercenaries to guard them, putting my trust in hirelings. But I hold to it that if I make my friends rich they will be my treasures themselves, and far better guards too, for me and all we have, than if I set hired watchmen over my wealth. 20. And I have somewhat else to say; I tell you, Croesus, there is something the gods have implanted in our souls, and there they have made us all beggars alike, something I can never overcome. 21. I too, like all the rest, am insatiate of riches, only in one respect I fancy I am different. Most men when they have more wealth than they require bury some of it underground, and let some of it rot, and some they count and measure, and they guard it and they air it, and give themselves a world of trouble, and yet for all their wealth they cannot eat more than they have stomach for – they would burst asunder if they did – nor wear more clothes than they can carry – they would die of suffocation – and so their extra wealth means nothing but extra work. 22. For my part, I serve the gods, and I stretch out my hands for more and more; only when I have got what is beyond my own requirements I piece out the wants of my friends, and so, helping my fellows, I purchase their love and their good-will, and out of these I garner security and renown, fruits that can never rot, rich meats that can work no mischief; for glory, the more it grows, the grander it becomes, and the fairer, and the lighter to be borne; it even gives a lighter step to those who bear it. 23. One thing more, C. 3 Croesus, I would have you know; the happiest men, in my judgment, are not the holders of vast riches and the masters who have the most to guard; else the sentinels of our citadels would be the happiest of mortals, seeing they guard the whole wealth of the state. He, I hold, has won the crown of happiness who has had the skill to gain wealth by the paths of righteousness and use it for all that is honourable and fair.'

24. That was the doctrine Cyrus preached, and all men could see that his practice matched his words.

Moreover, he observed that the majority of mankind, if they live in good health for long, will only lay by such stores and requisites as may be used by a healthy man, and hardly care at all to have appliances at hand in case of sickness. But Cyrus was at pains to provide these; he encouraged the ablest physicians of the day by his liberal payments, and if ever they recommended an instrument or a drug or a special kind of food or drink, he never failed to procure it and have it stored in the palace. 25. And whenever any one fell sick among those who had peculiar claims on his attention, he would visit them and bring them all they needed, and he showed especial gratitude to the doctors if they cured their patients by the help of his own stores. 26. These measures, and others like them, he adopted to win the first place in the hearts of those whose friendship he desired. Moreover, the contests he proclaimed and the prizes he offered to awaken ambition and desire for gallant deeds all redounded to his own glory as a man who had the pursuit of nobleness at heart, while they bred strife and bitter rivalry among the champions themselves. 27. Further, he laid it down that in every matter needing arbitration, whether it were a suit-at-law or a trial of skill, the parties should concur in their choice of a judge. Each would try to secure the most powerful man he knew and the one most friendly to himself, and if he lost he envied his successful rival and hated the judge who had declared against him, while the man who won claimed to win because his case was just and felt he owed no gratitude to anybody. 28. Thus all who wished to be

C. 2 first in the affections of Cyrus, just as others in democratic states, were full of rancour against each other, in fact most of them would sooner have seen their rivals exterminated than join with them for any common good. Such are some of the devices by which he made the ablest of his subjects more attached to himself than to one another.

C. 3 I will now describe the first public progress that Cyrus made. For the very solemnity of the ceremony was one of the artifices by which he won reverence for his government. The day before it he summoned the officers of state, the Persians and the others, and gave them all the splendid Median dress. This was the first time the Persians wore it, and as they received the robes he said that he wished to drive in his chariot to the sacred precincts and offer sacrifice with them. 2. 'You will present yourselves at my gates,' he added, 'before the sun rises, attired in these robes, and you will take your places where Pheraulas the Persian bids you on my behalf. As soon as I lead the way you will follow in your appointed order. And if any of you should think of some change to heighten the beauty and stateliness of our procession, you will acquaint me with it, I pray, on our return; it is for us to see that all is done in the manner you feel to be most beautiful and best.'

3. With that Cyrus gave the most splendid robes to his chief notables, and then he brought out others, for he had stores of Median garments, purple and scarlet and crimson and glowing red, and gave a share to each of his generals and said to them, 'Adorn your friends with these, as I have adorned you.' 4. Then one of them asked him, 'And you, O Cyrus, when will you adorn yourself?' But he answered, 'Is it not adornment enough for me to have adorned you? If I can but do good to my friends, I shall look glorious enough, whatever robe I wear.'

5. So his nobles took their leave, and sent for their friends and put the splendid raiment on them. Meanwhile Cyrus summoned Pheraulas, knowing that, while he was a man of the people, he was also quick-witted, a lover of the beautiful, prompt to understand and to obey, and one who had ever an eye to please his master. It was he who had supported Cyrus long ago when he proposed that honour

should be given in proportion to desert. And now Cyrus C. 3 asked him how he thought the procession might be made most beautiful in the eyes of friends and most formidable in the sight of foes. 6. So they took counsel and were of the same mind, and Cyrus bade Pheraulas see that all was done on the morrow as they had agreed.

'I have issued orders,' he added, 'for all to obey you in the matter, but to make them the more willing, take these tunics yourself and give them to the captains of the guard, and these military cloaks for the cavalry officers, and these tunics for those who command the chariots.'

7. So Pheraulas took the raiment and departed, and when the generals saw him, they met him with shouts and cried, 'A monstrous fine fellow you are, Pheraulas!' said one: 'you are to give us our orders, it seems!'

'Oh, yes,' said Pheraulas, 'and carry your baggage too. Here I come with two cloaks as it is, one for you and another for somebody else: you must choose whichever you like best.'

8. At that the officer put out his hand to take the cloak; he had clean forgotten his jealousy, and fell to asking Pheraulas which he had better choose. And Pheraulas gave his advice, adding, 'But if you inform against me, and let out that I gave you the choice, the next time I have to wait upon you you will find me a very different sort of serving-man.'

Thus he distributed the gifts he brought, and then he saw to the arrangements for the procession so that everything should be as fair as possible.

9. On the morrow all things were ready before day-break, ranks lining the road on either hand, as they do to this day when the king is expected to ride abroad – no one may pass within the lines unless he is a man of mark – and constables were posted with whips, to use at any sign of disturbance.

In front of the palace stood the imperial guard of lancers, four thousand strong, drawn up four deep on either side of the gates. 10. And all the cavalry were there, the men standing beside their horses, with their hands wrapped in their cloaks, as is the custom to this day for every subject

C. 3 when the king's eye is on him. The Persians stood on the right, and the allies on the left, and the chariots were posted in the same way, half on one side and half on the other. 11. Presently the palace-gates were flung open, and at the head of the procession were led out the bulls for sacrifice, beautiful creatures, four and four together. They were to be offered to Zeus and to any other gods that the Persian priests might name. For the Persians think it of more importance to follow the guidance of the learned in matters pertaining to the gods than in anything else whatever.

12. After the oxen came horses, an offering to the Sun, then a white chariot with a golden yoke, hung with garlands and dedicated to Zeus, and after that the white car of the Sun, wreathed like the one before it, and then a third chariot, the horses of which were caparisoned with scarlet trappings, and behind walked men carrying fire upon a mighty hearth. 13. And then at last Cyrus himself was seen, coming forth from the gates in his chariot, wearing his tiara on his head, and a purple tunic shot with white, such as none but the king may wear, and trews of scarlet, and a cloak of purple. Round his tiara he wore a diadem, and his kinsmen wore the same, even as the custom is to this day. 14. And the king's hands hung free outside his cloak. Beside him stood a charioteer – he was a tall man, but he seemed to be dwarfed by Cyrus; whether it was really so, or whether there was some artifice at work, Cyrus towered above him. At the sight of the king, the whole company fell on their faces. Perhaps some had been ordered to do this and so set the fashion, or perhaps the multitude were really overcome by the splendour of the pageant and the sight of Cyrus himself, stately and tall and fair. 15. For hitherto none of the Persians had done obeisance to Cyrus.

And now, as the chariot moved onwards, the four thousand lancers went before it, two thousand on either side, and close behind came the mace-bearers, mounted on horseback, with javelins in their hands, three hundred strong. 16. Then the royal steeds were led past, with golden bridles and striped housings, two hundred and

more, and then followed two thousand spearmen and after C. 3
them the squadron of cavalry first formed, ten thousand
men, a hundred deep and a hundred riding abreast, with
Chrysantas at their head. 17. And behind them the second
body of the Persian horse, ten thousand more, in the same
order, under Hystaspas, and then again ten thousand
under Datamas, and others behind them under Gadatas.
18. And after them the Median cavalry, and then the
Armenians, the Hyrcanians, the Cadousians, and the
Sakians in their order; and after the cavalry a squadron
of war-chariots, drawn up four deep, with Artabatas the
Persian in command.

19. All along the route thousands of men followed,
outside the barriers, with petitions to Cyrus. Accordingly
he sent his mace-bearers, who rode beside him for the
purpose, three on either side of his chariot, bidding them
tell the crowd of suitors, if they had need of anything, to
acquaint one of the cavalry officers and he would speak
for them. So the petitioners withdrew, and fell to marching
along the lines of the cavalry, considering whom they
should address. 20. Cyrus meanwhile would send messengers to the friends he wished to be courted, saying to them,
'If any man appeals to you and you think nothing of what
he says, pay no heed to him, but if his request seems just,
report it to me, and we will discuss it together and arrange
matters for him.' 21. As a rule the officers so summoned
did not loiter, but dashed up at full speed, glad to enhance
the authority of Cyrus and to show their own allegiance.
But there was a certain Daïpharnes, a person of somewhat
boorish manners, who fancied that he would make a show
of greater independence if he did not hurry himself.
22. Cyrus noted this, and quietly, before the man could
reach him, sent another messenger to say he had no further
need of him; and that was the last time Daïpharnes was
ever summoned. 23. And when the next officer rode up, in
front of Daïpharnes though sent for after him, Cyrus
presented him with a horse from his train and bade one of
the mace-bearers lead it wherever he wished. The people
saw in this a high mark of honour; and a greater crowd
than ever paid their court to the favoured man.

C. 3   24. When the procession reached the sacred precincts, sacrifice was offered to Zeus, a whole burnt-offering of bulls, and a whole burnt-offering of horses to the Sun; and then they sacrificed to the Earth, slaying the victims as the Persian priests prescribed, and then to the heroes who hold the Syrian land. 25. And when the rites were done, Cyrus, seeing that the ground was suitable for racing, marked out a goal, and a course half-a-mile in length, and bade the cavalry and the chariots match their horses against each other, tribe by tribe. He himself raced among his Persians, and won with ease, for he was far the best horseman there. The winner among the Medes was Artabazus, the horse he rode being a gift from Cyrus. The Syrian race was won by their chieftain, the Armenian by Tigranes, the Hyrcanian by the general's son, and the Sakian by a private soldier who left all his rivals half the course behind him.

26. Cyrus, so the story says, asked the young man if he would take a kingdom for his horse.

'No kingdom for me,' answered the soldier, 'but I would take the thanks of a gallant fellow.'

27. 'Well,' said Cyrus, 'I would like to show you where you could hardly fail to hit one, even if you shut your eyes.'

'Be so good as to show me now,' said the Sakian, 'and I will take aim with this clod,' picking up one from the ground.

28. Then Cyrus pointed to a group of his best friends, and the other shut his eyes and flung the clod, and it struck Pheraulas as he galloped by, bearing some message from Cyrus. But he never so much as turned, flashing past on his errand. 29. Then the Sakian opened his eyes and asked whom he had hit?

'Nobody, I assure you,' said Cyrus, 'who is here.'

'And nobody who is not, of course,' said the young man.

'Oh yes, you did,' answered Cyrus, 'you hit that officer over there who is riding so swiftly past the chariot-lines.'

30. 'And how is it,' asked the other, 'that he does not even turn his head?'

'Half-witted, probably,' said Cyrus.

Whereat the young man rode off to see who it was, and C. 3 found Pheraulas, with his chin and beard all begrimed and bloody, gore trickling from his nostrils where the clod had struck him. 31. The Sakian cried out to know if he was hit.

'As you see,' answered Pheraulas.

'Then,' said the other, 'let me give you my horse.'

'But why?' asked Pheraulas.

And so the Sakian had to tell him all about the matter, adding, 'And after all, you see, I did not miss a gallant fellow.'

32. 'Ah,' said Pheraulas, 'if you had been wise, you would have chosen a richer one; but I take your gift with all my thanks. And I pray the gods,' he added, 'who let me be your target, to help me now and see that you may never regret your gift. For the present, mount my horse yourself and ride back: I will be with you shortly.'

So they exchanged steeds and parted.

The winner of the Cadousian race was Rathines.

33. Then followed chariot-races, tribe by tribe as before: and to all the winners Cyrus gave goblets of price, and oxen, that they might have the wherewithal for sacrifice and feasting. He himself took an ox for his own meed, but he gave all his goblets to Pheraulas to show his approval of the arrangements for the march. 34. And the manner of that procession, then first established by Cyrus, continues to this day, the same in all things, save that the victims are absent when there is no sacrifice. And when it was over, the soldiers went back to the city, and took up their quarters for the night, some in houses and some with their regiments.

35. Now Pheraulas had invited the Sakian who had given him the horse, and he entertained him with the best he had, and set before him a full board, and after they had dined he filled the goblets Cyrus had given him, and drank to his guest and offered them all to him. 36. And the Sakian looked round on the rich and costly rugs, and the beautiful furniture, and the train of servants, and cried:

'Tell me, Pheraulas, do you belong to wealthy folk at home?'

C. 3   37. 'Wealthy folk indeed!' cried Pheraulas, 'men who live by their hands, you mean. My father, I can tell you, had work enough to rear me and get me a boy's schooling; he had to toil hard and live sparely, and when I grew to be a lad he could not afford to keep me idle, he took me to a farm in the country and set me there to work it. 38. Then it was my turn, and I supported him while he lived, digging with my own hands and sowing the seed in a ridiculous little plot of ground, and yet it was not a bad bit of soil either, but as good and as honest earth as ever you saw: whatever seed it got from me, it paid me back again, and so prettily and carefully and duly, principal and interest both; not that the interest was very much, I won't say it was, though once or twice, out of pure generosity, that land gave me twice as much as I put into it. That's how I used to live at home, in the old days: to-day it's different, and all that you see here I owe to Cyrus.'

39. Then the Sakian cried:

'O lucky fellow! Lucky in everything, and most of all in coming to wealth from beggary! I know your riches must taste the sweeter, because you hungered for them first and now are full.'

40. But Pheraulas answered:

'Do you really think, my friend, that my joy in life has grown with the growth of my wealth? Do you not know,' he went on, 'that I neither eat nor drink nor sleep with any more zest than I did when I was poor? What I get by all these goods is simply this: I have more to watch over, more to distribute, and more trouble in looking after more. 41. I have a host of servants now, one set asking me for food, another for drink, another for clothing, and some must have the doctor, and then a herdsman comes, carrying the carcase of some poor sheep mangled by the wolves, or perhaps with an ox that has fallen down a precipice, or maybe he has to tell me that a murrain has broken out among my flocks. It seems to me,' Pheraulas ended, 'that I suffer more to-day through having much than ever I did before through having nothing.'

42. 'But – Heaven help us!' cried the Sakian, 'surely,

when it is all safe, to see so much of your own must make C. 3
you much happier than me?'

'I assure you, my friend,' said Pheraulas, 'the possession
of riches is nothing like so sweet as the loss of them is
painful. And here is a proof for you: no rich man lies
awake from pure joy at his wealth, but did you ever know
a man who could close his eyes when he was losing?'

43. 'No,' said the Sakian, 'nor yet one who could drop
asleep when he was winning.'

44. 'True enough,' answered the other, 'and if having
were as sweet as getting, the rich would be a thousand
times more happy than the poor. And remember, stranger,'
he added, 'a man who has much must spend much on the
gods and his friends and his guests, and if he takes intense
delight in his riches, spending will cause him intense
annoyance.'

45. 'Upon my word,' said the Sakian, 'for myself, I am
not that sort of man at all: to have much and to spend
much is just my idea of perfect happiness.'

46. 'Heavens!' cried Pheraulas, 'what a chance for us
both! You can win perfect happiness now, this instant,
and make me happy too! Here, take all these things for
your own, make what use of them you please; and as for
me, you can keep me as your guest, only much more
cheaply if you like: it will be quite enough for me to share
whatever you have yourself.'

'You are jesting,' said the Sakian.

47. But Pheraulas swore with all solemnity that he spoke
in earnest.

'Yes, my friend,' he added, 'and there are other matters
that I can arrange for you with Cyrus: freedom from
military service or attendance at the gates. All you will
have to do will to be stay at home and grow rich: I will do
the rest on your behalf and mine. And if I win any treasure
through my service at court or on the field, I will bring it
home to you, and you will be lord of more; only,' he added,
'you must free me from the responsibility of looking after
it, for if you give me leisure from these cares I believe you
will be of great use to Cyrus and myself.'

48. So the talk ended and they struck a bargain on these

C. 3   terms, and kept it. And the Sakian thought he had found happiness because he was the master of much wealth, and the other felt he was in bliss because he had got a steward who would leave him leisure to do what he liked best. 49. For the character of Pheraulas was amiable: he was a loving comrade, and no service seemed so sweet to him or so helpful as the service of man. Man, he believed, was the noblest of the animals and the most grateful: praise, Pheraulas saw, will reap counter-praise, kindness will stir kindness in return, and goodwill goodwill; those whom men know to love them they cannot hate, and, in a way no other animals will, they cherish their parents in life and in death, and requite their care. All other creatures, in short, compared with man, are lacking in gratitude and heart.

50. Thus Pheraulas was overjoyed to feel that he could now be quit of anxiety for his wealth, and devote himself to his friends, while the Sakian was delighted with all that he had and all that he could use. The Sakian loved Pheraulas because he was for ever adding something to the store, and Pheraulas loved the Sakian because he was willing to assume the entire burden, and however much the cares increased he never broke into the other's leisure. Thus those two lived their lives.

C. 4   Now Cyrus offered sacrifice and held high festival for his victories, and he summoned to the feast those of his friends who bore him most affection and had shown most desire to exalt him. With them were bidden Artabazus the Mede, and Tigranes the Armenian, and the commander of the Hyrcanian cavalry, and Gobryas. 2. Gadatas was the chief of the mace-bearers, and the whole household was arranged as he advised. When there were guests at dinner, Gadatas would not sit down, but saw to everything, and when they were alone he sat at meat with Cyrus, who took delight in his company, and in return for all his services he was greatly honoured by Cyrus and that led to more honours from others. 3. As the guests entered, Gadatas would show each man to his seat, and the places were chosen with care: the friend whom Cyrus honoured most was placed on his left hand (for that was the side most open to attack), the second on his right, the third next to C. 4 the left-hand guest, and the fourth next to the right, and so on, whatever the number of the guests might be. 4. Cyrus thought it well it should be known how much each man was honoured, for he saw that where the world believes merit will win no crown and receive no proclamation, there the spirit of emulation dies, but if all see that the best man gains most, then the rivalry grows keen. 5. Thus it was that Cyrus marked out the men he favoured by the seat of honour and the order of precedence. Nor did he assign the honourable place to one friend for all time; he made it a law that by good deeds a man might rise into a higher seat or through sloth descend into a lower; and he would have felt ashamed if it were not known that the guest most honoured at his table received most favours at his hands. These customs that arose in the reign of Cyrus continue to our time, as we can testify.

6. While they were at the feast that day it struck Gobryas that though there was nothing surprising in the abundance and variety at the table of one who was lord over so vast an empire, yet it was strange that Cyrus, who has done such mighty deeds, should never keep any dainty for himself, but must always be at the pains to share it with the company. More than once also he saw Cyrus send off to an absent friend some dish that had chanced to please him. 7. So that by the time they had finished their meal all the viands had been given away by Cyrus, and the board was bare.

Then Gobryas said, 'Truly, Cyrus, until to-day I used to think it was in generalship that you outshone other men the most, but, by heaven! I say now it is not in generalship at all, it is in generosity.'

8. 'Maybe,' said Cyrus, 'at least I take far more pride in this work than in the other.'

'How can that be?' asked Gobryas.

'Because,' said he, 'the one does good to man and the other injury.'

9. Presently as the wine went round and round, Hystaspas turned to Cyrus and said:

C. 4 'Would you be angry, Cyrus, if I asked you something I long to know?'

'On the contrary,' answered Cyrus, 'I should be vexed if I saw you silent when you longed to ask.'

'Tell me then,' said the other, 'have you ever called me and found I refused to come?'

'What a question!' said Cyrus, 'of course not.'

'Well, have I ever been slow in coming?'

'No, never.'

'Or failed to do anything you ordered?'

'No,' said Cyrus, 'I have no fault to find at all.'

'Whatever I had to do, I always did it eagerly and with all my heart, did I not?'

'Most assuredly,' answered Cyrus.

10. 'Then why, Cyrus, why, in heaven's name, have you singled out Chrysantas for a more honourable seat than me?'

'Shall I really tell you?' asked Cyrus in his turn.

'By all means,' said the other.

'And you will not be annoyed if I tell you the plain truth?'

11. 'On the contrary, it will comfort me to know I have not been wronged.'

'Well, then, Chrysantas never waited to be called; he came of his own accord on our behalf, and he made it his business to do, not merely what he was ordered, but whatever he thought would help us. When something had to be said to the allies, he would not only suggest what was fitting for me to say myself, he would guess what I wanted the allies to know but could not bring myself to utter, since it was about myself, and he would say it for me as though it were his own opinion; in fact, for everything of the kind he was nothing less to me than a second and a better self. And now he is always insisting that what he has already got is quite enough for himself, and always trying to discover something more for me: he takes a greater pride and joy in all my triumphs than I do myself.'

12. 'By Hera,' said Hystaspas, 'I am right glad I asked you. Only one thing puzzles me: how am I to show my

joy at your success ? Shall I clap my hands and laugh, or C. 4
what shall I do ?'

'Dance the Persian dance, of course,' said Artabazus.
And all the company laughed.

13. And as the drinking deepened Cyrus put a question
to Gobryas :

'Tell me, Gobryas, would you be better pleased to give
your daughter to one of our company to-day than the day
when you met us first ?'

'Well,' said Gobryas, 'am I also to tell the truth ?'

'Certainly,' said Cyrus, 'no question looks for a lie.'

'Then,' said Gobryas, 'I assure you, I would far rather
give her in marriage to-day.'

'Can you tell us why ?' said Cyrus.

'That I can,' said he.'

14. 'Say on, then.'

'At that time, I saw, it is true, the gallant manner in
which your men endured toil and danger, but to-day I see
the modesty with which they bear success. And I believe,
Cyrus, that the man who takes good-fortune well is further
to seek than he who can endure adversity; for success
engenders insolence in many hearts, while suffering teaches
sobriety and fortitude.'

15. And Cyrus said, 'Hystaspas, did you hear the saying
of Gobryas ?'

'I did indeed,' he answered, 'and if he has many more as
good, he will find me a suitor for his daughter, a far more
eager one than if he had shown me all his goblets.'

16. 'Well,' said Gobryas, 'I have many such written
down at home, and you may have them all if you take my
daughter to wife. And as for the goblets,' he added, 'since
it seems you cannot away with them, perhaps I might give
them to Chrysantas to punish him for having filched your
seat.'

17. 'Listen to me,' said Cyrus, 'Hystaspas, and all of
you. If you will but tell me, any of you, when you propose
to marry, you would soon discover what a clever advocate
you had in me.'

18. But Gobryas interposed, 'And if one of us wants to
give his daughter in marriage, to whom should he apply ?'

C. 4   'To me also,' answered Cyrus; 'I assure you, I am an adept in the art.'

'What art is that?' Chrysantas inquired.

19. 'The art of discerning the wife to suit each man.'

'Then by all the gods,' said Chrysantas, 'tell me what sort of wife would do for me?'

20. 'In the first place,' he answered, 'she must be short, for you are not tall yourself, and if you married a tall maiden and wanted to give her a kiss when she stood up straight, you would have to jump to reach her like a little dog.'

'Your advice is straight enough,' said Chrysantas; 'and I am but a sorry jumper at the best.'

21. 'In the next place,' Cyrus went on, 'a flat nose would suit you very well.'

'A flat nose?' said the other, 'why?'

'Because your own is high enough, and flatness, you may be sure, will go best with height.'

'You might as well say,' retorted Chrysantas, 'that one who has dined well, like myself, is best matched with the dinnerless.'

'Quite so,' answered Cyrus, 'a full stomach is high and an empty paunch is flat.'

22. 'And now,' said Chrysantas, 'in heaven's name, tell us the bride for a flat king?'

But at this Cyrus laughed outright, and all the others with him. 23. And the laughter still rang loud when Hystaspas said:

'There is one thing, Cyrus, that I envy in your royal state more than all the rest.'

'And what is that?' said Cyrus.

'That though you are flat, you can raise a laugh.'

'Ah,' said Cyrus, 'what would you give to have as much said of you? To have it reported on all sides and wherever you wished to stand well that you were a man of wit?'

Thus they bantered each other and gave jest for jest.

24. Then Cyrus brought out a woman's attire and ornaments of price and gave them to Tigranes as a present for his wife, because she had followed her husband so manfully to the war, and he gave a golden goblet to

Artabazus, and a horse to the Hyrcanian leader, and many C. 4
another splendid gift among the company.

'And to you, Gobryas,' said he, 'I will give a husband
for your daughter.'

25. 'Let me be the gift,' said Hystaspas, 'and then I shall
get those writings.'

'But have you a fortune on your side,' asked Cyrus, 'to
match the bride's ?'

'Certainly, I have,' he answered, 'I may say twenty times
as great.'

'And where,' asked Cyrus, 'may those treasures be ?'

'At the foot of your throne,' he answered, 'my gracious
lord.'

'I ask no more,' said Gobryas, and held out his right
hand. 'Give him to me, Cyrus,' he said; 'I accept him.'

26. At that Cyrus took the right hand of Hystaspas and
laid it in the hand of Gobryas, and the pledge was given
and received. Then Cyrus gave beautiful gifts to Hystaspas
for his bride, but he drew Chrysantas to his breast and
kissed him. 27. Thereupon Artabazus cried:

'Heaven help us, Cyrus ! The goblet you gave me is not
of the fine gold you have given Chrysantas now !'

'Well,' said Cyrus, 'you shall have the same one day.'

'When ?' asked the other.

'Thirty years hence,' said Cyrus.

'I will wait,' said Artabazus: 'I will not die: be ready
for me.'

And then the banquet came to an end: the guests rose,
and Cyrus stood up with them and conducted them to the
door.

28. But on the morrow he arranged that all the allies
and all who had volunteered should be sent back to their
homes, all except those who wished to take up their abode
with him. To these he gave grants of land and houses, still
held by their descendants, Medes for the greater part, and
Hyrcanians. And to those who went home he gave many
gifts and sent them away well content, both officers and
men. 29. After this he distributed among his own soldiers
all the wealth he had taken at Sardis, choice gifts for the
captains of ten thousand and for his own staff in propor-

C. 5 tion to their deserts, and the rest in equal shares, delivering to every captain one share with orders to divide it among their subordinates as he had divided the whole among them. 30. Thereupon each officer gave to the officers directly under him, judging the worth of each, until it came to the captains of six, who considered the cases of the privates in their own squads, and gave each man what he deserved: and thus every soldier in the army received an equitable share. 31. But after the distribution of it all there were some who said:

'How rich Cyrus must be, to have given us all so much!'

'Rich?' cried others, 'what do you mean? Cyrus is no money-maker: he is more glad to give than to get.'

32. When Cyrus heard of this talk and the opinions held about him, he gathered together his friends and the chief men of the state and spoke as follows:

'Gentlemen and friends of mine, I have known men who were anxious to have it thought they possessed more than they really had, thinking this would give them an air of freedom and nobility. But in my opinion the result was the very opposite of what they wished. If it is thought that a man has great riches and does not help his friends in proportion to his wealth, he cannot but appear ignoble and niggardly. 33. There are others,' he went on, 'who would have their wealth forgotten, and these I look upon as traitors to their friends: for it must often happen that a comrade is in need and yet hesitates to tell them because he does not know how much they have, and so he is kept in the dark and left to starve. 34. The straightforward course, it seems to me, is always to make no secret of our own resources, but to use them all, whatever they are, in our efforts to win the crown of honour. Accordingly I am anxious to show you all my possessions so far as they can be seen, and to give you a list of the rest.'

35. With these words he proceeded to point out his visible treasures, and he gave an exact account of those that could not well be shown. He ended by saying:

36. 'All these things, gentlemen, you must consider yours as much as mine. I have collected them, not that I might spend them on myself or waste them in my own

use : I could not do that if I tried. I keep them to reward C. 5 him who does a noble deed, and to help any of you who may be in want of anything, so that you may come to me and take what you require.'

Such were the words of Cyrus.

But now that all was well in Babylon and Cyrus felt he C. 5 might leave the land, he began to prepare for a march to Persia, and sent out orders to his men. And when he had all he needed, the steeds were yoked and he set off. 2. And here we will explain how it was that so vast a host could unpack and pack again without a break of order, and take up a position with such speed wherever it was desired. When the king is on the march his attendants, of course, are provided with tents and encamp with him, winter and summer alike. 3. From the first Cyrus made it a custom to have his tent pitched facing east, and later on he fixed the space to be left between himself and his lancers, and then he stationed his bakers on the right and his cooks on the left, the cavalry on the right again, and the baggage-train on the left. Everything else was so arranged that each man knew his own quarters, their position and their size. 4. When the army was packing up after a halt, each man put together the baggage he used himself, and others placed it on the animals : so that at one and the same moment all the bearers came to the baggage-train and each man laid his load on his own beasts. Thus all the tents could be struck in the same time as one. 5. And it was the same when the baggage had to be unpacked. Again, in order that the necessaries should be prepared in time, each man was told beforehand what he had to do : and thus all the divisions could be provided for as speedily as one. 6. And, just as the serving-men had their appointed places, so the different regiments had their own stations, adapted to their special style of fighting, and each detachment knew their quarters and went to them without hesitation. 7. Even in a private house, orderliness, Cyrus knew, was a most excellent thing : every one, if he needed anything, would then know where to get it ; but he held it still more desirable for the arrangement of an army, seeing that the moment for action passes far more quickly in war and the

C. 5 evil from being too late is far more grave. Therefore he gave more thought and care to order and arrangement than to anything else.

8. His own position, to begin with, must be at the centre of the camp, as this was the safest place, and next to him must come his most faithful followers, as their habit was. Beyond these, in a ring, lay the cavalry and the charioteers. 9. For Cyrus held to it that these troops also needed a safe position: their equipment could not be kept at hand for them, and if they were to be of any use at all they needed considerable time for arming. 10. The targeteers were placed to left and right of the cavalry, and the bowmen in front and rear. 11. Finally, the heavy-armed troops and those who carried the huge shields surrounded the whole encampment like a wall; so that in case of need, if the cavalry had to mount, the steadiest troops would stand firm in front and let them arm in safety. 12. He insisted that the targeteers and archers should, like the soldiers of the line, sleep at their posts, in case of alarm at night, and be ready at any moment, while the infantry dealt with the assailant at close quarters, to hurl darts and javelins at them over the others' heads. 13. Moreover, all the generals had standards on their tents; and just as an intelligent serving-man in a city will know most of the houses, at any rate of the most important people, so the squires of Cyrus knew the ways of the camp and the quarters of the generals and the standards of each. Thus, if Cyrus needed any one they had not to search and seek, but could run by the shortest road and summon him at once. 14. Owing to this clear arrangement, it was easy to see where good discipline was kept and where duty was neglected. With these dispositions Cyrus felt that if an attack should be made, by night or day, the enemy would find not so much a camp as an ambuscade. 15. Nor was it enough, he considered, for a real master of tactics to know how to extend his front without confusion, or deepen his ranks, or get from column into line, or wheel round quickly when the enemy appeared on the right or the left or in the rear: the true tactician must also be able to break up his troops into small bodies, whenever necessary, and place each division

exactly where it would be of the greatest use; he must C. 5
know how to quicken speed when it was essential to
forestall the enemy; these and a hundred other operations
are part of his science, and Cyrus studied them all with
equal care. 16. On the march he varied the order constantly to suit the needs of the moment, but for the camp,
as a rule, he adopted the plan we have described.

17. And now when the march had brought them into
Media, Cyrus turned aside to visit Cyaxares. After they
had met and embraced, Cyrus began by telling Cyaxares
that a palace in Babylon, and an estate, had been set aside
for him so that he might have a residence of his own
whenever he came there, and then he offered him other
gifts, most rich and beautiful. 18. And Cyaxares was glad
to take them from his nephew, and then he sent for his
daughter, and she came, carrying a golden crown, and
bracelets, and a necklace of wrought gold, and a most
beautiful Median robe, as splendid as could be. 19. The
maiden placed the crown upon the head of Cyrus, and as
she did so Cyaxares said:

'I will give her to you, Cyrus, my own daughter, to be
your wife. Your father wedded the daughter of my father,
and you are their son; and this is the little maid whom
you carried in your arms when you were with us as a lad,
and whenever she was asked whom she meant to marry,
she would always answer "Cyrus." And for her dowry I
will give her the whole of Media: since I have no lawful
son.'

20. So he spoke, and Cyrus answered:

'Cyaxares, I can but thank you myself for all you offer
me, the kinship and the maiden and the gifts, but I must
lay the matter before my father and my mother before I
accept, and then we will thank you together.'

That was what Cyrus said, but none the less he gave the
maiden the gifts he thought would please her father. And
when he had done so, he marched on home to Persia.

21. And when he reached the borders of his fatherland,
he left the mass of his troops on the frontier, and went
forward alone with his friends to the city, leading victims
enough for all the Persians to sacrifice and hold high

C. 6 festival. And he brought special gifts for his father and his mother and his friends of old, and for the high officers of state, the elders, and all the Persian Peers; and he gave every Persian man and every Persian woman such bounties as the king confers to-day whenever he visits Persia. 22. After this Cambyses gathered together the elders of the land and the chief officers, who have authority in the highest matters, and spoke as follows:

'Men of Persia, and Cyrus, my son, both of you are dear to me and must needs be dear; I am the king of my people and the father of my son; therefore I am bound to lay before you openly all that I believe to be for the good of both. 23. In the past the nation has done great things for Cyrus by giving him an army and appointing him the leader, and Cyrus, God helping him, has made my Persians famous in all the world by his leadership, and crowned you with glory in Asia. Of those who served with him he has made the bravest wealthy for life, and given sustenance and full pay to numbers. By founding the cavalry he has won the plains for Persia. 24. If your hearts are still the same in future, all of you will bless each other: but if you, my son, should be puffed up by your present fortune and attempt to rule the Persians for your own advantage as you rule the rest of the world, or if you, my people, should envy this man's power and try to drive him from his throne, I tell you, you will cut each other off from many precious things. 25. Therefore, that this should never be, and only good be yours, I counsel you to offer sacrifice together, and call the gods to witness and make a covenant. You, Cyrus, shall vow to resist with all your strength any man who attacks our land of Persia or tries to overthrow our laws; and you, my people, must promise that if rebels attempt to depose Cyrus or if his subjects revolt, you will render aid to him and to yourselves in whatever way he wishes. 26. Now, so long as I live, the kingdom of Persia is and continues mine, but when I die it passes to Cyrus if he is still alive, and whenever he visits Persia it should be a holy custom for him to offer sacrifice on your behalf, even as I do now; and when he is abroad, it will be well for

you, I think, if the member of our family whom you count C. 6
the noblest fulfils the sacred rites.'

27. Cambyses ended, and Cyrus and the officers of
Persia agreed to all he said. They made the covenant and
called the gods to witness, and to this day they keep it still,
the Persians and the Great King. And when it was done,
Cyrus took his leave and came back to Media. 28. There,
with the full consent of his father and his mother, he
wedded the daughter of Cyaxares, the fame of whose
beauty has lasted to this day. And after the marriage his
steeds were yoked and they set out for Babylon.

When he was in Babylon once more, he thought it would C. 6
be well to appoint satraps and set them over the conquered
tribes. Yet he did not wish the commandants in the citadels
and the captains in charge of the garrisons throughout the
country to be under any authority but his own. Herein he
showed his foresight, realising that if any satrap became
insolent and rebellious, relying on his own wealth and the
numbers at his back, he would at once find a power to
oppose him within his own district. 2. In order to carry
out this plan, Cyrus resolved to summon a council of the
leading men and explain the terms on which the satraps
who went would go. In this way, he thought, they would
not feel aggrieved, whereas, if a man found himself
appointed and then learnt the restrictions for the first time,
he might well take it ill, fancying it a sign of personal
mistrust. 3. So it was that Cyrus called a council and spoke
as follows:

'Gentlemen and friends of mine, you are aware that we
have garrisons and commandants in the cities we conquered, stationed there at the time. I left them with orders
simply to guard the fortifications and not meddle with
anything else. Now I do not wish to remove them from
their commands, for they have done their duty nobly, but
I propose to send others, satraps, who will govern the
inhabitants, receive the tribute, give the garrisons their
pay, and discharge all necessary dues. 4. Further, I think it
right that certain of you who live here and yet on whom I
may lay the task of travelling to these nations and working
for me among them, should possess houses there and

C. 6 estates, where tribute may be brought them, and where they may find a place of their own to lodge in.'

5. With these words he assigned houses and districts to many of his friends among the lands he had subdued: and to this day their descendants possess the estates, although they reside at court themselves. 6. 'Now,' he added, 'we must choose for the satraps who are to go abroad persons who will not forget to send us anything of value in their districts, so that we who are at home may share in all the wealth of the world. For if any danger comes, it is we who must ward it off.'

7. With that he ended for the time, but later on when he came to know what friends of his were ready and willing to go on the terms prescribed, he selected those he thought best qualified for the work, and sent Magabazus to Arabia, Artabatas to Cappadocia, Artacamas to Greater Phrygia, Chrysantas to Lydia and Susia, Adousius, whom the Carians had asked for themselves, to Caria, and Pharnouchus to Aeolia and Phrygia by the Hellespont.

But to Cilicia, Cyprus, and Paphlagonia, Cyrus sent no satraps, because they had shown their willingness to march against Babylon; tribute, however, was imposed on them as on the others. 9. In accordance with the rules then laid down by Cyrus, the citadel garrisons and the captains-of-the-guard are to this day appointed directly by the king, and have their names on the royal list. 10. All satraps whom Cyrus sent out were ordered to do as they saw him doing: each was to raise a body of cavalry and a chariot-force from the Persians and the allies who went out with him; and all who received grants of land and official residences were to present themselves at the palace-gates, study temperance and self-control, and hold themselves in readiness for the service of their satrap. Their boys were to be educated at the gates, as with Cyrus, and the satrap was to lead his nobles out to hunt, and train himself and his followers in the art of war. 11. 'Whichever of you,' Cyrus added, 'can show the greatest number of chariots in proportion to his power, and the largest and finest body of cavalry, I will honour him as my best ally and most faithful fellow-guardian of the Persian empire. Let the best men

always have the preference at your courts as they have at C. 6
mine, give them seats of honour as I do, and let your table
be spread, as mine is, not only for your own household,
but for your friends also, and for the honour of him who
may accomplish any noble deed. 12. You must lay out
parks and breed game, and never touch food until you
have toiled for it, nor give your horses fodder until they
have been exercised. I am but a single man, with only
human strength and only human virtue, and I could not
by myself preserve the good things that are yours : I must
have good comrades to help me in goodness, and only thus
can I be your defender; and you likewise, if you are to
help me, must be good yourselves and have good men at
your side. 13. Remember that I have not spoken unto you
as unto slaves : what I say you ought to do I strive to do
myself. And even as I bid you follow me, so I would have
you teach those in authority under you to follow you.'

14. Such were the principles then laid down by Cyrus,
and to this day all the royal garrisons are appointed in the
same manner, the gates of all the governors are thronged
in the same way, the houses, great and small, are managed
in the same fashion, everywhere the most distinguished
guests are given seats of honour, every province is visited
on the same system, and everywhere the threads of num-
berless affairs are gathered into the hands of a few
superiors. 15. Having given these instructions, Cyrus
assigned a body of troops to each of his satraps, and sent
them out to their provinces, bidding them to be ready for
a campaign in the new year and for a review of their
soldiers, their weapons, their horses, and their chariots.
16. And here I may notice another custom, also instituted
by Cyrus, it is said, and still in force to-day : every year a
progress of inspection is made by an officer at the head of
an army, to help any satrap who may require aid, or bring
the insolent to their senses ; and, if there has been negli-
gence in the delivery of tribute, or the protection of the
inhabitants, or the cultivation of the soil, or indeed any
omission of duty whatsoever, the officer is there to put the
matter right, or if he cannot do so himself, to report it to
the king, who decides what is to be done about the

C. 7 offender. The announcements so often made, such as 'the king's son is coming down,' or 'the king's brother,' or 'the king's eye,' refer to these inspectors, but sometimes no one appears, for at any moment the officer may be turned back at the king's command. 17. We hear of another arrangement, devised to meet the huge size of the empire and enable the king to learn with great celerity the state of affairs at any distance. Cyrus first ascertained how far a horse could travel in one day without being over-ridden, and then he had a series of posting-stations built, one day's ride apart, with relays of horses, and grooms to take care of them, and a proper man in charge of each station to receive the despatches and hand them on, take over the jaded horses and men, and furnish fresh ones. 18. Sometimes, we are told, this post does not even halt at night: the night-messenger relieves the day-messenger and rides on. Some say that, when this is done, the post travels more quickly than the crane can fly, and, whether that is true or not, there is no doubt it is the quickest way in which a human being can travel on land. To learn of events so rapidly and be able to deal with them at once is of course a great advantage.

19. After a year had passed, Cyrus collected all his troops at Babylon, amounting, it is said, to one hundred and twenty thousand horse, two thousand scythe-bearing chariots, and six hundred thousand foot. 20. Then, seeing that all was got together, he set out for that campaign of his, on which, the story says, he subdued the nations from the borders of Syria as far as the Red Sea. After that there followed, we are told, the expedition against Egypt and its conquest. 21. From that time forward his empire was bounded on the east by the Red Sea, on the north by the Euxine, on the west by Cyprus and Egypt, and towards the south by Ethiopia. Of these outlying districts, some were scarcely habitable, owing to heat or cold, drought or excessive rain. 22. But Cyrus himself always lived at the centre of his dominions, seven months in Babylon during the winter season, where the land is warm and sunny, three months at Susa in the spring, and during the height of summer in Ecbatana, so that for him it was springtime

all the year. 23. Towards him the disposition of all men C. 7
was such that every nation felt they had failed unless they
could send Cyrus the treasures of their land, plants, or
animals, or works of art. And every city felt the same, and
every private person counted himself on the road to riches
if he could do Cyrus some special service, for Cyrus took
only such things as they had in abundance, and gave them
in return what he saw they lacked.

Thus the years passed on, and Cyrus was now in a ripe C. 7
old age, and he journeyed to Persia for the seventh time in
his reign. His father and mother were long since dead in
the course of nature, and Cyrus offered sacrifice according
to the law, and led the sacred dance for his Persians after
the manner of his forefathers, and gave gifts to every man
according to his wont.

2. But one night, as he lay asleep in the royal palace, he
dreamt a dream. It seemed to him that some one met him,
greater than a man, and said to him, 'Set your house in
order, Cyrus : the time has come, and you are going to the
gods.'

With that Cyrus awoke out of sleep, and he all but
seemed to know that the end of his life was at hand.
3. Straightway he took victims and offered sacrifice to
Zeus, the god of his fathers, and to the Sun, and all the
other gods, on the high places where the Persians sacrifice,
and then he made this prayer :

'Zeus, god of my fathers, and thou, O Sun, and all ye
gods, accept this sacrifice, my offering for many a noble
enterprise, and suffer me to thank you for the grace ye
have shown me, telling me all my life, by victims and by
signs from heaven, by birds and by the voices of men,
what things I ought to do and what I ought to refrain from
doing. Deep is my thankfulness that I was able to recognise
your care, and never lifted up my heart too high even in
my prosperity. I beseech you now to bless my children
also, and my wife, and my friends, and my fatherland ;
and for myself, may my death be as my life has been.'

4. Then Cyrus went home again and lay down on his
bed, for he longed to rest. And when the hour was come,
his attendants came to him and bade him take his bath.

C. 7 But he said he would rather rest. And others came afterwards, at the usual time, to set the meal before him; but
he could not bring himself to take food: he seemed only
to thirst, and drank readily. 5. It was the same the second
day, and the third, and then he called his sons to his side –
it chanced they had followed him to Persia – and he
summoned his friends also and the chief magistrates of the
land, and when they were all met, he began:

6. 'My sons, and friends of mine, the end of my life is at
hand: I know it by many signs. And when I am dead, you
must show by word and deed that you think of me as
happy. When I was a child, I had all the joys and triumphs
of a child, and I reaped the treasures of youth as I grew
up, and all the glories of a man when I came to man's
estate. And as the years passed, I seemed to find my powers
grow with them, so that I never felt my old age weaker
than my youth, nor can I think of anything I attempted or
desired wherein I failed. 7. Moreover, I have seen my
friends made happy by my means, and my enemies crushed
beneath my hand. This my fatherland, which was once of
no account in Asia, I leave at the height of power, and of
all that I won I think I have lost nothing. Throughout my
whole life I have fared as I prayed to fare, and the dread
that was ever with me lest in days to come I might see or
hear or suffer evil, this dread would never let me think too
highly of myself, or rejoice as a fool rejoices. 8. And if I
die now, I leave my sons behind me, the sons the gods
have given me; and I leave my fatherland in happiness,
and my friends. Surely I may hope that men will count me
blessed and cherish my memory. 9. And now I must leave
instructions about my kingdom, that there may be no
dispute among you after my death. Sons of mine, I love
you both alike, but I choose the elder-born, the one whose
experience of life is the greater, to be the leader in council
and the guide in action. 10. Thus was I trained myself, in
the fatherland that is yours and mine, to yield to my elders,
my brothers or my fellow-citizens, in the street, or in the
place of meeting, or in the assembly for debate. And thus
have I trained both of you, to honour your elders and be
honoured by those who are younger than yourselves. These

are the principles that I leave with you, sanctioned by time, C. 7
ingrained in our customs, embodied in our laws. 11. The
sovereignty is yours, Cambyses; the gods have given it to
you, and I also, as far as in me lies; and to you,
Tanaoxares, I give the satrapy over the Medes and the
Armenians and the Cadousians, these three; and though I
leave your elder brother a larger empire and the name of
king, your inheritance will bring you, I believe, more
perfect happiness than his. 12. I ask myself what human
joy will be lacking to you: all things which gladden the
hearts of men will be yours – but the craving for what is
out of reach, the load of cares, the restless passion to rival
my achievements, the plots and counterplots, they will
follow him who wears the crown, and they are things, be
well assured, that leave little leisure for happiness. 13. And
you, Cambyses, you know of yourself, without words from
me, that your kingdom is not guarded by this golden
sceptre, but by faithful friends; their loyalty is your true
staff, a sceptre which shall not fail. But never think that
loyal hearts grow up by nature as the grass grows in the
field: if that were so, the same men would be loyal to all
alike, even as all natural objects are the same to all
mankind. No, every leader must win his own followers for
himself, and the way to win them is not by violence but by
loving-kindness. 14. And if you would seek for friends to
stand by you and guard your throne, who so fit to be the
first of them as he who is sprung from the self-same loins?
Our fellow-citizens are nearer to us than foreigners, and
our mess-mates dearer than strangers, and what of those
who are sprung from the same seed, suckled at the same
breast, reared in the same home, loved by the same parents,
the same mother, the same father? Must they not be the
nearest and dearest of all? 15. What the gods have given
to be the seal of brotherhood do not make of none effect
yourselves. But build upon it: make it the foundation for
other loving deeds, and thus the love between you shall
never be overcome. The man who takes thought for his
brother cares for his own self. For who but a brother can
win glory from a brother's greatness? Who can be honoured as a brother can through a brother's power? Or

C. 7 who so safe from injury as the brother of the great?
16. Let no one, Tanaoxares, be more eager than yourself
to obey your brother and support him: to no one can his
triumph or his danger come so near. Ask yourself from
whom you could win a richer reward for any kindness.
Who could give you stouter help in return for your own
support? And where is coldness so ugly as between
brothers? Or where is reverence so beautiful? And remember, Cambyses, only the brother who holds pre-eminence
in a brother's heart can be safe from the jealousy of the
world. 17. I implore you both, my sons, by the gods of our
fathers, hold each other in honour, if you care at all to do
me pleasure: and none of you can say you know that I
shall cease to be when I cease to live this life of ours. With
your bodily eyes you have never seen my soul, and yet you
have discerned its presence through its working. 18. And
have you never marked the terrors which the spirits of
those who have suffered wrong can send into the hearts of
their murderers, and the avenging furies they let loose
upon the wicked? Think you the honours of the dead
would still abide, if the souls of the departed were
altogether powerless? 19. Never yet, my sons, could I be
persuaded that the soul only lives so long as she dwells
within this mortal body, and falls dead so soon as she is
quit of that. Nay, I see for myself that it is the soul which
lends life to it, while she inhabits there. 20. I cannot believe
that she must lose all sense on her separation from the
senseless body, but rather that she will reach her highest
wisdom when she is set free, pure and untrammelled at
last. And when this body crumbles in dissolution, we see
the several parts thereof return to their kindred elements,
but we do not see the soul, whether she stays or whether
she departs. 21. Consider,' he went on, 'how these two
resemble one another, Death and his twin-brother Sleep,
and it is in sleep that the soul of a man shows her nature
most divine, and is able to catch a glimpse of what is about
to be, for it is then, perhaps, that she is nearest to her
freedom. 22. Therefore, if these things are as I believe, and
the spirit leaves the body behind and is set free, reverence
my soul, O sons of mine, and do as I desire. And even if it

be not so, if the spirit must stay with the body and perish, C. 7
yet the everlasting gods abide, who behold all things, with
whom is all power, who uphold the order of this universe,
unmarred, unaging, unerring, unfathomable in beauty and
in splendour. Fear them, my sons, and never yield to sin or
wickedness, in thought or word or deed. 23. And after the
gods, I would have you reverence the whole race of man,
as it renews itself for ever; for the gods have not hidden
you in the darkness, but your deeds will be manifest in the
eyes of all mankind, and if they be righteous deeds and
pure from iniquity, they will blazon forth your power: but
if you meditate evil against each other, you will forfeit the
confidence of every man. For no man can trust you, even
though he should desire it, if he sees you wrong him whom
above all you are bound to love. 24. Therefore, if my
words are strong enough to teach you your duty to each
other, it is well. But, if not, let history teach you, and there
is no better teacher. For the most part, parents have shown
kindness to their children and brothers to their brothers,
but it has been otherwise with some. Look, then, and see
which conduct has brought success, choose to follow that,
and your choice will be wise. 25. And now maybe I have
said enough of this. As for my body, when I am dead, I
would not have you lay it up in gold or silver or any coffin
whatsoever, but give it back to the earth with all speed.
What could be more blessed than to lie in the lap of Earth,
the mother of all things beautiful, the nurse of all things
good? I have been a lover of men all my life, and methinks
I would fain become part of that which does good to man.
26. And now,' he added, 'now it seems to me that my life
begins to ebb; I feel my spirit slipping away from those
parts she leaves the first. If you would take my hand once
more, or look into my eyes while life is there, draw near
me now; but when I have covered my face, let no man
look on me again, not even you, my sons. 27. But you
shall bid the Persians come, and all our allies, to my
sepulchre; and you shall rejoice with me and congratulate
me that I am safe at last, free from suffering or sorrow,
whether I am with God or whether I have ceased to be.

C. 7 Give all who come the entertainment that is fitting in honour of a man whose life on earth was happy, and so send them away. 28. Remember my last saying: show kindness to your friends, and then shall you have it in your power to chastise your enemies. Good-bye, my dear sons, bid your mother good-bye for me. And all my friends, who are here or far away, good-bye.'

And with these words he gave his hand to them, and then he covered his face and died.

EPILOGUE

OF all the powers in Asia, the kingdom of Cyrus showed C. 1
itself to be the greatest and most glorious. On the east it
was bounded by the Red Sea, on the north by the Euxine,
on the west by Cyprus and Egypt, and on the south by
Ethiopia. And yet the whole of this enormous empire was
governed by the mind and will of a single man, Cyrus: his
subjects he cared for and cherished as a father might care
for his children, and they who came beneath his rule
reverenced him like a father.

2. But no sooner was he dead than his sons were at
strife, cities and nations revolted, and all things began to
decay. I can show that what I say is true, and first I will
speak of their impiety. In the early days, I am aware, the
king and those beneath him never failed to keep the oaths
they had sworn and fulfil the promises they had given,
even to the worst of criminals. 3. In fact, if such had not
been their character and such their reputation, none of the
Hellenic generals who marched up with the younger Cyrus
could have felt the confidence they did: they would not
have trusted a Persian any more than one trusts them to-
day, now that their perfidy is known. As it was, they relied
on their old reputation and put themselves in their power,
and they were taken up to the king and there beheaded.
And many of the Asiatics who served in the same war
perished as they did, deluded by one promise or another.

4. In other ways also the Persians have degenerated.
Noble achievement in the old days was the avenue to fame:
the man was honoured who risked his life for the king,
or brought a city or nation beneath his sway. But now,
if some Mithridates has betrayed his father Ariobarzanes,

C. 8 if some Reomithres has left his wife and children and the sons of his friend as hostages at the court of Egypt, and then has broken the most solemn of all pledges – it is they and their like who are loaded with the highest honours, if only they are thought to have gained some advantage for the king. 5. With such examples before them, all the Asiatics have turned to injustice and impiety. For what the leaders are, that, as a rule, will the men below them be. Thus has lawlessness increased and grown among them. 6. And injustice has grown, and thieving. Not only criminals, but men who are absolutely innocent are arrested and forced to pay fines for no reason whatsoever: to be known to have wealth is more dangerous than guilt, so that the rich do not care to have any dealings with the powerful, and dare not even risk appearing at the muster of the royal troops. 7. Therefore, when any man makes war on Persia, whoever he may be, he can roam up and down the country to his heart's content without striking a blow, because they have forgotten the gods and are unjust to their fellow-men. In every way their hearts and minds are lower than in days gone by.

8. Nor do they care for their bodies as they did of old. It was always their custom neither to spit nor blow the nose, only it is clear this was instituted not from concern for the humours of the body, but in order to strengthen themselves by toil and sweat. But nowadays, though this habit is still in vogue, to harden the body by exercise has quite gone out of fashion. 9. Again, from the first it was their rule only to take a single meal in the day, which left them free to give their time to business and exercise. The single meal is still the rule, but it commences at the earliest hour ever chosen for breakfast, and the eating and drinking goes on till the last moment which the latest reveller would choose for bed. 10. It was always forbidden to bring chamber-pots into the banquet-hall, but the reason lay in their belief that the right way to keep body and brain from weakness was to avoid drinking in excess. But to-day, though as in the old time no such vessels may be carried in, they drink so deep that they themselves are carried out, too weak to stand on their own legs. 11. It was a national

custom from the first not to eat and drink on the march C. 8
nor be seen satisfying the wants of nature, but nowadays,
though they still abstain, they make each march so short
that no man need wonder at their abstinence.

12. In the old time they went out to hunt so often that
the chase gave enough exercise and training for man and
horse alike. But when the day came that Artaxerxes and
all his court were the worse for wine, the old custom of
the king leading the hunt in person began to pass away.
And if any eager spirits hunted with their own followers it
was easy to see the jealousy, and even the hatred, aroused
by such superiority.

13. It is still the habit to bring up the boys at the palace-
gates, but fine horsemanship has disappeared, for there is
no place where the lads can win applause by their skill. The
old belief that the children of Persia would learn justice by
hearing the judges decide the cases has been turned upside
down: the children have only to use their eyes and they
see that the verdict goes to the man with the longest purse.
14. Children in former times were taught the properties of
plants in order to use the wholesome and avoid the
harmful; but now they seem to learn it for the mere sake
of doing harm: at any rate, there is no country where
deaths from poison are so common. 15. And the Persian
of to-day is far more luxurious than he was in the time of
Cyrus. Then they still clung to the Persian style of education and the Persian self-restraint, merely adopting the
Median dress and a certain grace of life. But now the old
Persian hardihood may perish for all they care, if only they
preserve the softness of the Mede. 16. I might give
instances of their luxury. They are not content with soft
sheets and rugs for their beds, they must have carpets laid
under the bed-posts to prevent any jarring from the floor.
They have given up none of the cooked dishes invented in
former days; on the contrary, they are always devising
new ones, and condiments to boot: in fact, they keep men
for the very purpose. 17. In the winter it is not enough to
have the body covered, and the head and the feet, they
must have warm sleeves as well and gloves for the hands:
and in the summer they are not content with the shade

C. 8 from the trees or the rocks, they must have servants standing beside them with artificial screens. 18. To have an endless array of cups and goblets is their special pride: and if these are come by unjustly, and all the world knows it, why, there is nothing to blush for in that: injustice has grown too common among them, and ill-gotten gain. 19. Formerly no Persian was ever to be seen on foot, but the sole object of the custom was to make them perfect horsemen. Now they lay more rugs on their horses' backs than on their own beds; it is not a firm seat they care for, but a soft saddle.

20. As soldiers we may imagine how they have sunk below the ancient standard; in past times it was a national institution that the land-owner should furnish troopers from his own estate, and men were bound to go on active service, while the garrison troops in the country received regular pay; but now the Persian grandees have manufactured a new type of cavalry, who earn their pay as butlers and cooks and confectioners and cupbearers and bathmen and flunkeys to serve at table or remove the dishes, and serving-men to put their lords to bed and help them to rise, and perfumers to anoint them and rub them and make them beautiful. 21. In numbers they make a very splendid show, but they are no use for fighting; as may be seen by what actually takes place: an enemy can move about their country more freely than the inhabitants themselves. 22. It will be remembered that Cyrus put a stop to the old style of fighting at long range, and by arming men and horses with breastplates and giving each trooper a single short spear he taught them to fight at close quarters. But nowadays they will fight in neither one style nor the other. 23. The infantry still carry the large shields, the battle-axes, and the swords, as if they meant to do battle as they did in Cyrus' day. 24. But they will never close with the enemy. Nor do they use the scythe-bearing chariots as Cyrus intended. By the honours he gave he raised the dignity and improved the quality of his charioteers till he had a body of men who would charge right into the enemy's ranks; but the generals of to-day, though they do not even know the charioteers by sight, flatter themselves

that untrained men will serve their purpose quite as well C. 8
as trained. 25. So the chariots will dash off, but before
they reach the enemy half the men have fallen from their
boxes, and the others will jump out of their own accord,
and the teams, left without their drivers, will do more
harm to their friends than to their foes. 26. And since in
their hearts the Persians of to-day are well aware what
their fighting condition really is, they always give up the
struggle, and now none of them will take the field at all
without Hellenes to help them, whether they are fighting
among themselves or whether Hellenes are in arms against
them: even then it is a settled thing that they must have
the aid of other Hellenes to face them.

27. I venture to think I have shown the truth of the
statement that I made. I asserted that the Persians of to-
day and their allies are less religious than they were of old,
less dutiful to their kindred, less just and righteous towards
other men, and less valiant in war. And if any man doubts
me, let him examine their actions for himself, and he will
find full confirmation of all I say.

NOTES

Book I

1.4 Xenophon's remark about the Scythians is misleading, since Scythian tribes did dominate northern Iran, Armenia, and parts of Syria and Palestine around 600 BC.

This list of peoples conquered by Cyrus agrees with that given by other sources, except that according to Herodotus (II.2, III.1–13) it was Cyrus' son Cambyses who accomplished the conquest of Egypt (cf. Olmstead 86 ff.). The Magadidians are otherwise unknown. The inclusion of Egypt in Cyrus' conquests is repeated at VIII.6.20–2. Hirsch 79 suggests that Xenophon is here following a Persian oral tradition, perhaps one that circulated as part of the propaganda of the Younger Cyrus. It may be simpler to assume that Xenophon is simply mistaken.

2.1 The celebration of Cyrus 'in song and story' may be an indication of the kind of sources used by Xenophon (Hirsch 67 f. argues that he made considerable use of Persian oral traditions), or it may be no more than a manner of speech. Other references to legends and sources occur at 4.25, V.2.20, VIII.6.16, 6.20. Strabo XV.3.18 says that it was a Persian custom to celebrate 'both with song and without song' the deeds of the gods and the noblest men.

2.2 On the ancestry of Cyrus cf. Introduction. A much more elaborate account is given by Herodotus I.96, 107 ff., which should be compared generally with Xenophon's version.

2.3 Free Square. Herodotus I.153 asserts that there are no markets for buying and selling anywhere in Persia. Trade and exchange, then as now, were confined to a permanent commercial quarter or bazaar.

2.6 ff. Persian education. There is a closely similar account of the upbringing of Cyrus the Younger in the *Anabasis* I.9.2–6. See Hirsch 64 ff. Herodotus I.135 says that Persian education for boys between five and twenty consists of learning three things: riding, archery and telling the truth. Truth-telling is a central pillar of ancient Persian ethics, reflected in the name of the god Mithra, 'bond', and the inscriptions of the Achaemenid and Sassanian kings regularly refer to their enemies as having 'lied' to the Persians. On Persian trustworthiness see Hirsch 20–38. It is surprising that Xenophon, who makes a good deal of truth in the *Anabasis*, does not refer to it in this context. The virtue of eating little (2.8 and 11) is one which Greeks generally admired, and is praised in a Spartan context by Xenophon, *Lac. Pol.* II.5.

2.8 The nasturtium diet is also mentioned by Cicero, *De Finibus* II.92.

2.9–10 Hunting was and is the major leisure pursuit of the Persian upper classes, and Xenophon is right to emphasise it. Cf. VIII.1.34. Persian art of all periods provides copious examples of hunting scenes, not least the relief sculpture on the wall of the cave at Taq-e-Bostan with its depiction of Chosroes II hunting.

2.12 Games for prizes are a very Greek institution. Xenophon expresses admiration for them also at *Lac. Pol.* IV.1–2, as an institution of Lycurgus. Cf. below, II.1.22.

2.16 Persian decorum over bodily functions is mentioned also by Herodotus I.134. This passage is the first occurrence in *The Education of Cyrus* of the theme of sweating as a valuable tonic for the body. Cf. Due 108.

3.4 The Persian austerity is contrasted with Median luxury in the same way as fifth-century Greeks contrasted Hellenic austerity with Persian (or Median) luxury. The same point is made in Cyrus' pronouncement about drunkenness at 3.10.

3.9 On the commonness of poisoning in Persia cf. VIII.8.14.

3.10 Cyrus' pert joke to his grandfather about 'free speech' (*isegoria*) is based on an anachronism. *Isegoria* was one of the points on which the Athenian democracy prided itself; Xenophon indulges in a sour stab at Athenian mores. Cf. Due 39. The custom of the birthday party is also mentioned by Herodotus I.134; Plato, *Alcibiades* I.121c.

3.12 The boy who delights his elders with his wisdom was destined to become a stock figure of the biographical narrative; cf. the teaching of the young Jesus in the Temple, Luke 2.41–52.

3.14 Paradises. Xenophon is the first Greek author to use correctly this Persian term (the original is something like *paradayada*, cf. modern Persian *firdus*) for a hunting park. Hirsch 149.

3.17 Xenophon's Socratic training makes itself apparent in this rather simplistic piece of philosophical reasoning, though Socrates would hardly have allowed a pupil to claim that he 'had the whole of justice at his fingers' ends'. Cf. Xenophon, *Memorabilia* IV.4.8 ff. where he talks down the young Hippias who is 'quite confident that I have something to say that neither you nor anyone else could contradict'.

3.18 The contrast of legitimate king and tyrant is a standard piece of Greek political philosophy; cf. Xenophon, *Memorabilia* IV.6.12; Plato, *Statesman* 291d; Aristotle, *Politics* III.7.5. This is the first entrance of Cyrus' uncle Cyaxares, who is named only at 4.9. Cyaxares is one of the most important characters in the work, and he is entirely fictional. His role is to provide a contrast and foil to Cyrus, and to display Cyrus' skill in managing people. His imperious ways and intolerance of Cyrus' independence show themselves in both small things and great, and he exhibits many of the characteristics of the textbook tyrant of Greek thought. Good discussions are Due 55–63, Tatum 115 ff.

4.13 The mode of persuasion or argument by analogy is one that Xenophon had learnt from Socrates; cf. *Memorabilia* III.4, for example; the style of argument is very common in the earlier Socratic dialogues of Plato.

4.16 Like Herodotus (I.189), Xenophon refers to the kingdom of Babylon as Assyria, although the Assyrian Empire had ceased to exist in 612. If the young prince of Assyria is meant to represent a historic person, it must be Belshazzar, the son of Nabonidus. But the mode of his introduction suggests that his role is a fictional one.

4.26 The unnamed comrade to whom Cyrus gives his cloak is revealed at V.1.2 to be Araspas; cf. VI.3.14. The introduction of characters without names, only to be named later on, is a characteristic of Xenophon's narrative style in this work, and perhaps one of the ways in which he gives the impression of a narrative that corresponds to life as it is lived.

4.27 The 'certain Mede', Cyrus' lover, is later named as Artabazus: cf. IV.1.22, V.1.24, VI.1.9, etc. The fashion of a kiss on the lips as a greeting between equals is referred to by Herodotus I.135 and by Xenophon, *Agesilaus* 5.4. Herodotus in the same chapter asserts that the fashion of an older man becoming the homosexual lover of a teenage boy was adopted by the Persians from the Greeks. It was certainly a common practice among Greek aristocrats up to the fifth century, and particularly characteristic of Sparta: Xenophon, *Lac. Pol.* 2.12 ff. See in general K. J. Dover, *Greek Homosexuality* (London 1978).

5.2 According to our other sources, the 'Assyrians' (i.e. Babylonians) did indeed attack the Medes; but they did so as allies of Cyrus. He used their aid to make himself king of Media, overthrowing his grandfather Astyages, who was unpopular in Media (Diodorus Siculus 9.23). Xenophon's story excludes the overthrow by Cyrus of Media, leaving Cyaxares in charge of the Medes. The reason is part literary (Cyaxares is needed as foil to Cyrus), part ethical (Cyrus would not do anything so base as revolt against a kinsman). But cf. IV.2.9 ff. and note.

5.5 The Peers, *homotimoi*, sound rather like the Spartan Peers, known as *homoioi*. Xenophon may be trying to assimilate Persian social structure to Spartan. This form of army organisation is also described at length at II.1, and is often accepted as historical. In the actual battles, as described by Xenophon, however, Cyrus makes no use of this structure. See Cook 101.

6.12 'The teacher who professed to have taught me generalship.' Teachers could be found in Greece for most professional skills. The *Memorabilia* III.1 introduces one Dionysodorus who professed to teach generalship at Athens; the chapter consists mainly of a discourse by Socrates on the art of generalship from the philosopher's point of view.

6.22 The same observation is made in Xenophon, *Memorabilia* 1.7.2

6.24 Friendship is also treated at length by Xenophon at *Memorabilia* II.3–6.

6.31–4 The ancient teacher does not seem to be a portrait of any known Greek thinker, though the amorality of his doctrine might recall some of the more extreme of the sophists pilloried by Plato. The laws of Lycurgus at Sparta institutionalised stealing (*Lac. Pol.* II.6 f.), but only as a lesson in self-reliance and not through any putatively altruistic motive such as is given here.

6.39 On hunting with nets cf. Xenophon, *Art of Hunting*, esp. chs. 2 and 6.

6.44 Religious observance was very important to Xenophon, as is apparent from many passages of the *Hellenica*: see Cawkwell, *History of My Times* 45. No good Greek general would neglect sacrifices and omens in the course of a campaign. Other passages in *The Education of Cyrus* which emphasise this theme are I.5.6, III.3.21, 34.

Book II

1.1 Praying to the local gods and heroes is certainly a Greek custom, whether or not it may have been Persian. The heroes might accompany the army in the form of images: Herodotus 5.80 f., Aeschylus, *Agamemnon* 516.

1.5 Apart from the famous Croesus, none of the rulers named in this chapter is attested independently, and they may well be fictional. The neat round numbers of troops are to be presumed imaginary. The 'Lord of Assyria and Babylon' should be Nebuchadnezzar, though Herodotus (I.189) makes Cyrus' opponent king Labynetus, the son of queen Nitocris.

2.1 ff. The importance of table talk is a topic also in *Lac. Pol.* V.5 ff., where the ideal conversation will turn on 'the great deeds wrought in the state'.

2.2 Hystaspas is introduced here without further explanation. He is a prominent character throughout the work: cf. IV.2.46 ff., VI.1.1–5, VII.1.19 f., 39, 4.8 ff., VIII.2.15, 4.5. His most characteristic feature is his wit. See Due 68 ff. The name is that of the father of king Darius, who ruled Parthia in the reign of Cyrus' son Cambyses, but Xenophon gives no indication that he intends his character to be the historical one.

2.11 The ill-tempered Aglaïtadas does not appear again in the work; there is no place for him in Cyrus' empire. Tatum 199 f.

2.17 Chrysantas is introduced without further explanation, but like Hystaspas he develops into an important and distinct personality in the course of the work. Cf. II.4.2 ff., III.3.48 ff., VIII.4.18 ff. He is plainly a clever man and at VIII.6.7 receives his reward by being appointed satrap of Lydia and Ionia. Due 73 ff.

2.24 The paths of Vice and Virtue feature in the myth of the choice of Heracles recounted by Xenophon at *Memorabilia* II.1.21 ff.

2.28 The episode of Sambulas reveals a very Greek prejudice, that love should only be bestowed on the physically beautiful. On Persian pederasty see note on I.4.27.

3.8 Pheraulas' observation explicitly contradicts the gradations of valour by class enunciated by Odysseus in *Iliad* II.188 ff. It is notable that the observation is put in the mouth of a 'man of the people', designed as a counterpart to the disagreeable lower-class soldier Thersites in the same scene of the *Iliad*. The attitude evinced by Xenophon is a good deal more 'democratic' than that of Homer.
Pheraulas reappears at VIII.3.1ff., where again he is presented as a good fellow and an acute organiser and lieutenant. See Due 73 ff.

4.12 The involvement of the Armenians in Cyrus' campaigns is not
mentioned elsewhere in the Greek sources. Armenia had been tributary
to the Medes since about 590 (D. M. Lang, *Armenia* (London 1970)
110; M. Chahin, *The Kingdom of Armenia* (London 1987) 206 f.).
The eventual contribution of the Armenian nation to the overthrow of
Babylon is mentioned by the prophet Jeremiah (51.24–9). Armenia
was a region that Xenophon knew well, having marched through it
with the Ten Thousand in 401/400. Much of the later detail about
Armenia must come from personal observation.

4.19 The omen of the eagle and the hare is an imitation of the similar
omen in Aeschylus' *Agamemnon* 114 ff., which foretells the fall of Troy
to the Greeks.

4.20 The plentifulness of wild asses in the region is also mentioned at
Anabasis I.5.2.

4.21 'Eight miles off'. The Greek term is 'two *parasangs*'. The *parasang*
(modern Persian *farsakh*) is the distance that may be covered on foot in
an hour, and varies according to the terrain.

4.32 Cyrus' magnanimous treatment of the Armenians may be inspired
by Xenophon's own good experiences of the Armenians, who provided
him and his troops with plentiful food during their march through the
region: *Anabasis* IV.5.30 ff.

Book III

1.1 The king of Armenia is never named by Xenophon. Several rulers
of Armenia are listed by the Armenian historian, Moses of Choren,
who might fit the dates (Chahin 207). Presumably Xenophon did not
know the name of the king. His son is unhistorical: see note on 1.7.

No location is given for the battle, which thus betrays itself as fiction.

1.7 Tigranes is an authentic Armenian name, but its first known holder
is the Achaemenid Tigranes who led troops for Darius in 490 and for
Xerxes in 480 (Herodotus VII.62). Moses of Choren (I.24–30) has a
long narrative about the assistance given to Cyrus by Tigranes in the
former's revolt against Astyages (Azhdahak); however, he describes
Tigranes as the son of Eruand, thus confusing him with Tigranes the
Great (first century BC). See Moses Khorenats'i, *History of the Armenians* (tr. Robert W. Thomson, Cambridge, MA 1980) 113–22; Chahin
209.

1.19 ff. The debate in these chapters, centring on what might be called
the casuistry of advantage, recalls, though in gentler form, the bleak

presentations of the doctrine that might is right in Thucydides' Melian Dialogue (V.84–114), or in Plato's *Gorgias*.

1.38 The brave and beautiful teacher whom the Armenian king put to death is certainly meant to recall Xenophon's own teacher Socrates, put to death by the people of Athens. The accusation of corrupting the young is exactly that levelled by the prosecutors at Socrates: cf. *Memorabilia* I.2.49 ff. The teacher's forgiveness of his executioners on the grounds that their action is due to ignorance reproduces Socrates' oft-repeated doctrine that no one does evil unwillingly (Plato, *Protagoras* 358c). See the discussions by Due 77 f., Tatum 114. The Armenian teacher is of course fictional. The death of a noble teacher at the hands of a tyrant becomes a topos of Greek fiction; a nice example is the treatment of Barlaam by king Abenner in *Barlaam and Ioasaph*, the novel attributed to John Damascene.

1.41 The coda of the pleasures of love after suffering recalls the conclusion of Odysseus' adventures in the arms of his wife, *Odyssey* 23.230 f., 300.

2.1 and 7 The Chaldaeans are not the Babylonian astronomers but a people of the Armenian mountains, perhaps to be equated with the original Urartian inhabitants of Armenia (D. M. Lang 113). Xenophon had encountered them in Kurdistan, in the mountains south of Lake Van (*Anabasis* IV.3.4, where again they take the part of mercenaries; cf. *Anabasis* V.5.17 where it is stated that they were not subjects of Persia).

2.24 The treaty between the Chaldaeans and the Armenians, reached in a spirit of compromise worthy of a clever hero like the Alexander of the *Romance*, is clearly known to Xenophon from his experience of the region as still in force in his own day.

3.21, 22 The Heroes of Media and of Assyria. Cf. II.1.1 and note.

3.25 A parallel for the use of fires to deceive the enemy about the size of the army is found in the *Alexander Romance* II.13, where the hero has branches tied to the tails of flocks of sheep to raise a great dust, and at night ties torches to their horns to make it look as if the number of camp fires is immense. The same stratagem is attributed to Cyrus by Polyaenus 7.6.9, the occasion being his retreat to Pasargadae after a first defeat in his rebellion against the Median king. Cyrus had been advised by Cambyses of the value of deceiving the enemy at I.6.27.

3.26 At *Anabasis* I.7.14 the Persian king has a great ditch constructed to impede the advance of Cyrus' army. Xenophon writes from first-hand experience of these tactics.

Book IV

2.1 The subjection of Hyrcania by Cyrus is historical; cf. Olmstead 45 f., though no details are available to corroborate Xenophon's narrative.

Skirites. Skiritis was a region on the borders of Laconia and Arcadia, whose inhabitants had the status of *perioeci* in the Spartan state but functioned as an élite in the Spartan army; they performed the role of sentries and preceded the king on the march: *Lac. Pol.* XII.3, XIII.6, Thucydides V.67.1, etc.

2.9 ff. Hirsch 81 argues that this episode is effectively a coup by Cyrus against Cyaxares, in that he now attaches the Median troops to his army. Herodotus skates in the lightest possible way over this, the central element of his rise to supremacy. At 5.10 Cyaxares realises that all his Medes have deserted to Cyrus and is thoroughly embittered. By the use of the fictional Cyaxares, Xenophon has avoided the need to have Cyrus revolt against his grandfather and has created an interesting study in leadership. See also note on VIII.5.19.

2.15 This is the only supernatural event in *The Education of Cyrus*. Maybe the derivation from Persian legend is authentic.

3.4 ff. Cavalry were of central importance to the Persian army and were never outclassed until the campaigns of Alexander the Great. Herodotus VII.84–8 gives a description of the Persian army and the place in it of cavalry. Unfortunately, there are no pictorial representations of Achaemenid cavalry. In later (Sassanian) times the cavalry became more and more heavily armed, until they resembled medieval knights and were dubbed by the Romans *clibanarii*, 'oven-men'.

5.14 On the Magi see note on VIII.1.23.

6.1 Gobryas is, for once, a historical character, his Babylonian name being Gubaru or Ugbaru. He plays an important role in the campaign against Babylon, and became its satrap after the conquest: Cook 168. In general, Due 83 ff.

6.3–4 The explanation of the prince's dislike for Gobryas' son belongs to a common story-pattern. Alexander took against Hermolaus for a similar offence of spearing a quarry before him: *Anabasis* IV.3.1–2. The same motive is adopted by Zonaras 12.24 to explain the murder by Maeonius of Odenathus the king of Palmyra in AD 267.

6.11 The unnamed lady of Susa is Pantheia. At V.2.3 she is described as the wife of Abradatas, but is only named at VI.1.41, after being for more than a whole book merely the 'lady from Susa'. This is one of the most striking examples of Xenophon's technique of delaying the naming of his important characters.

Book V

1.2 See note on IV.6.11.

1.8 The account of the persuasive force of beauty recalls the encomium of Helen by Gorgias in which he argues that Helen could not be blamed for succumbing to the irresistible force of Persuasion. It was Persuasion that the sophists promised above all to teach. The discussion between Cyrus and Abradatas centres on the Socratic theme of a man's responsibility for his feelings and actions, and there is a Socratic tone to the discussion of the voluntary or involuntary nature of love. Abradatas' proud boast of his ability to resist is belied in paragraph 18. Sophists one, Socrates nil, one might conclude.

2.7 The coins named darics were introduced by king Darius (548–486 BC); the reference to them at this date is anachronistic. The same anachronism is committed by the author of I Chronicles 29.7.

2.20 'The story runs . . .' Again Xenophon hints at a knowledge of Persian oral traditions. Yet the epigrammatic quality of the phrase may suggest a Greek origin, i.e. invention by Xenophon.

2.25. The Cadousians or Kadousioi are a people dwelling to the southwest of the Caspian Sea, within the territory of Media: Xenophon, *Hellenica* 2.1.13, Strabo 11.508, 523. The Sakians or Sakai are an Iranian nomadic people, one of the group known generally to the Greeks as Scythians. Herodotus 7.64 says that the Persians call all Scythians Sakai. It is characteristic of Xenophon to use the correct Persian ethnographic term.

2.28 The young man introduced anonymously here is named at V.3.10 as Gadatas. Due 85–7. In keeping with the moral tone of the work, Gadatas' defection to Cyrus is justified by the preceding offence by his master.

3.38 The names of individuals given here have no external support but are probably chosen by Xenophon as appropriate to members of their nations. Empas the Armenian is rather optimistically identified by Chahin (208) with one Ampak (or Ambag) named by Moses of Choren (I.19) in a long list of early Armenians, who may have been satrap of western Armenia at about the right time.

3.47 The analogy of the general with the craftsman is a very Socratic one. Socrates was sometimes mocked for his constant use of analogies from lowly occupations : see Xenophon, *Memorabilia* I.2.33–7, Plato, *Gorgias* 491a.

Book VI

1.20 Siege-engines were a development of fourth-century warfare, brought to a peak by Philip of Macedon in the years immediately following Xenophon's death ; the reference to such tactics is anachronistic for sixth-century Persia. However, simple battering-rams may have been used, as at Miletus (Herodotus VI.18) : Cook 105.

1.27–30 The use of chariots with scythed wheels was a famous Persian speciality. Cf. Xenophon, *Anabasis* 1.7.10. Cook 102 states that they were used in small numbers to break up a mass of infantry before the main onslaught. On Trojan and Cyrenaean charioteering see J. K. Anderson, 'Homeric, British and Cyrenaic Chariots', *Amer. Jnl. of Archaeology* 1965, 349–52.

1.30 Camels were used as pack animals by the Persian army : Cook 102. See also on VII.1.27.

1.41 This is the first point at which Pantheia is named.

1.50–5 For Abradatas' siege-towers, cf. note on VI.1.20.

2.1 No other source mentions these Indian allies of Cyrus.

2.9–11 Croesus' attack on Cyrus is described also by Herodotus, I.71, who mentions the alliance with Sparta (I.69). Strictly speaking, the object of his attack was Cyrus' territory of Cappadocia, not Cyrus himself. Xenophon, in contrast, makes Cappadocia one of Croesus' allies. Croesus' other allies are not otherwise attested.

2.11 The Pactolus is the river running through Croesus' capital of Sardis ; Thymbrara was apparently situated about 25 km northeast of Sardis. The battle took place in 546/5.

2.21 Lydia is indeed a land of wine and oil and fig trees. It is perhaps a little surprising that Chrysantas does not also mention the wealth it extracted from the gold-bearing river Pactolus.

3.1 ff. The complete lack of topographical information on Cyrus' march to Lydia is remarkable in an author who in the *Anabasis* devotes such attention to topography. But for a similar vagueness about a region Xenophon must have known well, cf. Xenophon, *Hellenica*

IV.5. According to Herodotus I.80, the battle took place on 'level ground before Sardis'.

3.3 Cf. Xenophon, *Cavalry Commander* 4.3.

3.20 The Egyptian positions, like the rest of these details, are fiction.

3.21 The phalanx, a long but shallow line of infantry, is a typical deployment of Greek warfare and was also used, according to Xenophon, by Cyrus the Younger: *Anabasis* I.2.17, etc. However, it was probably not typical of Persian infantry tactics, as Persian infantry were more lightly armed than Greek.

3.28 ff. The names seem all to be intended for Persian ones. For Carouchas, some MSS have Cardouchos, a national designation (Kurd).

4.1 Scarlet tunics were worn by the Spartan army (*Lac. Pol.* 11.3) and by the troops of Cyrus the Younger (*Anabasis* I.2.16).

4.2 The episode of Pantheia bringing Abradatas his armour recalls the Homeric scene where Thetis brings divine armour to her son Achilles: *Iliad* 18.

4.5 Abradatas' leavetaking from Pantheia recalls another Homeric scene, the farewell of Hector to Andromache, *Iliad* 6 (cf. Due 81). The departure of a warrior in a chariot is also a common theme on Attic vase-painting of the fifth century.

Book VII

1.27 The effect of camels on horses is also mentioned by Herodotus I.82 f., and by the strategic writer Polyaenus VII.6.6.

1.30 'Of all strong formations the strongest is a band of friends.' The principle is a Spartan one, and it is the justification for the Spartan employment of the mess-system and homosexual pairing of older and younger warriors.

1.40–5 This defection of the Egyptians is not mentioned by Herodotus; as it is given as a cause for the existence of cities in Persia known as 'cities of the Egyptians', Xenophon may be relying here on Persian traditions.

2.2 ff. Xenophon's account of the capture of Sardis is similar to that in Herodotus (I.84). The siege-engines which Xenophon (anachronistically) mentions are not used in the eventual capture. Ctesias FGrH 688 F 14 §38 and Polyaenus (VII.6.10) have a story of Cyrus getting his men to mount dummies with beards on long poles and raise them above the walls of the city; the Lydians, inside, thinking the enemy had scaled their walls, panicked and opened the gates to escape. Then the Persians marched in.

2.9–29 Xenophon's version of the meeting between Cyrus and Croesus is written with knowledge of the other accounts given by Herodotus (I.84 ff.), Ctesias (reported for us by Nicolaus of Damascus, FGrH IIA 90 fr. 66) and perhaps the poet Bacchylides (Ode 3). We are here in a particularly good position to assess Xenophon's literary method. Certain features are common to all the accounts: the occurrence of the dumb son, Croesus' recognition of the instability of his fortune, Cyrus' eventual leniency. However, Xenophon omits the point of the son's dumbness, which is that he learns to speak only at the moment of Croesus' downfall – in Herodotus to save Croesus' life by warning a Persian soldier not to kill him, in Ctesias to call on the gods; in Xenophon his dumbness is merely one of many misfortunes. Again, Xenophon omits all mention of the pyre on which Cyrus prepared to burn Croesus until the latter called on Apollo, upon which, in Ctesias and Bacchylides, the god sent a heavy rainstorm to quench the flames, and, in Herodotus, Cyrus relented when he heard Croesus call on the name of Solon. Solon's part is also omitted by Xenophon, though his role in Croesus' achievement of self-knowledge is crucial in Herodotus, and his naming him while on the pyre appears in both Herodotus and Ctesias. Croesus' devotion to Apollo and his oracle at Delphi is common to all sources; however, it is only Xenophon who suggests that Croesus has erred in testing the god rather than trusting him (15), thus giving a moral reason for the king's downfall. Croesus' emphasis on self-knowledge (22, 23, 25) recalls the theme raised by Solon in Herodotus, and also fits well with Xenophon's interest in Socrates, one of whose key maxims this was. Xenophon can be seen to have removed the miraculous elements (the rainstorm and the dumb son's speaking), as well as the evidence of Cyrus' cruelty (the pyre), while laying more stress on the ethical significance of Croesus' behaviour and the magnanimity of Cyrus' final release of the king. It is a pity that he also omitted the Lydian king's devotion to the Athenian Solon, but in so doing he emphasised the Socratic aspect of Croesus' introspection.

3.14 Pantheia's suicide over the body of her husband is a romantic narrative motif already common in fifth- and fourth-century Greek literature: in Ctesias, in tragedy (Sophocles' *Antigone*, cf. Euripides' *Helen*) and in new comedy: see S. Trenkner, *The Greek Novella in the Classical Period* (Cambridge 1958) 62 f., 71, 111. Cf. Thisbe's suicide over Pyramus in Ovid, *Metamorphoses* 4.162. Pantheia's suicide was the theme of a painting described by Philostratus, *Imagines* II.9, and there are similar stories in the Hellenistic author Parthenius, *Amatory Tales*, e.g. 13, 31. Comedy, and the later Greek novel, generally do not allow the suicide to be more than a threat or an illusion. See further Anton van Hooff, *Autothanasia : from self-killing to suicide in classical antiquity* (London 1990).

3.15 At the end of this paragraph the MSS have the sentence : 'And the monument erected to these eunuchs is said to be standing even to this day ; on the upper part of the monument the names of the man and the woman are said to be inscribed, and below the monument is in three parts, inscribed "Sceptre-bearers".' The sentence is deleted in the Oxford text, which has no chapter 17 in its numbering.

4.1 ff. According to Herodotus I.171–5 the subjugation of Caria was the achievement of Cyrus' general Harpagus. Xenophon's account is remarkable for its lack of circumstantial detail. (What is the city being besieged in Book VI) In the fifth century Caria became a hereditary satrapy under Hecatomnus and his descendants.

5.1 ff. The siege of Babylon (October 539) is also described by Herodotus I.190–2 and in the *Chronicle of Nabonidus* : 'In the month of Tashritu, when Cyrus attacked the army of Akkad in Opis on the Tigris, the inhabitants of Akkad revolted, but he (Nabonidus) massacred the confused inhabitants. The fourteenth day Sippar was seized without battle. The sixteenth day Gobryas (Ugbaru), the governor of Gutium and the army of Cyrus entered Babylon without battle. Afterwards Nabonidus was arrested in Babylon when he returned there.' (Cited from Richard N. Frye, *The Heritage of Persia* (London 1962) 89.) Both Herodotus and Xenophon agree against the *Chronicle* that there was a battle before Babylon fell : see Hirsch 78 for an assessment of their reliability.

5.9–17 The diversion of the river as a means of entering the walled city is similarly described by Herodotus I.190, and recounted as a famous stratagem by Polyaenus *Stratagemata* VII.6.5, Frontinus III.7.3. In the *Hellenica* (V.2.7) Xenophon remarks that the similar destruction of Mantinea was a lesson to its inhabitants not to let a river run through the midst of their city.

4.60–5 The Persian use of eunuchs was common knowledge in the Greek world. Xenophon treats the use of these 'grateful geldings' (Tatum 199) as if it were entirely analogous to a problem of estate-management, an analogy central to Xenophon's view of leadership (Due 211–12).

5.80 The idea that enjoyment is a direct result of proportionate pains is a very Greek one, and is prominent in the aristocratic ideology of the poet Pindar (*Nemean* 3.17–18, *Pythian* 5.103–7, *Nemean* 4.1–3,

Nemean 8.49–50, *Isthmian* 8.1–3): Kevin Crotty, *Song and Action: the Victory Odes of Pindar* (Baltimore 1982), 55 ff.

Book VIII

1.1 The treatment of the ruler of an empire as the head of a household is paralleled at Xenophon, *Oeconomicus* IV.4 ff. Cf. Due 211–12.

1.23 The Magi seem originally to have been a tribe or clan among the Medes with special priestly responsibilities, rather like the Levites among the Jews; they functioned as guardians of the Sacred Fire. For brief discussions see Strabo XV.3.13–15; Frye 82–4, Cook 154 f. They were of course in existence long before Cyrus. The attribution of their establishment to a founder-figure may, like much else in this chapter, be derived from Persian traditions, or it may be the result of the Greek propensity for attributing all long-established structures to the fiat of a single legendary ruler.

1.34 Cf. note on I.2.9–10.

2.5 Division of labour is one of the pillars of the efficient state envisaged by Plato and put into the mouth of Socrates in the *Republic*. Cf. II.1.21 on military specialisation.

2.10–12 It was a common belief among Greeks in the fifth and fourth centuries (as evidenced by Aristophanes, *Acharnians* 91–125) that the Persian king maintained a single official called the 'King's Eye'. Plutarch (*Life of Artaxerxes* 12.1–3) attributes to Ctesias information about such an official. Other writers imply that there were a number of officials with this name and also a number of 'King's Ears'. Xenophon here (and at VIII.6.16) gives the lie to this belief, asserting that the king could rely on any number of informers who could all be described as 'King's Eyes' and 'Ears'. Hirsch, in a detailed discussion (101–39), shows that no known Persian term can be interpreted as having this meaning and argues that there was no systematic system of informers in the Persian Empire. If this is so, Xenophon, as befits the authoritative tone of his statement, is imparting more correct information about the alleged institution than any other Greek writer.

3.1 Pheraulas: see II.3.8.

3.11 The sacrifice to Zeus is obviously not appropriate for Persians; Xenophon writes as if he were describing a Greek leader.

3.14 The episode is an explanation for the Persian custom of *proskynesis*, obeisance by prostration, which so shocked the Greeks and was one of the main contributory causes to conspiracy against Alexander the Great when he, as heir to the Persian throne, demanded the honour for himself from Greeks and Macedonians.

3.25 The conclusion of the festivities with competitive games is inappropriate for Persians, being a thoroughly Greek practice, and one with a good literary precedent in the funeral games for Patroclus in *Iliad* XXIII.

3.27–32 This puzzling story seems to be intended as amusing.

3.46–50 The exchange of goods of obvious value for intangible goods seems to recall the episode in *Iliad* VI when Glaucus and Diomedes exchange armour, the one acquiring a golden set, the other a greatly inferior sort.

4.12 The joke is baffling.

5.19 Cyrus' marriage to the daughter of Cyaxares represents the reconciliation of the two men, and Cyrus' final assumption of lordship over the Medes as well as the Persians. According to Ctesias (fr. 9, 9a) Cyrus married the daughter of Astyages.

5.25–7 The covenant between the Persian king and his people is anachronistic, and is interestingly paralleled by the similar covenant between king and state at Sparta, described by Xenophon in *Lac. Pol.* XV – 'the only government that continues exactly as it was established' (like the 'Law of the Medes and Persians which changeth not').

6.1–17 The establishment of satrapies, and of the royal mail, describe the administration of the Persian Empire as it functioned in Xenophon's own day. The satrap was responsible for civil, especially financial, administration in his province.

6.19 The conquest of Egypt is normally ascribed to Cyrus' son Cambyses. Cf. I.1.4 and note.

7.1 The 'Education' of Cyrus is now effectively concluded, and the narrative jumps to the end of Cyrus' life.

7.2 The dream that foretells his death is a Homeric mechanism which becomes a prominent determinant of action in the later Greek romances.

7.9 ff. The disposition of Cyrus' kingdom, a natural conclusion to the narrative, seems to be derived by Xenophon from Ctesias (fr. 9). It looks forward to the very similar episode at the end of the *Alexander Romance* (III.32) where Alexander dictates his will.

7.11 Tanaoxares is called by Ctesias Tanyoxarkes, by Herodotus Smerdis, by Aeschylus (*Persae* 774) Mardos, by Hellanicus (fr. 164) Marphius: see Hirsch 83 and 178 n. 72.

7.21 Death and his twin brother Sleep: Homer, *Iliad* XVI.682.

7.22 Cyrus' reflections on the immortality of the soul recall the last discourse of Socrates before his execution, as described by Plato in the *Phaedo*.

7.27 The peaceful death of Cyrus is one of the most remarkable of Xenophon's divergences from the other versions known to us. It is closest to that of Ctesias, who likewise has him die in bed surrounded by his chosen successors, but as the result of a wound sustained in battle against the Derbici, a Central Asian tribe. According to Herodotus (I.204 ff.), Diodorus (II.44), Strabo (XV.8.413–14), Berossus (III.15) and Polyaenus (VIII.28), he died in battle against the Massagetae, who inhabited modern Turkmenistan. Herodotus says that his corpse was beheaded by queen Tomyris and immersed in a goatskin of blood; Diodorus says that she had him crucified. The sources are assembled by J. Gilmore, *The Fragments of the Persika of Ctesias* (London 1886) 135–6. Hirsch 84 argues that the existence of the tomb of Cyrus at Pasargadae, which was not a cenotaph, proves Xenophon to have been closer to the truth; but the argument does not seem a strong one.

8. For the problems of the epilogue see Introduction.

8.2 The outbreak of civil war between Cyrus' sons is described by Plato, *Laws* 694, 695ab. Cambyses' rule (529–521) receives a generally bad press from Greek writers.

INDEX